Praise for *A No Life Story*

"Bill Pagum has given us a lesson in sweet ticklish ever trudging-onward reality. And this story of the life of Bob O'Neil is lyrical. With the rhythm of a big kindly, cautious, tenacious heartbeat. Indeed, this is a BIG LIFE but one not marked with fanfare, for fanfare is for the few. Clap!Clap!Clap!Clap!Clap! for the few. Boom pause Boom pause Boom pause Boom pause for the truly wonderful Bob O'Neil."

Carolyn Chute, author of *Beans of Egypt, Maine*

"Bill Pagum's book is terse, spare, gotcha! His book pulls you along . . . so keep your ears and eyes open for this witty, knowing spin."

Doris "Granny D" Haddock, author, activist, and former candidate for the U.S. Senate

"Engrossing, witty, compassionate and psychologically telling—this book offers insight into recovery from mental illness that will be valued by those in the process and by their helpers, family, and friends."

Andrew LeCompte, author of *Creating Harmonious Relationships*

"Bill Pagum has written a book which will open eyes and your heart. Each chapter is a subtly-sketched vignette in which Bob O'Neil encounters his not so ordinary life with intelligence and gentle irony. Little does one expect, at the outset, how much this narrator will endear himself to you, and to the rich array of characters that make up his cast."

Carol Hochstedler, Ph.D.

"Full of understanding and enjoyment. A great read!"

Sue Madden, RN

A No Life Story

A Novel by

Bill Pagum

Peter E. Randall Publisher LLC
Portsmouth, New Hampshire
2005

ISBN: 931807-33-7
Library of Congress Control Number: 2004099598

Additional copies available from:
   www.billpagum.com

Peter E. Randall Publisher LLC
Box 4726, Portsmouth, NH03802
www.perpublisher.com

to the memory of my mother and father
Doris and Joseph Pagum

"I asked for health, that I might do great things;
I was given infirmity, that I might do better things."
—Anonymous
from "The Asking Prayer"

Acknowledgment

To Kenneth Butler, a fine editor and good friend, who helped make this book possible.

A No Life Story

Frozen Soul

Bob O'Neil fidgeted in his chair. Shame pulsed blood into a reddening face. His shrink, a large-boned Australian, triggered Bob whenever they discussed his not working due to an emotional disability. He turned away from the shrink's dull gray eyes and stared at the various salt-water aquariums built into the walls of the office. The doctor collected tropical fish. Bob watched as one brightly colored striper gobbled up pink sediment from the bottom, returned his stare, and, tail wagging, threw up at him.

"I have a possible solution to your work dilemma," said the doctor, smiling.

Bob never knew what to expect when the doctor smiled. Secretly, he thought she was depressed.

"What kind of solution?" asked Bob. He didn't grin back.

"An associate of mine is on the board of the new beer brewing company—Blue Twist Ale—that is opening in Fiston. He has some influence with the hiring manager. He says they could use a good chemical engineer with your experience," said the doctor, whose voice had returned to the toneless quality appropriate for therapy.

Bob hadn't had a drink in almost ten years. Beer had been his favorite. He cringed at the thought of making booze. Liquor killed people everyday. He wondered what his friends in recovery would think. Bob said nothing to the doctor, grimacing slightly as icy tendrils twisted in a hole deep in his chest.

Taking Bob's silence for assent, the doctor gave Bob an "attaboy" for licking his own booze problem, mentioned that a niece had built an alcohol distillation plant for processing sugar cane in Indonesia, and warned him to keep away from any taste testing—since taking a drink might still kill him, let alone interfere with the action of his meds.

"You don't want to end up dead of alcoholism like the actor, William Holden," said the doctor. "By the way, my niece has come here to the States to get her PhD. You did your post-grad work at Columbia, right?"

Bob shook his head. All he had was a BS. "Bull Shit," "More Shit," and "Piled higher and Deeper" he used to say with his college friends.

Hearing that Bob had just a Bachelor's degree, the doctor changed the subject.

"Need any scripts?" asked the doctor.

Bob nodded while he inwardly obsessed on the doctor's statement about work. *A job*, he thought, *what about my pension?* The answer soon followed. He would lose it when he cast himself adrift in the free-market. While shaming and meager, the security the pension offered in case of another breakdown had advantages. The tendrils twisted again and Bob shuddered.

"Doctor, isn't returning to work premature?" asked Bob.

"Nonsense, you've been out of the hospital for two years, your symptoms are in remission, and your meds are stable," said the doctor.

Bob feebly mentioned he had suffered a number of close calls every year, in spite of not having stressors such as work, family, or significant others in his life, but the doctor's head shook. "Close calls don't count," he was told. In a final plea, Bob mentioned the inner turmoil he now felt.

The doctor said it was probably indigestion. Next, scribbling briefly on the script pad, the doctor punctuated the undecipherable scratches with a flourishing signature, then ripped off the sheet, and handed the paper to Bob.

"These tranquilizers are fast-acting and only mildly addictive, take them whenever you feel uncomfortable," said the doctor. Looking at the clock, the doctor mentioned the impending arrival of another patient and told Bob the session had ended.

✦ ✦ ✦

"How did you hear about me?" asked Dr. Howser Dumas.

"Well, Dr. Dumas," Bob paused, looking into the phone's receiver.

"Call me Howser, Bob," said Dr. Dumas.

"My friends in recovery recommended you," said Bob.

"Do you go to meetings, too? I have fifteen years of recovery," said Dr. Dumas.

Bob told Dr. Dumas he was having a problem connecting with his current doctor, that he was on medication, and not working. Then he started to relate that his old career was too thankless and stressful for him to handle now, that he lived comfortably on a pension, and that he was feeling his way back to the working world through community service projects—but the doctor cut him off.

"Before you go any further, can you pay my fee?" asked Dr. Dumas.

Bob assured him money was not a major problem and he did carry insurance.

"OK Frank, tell me about yourself," said Dr. Dumas.

"It's 'Bob,'" he said.

Bob went through his now familiar litany of lost jobs, lost career, breakdowns and mend-ups, with familial alcoholism, insanity and suicide added to show that he didn't have to shoulder the blame alone.

"Wow, you have had a tough time. Med visits are one thing, but I think you must have a lot of unresolved anger that you need to tap. It just so happens I'm starting a men's group. For an additional thirty-five dollars a week you can learn to emote with other men, reach your feelings, punch pillows, cry, and share your experiences in an open, safe, non-judgmental format. Are you interested?" asked Dr. Dumas.

"Actually, I'm satisfied with my current therapist. But the men's group does sound attractive."

"I do a lot of individual therapy too. Who is your therapist?... oh...that's OK, you don't have to answer, I understand, you have a trust issue. Bob, I know a great way we can meet and get to know each other. I'm conducting a men's retreat next weekend. For $375 dollars, you can meet the group, see how I work, and just get away from it all. How does that sound?" asked Dr. Dumas.

Bob frowned. Next weekend was Super Bowl Sunday. He wasn't much of a fan, but he did commit to visiting his cousin and her ex to rebuild the only remnants of his shattered family. Vaguely, Bob asked himself what kind of guy went on retreat during the Super Bowl.

"I have already made plans to visit my cousin," said Bob.

"You won't be disappointed if you go, the retreat would ease your introduction into my practice and my group. Of course, you'll still have to visit with me first for final approval because I don't know you and you do have a lot of baggage," said Dr. Dumas.

Bob's frown deepened.

"Dr. Dumas, I don't know you either. Consider my perspective. If I go

3

on the retreat, I'll be in a strange place with strange people all weekend. I'm not sure I need to put myself in that kind of situation," said Bob, his voice cracking.

"Frank, that's where a leap of faith comes in. I hear fear in your voice. Let me help you face that fear. I'll send you a flier about the retreat. When would you like to schedule a visit?" asked Dr. Dumas.

Bob gave up correcting the doctor, gave out his address for the flier, and gave in to scheduling an appointment. But Bob's chest hurt. It was tight and twisted, like a deepening hole filled with sharp ice.

Tuesday was therapy day. Trisha met Bob with a smile. She was tall, blonde, and radiant as ever in a black pants suit and red sweater-vest. Sometimes, Bob thought she was too pretty to be his counselor.

"What's been happening, Bob?" asked Trisha.

Bob shrugged.

"My shrink may have a job for me—in a brewery. I'm afraid I'll lose my disability pension. When I tried to run to another doctor, the guy kept figuring ways for me to spend money and he couldn't even remember my name," said Bob.

"Doesn't your current doctor know about your alcohol problem?" asked Trisha.

Bob nodded.

"So how do you feel about this?" asked Trisha.

Bob hesitated. Feelings were elusive. In the last few days, he had tried to determine the right thing to do; he talked to friends, wrote in a journal, and cleaned his house. He even took his dog for a long walk in the freezing winter weather.

"A cold, icy feeling prickles my chest," said Bob.

"Have you ever heard of the still, quiet voice within?" asked Trisha.

"Yes, but I don't have it. If I hear voices I need more medication," said Bob.

"We all have the voice. We only become lost when we stop listening to it. Do you feel icy now?" asked Trisha.

"No, I feel warm. Do you think I'm hearing the voice?" asked Bob.

"I think you can answer that for yourself," said Trisha.

"Guess what I did? I threw out Dr. Dumas's flier and cancelled my appointment. He wanted to interview me but he flunked my interview."

"Great, Bob," said Trisha, "I'm really impressed with the growth of your self-esteem."

"But I really need help with my doctor. Will you say something on my behalf?" asked Bob.

"I think periodic consultations between professionals are a good idea, but you have a long relationship with your doctor. Maybe you misread the situation. Don't you think you should check it out?" asked Trisha.

Bob twisted in his chair.

"The doctor could forget what happened," said Bob.

"Aren't your feelings important enough to discuss?" asked Trisha.

Suddenly, the light dawned on Bob. He was beginning to react to situations as they occurred. The reactions were primitive, simply "hot" and "cold" but who knew where they could lead?

"So I guess the best choice is that I face my doctor. Face the fear. I need to remember too that this is America, and no one can force me to take a job or enter a career that makes me crazy," said Bob.

"You really need to believe that, Bob," said Trisha.

"What if the doctor still doesn't hear me?" asked Bob.

"Then we'll face that together," said Trisha. "Perhaps beginning a search for a new doctor would be an appropriate response."

Bob smiled. Someone else was on his team.

When he left Trisha's office, he was fortified with a new resolve. He would talk to the shrink, and if the differences were irreconcilable, he would find another. Then his thoughts turned to the warm glow in his chest. He pressed his hand against his solar plexus. He was eager to know more about his new friend, the quiet voice within.

I Want My Share

Bob O'Neil started awake at the shrill ring, struggled to pull his arm free from the bedcovers, and groped for the phone. The dimly lit clock read 5:00 am. Who the hell could be calling at this hour?

"Paul? What's happening?" Bob asked, sitting up in bed.

"Are you awake?" asked the familiar voice.

Bob wiped his eyes of sleep before he answered his brother.

"I am now," he said.

"Don't freak out or anything but the old man killed himself," said Paul.

Bob's eyes caught the sunrise glowing between the trees beyond his bedroom window and they glazed over as he recalled his last conversation with Dad only the week before.

✦ ✦ ✦

Bob came home from work after another long hot day at the muggy office. After being laid-off from a Fortune 50 company, his hard-working reputation had landed him a job at a start-up engineering firm in Cincinnati. Eight hours of meaningless work in the sweatshop had left him with a hole in his gut. A quick glance at his answering machine sparked the hole a little. Its blinking red light sent a thrill through him. Had that nurse from Kentucky called? He met her through the personals. Relishing the moment, he waited a bit to tease himself. First, he opened the fridge and grabbed a beer. Then he opened the cabinet and grabbed a bag of chips. Dinner time. Bob sat down on the couch with his food nestled in his lap. After munching potato chips, he sucked a long gulp from his cold one and winced as the beer burnt his throat and tingled his stomach. The dark hole disappeared.

He was ready to hear the message.

"Bob," said a man's voice—it was Dad, he realized, "Please call home, I need to talk with you about some family matters."

Dad hardly ever called Bob—much less left him a message. Mom controlled the phone. What could he want? He decided to call home. His fingers raced through the 12-digit access code he used to save money. Making numerous long-distance phone calls was his form of therapy—in concert with his weekly shrink visits and his nightly consumption of prescription medication. His daily drinking habit was merely a reward for his daily work routine. Drinking played no part in his therapy. He did not self-medicate. The doctor even knew he had "a couple" every night—Bob never drank just one—although he himself was not sure how much "a couple" actually meant.

"Hello Mom? It's Bob. Dad called me. Is anything wrong?"

"Well...nothing's been right here for the last twenty-five years, only he's just realizing it now. He's been retired for three months and hasn't got off his arse yet to do something. All he does is sit and drink beer—either in the cellar or at the club."

Mom paused briefly to drag on her Lark or sip her Miller Lite. Bob took advantage of the lull to tilt his sweating sixteen-ounce as well.

"I need to speak with him," said Bob. "Is he there?"

"Him? You want him? So you're through with me!" said Mom.

"No, I'll talk to you," said Bob. "It's just he called me."

"Right, forget me, screw your mother, the one who brought you into the world. He called you, so go ahead and talk to him," said Mom. "Jim! Jim!" She screamed only slightly away from the phone receiver. He held the receiver six inches from his ear to modulate The Voice.

"Your first born answered your distress call," said Mom. "Get up here and speak to him."

He imagined Dad, below deck, nestled in his deep leather chair in the cellar, nodding awake with a beer in his hand, cursing the witch, and trudging up the stairs to the phone.

Bob heard a sudden scuffle for the phone, a bang of chairs, and then the crackle of Dad's congested lungs.

"How's retired life, Dad?"

"Awful," said Dad, "I'm going back to work a week from Monday. I need to send back all the Social Security checks. Lots of problems."

"You're retired. Take advantage of it," said Bob. "You have your health, your family, and friends. Just develop some new interests to spend your time."

"Bob, she says I can't live here anymore."

"What else is new? You know she's nuts," said Bob.

"You don't get it," Dad said, coughing into the phone. "I don't want to retire and I don't want to work. But most of all, I don't want to leave here."

"You don't have to," said Bob. "Work in the garden. Forget her."

He knew Dad loved raising tomato plants, pulling suckers, digging weeds, and killing the occasional tomato bug.

"But she wants me out and she says she's got a lawyer. She wants everything that's coming to her. She wants her share," he said.

"She's been saying the same thing for twenty-five years."

"But now she means it." Dad sounded convinced. He coughed again.

"You better take care of that cold," said Bob.

"It's just extra congestion from all the smoking I'm doing."

Dad was smoking again after a ten-year hiatus.

"Have you talked to your sister about rooming at the ancestral home?" asked Bob.

"She refused," said Dad.

"You could come here," said Bob.

"What would I do in Ohio?" asked Dad.

"Hell, I don't even know what I'm doing here anymore," said Bob. He had lost his Big Job, which had given meaning to his life.

"I should never have started her on beer. I told her beer relieved constipation. She drank more and more. Now she's worse than ever," said Dad.

Bob knew that conditions at home were hard as a result of Mom's untreated personality disorder but her drinking made life unbearable.

Dad's tone sharpened. "Are you drinking?"

He looked at the beer can between his legs, salivated over the case in the fridge, then thought about the pills the shrink gave him to stay calm.

"Yes," said Bob flatly.

"You know, you're just like your mother. You've already been to two hospitals to unscramble your brains. Are you looking for a third?" asked Dad. "I think you'll turn out just like her—just as sick, unhappy, and lonely."

Bob silently shook his head against the phone.

"I wish I never drank in front of you and your brother," said Dad. "Hell, I wish I never drank period. Your brother's turning out fine. But you—especially if you listen to that witch—you'll go down the tubes. She'll sink you."

"I started drinking in college, Dad," he said. "You had nothing to do with it. But maybe I should have it under better control. I'll try."

"Love you Bob," said Dad.

"See you later, Dad," said Bob.

Before hanging up, he heard a scuffle, then Mom's voice.

"Don't listen to him, Bobby," said Mom. "We think the world of you. Look at what you've accomplished."

He looked at his tiny, air-conditioned one-bedroom apartment strewn with empty beer cans and pizza cartons. His diploma from Cornell University hung above the TV set. The place smelled of stale beer and rotting onions.

"Thanks Mom. Bye," said Bob.

Bob swigged the rest of his beer, burped, and rested the empty can on the rug next to a half dozen others. Dad, he thought, sounded angry and depressed.

Bob's eyes refocused on the sunrise as his mind cleared and he returned to the bedroom where he was talking to his brother in semi-darkness. Bob shook himself back to reality.

"What happened?" asked Bob.

"This is how he did it, Bob," said Paul. "He rose out of the black leather chair, turned off the TV, walked across the cellar floor to the cardboard-box filled with books, finished off his beer and set it down next to him. He sat on the cardboard box to keep from staining the leather chair with blood. Then he held the three-fifty-seven magnum against his forehead and pulled the trigger. The witch found him. She heard the shot. She took one look and called me and then the police."

"Did he leave a note?" asked Bob. He propped himself up with his right elbow.

"Yes," he said. "I found the note on the Ping-Pong table. He wrote a couple sentences about how he was sick of buying houses and cars for the witch—that he was Catholic and didn't believe in divorce, and that he was from the old school. He couldn't bear to leave home. He blamed her. He wrote the note with a thick black marker on the back of a big paper bag from a grocery store. The cops told me not to show her. We had all kinds of cops—the locals and staties, marked and unmarked cars. Over a dozen cops showed."

"What else happened?" asked Bob. His eyes were closed.

"He had two more bullets loaded in the revolver—he might have shot the dog and Mom but thought better of it at the last minute," said Paul.

"He'd never kill them. He could've spun the cylinder. What a mess," said Bob, grimacing.

"Yes, I know. I had to clean the blood off the cellar floor with a shovel. It had congealed on the cold tile."

"Jesus, Paul," said Bob. "We'll hire a cleaning company."

"No. It's finished. She always wanted her share. I guess she got it," he said.

Bob looked at the ceiling.

"He called me last week. Said Mom and I were two screwballs that drank too much."

"He never called me. Bob, I have to go—the arrangements and all. Give me a call when you fly in. See you."

Bob hung up the phone. He thought about a beer. He looked back at the window. Clouds had obscured the sunrise. Would it rain? He decided a walk in the rain would clear his head. Bob dressed quickly, walked past the beer cans in the living room without even a glance, and opened the front door.

How God Drove Bob Crazy

Bob O'Neil awoke with a start, his mind chanting the same prayer for help he had used from the previous night. Getting out of bed he knocked over the telephone receiver and left it dangling while he dressed from the pile of clothes beside his bureau. Breakfast was quick; while he stared at his corn flakes, God said, "TIME TO GO." He didn't question the voice, he had tapered off his meds by joint agreement with his shrink the week before. He simply complied and went out to start the car.

God told him he couldn't wear his glasses for driving, nor secure his seat belt for safety, nor use the windshield wipers for clearing the rainy mist. "What?" he said to himself.

"JUST DRIVE BY MY INSTRUCTIONS," said God.

Bob obeyed, his tension eased as God gave him explicit directions. But what if he had an accident and the police arrested him for not wearing his glasses? He wondered briefly then realized that, like being the hero in his own movie, he was above the laws that applied to ordinary people. God had given him a destiny and a purpose and he needed to follow His divine orders.

On command, Bob drove up the wrong way on a one-way street, then he made a series of turns on the coastal back roads and became totally lost. He relied on instinct and His sense of direction. Along the winding two-lane highway that paralleled the ocean, he drove faster and faster, passing a slower blur of a car on a blind curve. The little Honda hugged the wet road well. He handled the car like a professional. "I'm a race car driver," he thought.

"FASTER – FASTER – DRIVE FASTER," said God.

Bob pressed on the pedal harder and harder until he floored it. Up ahead, through the misted windshield, he noticed the hairpin curve and a yellow signpost with a black arrow showing an impossible angle. He could just see rocks and brush outlined against the horizon—with the ocean below—before the car veered across the double yellow lines and sailed over the embankment. He never attempted to brake the car. The thought hadn't occurred to him. His last feelings were not of horror but of bewilderment at God having led him astray. He didn't remember the accident itself, but awoke from the blackout standing on a rock above the car. Luckily the ocean was at low tide so he stayed dry. The car was balanced on a couple of rocks and appeared to him in perfect condition. After a 70-foot airborne journey at high speed, the car had flipped over on its roof with the nose pointed into a few beach rocks. Bob didn't even notice a paint scratch or cracked window.

He checked himself over. Blood stained his palms and jacket from a nosebleed that had stopped by itself. As he climbed the rocks to the road, his left eye began to close over, making his progress unsteady. At the roadside, on cue, a pickup truck stopped to give him a lift. Bob asked the driver how his eye looked. The driver turned to Bob, grimaced, then looked away without a word.

Bob liked the ambulance guys. They said he had survived a nearly fatal crash but that his car was crushed beyond repair. Bob told them the car was undamaged. They stared and asked him if had been drinking. He told them he was a recovering alcoholic and took lithium but said nothing about the other meds; it was none of their business—besides they might think he was crazy.

Upon arrival at the ER, Bob became a reluctant patient. The doctor kept asking him how much he had been drinking and Bob thought it was a trick question so he refused to answer. Then the doctor said his blood alcohol content was zero. Why did he keep asking questions, wondered Bob? The badgering continued. "Do you use drugs?" asked the doctor.

Next Bob upset the nurses. He kept rotating his head while inside the CAT Scan chamber. The movement blurred the pictures and the professionals couldn't determine if his head was cracked. For the upper body x-ray, he twisted out of the grip of a bruiser trying to hold him still. Then he lost his concentration for a few moments and they snapped the picture of his broken face and injured eye. He apologized to God and He forgave him.

Bob hated the stomach pumping. They made him swallow yards of plastic tubing. During the procedure, a doctor said that when the cheekbone and nasal passage were broken, as in Bob's case, air might vent through the eye socket, blowing it out. Bob worried while coughing and vomiting that his eye might pop from its socket and land on the floor. As

Bob wondered if his eyeball might bounce away, a tube reamed out his guts. They extracted lots of blood, bile, and breakfast. He realized then that hospitals were not interested in curing people but killing them.

Bob fell asleep between clean white sheets but awoke in the early evening, walked into the bathroom, and locked the door behind him. He faced the mirror and, looking straight into the image of his face, he saw his eyes melt away into dark hypnotic pits. He meditated from a standing position, arms crossed, hands interlocked behind his back. The images swirling in the mirror frightened him but he forced himself to look at them and those beyond. "Bob," said a nurse, "Bob?" She jiggled the door handle. "Bob! There shouldn't be a lock on this door. Security!" They broke down the door and twirled out his tense body like he was a pine plank.

They left as soon as he pretended to fall asleep. When he opened his eyes, he saw the foot of his bed drop to the floor and felt the headboard lift straight up to the ceiling. He was standing, surrounded by the silver-colored control panels of a single-man star ship. He watched the video display on the closet door of the opposite wall. Military armor moved across desert terrain. A four-foot tall translucent light being stayed behind him, tapping his injured left cheek with a wand and emitting a buzzing sound to emphasize the major points of his up-coming mission.

Metal microbes entered his arm through the open IV in his left hand. They traveled to his left eye and other injured body parts to heal them. The metal microbes also caused corrosion and accidents like the shuttle disaster. They took advantage of the expansive space between molecules to translate them into new shapes. They gave him enhanced ability and insight.

He received the Word around 5:30 pm on Wednesday. He resisted the Call to Action—which would be his Run to Glory—but He said, "MOVE, SOLDIER. MOVE!" Bob jumped over the side rail of the bed and ran out of the room. "TURN RIGHT!" He ran past the nurses' station and one nurse ran after him screaming, "Stop!" He ran in his stocking feet, wrapped in a bath towel and johnny. The alarm sounded when he pushed open the emergency door. The nurse stayed right behind as he ran down five flights of stairs. Luckily, Bob thought, she didn't hurt herself.

Outside in the dark December night, he hesitated. "God, I can't run barefoot on pavement," he said. "YOUR FEET ARE CLOTHED IN IRON."

Without another thought, he ran down the street. He held his towel securely around himself to show people he was still a man and not an animal or simply crazy. Half naked, he ran past a policeman at the roadside writing someone a ticket.

He crossed the busy road, crashed through backyards and brush, then moved into the woods and saw the demonstrators. They were supporting his journey by witnessing his adventure. All through the woods, the shadows became full of friendly images. He saw faces, heads, even bodies in misty profile. While on his historic mission, they would do whatever possible to protect him from the authorities. They were the legendary people of the wood, very silent but real. He was glad for the help because, as a result of his frequent falls into the river, the cold breeze was freezing his body and numbing his brain.

After fording one last section of river, a deep one, where water lapped his armpits, he heard the voice exhort him, "MOVE FORWARD. UP AND OUT... TO THE LAST FULL MEASURE OF DEVOTION." The reeds were thick and tall, over eight feet at least. He had the feeling safe people would rescue him. He saw two multi-colored flashlights. Were they from a UFO? "Hello, it's Bob! Hello!" Bob yelled to them.

Two cops came into view. They plodded across the reed-strewn marsh with a short-haired, medium-sized yellow dog. Bob shrugged, accepting the situation. He wasn't to be taken prisoner crouched in the weeds like a criminal. He outstretched his hands and they clamped on the steel bracelets. After the climb up the hill to the parked cruiser, they threw him in the back seat. Although sick and injured, they drove him to the county jail for confinement and observation. He hoped they would not send him to the State Hospital again, meals there were lousy. Only God knew for sure.

Earth Lights

Bob O'Neil tried not letting the large heads and slit eyes of his captors bother him. Naked, he was strapped to a cold metal table with laboratory equipment poking into every orifice of his body. The head honcho, slightly taller and bluer skinned than the rest, smirked down at Bob. Then he patted Bob's head. Through telepathy, Zack said they were pleased with Bob's progress but now expected more. Zack cautioned that the operation to implant him with the dream maker might be uncomfortable.

Bob closed his eyes as the long needle-like device entered his left nostril but the worst was Zack's two diminutive hands helping guide it up his nasal cavity. When the drilling punctured a hole in the membrane to the brain, Bob groaned and swallowed blood in gulps. Then the device slipped out of Zack's fingers, slithered up his nostril, and, he suspected, coiled around his brain.

Bob awoke screaming. He examined the room: White washed walls, a straight-backed chair, and a window covered with wire mesh. He wore bedclothes with a crisp institutional smell. The sun shone through the window. Memories flooded in: the manic high, a sudden twist of fate, and the incident, which led to a kangaroo court convening at the hospital where the judge had involuntarily committed him. Suddenly, a key jiggled in the door and an orderly, clad in whites, entered the room carrying a tray of food and a paper cup full of pills.

"Hello, Mr. O'Neil," the orderly said in a cutesy singsong voice. "Are you ready for breakfast?"

Bob nodded. He decided to keep the dream about the aliens a secret.

"If you take your meds, we'll walk the halls later," said the orderly. He smiled, holding out the meds and a glass of orange juice.

Bob knew the routine at hospitals. He'd be out quicker if he took the meds, gave the orderlies respect, kissed up to the nurses, and told the doctors what they wanted to hear.

Bob swallowed the pills.

"Very good, Bob," said the orderly. "Now eat your breakfast and we'll go for a little walk later."

Bob ate the eggs, ham, and home fries but left the burnt white toast. The orderly pursed his lips at the toast but said nothing. When the door clicked shut, Bob slapped his gut reflectively, then stretched back down on the bed. Rack time. He yawned. The meds were kicking in. As usual for the first few days, the staff preferred sheet therapy to talk. Just as long as he didn't dream about Zack the alien again. His life was complex enough.

At first Bob didn't recognize the man sleeping on the bed. He was unshaven, fully clothed, and haphazardly covered with a red-plaid comforter. Then Bob saw the two empty pill bottles on the nightstand by the lamp and an empty fifth next to the clock radio. Cam, a depressed member of The Group, was unable to forgive himself for molesting his two younger sisters as a drunken teen. The haunting memories jammed up his head. Bob had met Cam at the hospital on an earlier stint. Cam was released as soon as his insurance expired. He was working part-time for the city until he could qualify for Social Security Income and Medicaid.

Bob shook him by the shoulders. Cam groaned. Bob stopped shaking Cam and grabbed the black telephone with the old fashion dial sitting on the clock radio. The red digits of the clock read 9:00 am.

"I'm reporting an attempted suicide. I need an ambulance at...where am I...I don't know...The phone says 555-5566. Get an address from that while I try to find somebody."

Bob took another look at Cam. He moved. Bob slapped him across the face lightly. Then shook him by the shoulders.

Somebody was shaking him.

"Wake up Bob," said the orderly.

Bob opened his eyes to the grinning orderly. Why did he grin? Because he was holding the keys? Bob wondered.

"It's lunch time, Bob," said the orderly. "Are you hungry?"

Bob blinked at the food tray.

"We'll walk the halls as soon as you finish," said the orderly. He watched Bob consume the Rueben sandwich, green beans, and milk. Bob ignored the grape Jell-O.

"Let's go to the nurses' station," said the orderly. "You can buy change there for a soda. Would you like a cool drink, Bob?"

"I'd like a Coke," said Bob.

With his shadow next to him, Bob padded over to the nurses' station in his green Styrofoam slippers to make change for a dollar. Then he saw the Big Door open and Cam walk in escorted by hospital security and two large-boned orderlies.

"Hey, Cam," said Bob, "what happened?"

Cam looked straight ahead. He never heard a word.

"Change in plans, Bob. We need your room. You're moving into a double," said the nurse. She smiled. "See, you're getting better."

Bob sucked on the Coke while orderlies moved his things out of the Quiet Room. Cam was guided in, tucked in, and then locked in.

"It's time for your pills, Bob," said the nurse. She held a tiny white paper cup filled with pink and blue pills and a fat yellow capsule.

"I don't want them. I don't want to sleep. The dreams won't stop."

The nurses exchanged glances.

"If you're good, tomorrow we'll escort you around the grounds for twenty minutes," said the nurse.

"No way," said Bob. "The aliens are following me, Cam's here because of me, and I'm not going to sleep."

Both nurses tried to reason with him. They weren't even pretty, thought Bob.

"You're safe here, no one can 'get' you and you had nothing to do with Cam's situation."

He snorted. "I called in his OD from his own room."

Bob swatted the pills out of the nurse's hand and they bounced off the floor, scattering between the patients. He tried turning the silver knob of the Big Door. Locked. Then he ran down the hall. Two orderlies clamped his arms behind his back and a nurse moved forward with a hypodermic needle. Bob relaxed immediately to delay the drug's effect on his body. They dragged him to his bed and covered him with a sheet. Bob listened.

"How did he know Cam was an OD?" asked the nurse.

"Just a lucky guess," replied another.

Bob awoke on the cold metal table in a dim laboratory with Zack, his handler, grinning at him. Zack made it clear he would be leaving soon on a trip but promised to return. Bob struggled to free his arms. The four-point restraints bothered him less than the stirrups into which his legs were shackled. He saw Zack nod to the three smaller aliens around the table to get to work. Bob screamed when several metal devices clamped into his groin. Then Zack bent down into Bob's face and stared at him with his huge, black, hypnotic eyes. Bob slowly relaxed as he lost himself in the black bottomless pits before him. Helpless at his loss of control, he wondered if he would father half-human aliens or become completely sterile. Zack told him not to worry; if he could have kids before the examination, he could have them afterwards.

Bob cut his thin slice of roast beef in the Common Room with a flimsy white plastic knife. He ate the beef, mashed potatoes, and watery mixed veggies slowly to aid digestion and maintain a satiated feeling longer. After dinner the staff promised to take a small group of patients with grounds privileges on a walk around the hospital. A nurse and an orderly marched five patients through the Big Door and out into the hospital lobby. Bob wore a light jacket. The sun had set. As they entered the cool evening air, a shiny saucer-shaped object whisked into view, hovered above the parking lot for several seconds amid shouts from the patients and staff, then veered almost vertically into the twilight sky.

"We saw a UFO!" chanted all the patients except Bob.

"They were 'earth lights,' an unusual but completely natural phenomena," replied the nurse.

"We saw a UFO!" continued the chant.

Bob grinned. Seeing the saucer scoot away gave him hope that Zack was really gone, the dreams would stop, and he could get on with his life.

"What did you see, Bob?" asked the nurse.

"Earth lights."

How Bob Shrank at the Shrink's

Bob O'Neil was a very depressed patient on his way to visit a well-known psychiatrist. In his confused state, he was never sure, when he went for an appointment, if he had the right day or time. The Doctor was very busy with other patients and scheduled Bob's weekly appointments randomly. Perhaps, one day, Bob would merit a designated time slot of his own.

When he did see Dr. T, it was 't' for terrific.

The Doctor would charge him if Bob came late or if he missed the 'meet' entirely. Bob hated paying for the second 'meet' of the week. But he loved Dr. T's calm manner, Nordic looks, and thoughtful stare. Was Dr. T really looking at Bob or just thinking about his wife?

Bob pulled into the driveway of the beautiful townhouse office. Calmness befell Bob when he saw Dr. T's Mercedes, light brown and regal. The Doctor was "in" but he charged more than a nickel. When Mrs. T used the Mercedes, the Doctor drove the late-modeled black BMW.

Bob plodded up the stairs to the office. It was deserted. Dr. T had sent the secretary home early again to save money. Too bad she got short hours while her husband was unemployed.

The Doctor kept Bob waiting just ten minutes this time. Dr. T entered the room excusing himself with a smile—he was always late. They shook hands.

"Sorry I'm late Sir Robert. Ready to meet?" he asked.

Dr. T liked nicknames and thought Bob had a royal bearing.

"Sure," said Bob, shrugging. If he was there, he was ready.

Dr. T turned around and Bob followed him up the stairs to his private office. Bob liked visiting Dr. T because they discussed feelings.

Dr. T sat behind his desk in a large chair that let him stare down at Bob like he was a bug in his insect collection. Looking at the walls, Bob was always impressed with the MD and MBA degrees from Dartmouth. Dr. T said business was his hobby.

"So how are you, Bob? On a scale of one to ten," asked Dr. T.

"I'm a two, maybe less. I feel anxious and depressed," said Bob.

"Do you need help with your investments? Do you need more medication? What is it that you take?"

Dr. T opened Bob's folder.

"Doctor," said Bob, "I feel shaky. The medication isn't working; I'm losing my mind. My girlfriend left me. My friends are turning their backs on me. My emotions are tearing me apart."

"Bob," Dr. T said, smiling, "I just checked your medication levels and they're fine. I'm glad to see you looking so much better."

"But, Doctor, I'm at the edge. I could fall either way," said Bob.

"Just keep seeing me, Bob. I have the power to heal you. I don't care if you stuff the feelings back inside or crack up again and admit yourself to the mental hospital. Keep up the office visits. Remember, you're receiving the best psychotherapy money can buy. Some magic day we'll find the key to unlock your 'ism' and free your soul," said Dr. T.

"But Doctor I feel I may take my life," said Bob.

"Don't do that. Keep your appointments with me, take your medication, and control your emotions. Time's up for today," said Dr. T, rising from his chair. "Hope to see you next week."

The session was over. As Bob turned to leave, Dr. T looked up from his file folder of copious notes and financial records.

"I see you're behind on your bill. You must continue to make your payments or we will have to take action," said Dr. T.

Outside in the parking lot, Bob sighed. Nearby, in the park, he heard the birds sing, the trees sway, and the river gurgle. Bob always felt better after an office visit. Did relief come because he was crazy and the Doctor so good? Or was it something else? Too bad the feeling didn't last long. It was an expensive high.

Mad about Molly

On the way to meditation class, Bob O'Neil stopped at the beach to pray. Molly's face blew in from across the Atlantic—her home was Ulster. Molly was Bob's latest obsession. She was a pale-complexioned woman with raven black hair down to her shoulders and sparkling blue eyes raw with emotion. The guy he had seen her with the week before couldn't be her new boyfriend. The long looks they had exchanged, the sympathetic hand holding, and laughs over Irish stories shared at coincidental meetings were the work of fate. She said Americans had treated her well during her long stay here.

Driving into downtown Fiston, he was especially happy this evening since Molly finally had said she would ride bikes with him on Saturday. He only needed to confirm the date later in the week. He nearly blew his first attempt to ask her out because every time she suggested a day to bike, he told her he was busy. Nerves! He was sure she knew he was completely in love with her. They had talked so often at the local coffee shop.

At the small class in a tiny walk-up apartment, Bob noticed the Buddhist icons and framed pictures of angry gods. The instructor burned incense, sat cross-legged, and then struck a bell. Bob nodded to Gus, his roommate, who was entering late, then closed his eyes and let the slow, dull, muffled gongs wash over his mind. Next, he entered a trance so deep that he never heard the passing truck shake the building. Only when the instructor spoke louder, then louder, did he awake, amazed.

Bob arose weakly from his sitting position, guided by the steady hand of Gus, tall and dark-haired, with a surprising amount of commonsense. They left the class, exited the building, and walked over to the pier to relax, watch the moon, and listen to the waves break. An eclipse was to occur, but Bob was too shaken to marvel at the impending celestial event. He didn't feel good. His sudden crying under the full moon was a surprise. He never cried. Not for lost loves or dead-end jobs. Then the earth's shadow passed across the moon, the eclipse culminated, and the moon's sliver grew. He found more hope.

The next morning Bob told Gus about his new resolve to straighten out his position at work and call Molly. He also complained about feeling drained before the day began from a lack of sleep.

"Bob, just work on the relationship for now. One thing at a time. The job has been a problem for a while."

"You're right. But I feel so weird. No sleep."

Morning at the office was uneventful. Don, a power-hungry co-worker slightly younger than Bob, was substituting for the section leader who was out sick. Steve, a favorite co-worker with wispy blonde hair, translucent skin, and pink eyes, still looked like a concentration camp survivor. He was now a vegetarian and needed to purge his system of undesirable chemicals with a starvation diet. Upon attaining the proper spiritual attunement, he expected to receive his nourishment directly from the sun.

Many workers at the government facility regarded their status in terms of "time left." Like a prison sentence. Phil, a government "lifer" and full-time cynic, was the most senior member of the section, but he was out sick as well that day. Going bald at forty, he had been taking hormone shots to stimulate hair growth. But the cure was blinding him and the doctor was experimenting with a variety of pills to recover his eyesight.

After lunch, Bob rested in his office cubicle reviewing work procedures and thinking about Molly. She said living in Ulster was no more dangerous than New York City. But who expected Ireland to be like the city? Then Don gave him the time sheets to add up and Bob's brain exploded. He slumped in the chair while his brain swelled in his skull. Then, like an over-stretched elastic, it snapped back again, hard. Bob tried to add the numbers but couldn't even write them legibly.

The guys in an adjoining office started laughing.

"He's downtown today setting a trap for illegal Irish immigrants."

Bob rose unsteadily. Don's brother was an immigration officer.

"Is there a woman named Molly involved?" Bob asked.

They pretended not to hear him. Bob collapsed into his seat—too dizzy to think. Had he lead her into a trap? Had he divulged her illegal status to anyone? "Someone please tell me I'm innocent," he mumbled to himself. His thoughts whirled around him. His hand pawed at the buttons on his dress shirt as though feeling his chest might confirm his existence.

Don shouted for Bob to enter his office.

"Hey, where are those time sheets?"

Bob's face flushed bright red.

"I tried to add the numbers but couldn't."

His brains were scrambled. Maybe he had had a stroke like his dead mother. Was he dying while futilely trying to add one digit numbers?

Don dismissed him with a grimace and a wave of the hand. He gave the time sheets to someone else.

Bob stepped into Steve's office to look up a psychologist he had once seen. Clearly, he had to seek professional help, tell Molly he loved her, and resolve his "on loan" status at the office. After making a doctor's appointment, Bob decided to enter the division leader's office. He was a short round man with a square jaw and red face.

"Yes, Bob. How can I help you?"

"I like working here. I want to be part of the group. Can you admit me to the training program so I can merit a more responsible position?"

"I can see you have really thought this through. Have you had any word from the front office on the status of your security clearance?"

Bob looked down. He wore a "meatball" badge. The lack of a full clearance postponed Bob's admittance to his own group and relegated him to filing papers for this group. His was a Cinderella story.

"No. But I'd like to explain." Bob was totally honest with his feelings.

The big boss mulled over his reasons for wanting admittance to the training program. He said he would give the idea due consideration. His intense scrutiny suggested he noticed Bob's stammering, loud gasps for air, and wide-eyed stare. Bob felt his trembling was justified under the circumstances.

"I must be honest about how I feel." The thought kept revolving around his head. Bob had even told him he was very nervous.

When Bob arrived home, he fell into bed shaking and exhausted. "Did I feed my dog Teddy or didn't I?" he wondered.

Then the phone rang.

"Bob, feed Teddy," said Steve. "Phil could use cheering up. Why don't you call him?" Then Steve said goodnight.

Bob gave Teddy, his black Scottie, a bowl of food and then called the ailing Phil.

"How are your eyes today?" asked Bob.

"I think they're better," said Phil.

"Phil, I'm worried your hormone treatments will permanently blind you."

"I trust my doctor. But thanks for the concern." He hung up.

Bob called Steve back—late. His mind was in spasms. Steve said whenever you do something that causes your mind to crash, it's good not to do it again. Bob's mind kept crashing that night and he was so sorry about what he did. Only he didn't know what it was. He didn't call Molly; she might get upset and cancel the bike trip.

Shaking on the bed a few more hours finally tired Bob enough to sleep briefly. God awakened him. He said the end of the world was near, a chosen few could prevent it, and Bob needed to prepare. First, he showered and shaved. God said the nuclear holocaust was coming from the east—from Russia, the boats in the shipyard, or the nuclear power plant. Second, Bob submitted a sell order on his life savings of stocks to have funds to live on. Gus was asleep in the next room. Poor devil, thought Bob, he would never know what hit him.

Then Teddy and Bob drove to the northern edge of Fiston to find Phil. Intuitively, he knew that Phil's presence would spark a special connection and give him the insight needed to continue. Like in the movie, *Field of Dreams,* he needed to convince Phil to join him on a mission. At times, Bob could even see the silver cord that connected him to the Almighty.

Phil was surprised to hear from him at 5:30 am calling from a rural gas station.

"But why do you want to see me this early?"

"Phil, this is too important to explain now. Where do you live?"

Exasperated, he gave Bob terse directions and hung up.

Somehow Bob remembered the directions, navigated through the twists of roads, and found the house. He lived in an oversized cape with skylights that he had built himself. Phil didn't answer the front door, so Bob ran around back and banged on the doors and windows. He opened the back door wearing a bathrobe. By now his hair disease had made him completely bald. He was also nearly blind.

"Phil, I've come to take you to the Eye and Ear Hospital. Otherwise, you'll go blind and we need you. We need your help. Even I'm not sure what it's about. But we are on a mission to save the earth from destruction."

"Sorry Bob, but I can't go with you. My doctor says I'm going to be all right."

24

"Phil, you're dying. This planet's dying."

Bob fell to his knees and Phil joined him reluctantly.

"We must pray to God for forgiveness and guidance."

They recited scripture and prayed. Bob revealed to Phil his most intimate life secrets to convey his sincerity.

"Bob, I need sleep. I can't go with you. Please go home and get some rest yourself. Sounds like you need it."

"I'm sorry for you, Phil. Good luck."

Bob climbed into the car, patted Teddy on the head and asked God for help. Lost in rural Fiston, he drove home without knowing how he got there. Upon arrival, he went inside and decided to call the broker to cancel the sell order. Maybe the world was not ending after all.

Then he called Molly to tell her the most obvious thing in the world. He loved her.

"Hello?"

"Molly?"

"This is her roommate. Who are you? It's early you know."

"I'm Bob. Where is she? It's important."

"She's staying at her boyfriend's right now. What's the message?

"Tell her we need to reschedule the bike trip."

"Good enough, Bob. Thanks."

As soon as he hung up, the phone ringer went off.

"Hello?"

"Bob, we are very concerned about you. Someone will be over soon to help you. Remember to stay in the house," said the big boss.

"I may be a little sick, but I'll keep my job, right?"

"You work in a government facility that requires a high-level security clearance. I'm not in a position to answer that question."

The ambulance arrived shortly afterwards. Two men appeared at the door and asked if Bob would like a ride to the hospital. One was carrying a pullover shirt with extremely long arms.

"I feel sick."

"We'll take care of that. The doctors have lots of meds to make you feel better."

As the ambulance drove him away, Bob thought about how far his personal plan had diverged from God's. Now he was back on track in a new adventure in uncharted waters.

Branded

Bob O'Neil held the badge up for the scowling guard to see. The guard was probably a lowly GS-3, making a fraction above the minimum wage, but he did carry a gun. Bob wore the badge on a chain around his neck, so when the guard brought the badge to his eyes for a closer look, he dragged Bob along. Bob's badge was white—the color for undesirables. Bob stared down at his work shoes until he felt the badge bounce against his chest. He turned away and looked up the main street. Today, he thought, is my last day at the Fiston Navy Yard.

Bob walked slowly passed the brick buildings on either side of him. To the left, stood Personnel, where he had been introduced to the Shipyard's policies and procedures and, more recently, had his picture taken for his downgraded security pass. To the right lay Benefits, where he had just been stripped of his health insurance and opted to withdraw his meager retirement savings; he figured he'd need the money. Spending almost a hundred dollars a week on therapy without a job would drain his checking account in a hurry. A friend had told him what he really needed was a lawyer to save his position. But Bob thought legal action against the government would work against him. Besides, he didn't want to work for a place that didn't want him. He'd find another job. He'd had a number of interviews already but none had led to anything.

Bob closed his eyes for a moment and felt the sun warm his cheeks. He chuckled to himself. A couple of riggers pointed in his direction. Then he opened his eyes and noticed some spring color in the grass beside the Benefits building. He stooped, picked the yellow-blossomed dandelion, and held the flower beneath his cheek, trying to remember what the childhood practice signified. Absently, he deposited the memento in his shirt pocket.

He passed on his right a complex of offices that contained the Employee Assistance Program counselors. They had been very nice. One in particular had spoken on his behalf at the five person high-level meeting, which had ultimately led to his termination. Bob was not invited to attend. The union, which Bob had joined as soon as he returned from the hospital, had said the Shipyard officials had followed proper procedures and had not discriminated against him in any way. Bob kicked a stone into the street.

To his left, walking in the opposite direction, a small round man wearing a high-security red badge waved. Freddie! Another friend from the Labor Pool. Bob waved back. Although classed as a nuclear engineer, Bob had been placed in the excess labor pool of the Shipyard until his status was finalized. Men from the trades usually were deposited there when their shop foreman, short on work, had a chance to get rid of them. The labor pool contained the low-lifes, the misfits, and the shiftless of the Shipyard.

Briefly, Bob reminisced with his friend. Being a laborer would have been more comfortable to Bob if he'd had bigger muscles and any trade skills. Memories flooded back to him. He had shivered stacking pallets on a cold January morning. He had smiled watching harbor seals play alongside his window as he laced rubber insulation around stainless steel flexible hose. He had even painted the Officer's Club bathroom. Once, while laying rug in the Chapel, the Chaplain had asked him and his two co-workers what they had done to deserve their white badges. The muscular black man, Hugh, had said he was being disciplined for starting a drunken brawl. Freddie, a first-rate carpenter, had confessed to holding his wife and two young children hostage with a hunting rifle. The Fiston SWAT team had eventually hauled him off to jail until his lawyer argued a great misunderstanding had occurred. Then the Chaplain eyes gazed into Bob's. Bob told him simply that he'd had a nervous breakdown. The Chaplain had turned on his heel and had said his place of worship wasn't meant to house liars. Bob had shrugged.

Bob shook hands with Freddie. Congratulations were offered for his friend's returned job and condolences were accepted for Bob's lost job. Next, Bob hummed. The tune was from the theme song of the movie *The Bridge On the River Kwai.* The movie was about how a group of British POWs built a bridge for the Japanese. A funny thing about working for the government, Bob noticed, was that the employees acted like prisoners. Anyone staying longer than three years was "tenured" on a kind of career track and was suspected of being a "lifer," someone who intended to retire off the Shipyard. Many "lifers" penciled in the number of days left for retirement on their calendars. Lots of workers referred to the Yard as "The Prison" or "Devil's Island." Bob had been a couple of months away from being tenured when he became ill. Actually, Bob had liked the slow, steady pace of the Shipyard and the security of working for the government; it made up for the relatively low pay he received.

Bob could see a dry dock now. His stomach tightened. He never connected "the boats," as the submarines were called, with their ultimate mission: to torpedo vessels or to launch ballistic missiles and blow up the world. He could see the conning tower of one in the dry dock. He pulled his dandelion out of his shirt pocket and held it in his right hand as the black shadow disappeared behind a water truck. They weren't his "boats" any longer. He wasn't protecting the world for democracy; now that the government was protecting the world for Exxon, IBM, and Dupont.

Bob hefted the blue file folder in his left hand. The woman at Personnel had scrawled "Exiting Interview" across the front cover. He approached the guard shack that allowed access to the inner sanctum of the Shipyard. A large three-story gray stone building housing his former engineer co-workers loomed above him. Bob wondered if anyone was staring at him through the windows.

Filing into the steady stream of traffic that passed the guardhouse, between the jersey barriers, Bob paused in front of the guard.

"You! You! What's that?" demanded the guard.

"A flower," said Bob, looking at the dandelion.

"Not the weed you idiot! The badge! A white badge," said the guard grabbing him by the shoulder. "Step aside to clear the passage."

"But I have to see my department head. He's right up there." Bob pointed. "Today's my last day."

"Larry, I have to deal with this, take my position," said the guard.

As soon as Bob began following the guard around the jersey barrier, he noticed the dandelion was no longer in his hand. Looking back, he saw the flower being trampled by the faceless workers filing to and fro across the high-security checkpoint.

"Now, who are you?" asked the guard.

"I'm Bob O'Neil and I need to see...ah," he peeked into his file folder, "Ah, Davis McKinney."

The guard rang up the office and told McKinney that if he needed to interview a white badge, he had better do it outside the high-security zone because there was no way on earth the guard would allow O'Neil to enter.

Bob waited. The story behind all government work: hurry up and wait. In due course, McKinney appeared, wearing a jacket and tie, a military style haircut, and a moustache waxed at the tips.

"Good to see you, Bob," he said.

They shook hands.

"I guess this is it," said Bob. "Sorry to drag you out of your office."

"No trouble, if need be we can always bring the mountain to Mohammed," said McKinney.

"I do feel more spiritual now," admitted Bob.

McKinney looked away. "Have you come to a decision?"

"Oh yes," said Bob, "I want to resign. It's no good fighting. They'd give me an indefinite suspension. I'm not disabled. I'm as fit as anyone, only the government has rules about being in the hospital for breakdowns," said Bob.

He stared into clear blue sky, amazed at how strong his voice sounded.

Now McKinney stared into the sky.

"Where's the document?" he asked.

Bob blew air out of his mouth like a spouting whale. He opened the file folder and searched its contents. Then he withdrew the papers individually. Nothing. All he had was a couple of pieces of blue-lined graph paper.

"Do you have a pen?" asked Bob.

"Sure," said McKinney. "Let's go over to the picnic table."

Beneath the rustling flag, next to the steel-gray cannon where the drill team fired a volley every Memorial Day, Bob scribbled out a sentence with a wavering hand. He was leaving his job for "personal reasons" to "pursue other interests." McKinney briefly read the statement then tore it up.

"I couldn't understand your writing," said McKinney, "I want you to sign my printed statement. You simply tell me what you wrote, and sign with the guard as a witness." He called the guard over with a wave and a yell.

Bob gave McKinney the pen and a blank piece of blue-lined graph paper. He repeated his resignation statement in a quavering voice and McKinney transcribed the sounds into large bold letters.

"Is this what you said?" asked McKinney, staring at the document.

"Yes," said Bob.

"Then sign it," said McKinney. He motioned to the guard. "I want you to witness it." Bob's hand shook as he added his scrawling signature beneath the clearly printed lettering. He gave the pen to the guard for his signature. Then, at McKinney's request, they repeated the procedure a second time so Bob could retain a copy.

"I think you made the right decision, Bob," said McKinney as he shook Bob's trembling hand.

Bob nodded. The guard walked over to the flagpole.

"Now that we're finished here, are you any calmer? Do you need any medication?" asked McKinney.

Bob said he was well-medicated. He told McKinney he took lithium salts for his chemical imbalance, anti-seizure medication for his mood disorder, a neuroleptic for his psychosis, a tranquilizer for his nerves and two additional medications to counter the potential side effects of the previous four.

McKinney nodded but avoided looking at Bob directly.

"Good luck to you, Bob," he said and disappeared behind the gate.

"Mr. O'Neil," said a voice.

Bob jumped.

"My orders are to take your badge and escort you out the front gate," said the guard.

Bob lifted the badge above his head and wriggled through the metal chain. He presented the guard with his badge but stared at the flag now rippling in the afternoon breeze.

"Let's go," said the guard.

Bob looked at the guard's side arm and the cannon beside him. He shrugged, then fell into step next to the guard. The walk out to the main gate was much faster than the walk in. He didn't look for familiar faces. He stared at the hard bare asphalt. He stared at the crystal blue sky. At the main gate, he stopped at the white and red checkered crossbeam. The guards conferred. The crossbeam rose. Bob walked on. He sighted an island of grass, brush, and a tall maple. Bob stooped, pulled at the grass, and placed a fresh dandelion in his shirt pocket.

True Friends

Back from his walk, Bob O'Neil collected the rags, paint cans, steel scrapers, and sand paper from the back yard and stored them in the shed. Then he carried the new orange fiberglass ladder, already stained with white paint, to where the blue tarp hid his other valuables beside the deck. Bob noticed that Rudy, his roommate, had thoughtfully washed Bob's brand-new two-inch brush made of high-quality nylon. As Rudy said, a paint job was only as good as the brush used. Rudy was helping to paint the white trim of Bob's house. Luckily Rudy had not held a grudge after the argument over Tess. Bob had forgotten he left the wet brush on top of an open can of white latex before the lunch break.

While eating his turkey bologna sandwich, he had fallen for yet another of Rudy's humorless digs, this time about Bob's newest love interest. Rudy tricked him into confiding his feelings about Tess when Rudy hinted she was back with her old boyfriend. Then Rudy zinged him with a guilt trip about romancing a highly medicated woman fresh from the psych unit. Bob had growled at Rudy then stormed out of the house and taken a long walk.

Tugging at the snagged blue tarp, he mulled over the relationship with his roommate. Bob refrained from kicking Rudy out because he paid the rent promptly and Bob needed the money. Besides, the next guy could be worse. At least Rudy had stopped drinking and was back in therapy. Perhaps, if Rudy found a woman, he would settle down and leave him alone.

While Bob struggled with a stuck flap of blue tarp, he saw a pickup truck pull in the driveway. He paid no attention to the two men in the cab. They might be Rudy's friends. He did notice the beige truck—surface rust a foot across ate away the metal. He tugged harder, ripping the fabric. Suddenly, the screen slider opened and Ken walked out on the deck. Bob had seen too much of Rudy's friend these past two weeks. He was one of Rudy's old drinking buddies that had dried out. On his first visit, he

31

showed Bob an easy way to strum the guitar, and then he patted Bob's black Scottie dog, and asked Rudy for twenty bucks. Rudy pointed to Bob and said that he was loaded. Ken returned Bob's money the next day. But he kept coming back.

Bob's guts churned as he greeted Ken. Unasked, Ken helped Bob move two canoes, the ice fishing rig, and a twelve-foot-long wooden ladder with a couple of cracked rungs. Then they covered the sixteen-foot fiberglass pushup easily with the tarp.

"Thanks Ken," said Bob. "What's up?"

Ken looked apologetic. He owed Bob $20. He had asked to borrow $20 on his last two visits but Bob had only given him $10 each time. People desperate enough to bare their souls and ask for money tore at Bob's insides. Giving away cash assuaged Bob's delicate stomach.

Ken worked outside in construction. His body was hardened through years of walking steel. He was a hunk with rugged features chiseled from stone. His mustache was neatly trimmed and his cheeks were burned red from wind and sun.

"Bob, I'll give it to you straight, I'm broke. I need twenty dollars. I know I owe you from before, but you will get it back. By tomorrow."

Tomorrow was Tuesday. Bob knew Ken was paid Friday. He either was going to steal, panhandle, or stiff him for it. Bob figured the last was more likely. Bob's stomach turned slightly.

"Ken, I can't give you the money. You still owe me twenty dollars," said Bob.

"But Bob," said Ken, "I need the money. I really do."

Ken gradually worked Bob, back stepping, to the far corner of the back yard. Bob felt the cedar fence nudge his shoulders. He stopped.

"Ken, my therapist and I made a pact," said Bob, "I agreed not to give away money or loan money. I contribute to charities. I even sponsor a Filipino boy from a penniless family."

Actually, Bob's therapist didn't mind him lending money to people in principle. He just was never repaid. Hardly ever. His old roommate Richard had repaid him, then skipped on the last month's rent. So did Cindy, the friendly woman down the street. Then Cindy asked him to co-sign a house loan to improve her chances of owning a home with her two kids. She shut up when he mentioned they might as well marry.

Ken changed his tune.

"Bob, really, I need the money because that guy in the truck out front wants the twenty dollars I borrowed from him. He wants it now and he's not taking no for an answer."

Bob folded his arms on his chest so his hands wouldn't shake as noticeably.

"You can keep the twenty you borrowed from me. Put it away in a drawer. When you need to borrow money, just pull it out and think of me. As far as that guy is concerned, let him wait until Friday. I waited. I don't even expect my money back. I don't want it. Consider it a gift," said Bob.

The last time Bob handed out a ten, Ken confided that his newly acquired girlfriend was three months pregnant. Ken was freshly sober and had just graduated from a homeless shelter to a one-room studio two months ago.

"Bob," said Ken, "I'm not going to fight you. Twenty is nothing to you. I can't find steady work, I drive a shit-box car, got bills up the yin-yang, and I'm behind on my rent. You've got it made—money, income, and a house. Be a sport."

"No Ken, I can't", said Bob. He could see Rudy peering out the slider with an apparent grin creasing his face.

In a way, Bob wanted to give him the money. But he didn't like going from a sport to a chump to a victim of extortion. Ken would return.

Finally, Ken told the real story.

"Bob, I'll tell you the truth. That guy drove me here to get more drinking money. I'm drinking again. I came here for money to go back to the Legion and buy drinks. I need a drink—it's that simple."

"I'm not funding your drunk," said Bob. "If you want a ride to a rehab or detox I'll drive you. If you want to go to a meeting I'll take you. But I refuse to give you money."

Ken steadied himself. His pale blue eyes twinkled as he shared one last confidence.

"Bob, I believe we have a special rapport, a bond, a spiritual connection that transcends material concerns. I know you feel it too. How about the money?" asked Ken.

Bob inhaled deeply. He stared Ken down.

"I can see you're not ready for help. When you do reach bottom, give me a call. In the meantime, please leave me alone. I can't afford an active drunk in my life."

Ken turned and ambled away to the pickup truck, arms outstretched to steady his swinging gate. The pair drove away with tires squealing. Inside Rudy was smoking a cigarette against the advice of his cardiologist. His next heart attack could be his last. Rudy's stomach spilled over his belt, his mustache contained leftovers from his steak and cheese sub, and his hand held the ever-present cup of coffee. His eyes were colorless gray and his movements were slow and ponderous from the meds, an effect that his coffee drinking was unable to counteract.

"Did you give that drunk any money?" Rudy asked about his latest ex-friend. "What nerve he had coming here like that."

"No," Bob snorted. "And thanks for the help out there. He considered fighting me for twenty bucks."

Rudy whistled. "You need to learn to face these people yourself. Besides, think of my heart condition."

Looking away, Bob tried to cool down but the silent treatment to Rudy lasted about five seconds. He angled the conversation to his love obsession.

"How did you know Tess was back with her ex?" he asked.

"I lied," Rudy said.

"First I'm being conned for money by a drunk. Now you're conning me about women in my own house," moaned Bob.

Bob let the waves of anger whip through his body. The tingling in his head made his scalp itch. Rudy instantly apologized. But he said Bob was overly sensitive and did not appreciate his humor. As Rudy left, grinning, he advised Bob discreetly to do a good job scraping the cedar shakes; after all, a paint job was only as good as the surface preparation.

The Broken Steps

Bob swore. He had almost fallen down the porch steps at the side door of his house. The rotten stringer let the boards bend dangerously. Rudy, his housemate, had warned him someone could fall and sue his ass. When Bob threw open the side door, he peered into the kitchen. His eyes adjusted to the dim light. He ignored the hanging cobwebs and looked away from the previous night's half eaten meal—just as long as nothing moved was his motto.

Rudy looked up from the newspaper he was reading on the couch. He dropped his boots from the flowered fabric as he met Bob's eyes. Rudy told him Lori still hadn't called back. Bob felt his stomach knot; he always had to crap when it was time to let go.

"I guess she's not only screening her calls, she screening me," Bob said.

"Forget her. Just a girl. Hey, Bob, how was the dentist appointment?"

"Oh real fun," said Bob. "Before he did any work I told him how my day was going: 'No, I haven't used the new mechanical toothbrush, I forget to floss, my head aches, my dog's sick with a mysterious disease, and a new guy at my volunteer job was sitting at my desk doing my work ten times better than me.' You know I'm trying that new therapy—talk about how you feel or at least talk period. The doc treated me real gentle after that and…no cavities."

Rudy started. "Right, the vet called. You can pick up Teddy any time now. He's holding his food. Hell, it's just been a day and I already miss the little guy—his messes in front of the bathroom door, the way his paws track urine across the hardwood floors, and his obliging practice of eating his own vomit."

Bob's gaze shifted to the framed picture of Teddy and himself taken by a professional photographer. Teddy was a jet-black Scottish terrier with a few streaks of gray. When Bob told friends that Teddy, now ten years old, was suffering from some form of colitis that might indicate any number of organ problems, they immediately said, "He's had a good life." Then Bob would insist Teddy had five more good years ahead.

"Good, I'll pick him up as soon as I drink some Coke. I need to dirty my teeth," said Bob.

The phone rang as he swigged from a two-liter bottle. Cousin Vicky was on the line. She asked if he received the message to call her. Then he noticed the blinking light of the answering machine. She told him to sit down. He placed the bottle on the floor and took a deep breath to nestle into the sofa. Vicky never called long distance; she was too cheap. He wondered who was ill.

She began by telling him "something's happened to Nancy." She was his favorite aunt and closest living relative. Both his parents had died relatively young, killed by alcoholism Bob believed. His aunt Nancy was his last blood connection with the previous generation of family. She filled the gap left by his parents. She always sent him cards and never forgot his birthday.

Next Vicky said, "Nancy died last night." Bob squirmed on the couch. He set his feet down and straightened his back. His chest tightened as he asked about the particulars. He mulled over the how and when, the why now and what if I'd called just one more time.

"She was very sick, Bob. She may have even starved herself to death. Dropping to only ninety pounds after that bypass surgery didn't help her any. We did our best to keep her alive this long. She didn't drive you know. She lived a lot closer to us than to you. I've been very busy with her. Now my own family needs me.

"I have to go, my father's sick and my daughter's a hellion. You'll have to come down and make the arrangements—it's time you did your share. Be seeing you."

Bob hung up the phone and told Rudy what had happened.

"How do you feel?" asked Rudy.

"I don't have feelings, I have nervous breakdowns. I don't feel anything," Bob said.

"Everyone has feelings."

His aunt had been worried about his nervous condition. She was always fretting over other people's problems and never taking care of her own. She gave advice freely to her two favorites—Vicky and Bob. She told Vicky that she should never have married that cold-hearted man she ultimately separated from. As for Bob, she told him never to marry—his mind was too fragile. He could never tolerate the psychological abuse involved

36

in a love relationship. Childless herself, she had buried two husbands.

Bob paced the floor as he talked to Rudy.

"She wanted most of the estate to go to me. I never saw the will. I wonder if she has updated the will since she last spoke to me."

"How much money is really involved?" asked Rudy.

"I don't know."

Bob was a little shocked finding himself talking about money and wondering if he'd have to feud with Vicky over the estate. Rudy said nothing. He just listened, then suggested they retrieve Teddy and eat dinner.

Before Bob started the car, he exclaimed what a coincidence—his aunt had died about the time his dog was very ill. He thought his psychic reader might deepen the connection. He wondered aloud whether or not to tell his therapist. Rudy shook his head. Then Bob put the car in gear to back out the driveway. The car surged forward, crushing the old porch steps. He had confused "Reverse" with "Drive."

"Looks like I'll be fixing those porch steps sooner than expected," said Bob.

"A minor carpentry project," said Rudy, buckling his seatbelt.

Bob took the hint, pulled his own seatbelt across his chest, and gently tapped the accelerator.

Under the Pavilion

Bob O'Neil climbed into his dependable burgundy Dodge and drove to the State Park in Fiston, NH. The Group was having its annual summer cookout. The Group was a loosely organized fellowship of people that shared insights about their common problem—mental illness. Individual support, along with medication and therapy, allowed for the hope of leading a normal life—although Bob wondered what was normal about not working. His disability wouldn't allow him to work, wouldn't allow him to earn more than a few hundred dollars a month. He was under the thumb of the Government. The blood that now suffused his cheeks was not anger but shame, a feeling that nearly overwhelmed his already sensitive nature. His father once joked that Bob was so sensitive—actually he had said self-centered—that he would blush at an inappropriate thought while alone in a room. The trouble was the old man was right—only the "problem" was never treated. Fear crippled Bob's ability to act spontaneously.

Bob turned right, yielded to on-coming traffic, then accelerated onto the highway. He fidgeted at the thought of mingling with the Group members. They were less than acquaintances, but knew his innermost thoughts. Would there be games at the cookout as well as food? The only game that allowed Bob to get out of himself was Ping-Pong. As a child he spent hours playing Ping-Pong with Dad in the cellar on hot summer days, his feet cooled on the damp tiled floor—the same cellar floor where Dad murdered himself. And where Bob's brother cleaned up the congealed blood with a shovel—a final gesture of familial support before he left Bob's life. No wonder Mom moved. She sold the ancestral home, gave away the Ping-Pong table, and left town to live in a trailer park next to her sister. Bob had to visit the hospital for a psychiatric vacation shortly after she died of a stroke. She didn't live long or prosper at the trailer park. Her sister discovered the body face down in a TV dinner. The place smelled of old chicken bones, cigarette butts, and stale beer.

Bob glanced at the tree-lined park on his left, slowed, and pulled into the parking lot. Now that he had lost his job, his career, and his family, he was dependent on a new support system. He visited his shrink for meds monthly, discussed his emotions with his therapist weekly, swallowed his medication daily, and occasionally leaned on his fellow Group members for comfort. Although he still believed theoretically in God, he wasn't grateful for being alive in His universe.

Bob stopped the car, hesitant to leave its safety. He saw the Group beneath the Pavilion. The old fear of not fitting in gnawed at his soul. They sat, blank-faced, on picnic tables next to a gas grill. He tried to shake away the odd-man-out feeling that came to him. Why had he bothered to come? He wiped away the sweat beading on his forehead from the hot August sun. The Group did have its good points. They understood, they tolerated, and they shared. They even exchanged opinions about the best doctors and latest meds. They listened while he openly expressed his contempt for the medical profession. Would switching to the right therapist with the right diagnosis and follow-up treatment plan mean a cure? Perhaps a functional life? What about reading the latest self-help book on feel-good thinking? Or would the body heal itself with time and chicken soup? Bob dismissed these purposeless questions and joined the Group. He needed fellowship.

Bob left his car in the lot with its windows rolled down, wistfully noticing the dozens of Little Leaguers playing baseball under the bright sun in a far away field. He walked toward the Group alone and empty handed. *Should have brought someone or something,* he thought. Finally, he ducked under the Pavilion. He welcomed the cool shade beneath its strong timber-lined roof. A double row of picnic tables was set on top of a concrete slab. The twenty-by-forty open air Pavilion was nestled at the foot of a great hill, covered with a forest of thick pine trees. The opposing two sides faced the parking lot and highway.

Betsy called greetings to him. With thinning white hair wrapped in a light blue scarf, she was short, thin, and liked to point her index finger at people. She had told Bob she was "cured" at the last Group meeting. He was curious.

"I'm interested in your recovery story and subsequent release from treatment," Bob said. "Release from treatment" was a rare event.

"I just willed myself to run my life like a normal person and you could do the same," she said, pointing her finger at Bob.

"How?" Bob asked.

"Just pull yourself together, stop taking those meds, go back to work, and get off that disability," she said, thumping his chest with her finger.

Her strident tone annoyed Bob. He shrugged and walked away. They didn't connect. She didn't have the answers to life for him; those answers had to come from inside.

The picnic was glum. Bob longed for connection and sought to satisfy that urge with food. He walked towards the grill, passed an auburn-haired lady discussing her relative under psychiatric care in a long-term state run facility, and paused next to the grill. Grey was roasting hamburgers and hot dogs. He had an alcohol-induced red face, a potbelly, and thick thatch of white hair. The smell of cooking flesh mixed with the aroma of vodka. A newcomer stared silently into the fire.

Grey had earned a good living selling dough-kneading equipment, built a house, acquired toys, and saved lots of money. Then he had lost it all, including the dough-kneading business, when his wife left him. He still hadn't found bottom after numerous visits to dry-out farms, fat farms, and psychiatric units. He liked to diagnose behavior, quote the Physician's Handbook, and push shrinks. Bob squirmed at the thought he was figured out. Bob chose not to listen to his "cure" for that day and introduced himself to the newcomer. They shook hands. The newcomer's name was David.

"Hungry?" asked Grey.

He offered to cook them a few burgers but the Group needed last minute supplies.

"I'll go to the store," said David. "Want to come, Bob?"

David drove. He was the real stranger to the Group – Bob just felt like one. Noticing the Little Leaguers in the distance playing ball, he said he liked baseball but that watching the Red Sox was a recipe for depression. He was tall, dark, and heavy. On the way to the convenience store they traded hospital horror stories, compared notes on medication side effects, and wondered what they could expect from the Group. At the store, David bought a pound each of potato salad and macaroni salad. Bob bought popcorn for himself—it acted as a cheap anti-depressant—and a bag full of tonic for the Group. On the way back, Bob ranted about his $120 per hour shrink that gave him a thirty percent reduction for being disabled.

"I want a second opinion from MacLeod's Hospital," said Bob.

"They're good, but I like Temple," said David.

By the time they had returned to the park, Bob wasn't alone; he had connected with a new friend. But the weather was souring. Bob stared at the slate blue sky with dark thunderheads billowing in from the west. Bob looked around the park and saw the ball players had left, as well as nearly everyone else. The Group was underneath the center of the Pavilion. An elderly couple, the man's leg in a cast, sat on a picnic bench near the western edge. The man raised a crutch to Bob, saluting, and said "Golfing accident," with a smile.

Bob looked at the sky again. He expected a thunderstorm lasting a few minutes, then bright sunshine again. But, with a cold front speeding across the East Coast, and Hurricane Bill rushing up the eastern seaboard, who could know for sure? Typical New England weather, one never knew what was happening next—least of all the weatherman.

Grey was still cooking Bob's hamburger when the storm arrived. The lightning and thunder splintered the summer afternoon. No rain, no wind, just fireworks. Grey saw Bob flinch at the show.

"No need to worry," he said. "If you see lightning, the danger is already passed, and remember, you never see the bolt that kills you."

"Thanks a lot, Grey," said Bob.

Everyone prepared for the storm. Grey finished cooking the burgers, handed them out, and shut down the grill. The salads stayed covered. They would wait on the veggies until the storm passed.

Bob took a couple of bites out of his hamburger before noticing the next phase of the storm. The wind rose from the west and picked up lots of loose sand and gravel. A biting yellow wind stung the Group.

The women said, "Oh, I don't like this."

The men said, "Ah, it'll blow over. Just you wait and see."

Then the wind tossed Bob's popcorn carton across the picnic table, and Bob shoved the container in the paper bag full of tonic. People raced around to secure the plates and paper flying off the tables. Bob was excited.

Betsy said, "I'm a little scared, Bob. What should we do?"

Bob said, "Don't worry Betsy. These storms never last long."

She clenched her hands together and walked over next to Bob. Slowly, Bob stopped thinking about the half-eaten hamburger in his hand. The rains came and the wind blew harder, no gusts, just a wall of wind that whipped a soaking rain against their faces. The hot August air chilled.

Bob noticed the elderly couple shout something to the group, rise from their picnic table near the western edge, and hobble across the rain slick concrete. Suddenly, the old man with the cast, slipped, dropped his crutch, and grabbed his wife's shoulder. David ran over to aid the couple. He guided them back to the picnic table and shielded them from the rain with his body.

A couple of women in the party went to the ladies room—made of concrete. The rest of the Group, including the kids, stayed put beneath the Pavilion's center simply because they had no better ideas. Betsy touched Bob's arm with her hand.

"Everything will be all right," Bob said, holding his hamburger tighter.

The wind and rain blew even colder and gusted from all sides. Bob's body tensed and shivered in waves—his wet, skimpy t-shirt and shorts offered little protection from the chill. Bob was not afraid but angry, that nature had fooled them. Then the wind, the rain, and anything loose on the ground was thrown into a gigantic blender and sprayed across the Pavilion from the west. Cold filthy water—full of silt and debris—instantly drenched Bob. Lots of paper plates and plastic dishes full of food blew away but no one ran to retrieve the party materials this time.

"We have to get out of here," said Betsy.

She held onto Bob's arm.

"Betsy, this is the best protection we have!" Bob said.

Bob heard tree limbs crashing. Tall heavy pine trees dotted the hillside next to the Pavilion. The winds from the fierce storm were tearing the trees. Bob heard large pieces crash on the roof. They sounded like shells exploding. Then the limbs and trunks rolled off the south edge with a thud.

Now Bob was scared. He peered at the roof. Would the beams hold? The air crackled between thunderclaps and exploding trees. Bob felt Betsy's grip on his arm tighten with each new volley of shelling. The rising crescendo of wind hurled more trees onto the roof. Then, as Bob stared at David shielding the elderly couple from the horizontal rain, the three simply disappeared in a sudden *crump*. Twisted pines and split timber from the roof pancaked all three people.

Bob reacted as the pine trees crumbled the rest of the Pavilion. Bob's mind went into overdrive. *Get out, out, out,* he thought and ran north toward the highway. Betsy's hand dropped from his arm. He passed the picnic tables, saw a piece of framing from the structure pass by his head, and then dodged a falling trunk. He ignored a thud against his hand. Next the roof lifted up, he saw the sky—and kept running. When Bob looked back, everything was flat. Nobody moved.

Bob wondered if everyone was dead.

He crawled to a large tree and, holding it, watched the storm tear trees in two and toss them aside. He held onto his tree for life. But what if the wind blew it away too? He crouched against the wind and struggled away from the tree. Voices from the wreckage yelled for him to lay flat. Somebody was alive! Bob hunkered down and felt the rain turn to hail. The storm calmed, then the full power returned, but only briefly.

Someone climbed out of the wreckage.

"Take the kid and get us help," the man yelled.

Then Bob saw a little boy scamper out. His red jersey was water-soaked and black with dirt. He looked about twelve years old.

"Find the injured. I'll be back," said Bob shouting to the man. Then he looked at the boy. "What's your name?"

"Richie," he said.

"Follow me, Richie."

They ran to the relative warmth and safety of Bob's car. Bob gave Richie a beach towel to wrap himself. His family was trapped, or maybe worse. Bob wiped his glasses with a spare shirt, then started the car, increased the heat, and turned the ventilator to full defrost. The windshield fogged. He was soaked and shivering uncontrollably.

"Will the storm come back? Where are my mother and father? Are they hurt? What about my brother?" Richie cried.

"No Richie, the storm is gone. We need to find a fireman to bring help," said Bob.

"But what kind of storm was it?" he asked.

"A tornado," Bob said.

Bob guided the car into traffic and steered around downed tree branches. Traffic snarled. Bob ran over to the man stepping out of his pickup and speaking into a two-way radio. He wore a heavy brown jacket stenciled with "FFD." Bob yelled that people where down at Fiston's State Park by the Pavilion. The fireman asked Bob to repeat himself more slowly. Then he spoke into his radio. Bob had to turn his car around, a tree blocked the road. He drove back to the Pavilion.

When they returned to the park, dozens of people and emergency vehicles surrounded the Pavilion. The lady with auburn hair pointed and told the nurse Bob was also a victim. The nurse told Richie his family was safe. Then the nurse had Bob and Richie lie side by side on blue plastic mats. Bob saw the sky was brighter although a light rain still spattered his glasses. The pretty nurse gently pressed Bob's injured hand while his body shook.

"Hurt? Just relax and take deep breaths, Bob. My name is Linda and I'm a nurse. Over a hundred rescue workers, all volunteers, are here to help everyone that needs help," said Linda. "Now let's put some ice on that hand, it may be broken."

The young, blonde nurse wore a skimpy, stretched-out, yellow halter-top. She straddled Bob, bent low, and completely revealed her curves.

A man in a navy blue jogging outfit knelt beside Bob and announced to the nurse, "I'm a doctor. Where can you use an orthopedic surgeon?"

He briskly examined Bob's injured hand and bruised forehead then strapped a gray tag on the wrist of Bob's good hand. Next, he signaled to the ambulance guys "OK." They drove Bob to the hospital. The ER doctor read Bob's chart and told him he could take an extra pill that day for anxiety. Bob declined. Then the doctor asked him if he knew the picnickers. Bob nodded. The doctor cleared his throat. "There were fatalities." Bob nodded again. The doctor continued saying that at least three had died and others were missing. Bob's mind flashed back to the image of the people he saw disappear. The ER doctor offered his congratulations; he thanked Bob for quick action and clear thinking.

"You're a hero," said the ER doctor.

"No, the real hero was David," said Bob.

He told the doctor about the way David had comforted the elderly couple before they had all vanished. The doctor touched Bob's shoulder and said he was discharged. As Bob walked down the hall to call a friend for a ride, he regretted that the old man had missed this segment of Bob's life.

Chasing the Cornell Tale

Bob O'Neil's meandering drive through the rolling hills and farm-lands of the state's southwest did not loosen the knots in his belly. He was alone, a newcomer, journeying to a party of strangers loosely connected by his old school tie. He was on his way to the Cornell Alumni Club's annual state cookout where he expected to meet pretty yuppettes and to possibly network his way into a new career. Surrounding himself with successful people might pull him out of his current jobless rut, career questioning, and emotional crisis. It might even give him a girl to hold his hand. He hated spending his life alone. Bob breathed deeply and focused on the scenery. He passed hand-drawn signs for "CORN" every mile or so. Vegetable stands in front of rambling farmhouses sold corn, tomatoes, peppers, squash, and orange-ripe pumpkins. He had sold home grown tomatoes door to door as a kid. Now what did he sell? What could he be?

Bob slowed the car to see "#29 Williamson" stenciled on the mailbox, then pulled into the driveway, ignoring the half-dozen high profile car makes parked in the yard. His Dodge was good enough. The three-story house had an adjoining rental and was newly painted blue with red trim.

"Oh, another guest," said the hostess, "I'm Amy."

"I'm Bob."

He shook hands, then patted down his wind blown hair. He sucked in his growing mid-thirties gut and guided his tall frame through the narrow doorway of the old house.

"So nice to meet you. Here's your nametag. Join the guests and have fun," said Amy.

Although overweight, Amy flitted around the room like a butterfly. Bob bent over the coffee table to fill out his name tag. He wrote his name and graduation year. College major? Does that apply? What am I current-ly working on—a job or myself? He simply answered the question and wrote "School of Chemical Engineering." So what if his major no longer applied to his life?

"If you're a chemical engineer, who do you work for?" asked a pretty brunette with a loose fitting turquoise top. Her top fell open as she crouched down to lift her drink. Bob stared down her shirt. She hesitated above him. Eyebrows lifted, she stooped to read, upside down, the name tag Bob was filling out.

"Now I'm a technical writing contractor," said Bob. He paused, hoping the conversation moved on.

"But what do you do?" she asked, persisting.

Bob stood. He retreated to the wall behind the couch and shoved his nametag in his pocket. The brunette's tag said "Carolyn." Carolyn pursued him.

"I write technical processes and procedures for companies," said Bob.

His voice cracked a little because he was actually just resting from being a chemical engineer and only thinking about other possibilities like technical writing. But he didn't feel comfortable disclosing that or much else about himself in front of strangers.

"Well, I still don't understand. What companies do you work for?" Carolyn asked.

The knot in Bob's stomach tightened. Reflexively, he lifted his left knee from the floor and held it tightly in his arms in a return-to-the-womb like gesture. She stared at the suspended leg.

"Any company in the Seacoast area that needs me. Everyone is reducing staff these days. I want to expand to product development and promotion. I write slogans too," said Bob.

Now pain had crept into Bob's eyes and voice. *Funny,* he thought, *these throwaway lines about work weren't as comfortable to share now as when he rehearsed them in front of the bathroom mirror several hours before.*

Carolyn's face grew solemn.

"I recently graduated from Cornell Law School. Now I'm an attorney at Barren & Barren in Concord," she said.

Then she squinted narrowly at Bob, and with a slight nod, left him to introduce herself to a tall mid-forties gentleman just entering the front door.

Bob looked over at an elderly couple. They drove a Cherokee jeep and wore matching green L.L. Bean outfits. They introduced themselves as Maude and Bernie. Apparently, Bernie had only partly overheard the previous conversation.

"So, you're a chemical engineer," he said, slowly approaching.

"Yes," said Bob. Here it comes again, he thought.

"Still doing it?" he asked, rounding Bob's perimeter.

"Now I write," said Bob.

"What kind of writing?" he asked. He wasn't stopping at all.

"Technical stuff, procedures and processes, and some creative short stories," said Bob. *Is this better?* He asked himself.

"You know, that's fine if you can make any money at it," Bernie shot back. Then he turned on his heel, but looked Bob straight in the face. "My son did that, now he practices law," he said.

Later, the hostess told Bob that Bernie was a retired vice president of engineering at Bucktite Corporation with a chemical engineering degree from Cornell. Bob wondered how his first impression went. Was Bernie referral material?

Bernie guided Maude out on to the deck where the grills were set to boil lobster and corn. Bob joined the latecomers for a tour of the house. Amy, the hostess, walked them through the plant room. Floor to ceiling glass windows facing the south for maximum sun exposure gave the greenery plenty of light. Bob stared through the glass at the mountains in the southwest that hung low on the horizon. Then the hostess called their attention to the inner wall of the room where the couple had hung animal skins. Amy pointed out that the large russet skin was from a Norwegian reindeer slaughtered on a local farm while the dark brown skin was from a moose killed by a neighbor in the mountains. She smiled remembering the pleasure of the unexpected gift.

Debra, an interior designer, complained that the moose fur did not feel as soft as the reindeer fur. The hostess explained that although both animals were kept warm with hollow air-filled hairs, only the reindeer had been killed during the optimum pelt season. Next, Bob studied the trophy-sized stuffed salmon hanging above the fireplace mantle and the full-length black bear skin rug, head intact, lying in front of the hearth. From a frozen growl on the tiled floor, the black bear's eyes bore into Bob. He turned away from the dead creatures decorating the room and gazed at the smiling guests sipping cocktails.

"Honey, the lobsters are ready," cried the host.

Bob walked onto the sunlit deck, sat down next to Bernie on a bench, and introduced himself to Brenda and her young daughter.

"Can you help me?" asked Brenda. "My son is applying to colleges for engineering. How was Cornell? He likes MIT. Stanford is a possibility. Perhaps you have some experience from your background?"

She was a blonde, in her mid-forties, who had temporarily given up her law partnership to raise her daughter.

Bob told her he had no regrets about Cornell, although it was isolated and lacked a social life. He mentioned the places he had applied to, his current ignorance, and the importance of making a wish list to rate the schools visited.

"You might try the state schools, too. U Mass is very good," said Bob.

"U Mass is an excellent school," Bernie chirped. He was monitoring the conversation.

"What do you do for fun?" asked Brenda.

"Watch movies, walk my black Scotty, and write stories," replied Bob.

"Really?" asked Brenda, "What kind of stories?" She smiled.

"All kinds. Whatever strikes me," said Bob.

Bernie, his ear cocked, swiveled his head to direct a question.

"But what kind?" he asked.

"I don't have a specialty," said Bob.

"Tell me the last story you wrote," Bernie said simply.

"I picked up a guy hitchhiking to Berlin. The hourly news on the radio gave the progressive story of a missing boy – the circumstances around his last sighting, his apparent abduction, the discovery of the body, cause of death, and lastly the search and capture of the killer. Then the hitchhiker next to me snickered, pulled out a knife, and said they had the wrong man. Of course the last part didn't happen, " said Bob.

""No. Of course not. And you weaved a story from the event. I never pick up hitchhikers. Have you been published?" he asked.

"No. It's a hobby. I just collect them," said Bob.

Bernie suddenly rose from the bench to refill his plate. The loss of his countering weight upended the bench causing Bob and his lobster to slide down to the deck planks.

"Is there an engineer in the house?" yelled someone.

"The bench legs are too close together," said Bob, brushing himself off. "I'm OK—no harm done to the lobster either."

Bernie shook his head and mumbled something about a moment of inertia. Then Bob took a moment to reflect on why he had come to the cookout and mingled with Cornell alumni. What was he looking for? A nurturing community of friends? Single women? An opportunity for net-working?

"Ready for ice-cream?" asked Amy.

"No, thanks. I've had all the nourishment I can handle," said Bob. "Thank you for your hospitality, Amy."

He gave Bernie and friends a little wave, then left for home.

The Ice Man

Bob O'Neil fluttered the newspaper excitedly at the closing price of Junkcorps, his mutual fund. It was almost double. Then he traced a line with his finger across the numbers—the volume, the high, the low, to the final closing. Junkcorps was unchanged. He had cross-read Junkcorps with its neighbor. He didn't normally read the financial page but his aunt had died recently and left him her entire estate, which was fortunate for him. Now he owned shares in a mutual fund, some stock in National Oil Co., and a $107,000 deposit in the Fiston National Bank.

His first impulse upon receiving the inheritance was to spend, spend, spend. By nature he was frugal, so the intensity of the feelings surprised him. He restrained himself from buying a sporty Mustang, a camp by a country lake, or a couple of laptop computers. Then he wanted a new house. But he already owned a house. He wanted a new house on a wooded four-acre lot with nice far away neighbors in the better end of town. His friends told him to wait. Indecisive, he let the money collect interest in the bank. Procrastination had its good points.

But six months had passed since the will was probated and the property sold. Now he needed an investment advisor. An old friend had once said when the student is ready the teacher will appear. Bob stared at the *Journal.* Five thousand mutual funds and another five thousand stocks stared back. Somehow he needed to select a profitable mix—but how?

He sipped coffee at his favorite cafe, the Starlet Cafe, where pretty waitresses offered a bottomless cup of coffee. As he read more columns and rows of numbers, his eyes glazed over and his chin nudged his chest.

"Excuse me," said the man next to him at the counter. "Are you finished with the *Journal?*" He smiled. "Is it today's?"

"You can borrow it for now," said Bob. "I'm taking the paper home to study."

"Are you new to finance?" asked the man.

He was tall, broad-shouldered, dressed in a dark suit and navy blue tie. His brown eyes darted across the room. He sidestepped the waitress's offer of coffee and sipped ice water instead. He patted smooth a wisp of black hair that partially covered his shiny bald top. Then he folded the Journal next to his silverware and outstretched his hand to Bob.

"I'm Benjamin Quinn. How do you do?" he asked.

"Bob O'Neil," said Bob.

Bob noticed Quinn's tight grip—like a vise.

"More power to the individual investor I always say," said Quinn. He sipped his ice water.

"I'm just a beginner when it comes to investing," Bob admitted. He postponed financial decision-making. Even when he did act and buy shares, he'd watch the price shoot up and down never knowing when to sell.

"My hobby is stock picks," said Quinn. "I have a seventy percent hit rate. When I find the time I'll start publishing a newsletter; meanwhile I'm building a clientele of like-minded investors who want to make a lot of money."

He asked the waitress to refill his ice water. Then he extracted his wallet.

"Here's my card," he said.

He sipped the ice water as Bob read the business card.

"You have an 800 number—wow," said Bob. "Is it expensive?"

"It's cheaper than you think," said Quinn. He pointed to his beeper. "My secretary."

Suddenly he glanced at his watch, gasped, and excused himself. He was late for an appointment. Bob watched his new acquaintance stroll out the door, overcoat draped over one arm and hand clutching umbrella with the other. Bob asked the waitress if she knew Quinn when she returned to wipe clean the place setting. She said she didn't know him from Adam, but she did mention he didn't leave a tip. Bob looked over at the new setting. Then Bob noticed his *Journal* was missing. He studied the card again.

Bob finished his third coffee, dropped a dollar on the counter, and left a fifty-cent tip. He grinned. Bob was about to find his missing newspaper.

Bob called Quinn the next day. The 800 number was connected to an answering service and Quinn called back immediately. Bob asked if Quinn knew how to make money through a comprehensive investment strategy. He invited Bob to the office with the understanding his first hour was free.

Bob met Quinn that afternoon, on Tuesday, inside the Starlet, where pictures of Marilyn Monroe in a low neckline dress adorned the walls. Quinn greeted Bob warmly, then left his ice water on the counter and his waitress without a tip, and escorted Bob down the street to his office. They walked passed the "Big Men's" storefront with its hand stenciled "fifty percent off- Going Out of Business" sign, entered a side door, and paused at a flight of stairs in a dimly lit hallway. Quinn had to stop and rest. He said an old injury had acted up while sleeping last night. He told Bob to go ahead up and wait for him at the top. Bob watched, concerned as Quinn laboriously pulled himself up the handrail, his torso wincing each time he leaned on the right side of his body.

Inside the office, Bob sat in one of two deep leather chairs placed directly in front of a large oak desk. A four drawer file cabinet beside the desk held Quinn's paperwork Bob surmised, and two large bookcases held books and magazines on everything from debt recovery to investing strategies. Quinn groaned when he dropped into his big straight-backed executive's chair. He excused himself for letting his PTSD interfere with business. Then he pulled the gold chain hanging from the chin of his brass dolphin lamp.

"How did you get PSTD?" asked Bob.

"It's PTSD. Post Traumatic Stress Disorder. Do you mind closing the door?" asked Quinn.

Bob closed the office door. He heard the locking mechanism click like a vault door had just shut.

"I twist and turn and strike out at ghosts from my old job. I used to work on a high security detail—guarding sheiks and heads of state," said Quinn.

Bob nodded. Since the first hour of consultation was free, this turn in the conversation didn't bother him.

"I used to be a special deputy for the Boston police department," said Quinn.

"You were a cop?" asked Bob.

"Not really. I meant to be one but on the day I was supposed to take the exam my girlfriend agreed to marry me and we went to the Justice of the Peace instead. Fate intervened. But as a special deputy I had a lot of the same thrills—just none of the benefits. I did have a badge."

He withdrew a black box from his desk drawer. He opened the box and Bob saw the silver shield. He whistled.

"I used to apprehend criminals the cops were afraid to capture. The money was in the reward," said Quinn.

"You must have ice water in your veins," said Bob.

"Funny you should say that. My handle was "Ice Man." The cops thought we were crazy," said Quinn.

Finally Bob steered the conversation away from police protection, bounty hunting, and the two-step kill method for hand-to-hand combat. Actually Bob didn't want to know if Quinn had broken the foot of some man behind him with his big size twelve wingtip leather shoes then turned quickly around and jammed the bones of the man's nose into his brain with the palm of his hand.

"What do you know about the disability system and investment management? I have a lawyer but don't trust him. I definitely don't trust the government. I'm looking for someone that's unaffiliated with a major organization, that's qualified, that's willing to be paid an hourly rate."

"I just happen to be working on a similar disability case for an elderly lady," said Quinn. "I know the results of my inquiries will directly relate to your case. I won't even bill you for that question."

Bob smiled. He was piggybacking on someone else's fee for free help. After paying the enormous legal bill that brought his crooked lawyer up the learning curve, he was glad it was his turn to benefit now.

"As far as investing is concerned, I will need more time and data. But before you leave, take a flier."

Bob glanced at the flier. The "Investment Seminar" was being offered at a "special introductory rate."

"Thanks," said Bob.

"This is a four-week seminar about how to handle money and investments. It's a real bargain at $75. The price will be $150 next time."

Bob considered all Quinn's free help, the special price, and his need for investment advice.

"OK, I'll show up this Saturday with the check," said Bob.

"I need the money now," said Quinn. His tone was harder, more urgent. He said he needed the money to front the room, pay a reception-ist, and cover the cost of materials.

Bob understood. Quinn was a businessman. He peeled off $75 from his wallet. Usually he carried less but today he had withdrawn money from the bank to food shop. Now he'd need to return to the bank and extract more money. Never mind, he had plenty more where that came from.

Quinn said he could stop by anytime to talk, if he wasn't busy, off the meter so to speak. He also said he had a special proposition to discuss with him after Saturday's meeting.

✦ ✦ ✦

Bob followed the bouncing blonde receptionist into the conference room down the hall from Quinn's office. She wore a sleeveless black top and sported a tattoo on the back of her upper arm—a red rose with a long green stem. Bob ate two blueberry muffins and drank three cups of coffee from a plastic china service. Newspapers and magazines covered the con-ference table. Bob slipped a *Journal* into his leather portfolio.

The presentation covered stock and bond market history, clarification of terms, and quotes from a successful mutual fund manager. Quinn even recommended a book, *How to Manage Your Investments*.

Bob told Quinn he liked the seminar back in the office. Apparently he shared a closer confidence with Quinn than the others had. Although he was surprised that the session was the second in the series of four. Quinn apologized about the mistake but he could make up it up at the final ses-sion. Quinn was giving a complete review then. The session had merely introduced the eight attendees and reviewed financial terms. Quinn was sure Bob was already familiar with them. Bob said he understood the mar-ket well enough to get into trouble.

"Have you resolved the disability issue?" asked Bob.

"Bob, I'm working my way through that now and I promise to have an answer for you soon. I have about five separate businesses going at once and I'm a little sick of working twelve hours a day, seven days a week—every damn week," he paused. "I'm sorry."

Bob commiserated with Quinn. Bob worked part-time at a volunteer job. He wanted to work a paid job in some capacity but that might jeop-ardize his disability pension -- hence his question to Quinn.

"I'm finding the seminar elementary," said Bob.

"Not everyone is as sophisticated as you are," said Quinn. "Some of those people have never even looked at a financial page in their local newspaper."

"But I can't make a decision on investing. I need some help," admitted Bob.

"I'm at your service, Bob," said Quinn. "In the meantime let me explain how my business is diversifying, incorporating, and issuing stock. You may find a niche there. I'm being very selective."

He grinned at Bob.

"How would you like to get in at the ground floor," he asked.

"Sure," Bob said.

Quinn waved his hand across the blackboard. Scribbled across in wavy letters were the outlines of five corporations that Bob could invest with, all linked to Quinn, the President.

"You'd be part of the economy yet not earn any money. No taxes to pay. No disability jeopardized," said Quinn.

Bob shrugged.

"You'd be a part owner. As it grows, you'd get ten percent of the profits," said Quinn.

Then Quinn said sometime in the future when Bob was sure about his disability, he could form a business to take advantage of the opportunities the exchange offered. The only problem was the offer was good for a limited time. To draw up the necessary legal work and start up money to revive the corporations. Quinn had acquired it from a rather dry, inhibited man who had no business sense. Now Quinn required $600. Three hundred down and three hundred when they drew up the paper work and signed the contracts to make him owner of a Sub Chapter "S" Corporation.

Bob beamed. He'd be a businessman. He was on the road to financial independence. He'd attend meetings with successful people, build relationships, and eventually land a job or get work in a field that would provide him a rewarding way of life.

"When do you need the money?" asked Bob.

Quinn ignored the question. Then Bob asked to see the documents the lawyer was reviewing to draft the new corporation.

Quinn searched his desk and his file cabinet.

"The file is missing. The lawyer must have both the copy and the original," said Quinn.

"When you do find it, I'll take a look," said Bob.

He rose to leave.

"If you leave now, you'll regret missing this business opportunity the rest of your life," said Quinn.

Bob's stomach churned. He hated being impulsive, but sometimes, when the situation warranted, he needed to act decisively. He looked Quinn square in the face.

"Will I make my money back?" asked Bob.

"I can't promise, that but I can promise you'll have fun meeting business people in a low-pressure atmosphere," said Quinn.

Ordinarily Bob never kept checks in his wallet. But today, because of yesterday's cancelled therapy appointment, he could seize the moment. Bob became so nervous about owning a corporation that he wrote the check for the full $600. Quinn didn't mind. He instructed Bob to make the check out to him, "Benjamin Quinn." Quinn stared at the check after Bob signed it.

Bob made a speech while Quinn kept staring at the check. Bob verified they weren't really business partners, just associates, that they really had a complete understanding of the business deal, in spite of the lack of documentation. Plus, Bob didn't want to make too much money right away—that might jeopardize his disability pension.

Then Bob presented the check to Quinn—who quickly slipped it into his wallet. Then Quinn said they had a lot more to talk about. Next month all the associates would meet to discuss business opportunities. Quinn was also available for investment decision-making. Any strategy he might devise was free until they developed a contract. After that, he'd just charge by the hour.

"Drop by any time," said Quinn. "I won't charge you, we'll just talk."

On Wednesday of the following week, Bob visited Quinn's office to boost his sagging morale. Stocks had tumbled twenty percent the last two days. The bull market was correcting itself. Bob knew better days lay ahead but he did need professional guidance.

Quinn pardoned himself for not rising when he shook hands with Bob; his right lower leg was in a walking cast. A cane, crested with a wolf's head, rested against the desk. What surprised Bob was seeing Quinn's left arm in a cast. He said his girlfriend had hit him while he was driving her car. The resulting minor accident had broken him up, physically and emotionally, as well as their relationship. Since he didn't drive nor own a car, he had forgotten about renewing his license when he moved in with his parents after his divorce. He didn't think the wrap would be tough to beat. In any case, he was suing the state for failure to send him a renewal notice, his ex-girlfriend for assault, and the town for gross negligence—they had failed to properly reflector the tree he had sideswiped. Quinn said he'd enjoyed his previous court appearances so much, he was thinking about law school.

Bob stated his business after the usual condolences.

"I'd like to possibly hire you as a money manager," said Bob.

"How much money do you have?" asked Quinn.

"Do you really need to know about everything I own?" asked Bob.

"If you really want me to help you I do—just the liquid assets," said Quinn.

Bob sat down in the chair as Quinn struggled with a pen. Bob told him about the oil shares, his Junkcorps mutual fund, and the $107,000 bank deposit.

Quinn stopped writing for a moment.

"Did you forget anything?" asked Quinn.

"Like my checking account balance?" asked Bob.

"No. Some people have so many accounts, they forget to tell me them all, then I can't do my best," said Quinn.

"You know about everything," said Bob.

"My fee is $65 per hour and because I like you, I'll charge you just $60 per hour. Office time is free. But I expect four hours of research time is sufficient to complete the project. How does $240 sound?" Quinn said.

"I like it," said Bob. He thought the price was a deal. Quinn said he expected his work to take longer but needed to build goodwill since he was starting his business over after being embezzled by his partner and divorced by his wife back in Boston.

"Perhaps you'd like to see my resume?" asked Quinn.

He opened a folder containing a two-page resume. The second page listed all his hobbies and interests—a lot for a guy without a car.

"Can I have a copy?" asked Bob.

"Just made today. This is my only copy," said Quinn.

Bob reviewed the only copy.

"What does RICO mean?"

Bob was looking at his credentials.

"I'm a board-certified Registered Investment Counselor and Operator—this allows me to deal in stocks and bonds as well as advise the public," said Quinn. "RICO means rich in Spanish—you know."

"Yes, I know, I took Spanish in high school," said Bob.

Bob looked at the office walls—three brass-framed pictures of geese, flying in formation, presumably headed south decorated the walls. Then Bob gave Quinn a copy of the plan he devised which he didn't have the courage himself to implement. He needed Quinn to supply the confidence.

Quinn outstretched his hand for a shake. They'd meet after Saturday's session. Then he rose and hobbled to the door with Bob.

"I have to be in court shortly. My business has a cash flow problem. I'm taking former clients to court for bounced checks or failure to pay me for services rendered. I know they have the money. Just shows you the richer you are, the tighter you get," said Quinn.

Bob wished Quinn luck in the court battle, shook his hand again and left.

✦ ✦ ✦

Quinn was late for the third seminar. He arrived with his head in bandages, eye swollen, but his arm was out of its sling. He hobbled to the front of the class on his walking cast and announced in a frog voice that he'd been mugged on his way home from town. The police were investigating.

Class was simple. He turned on the VCR and the class watched a tape from *Evening Star*, a mutual fund tracking company that instructed newcomers to the market how to evaluate and monitor mutual funds.

After the show, Quinn invited Bob back to the office for coffee and doughnuts. On the way down the hall, Bob extracted a blank check from his wallet and folded it into his shirt pocket to be ready to pay for Quinn's services.

"How is the work going?" asked Bob.

"Bob, I have your portfolio in a form suitable for your review," he said.

Quinn scrolled back his notebook a page and scrutinized his handwriting next to a pyramid shaped investment strategy involving risk. Then he withdrew from his shirt pocket a folded paper – Bob's own attempt to figure his way to financial independence.

"I'm also assessing your remarkable first attempt at investment strategy," said Quinn.

"I've read a few newspaper articles and a book or two," said Bob.

"Bob, I have a proposition for you," said Quinn.

"Shoot," said Bob.

"I need to borrow a few hundred dollars," said Quinn.

"Why?" asked Bob.

"I'm suffering from a severe cash flow crisis. My clients are using the legal system to stall payments while my creditors are threatening legal action against me," said Quinn.

"How much exactly?" asked Bob.

"Nine hundred dollars," said Quinn. "I will then do your work for free."

"Sounds too good to be true," said Bob. "You said a few hundred dollars. How about $400? Will you still work for free?" asked Bob.

"Oh, sure," said Quinn.

"I still feel bad that I'm taking advantage of you," said Bob.

"Will you feel any better if you permit me to show your account to my other clients—under a John Doe name?" said Quinn.

Bob nodded.

"What about the $500 remaining? I still need $500," said Quinn.

"I can't help you," said Bob.

"Now I'll have to ask someone else," said Quinn.

"I'm sorry but I live on a fixed income," said Bob.

"Oh, I'll manage somehow. I always do. I shouldn't burden you with my personal problems anyway, but with our friendship, the line between business and personal can bend," said Quinn.

Bob made the $400 check to "Benjamin Quinn" and set the check on the desk. Quinn plucked it and examined the signature.

Then Quinn told Bob he had discovered another way for them to make money. He was starting an investment club: the members sign over a quantity of cash to the fund manager, Quinn, who would then invest the cash—with the input of the club members considered of course. Quinn expected to start at the $10,000 level and work from there. Nothing like learning through doing, said Quinn.

Intrigued, Bob wanted to know more, but he needed time to digest the day's events. He shook hands, walked to the door, and turned suddenly.

"By the way..." said Bob. He stopped. Quinn had just swallowed a mouthful of pills with a cup of coffee. Bob let it go and left.

Bob ran into Cindy, a class member, at the Starlet Cafe on the following Wednesday. She had a round pink face, large blue eyes, and mousy brown hair pulled into a pigtail. She spilled coffee on her black sweater as she told him Quinn was suing her for non-payment of work she had never requested him to do. Furthermore, the work she had retained him to perform with an up front payment, he had never done. Quinn said to her he had signed documents that supported his points. Cindy said she had only signed a letter asking for services to be performed.

Then Bob told his story. Cindy touched his hand to give him the confidence to continue—all told he figured he'd have to write off $1000—unless he sued Quinn. But Quinn knew the legal system, and he also knew a half dozen ways to kill a man. Quinn had even told Bob, in his former security firm, he had attached a sawed off shotgun beneath his desk to train on out of control clients.

Before leaving, Cindy gave Bob her phone number and said to call anytime. Bob told her not to worry about Quinn now that they were wise to him.

Bob skipped the last class, Quinn called about scheduling a meeting but Bob excused himself quickly—he had an important phone call on the other line—and couldn't talk. Actually, Bob had just one phone line. Then Bob hired a new lawyer, a middle-aged woman with a pleasant smile, who said Quinn was a fraud, the money gone, and legal retaliation fruitless—possibly even dangerous.

Bob never heard from Quinn again, although once he thought he could make out a fog-shrouded figure limping down the road carrying an umbrella—but when he slowed to look more closely, all he saw was a drunk urinating in an alleyway.

"...Shame on Me"

After being fleeced out of $1,000 by the con man from Black River Executive Services, Bob O'Neil decided to seek recommendations from the professionals he respected most on the best way to invest the $100,000 from his aunt's estate. She had left him money, property, and a year's supply of toilet paper. Now he needed help with his finances. The Irish undertaker, a decent chap who gave Bob a discount on the service (this being the third the family had arranged in a year) directed him to an honest lawyer to handle the estate. Bob liked the lawyer: he came in under budget and didn't nickel and dime him to death for the penny-ante stuff. Unfortunately his office was out of state, difficult to reach, and almost 100 miles away from Fiston.

Bob decided to ask the professionals he knew best locally: his therapist and his psychiatrist. Bob's chemical imbalance resulted in an emotional instability that prescribed medication controlled. Since he couldn't work at present, he was grateful that his aunt had fancied him in her later years.

His two soul keepers, Trisha Petersen and the shrink, both recommended Judith Spellman. She specialized in disability issues. His last experience with the law was winning two judgments against the government, yet the verdict was appealed to a higher court. He had paid his lawyer $8,000, then received notice the lawyer had left town for greener pastures after verbally committing to do the remaining legal work pro bono.

So much for justice.

◆ ◆ ◆

Bob drummed his fingers against the tabletop while he waited for Ms. Spellman. He was early, hot and sweaty from the July heat. Bob rhythmically turned the pages of *People* magazine looking at the pictures, reading the captions and leaving little smudge prints from fingers sticky with chocolate. He had bought a bar from the receptionist: a dollar to help send a poor kid to the hospital. Bob looked out the window at the harbor view and around the computer-laden office. *How much did she charge per hour,* he wondered? The Norman Rockwell portrait of a snug couple, joyful in their elder years, stared down at him. Bob couldn't imagine people that old being so happy and figured they must be sharing more than their lives with each other and that the bottle was hidden beneath one of their bulky winter jackets.

"Attorney Spellman will see you now," said the receptionist. She was at least fifty, with glasses and a strong protruding jaw.

Bob tossed the magazine on the table, stood, wiped the sweat from his palms on his gray camper shorts, and combed his curly hair into a slight part with the fingers of his right hand. Then he picked up the white plastic bag lettered in green "Save Our Shores" containing all his legal and financial papers and walked into the attorney's office.

"Hello Attorney Spellman, I'm Bob O'Neil," he said.

"Call me Judy," said the lawyer. Her firm handshake surprised Bob. She was forty-something, pleasant-faced and matronly, with wavy brown hair that was secured from behind with a comb.

"What I'd like to do," began Bob, "is create a trust to help me manage my money. I need a buffer in case I become sick or fall under the spell of another con."

"You want a revocable trust. You should be able to fire me after say a sixty-day cooling-off period. That's no problem," said Judy.

Then Bob looked in her eyes a long time. He saw a happy lady who had decided at twelve to be a lawyer and hadn't looked back since.

"I need to trust you," said Bob. He hoped he could.

She raised her eyebrows.

"Trisha told me you were already burnt once. I understand how you feel. But this is a standard document, Bob. I don't want your money. Do you realize how much I make? I have a question for you: Do you yell? I can't deal with people that like to yell."

Bob shook his head.

First she wanted to do the easy items. She asked about his insurance. Bob was lucky that he had great health insurance but at twenty percent of his monthly disability check plus hefty co-payments Judy thought she could find a cheaper plan. She asked her contact at Blue Cross about a supplemental Medicare plan. Unfortunately for Bob the six-month application window for coverage had passed. He'd been on Medicare for two years.

"I'm sorry Bob," said Judy.

"But how much money would I have saved? Did they cover drugs as well?" asked Bob.

"What does it matter? You're not eligible. Let it go," said Judy, touching him on the elbow.

Bob insisted she call her contact again. They found out that Bob might have saved $100 per month in premium costs but the supplemental plan didn't cover his $150 per month drug habit- unlike in his current package. In fact, if Bob's current Blue Cross package ever lapsed, he'd find himself in the uninsurable pool of people that the health insurance companies excluded from buying premiums.

So much for health insurance.

Bob enjoyed the muffin break; Judy's secretary brought in a tray of blueberry and corn muffins with a pot of coffee, sugar, powdered cream and Styrofoam cups. He fixed himself a regular coffee and grabbed a corn muffin.

Judy sipped a coffee while gazing briefly at the picture of her two grade school children, embraced by Mom, in front of their beach front island home.

"Your little girl looks a lot like you. She's very pretty," said Bob.

He realized the indirect compliment too late, then absently wondered where the father was. She had already touched him on the arm twice so Bob figured she must like him. Usually, Bob was smitten by emotionally twisted prom queens that later ripped his heart out. Suddenly Judy smiled and Bob decided she must not be dating anyone in particular. She was kind of pretty and very successful.

"Thank you, Bob, you're very sweet," said Judy. "Now for the next order of business—disability insurance."

She reviewed his private disability plan whose benefits were ending next year and confirmed the ironclad nature of his contract. Too bad he hadn't opted for the plan that covered him until he was 65.

Next she reviewed the government disability plan. She explained that any money received from employers or as an independent contractor had to be reported to Social Security. Since he received money from the government for being completely disabled, any indication that he was an able wage earner might affect his benefits. They might review his medical history. If he really made a lot of money, say in a trial work period, they might eventually suspend his benefits.

Lastly, she investigated the lawsuit against the government for disability income as a former government worker. She looked up from the paper work and shrugged.

"With two judgments in your favor, I expect you'll win your court case in time. As a result of the arrearages and supplemental income, you'll be able to lead a very comfortable life without working. I advise you not to work because of the benefits you may lose and focus your life on non-traditional forms of service.

"Your doctor has stated your prognosis is a cycle of recovery, relapse and remission. I suggest you enjoy yourself as best you can and live life," said Judy.

So much for work.

Bob wondered if she still liked him as much now that she had read his files.

"Now for the inheritance," said Bob.

Bob had spent four months interviewing banks, trusts, and investment advisors after being robbed by the shark. As usual, he didn't know who to trust and time was wasting. Judy said that after signing the trust, he'd need to have someone manage the money. Although she personally lost money in the market, her firm used Ted Wood. He was very good, if they could get him.

"I hope so," said Bob, knocking his fist on the oak table twice.

"I'm not speaking out of turn if I say someone you see regularly uses his services too—just between you and me," said Judy. "He talks fast, avoids neck ties, and wears suspenders."

"As long as they're not polka dotted I don't care what he wears," said Bob.

"He likes rainbow colored ones," she snickered. "Let's call him."

She dialed his office and left a message to call as soon as he returned from vacation. "Next Friday? We'll sign the trust and interview Ted. Call to confirm," said Judy.

"It's a revocable trust, right?" asked Bob.

"Yes, Bob, take the next week to feel this out," said Judy.

The computer chimed softly. Judy stood. Bob shook her outstretched hand. She squeezed his fingers slightly, then touched his elbow.

"Don't forget your corn muffin and coffee," said Judy.

As Bob left, sipping his free coffee and munching his muffin, he regretted not making more small talk. But, at over $2 per minute, his reluctance to spend time laying the groundwork to ask her out was understandable.

So much for romance.

Ted Wood arrived characteristically late to Judy's office. Bob had already reviewed the trust, made sure it was revocable, and signed the document in the presence of Judy's secretary and slender paralegal. He even had a bank check made out to himself that he could endorse to Ted if he liked him well enough. Judy wanted him to proceed at a comfortable pace.

"Hello Judy," said Ted. "Always good to see a friendly face."

He set down a leather portfolio beside the chair, greeted Bob with a quick shake, and pulled up his chino slacks as he sat down. Then he twirled his thumbs in his gold-colored suspenders.

"Ted, Bob has come into some money and seeks expert financial advice. You're one of our first choices," said Judy.

"Thank you," said Ted.

Bob explained his circumstances, his background, his prospects. Then Ted went into action. He told them what a great guy he was, showed him his resume, his client recommendations and explained all the fruit salad next to his name. He even hinted about loopholes to reduce health insurance expense and prolong disability coverage.

"God, that's great," said Bob.

"Ted, you're wonderful," said Judy.

Next Ted told them he was selling over 800 load and no-load mutual funds at a fixed rate of 1.0% per year. He flipped through a thick folder of charts and happy faced people enjoying their newly acquired wealth from the fifteen-year bull market, a time when just about any fund or fund manager could enjoy double-digit growth. Bob wasn't sure he liked Ted but he did like the service Ted offered.

"I am only allowed by law to explain the charts and not leave them here. I cannot recommend any fund not listed here without possibly losing my license," said Ted.

"We wouldn't want that Ted," bantered Judy.

"What does that star mean?" asked Bob, pointing to the chart with several graphs.

"That's a good question," said Ted. "They've changed the book recently. I can get back to you on that."

"Thanks, Ted," said Judy.

"Here's a list of recommended funds from various categories. Now I can't leave them or comment on them, besides saying what I have just said legally," said Ted.

"We wouldn't want you to go to jail, Ted," said Judy. "How was your vacation?"

Bob listened as Ted recounted his fabulous visit to his mother country—Great Britain. He stayed with the financial consultant for Devil's Food Cake Co. "Gone to the Devil," he joked to his associates. His buddy in Britain worked for one of the wealthiest families in the US and tracked their European holdings using three computers. Ted admitted to dreaming up software but he used programmers to connect the dots.

"Do you like computers, Bob?" asked Ted.

"I like to write," said Bob.

"That's a nice hobby," said Ted.

"Do you mind waiting outside for a few minutes, Ted," asked Judy, touching him on the shoulder. "We have to consult."

Bob figured the best way to overcome his indecisiveness and past failures was to surround himself with successful people like Judy, his hired gun, and Ted, a financial whiz. He nodded to Judy that he was ready to deal. Ted returned to the office and thanked him for the business but refused the bank check. He gave Bob the blank forms and told him to sign at the x when he was ready, then send the check. After reviewing the form, Ted said it was an old one and he initialed and dated several changes.

Just then someone knocked softly on the door and one of Judy's law partners sneaked in excusing himself. He embraced her with a kiss and apologized for needing to miss lunch. Bob realized her partner really was her partner and heard his stomach growl.

"Bob, I think you should call Ted next week to discuss specific investment plans," said Judy.

Bob folded his papers into the plastic bag, shook hands with his team of professionals, and left them talking about old times.

So much for being his own man.

✦ ✦ ✦

Ted greeted Bob at the door of his office wearing green suspenders. Then he pulled a slab of wood from his desk for Bob to drop his plastic bag of papers.

"How can I help you?" asked Ted.

"I received your recommendations and I have counter recommendations. I've simplified the portfolio from twenty-four to eight funds. I eliminated the funds with less than a five year history, kept more of my funds where possible, and threw out a few because they looked lousy. Other than that, I didn't change much," said Bob, pausing. "Except that I changed all the ratios. I wasn't comfortable with the model's make up."

"Fine," said Ted.

He stared at the papers. Everything had changed. Bob's suggestions weren't meant to hamstring Ted, just guide him so that he could trust him. He hadn't yet earned Bob's trust.

Ted pulled at his green suspenders.

"What fund is this?" he asked.

"That's a closed end high performer—'Sailor's' been around for twenty years at least—you must have heard of it," said Bob.

Ted switched to another fund.

"We'll put 'Lion' into the growth section," said Ted.

"Isn't 'Lion' really an aggressive growth fund?" asked Bob.

"I guess it is," said Ted.

"How about income and growth?" asked Bob.

"You like 'Blue Chips,'" said Ted, "Let's see the computer story on that."

Ted rolled his chair over to the terminal.

"Do you have any financial magazines here?" asked Bob, "I forgot my *Forbes*."

"No," said Ted as he pounded the keyboard, "I know 'Blue Chips' is on the system somewhere."

"What about the *Journal?*" asked Bob.

Ted avoided the question. He said he needed to call the home office. His computer was acting up. Then he turned back to Bob.

"What happened?" asked Bob.

"They updated the computer software, but haven't sent me a new manual. My office system is improving so fast it's tough to keep track," said Ted.

Ted faxed "Blue Chips" for their performance history. After the papers were spit out of the machine, he excused himself. His wife was sick and he needed to leave early to feed the kids.

Bob drove home wondering how the day had gone. His little dog yawned, but Bob's breathing was sharp and quick, he felt like he was buying a house. Did Ted know anything? What good was paying a fee if Bob did all the thinking? Bob walked his dog and thought some more. The thought dropped to his guts and became a feeling. He didn't have to entrust Ted with his investments.

"He's fired," said Bob to himself.

Bob felt immediately more comfortable. Like his father had said, "Fool me once shame on you, fool me twice shame on me." What did Bob really know about the lawyer either? He hadn't even seen her bill. Ted could be kicking money back to her from the clients she sent him. Was Trisha involved as well?

So much for the professionals.

Bob looked at the three solemn faces staring at him as they sat around the table in Judy's office. Ted wore a short sleeve white shirt, navy blue suspenders and, uncharacteristically, a matching bow tie. Trisha's black pantsuit highlighted her golden hair. Judy smoothed the ruffles of her snowwhite blouse then unbuttoned her dark gray suit coat.

"Bob," said Judy, "I'm speaking for all of us when I say we want you to be happy with our performance, comfortable in your decisions, successful in your investments, and even like us as people regardless of our professional relationship."

"I've been having my doubts," said Bob.

"You've retained me to be your hired gun and I've called this meeting in that capacity. Ted told me you wanted to fire him. You have that right but there will be consequences—money and time lost, perhaps needlessly. Plus I'll feel bad for introducing you two," said Judy.

Trisha's hand gestured gracefully to Ted.

"Bob, I don't know about financial matters," said Trisha, her voice tinged with concern, "But I can vouch for Ted's character, honesty, and intelligence. I've known him a number of years."

Bob fidgeted. Would Trisha, his therapist for the last three years, lie to him?

Judy handed him a sheet of paper.

"I know you've been anxious about the bill. Is the fee fair?" she asked.

After all the calls, conferences, and revisions to draft the revocable trust, Bob was surprised how little Judy charged for "Professional Services."

Bob nodded. Ted cleared his throat.

"I hope my performance is no longer a question," he said, and Bob dropped his eyes, embarrassed. "But I do admit to being too aggressive for your taste. We've already ironed out most of the new portfolio make-up. It'd be a shame to fire me and start at ground zero again. I think we can work well together.

"As far as my firm goes, there have been an unusual number of top down changes. I may switch to provide you with more consistent service. As far as not knowing everything about funds, there are over 5000 out there—it's impossible to know them all."

Bob studied the three professionals. Although successful high-achievers, they were fallible. Bob knew the next guy he picked would need to pass similar rigorous tests, and the selection process would begin from scratch.

"OK, I'll give Ted a year," said Bob. "Now that we've talked, I appreciate his efforts on my behalf, and perhaps we'll communicate better in the future."

"Great," said Judy, looking at her watch. "Why don't we adjourn to the coffee shop downstairs?"

Bob felt comfortable again.

Everyone smiled in agreement.

Judy, a minor-league baseball fan, joked about how many games out of first place her favorite team—the Hurricanes—were, and asked about the weather for tomorrow's game. Actually, they were all attending tomorrow evening's twi-night doubleheader. Here they were, all buddy-

buddy again. The knife of paranoia stabbed in his gut as he fought the thought they were all in a conspiracy to steal his money. He said a quick prayer. The thought passed. He knew his head was out of order. After all, they even invited him along to the game. Next, Judy offered Bob two four-dollar general admission tickets to next week's game against the first-place Thunderheads. As Bob slipped the free tickets into his wallet, he let go of his money issues and focused instead on his developing interest in minor-league baseball.

So much for the inheritance.

Unanswered Love

Bob O'Neil surveyed the room full of women from his end of the bar and thought the selection looked especially bleak at the Mermaid's Tavern. At least the tasty appetizers were free. Bob and Foster ate their dinner.

The door opened and a statuesque blonde walked passed them. Foster hurriedly finished his last chicken wing. He was handsome, fortyish, and charismatic. His curly brown hair was dyed to remove the gray, and his roving blue eyes were targeted to capture beautiful young women. He slapped Bob on the arm.

"Did you see the blonde come in? I think she's alone. Bob, she's gorgeous," said Foster.

Bob shrugged. Dating, in general, scared him. But picking up a beautiful woman in a bar made his chest constrict, palms sweat and hands shake. Foster sipped his tonic water and peeked across the tables.

"Bob, I swear she's staring at us. Who'll try first, you or me?" asked Foster.

Bob glanced at the woman. She sat alone at a table smoothing out the napkin next to her drink. Bob looked away before she caught him. He was ten years younger than Foster, much taller yet less noticeable. He didn't share Foster's charisma.

"Go for it Foster," said Bob, "that stuff makes me too jittery." Talking to women triggered Bob's nervous condition.

Bob waited a short time before he looked over. Sure enough, Foster had her talking. He turned away and swallowed more Coke. How ungrateful, he thought, Foster had left him alone at the bar—after all the scrapes Bob had pulled him through—not to mention the money Bob had "loaned" jobless Foster. Four years of continuous unemployment -- he lived on the grace of God and the goodwill of friends -- had pushed Foster back into his old profession… running for political office. A job in itself. Winning the nomination for state representative might allow Foster to trade influence for a real job. Who knows, Bob might even find himself friends with the man representing Fiston in the state legislature in Concord.

Bob scanned the Tavern. The place was dead. He'd never find a girl. *Perhaps*, thought Bob, *I'll leave and strand Foster with the blonde. Serve him right.* Then Bob reconsidered; stranding him at the Tavern might actually help Foster get lucky tonight.

Bob was looking deep into his cola when someone grabbed his arm.

"Hey, Bob. Regina said she wants to meet you. Coming?" asked Foster.

"What's the catch?" asked Bob.

"Simple. She likes tall men and I struck out on account of my height. Now it's your turn—if you want it," said Foster.

Foster walked Bob over to Regina's table. She wore her long wavy blonde hair in a black band down to the middle of her back. She smiled at him with bright green eyes that highlighted a flawlessly fair complexion.

"Nice to meet you, Bob," said Regina waving her long eyelashes.

"Nice to meet you, too, Regina," said Bob. He fell stupidly dumb as he slid in a wooden chair.

Foster jumped in to save the encounter. He showed Bob Regina's personal ad in the local paper. A true Romeo, he had crossed out her adjective "attractive" and had written "beautiful" instead. The ad mentioned she owned her own business selling novelty items in a scenic seaport town nearby.

"Bob, stand up. She can guess your height," said Foster.

Bob stood. She sized him up quickly and correctly. Before long, they were trading pictures of their dogs and attesting to the reality of ghosts. She saw a psychic who forecasted she'd meet a boat builder. Bob told her he worked at the Shipyard in a technical position. He didn't lie about being unemployed and currently disabled—he did say "worked"—the past tense. When he asked her to dance, he couldn't stop his hands from shaking. She asked him about it and he told her he wasn't used to holding such a beautiful woman. He didn't tell her the shaky hands were a medication side effect. Bob liked her simple style. He was even a little jealous when she danced with another guy.

"I've had a wonderful time," said Bob. "Perhaps we can get together again."

Regina agreed and they exchanged phone numbers. Then he drove Foster home.

Foster hesitated before leaving the car for his room in his friend's half a million-dollar house. A room paid for by a town welfare check. He asked Bob if he was really going to call Regina. Bob nodded. Foster complained that he had to campaign the next day and his car needed gas. Bob got the hint and gave him a ten-dollar bill. Foster ambled away holding his necktie and brushing lint from his only suit.

Bob waited until the following Sunday to call Regina for a date. Her little boy answered the phone. Bob asked him for his mom. When Regina answered, Bob talked about everything except the date. He had forgotten to even plan the date. Exhausted, before he had to hang up, he managed to ask her to dinner. She suggested Richfield's, an elegant seaside restaurant. Like a chicken, he hedged on setting a day for the date. Instead, he promised to confirm a time during the week.

Next, he called Richfield's to make a reservation. While on the phone with the cashier, he estimated the bill, wondered if Regina would think he was an alcoholic because he didn't drink, and thought about how difficult it'd be to play father to a 12-year-old boy if he came along. Being involved made life difficult, but boredom was painful too. Actually, neither Regina nor Bob had much luck meeting the opposite sex. Her last boyfriend had abused her and Bob's last serious romantic relationship ended in a one-sided wrestling match from which Bob still felt pinned. Perhaps this time fate had taken a hand.

Tuesday Bob left a message on Regina's answering machine asking her to call him about the date. On Wednesday he left the day and time of the date on her recorder. Regina left him a message on Thursday.

"Bob," said Regina, "I'm sorry I haven't got back to you sooner, but I can't find a baby sitter, extra work came up, and I don't think I can make the date. I'll call you Friday. Bye."

Bob counter-attacked in the early afternoon on Friday when he didn't expect her home. He was surprised at how steady his voice sounded when he acknowledged her Thursday message, repeated his invitation to Richfield's, and even offered to treat her son to dinner as well. He hoped his message allayed her fears and convinced her to dine with him.

Regina called back late Friday afternoon. The answering machine picked up the call since Bob had left the house with a case of phone phobia.

"Bob, I am real sorry to have to do this, but I won't be able to go out tonight. This weekend isn't a good time to meet either. Maybe I'll call you next week or something. Talk to you later," said Regina.

Bob listened to the message twice. October was half over. He had hoped to spend Thanksgiving with her. Now he felt like the turkey. She didn't call back and he let go of the idea of dating her.

❖ ❖ ❖

Two weeks before Thanksgiving, Bob's answering machine caught another hope-filled message.

"Hello Bob. This is Regina, from the Tavern, and I'm calling you back about our broken date. I didn't like the way I handled it. Perhaps you can call me back tonight or tomorrow after 8:00 pm. Bye," said Regina.

Bob practiced his lines before making the call. Then he dialed. Regina's son answered the phone. He checked and said his mother was busy. Bob left his name and number then lied on his bed praying that she got his message. Would she call? Was it a trick? Were they both laughing at him?

The phone rang.

"Hello, Bob. This is Regina," she said.

"Hi, Regina," said Bob.

"Thanks for returning my call. Would you like to get together for a drink at the Tavern? Singles dancing starts at 8:00 pm tomorrow night," said Regina.

Bob remembered the Quaker function. He figured he could play hard to get as long as the conflict was over a religious matter.

"I'm going to a church supper Friday night. Perhaps we can go to Richfield's Saturday," said Bob.

"I'd really like to go to the singles dance. I'm planning a trip to Disney World so I have to work extra hard at the store. Christmas will be here soon. Lots of presents to buy. Call me in December. Let's go then," said Regina.

December was almost a month away, thought Bob.

"So I can call you then to get together," said Bob.

"Yes, bye Bob," said Regina.

Bob didn't forget the attractive, no scratch that, beautiful blonde businesswoman. She was five foot four and slender but really put together. He called her about a month later and left a message on her answering machine. She must have missed his message so he called again the next night. Her son answered and checked to see if mom was in. Then he came back and asked for Bob's name and number. A twelve-year-old boy not knowing if his mother was home?

Bob didn't forget, but apparently the blonde had. She never called back. Funny, he hadn't even divulged his non-alcoholic life style, his emotional illness, or his lack of a job to boot. She jilted him simply for the way he was. He either needed to work on his personality or call more women. Only his therapist knew for sure.

Another Angel

Bob O'Neil knew someone famous had been born years ago on Christmas day, but he suspected one of his friends would die this Christmas Eve. A couple had heart conditions, a few held back homicidal/suicidal urges, one admitted himself to a psych unit, and another signed himself out of a hospital AMA. Christmas was a tough time of year for sensitives. Memories surfaced.

Bob stared at the Christmas tree. Pine needles littered the floor—the tree absorbed water poorly. Tinsel draped the boughs. Red ribbons decorated the little twigs. Christmas cards drooped from nooks in the branches. A bell hung from the crown of the tree. Occasionally he shook the tree, ringing the bell, and thought about the fledgling angel who had just won its wings.

Sitting on the couch directly opposite his roommate, Bob opened more Christmas cards from his fair holiday friends – people from the past that he rarely heard from otherwise. He tore apart the envelopes from his successful ex-co-workers and read the little notes with pursed lips. Dennis, his old boss from the Fortune 50 oil company, was still consulting on coke—the petroleum kind. Winston, the reclusive miser now in management, had graduated from merely staring at women in longing to stalking them in earnest. Lionel, the gay electronics whiz with the kleptomaniac partner, had bought a larger house to fill with glass and brass collectibles, proceeds from his work on the Sea Hawk missile guidance system. But Bob missed the card from his college buddy and former colleague who was now a VP of a Fortune 500 subsidiary.

"I bet Cliff is a company president and multimillionaire by now," Bob told his roommate Rudy.

He stared hard at Rudy's shoe clad feet scrunched under ample thighs on the couch as Rudy picked chicken flesh from a box of Dominoes Buffalo wings. The roommate shrugged, twisted his feet back to the floor, and nearly dumped his wings in the process.

"You want a wing, Bob?" he asked.

"Sure, here's a napkin," said Bob.

They shared the chicken. Bob stripped the meat clean from the bone, licking the grease from his fingers and wiping them with the napkin. He tore off some broccoli heads from the fridge and popped them into his mouth. Then he sucked up a bowl of twirling pasta. Dinner!

Bob grabbed the phone, address book, some chips and a Diet Coke. He punched in the numbers wondering what his buddy the VP was up to on Christmas Eve. Cliff was an entrepreneur who was politically astute in the corporate world; his hobby was stock market picks and company takeover candidates. Last Christmas, in the midst of the holiday blues, Bob moaned to Cliff about his depression, his disability, his dwindling inheritance, his lost career, and his lack of a steady honey. Then he asked to what Cliff attributed his own worldly success. He replied with "hard work." This Christmas, the blues had stayed away and he had invited over a dozen friends to celebrate the holiday the previous Sunday. Everyone said they had a great time.

Bob listened to the rings until a woman answered.

Surprised, Bob asked for Cliff. The woman, in response, asked who was speaking and then apologized.

"Cliff passed away last July. He was jogging and died suddenly on the side of the road. His phone rings in my home in Cleveland. Were you close to my son? I didn't know he had many friends."

"I tried to stay in touch," said Bob guiltily. "What was the cause of death?"

The roommate did a double take.

"Heart attack. He was thirty-eight," she said.

Bob was thirty-six and had stopped exercising routinely ten years ago. He stared at the chicken bones and chips and Coke on the table in front of him. Rudy was slugged away on the other couch with his big belly leaning against a pile of glistening chicken bones in his lap.

"He's dead."

Bob hung up the phone and looked at the roommate.

"What?" asked the roommate.

"He's dead. How do you measure success? I'm on disability, but today I'm happy. I have friends. I'm alive. Despite all his money, he didn't have close friends, and died of a broken heart. Now his mother's a rich lady."

Bob walked over to the Christmas tree. He shook the tree and rang the bell.

77

Heart Work on Valentine's Day

Bob O'Neil let Gloria push past him in the hallway adjacent to where the Group held their meetings. She didn't say a thing as he called to her. He watched Gloria saunter off to her newest confidant, a tall hunky blonde surfer type. She had snubbed Bob again. Bob clenched his teeth as she greeted the surfer with a smile. She talked rapidly and kept wiping invisible strands of brown hair out of her sky blue eyes. She turned around once and caught him staring at her. He decided to confront her in the street. Bob was sick of her endless games. *Did she really care about me?* He asked himself.

Soon, Bob gave up waiting. He looked back once on the way to the car and she appeared to be motioning him to follow the two of them. Bob guessed she was headed for the Starlet Cafe for coffee. He took one step in their direction then remembered that three is a crowd. He faded into the background. Actually, he could not bear the thought of hearing her tell the hunk, her newest obsession, the things he thought she only told him. Later, he walked passed the Cafe, stared at the couple briefly, and disappeared.

Gloria was a fitness trainer. She had lived the past ten years with an inattentive boyfriend. She said the boyfriend let her do her own thing to a point. What that point was Bob hadn't yet figured out. After a walk around downtown Fiston, Bob decided to stop by Gloria's to explain how he felt.

Gloria answered the door on the first knock and invited him to sit by the kitchen table. She sat across from him and flipped her hair. They drank tea.

"So, Bob, what is it you want?" she asked.

"You know I love you. But it's Valentine's Day and I can't even give you a card," said Bob, shrugging.

"I do have a boyfriend," said Gloria smiling.

Then she smiled even more sweetly and deeply.

"You would like to give me more than a card, wouldn't you," asked Gloria.

Bob stuttered as she batted her eyelashes and grinned.

"Yes," said Bob.

"You said you brought nutritional handouts for me on dieting," said Gloria.

Bob sighed to cool down; then he handed her the folder.

"It's about how to eat right and feel better. You certainly don't need to diet," said Bob.

"Thank you. Would you care to massage my back?" asked Gloria.

She turned around on the kitchen chair, sat with her knees on the seat, and leaned against the wall. Bob's long arms reached across the table. He dug into her neck and small shoulders. Her hair slid lightly across the back of his hands. He tried not to let his hands shake.

"MMMMMM, now for the other way," said Gloria.

She turned her kitchen chair around, straddled the seat to face him, and rested her upper body on the table. Her hands gripped the table edge. Once in a while, she peeked up at him with a smile as he kneaded her back. Her chest was prominently displayed over the table's edge. Playfully, he spread her hair across the table. He rose to drop his hands further and further down her back. She encouraged him with little sighs. As his hands lost their strength, his touch lightened to a feather. He stroked her neck then slipped his hand down the back of her loose fitting top. He felt her smooth round shoulders then slid his hands down to the small of her back, passed her silky bra, to explore where her narrow waste flared to her hips. Finally he just held her torso while he kissed the back of her neck.

She held his arms in her hands and smiled into his face.

"Thank you for a wonderful massage," said Gloria.

She stood, walked around the table, and gave him a rare kiss on the cheek.

Becoming the hostess, she said, "Are you finished with your tea?"

"Yes, but not with you," Bob quipped.

She smiled.

"Good. I'll see you out," said Gloria.

"But when will we meet again?" asked Bob.

"Soon," replied Gloria.

"Can we go somewhere?" asked Bob.

"How would you like to go somewhere right now?" asked Gloria. She opened her arms, arched her back, and pressed closed against him.

Although very short, Gloria was well proportioned. Bob bowed deeply to hug her close. He dropped his hand down her back and twirled her long hair.

She held him firmly and asked, "Is this better?"

Bob replied by squeezing her rear and she shuddered. She asked the question again. Bob simply nodded. He kissed her nose, her cheeks, and her neck. All of her face, except her lips. She wouldn't allow that. One day, perhaps, Bob hoped, his lips would finally meet Gloria's. Next, her little hands grabbed him on the hips.

"Now stop," said Gloria, "or something might happen. My boyfriend is coming home soon."

Bob let her go. He sighed while Gloria went over to the couch to pick up his things. She gave him his navy-blue winter coat and ushered him through the condo front door before he had a chance to put it on. He turned to ask her about the Group dance tonight, but she had already shut the door and disappeared. Just as well, he thought, she'd probably go with her boyfriend. Bob felt a little guilty and flustered. The cold air cleared his head and steadied his nerves. One of these days, thought Bob, she'd realize what a nice guy he was and ditch her boyfriend of ten years. Until then his life would be rather complicated.

On the way home, Bob remembered the woman from the Quaker church. Today was Valentine's Day. Bob stopped at the florist and bought the Quaker girl a bouquet of yellow marigolds. Cathy was pretty, direct, and available. Qualities that both appealed to Bob and scared him. Did he know her well enough to deliver flowers to her house? Was he being too forward? What would she think he meant? Instead of simply leaving the flowers on her doorstep, Bob went home, placed the flowers on the kitchen table, and lay on the couch to consider these imponderable questions.

Cathy knocked on the door a few minutes later. She was tall, blonde, and very pretty. Today she appeared very pale and shaky from a fight with a neighbor. She talked constantly about her thoughts and feelings, as her therapist suggested, to relieve the stress within her. But she kept the actual nature of the problem a secret. Finally she asked if she could sit on Bob's end of the couch.

"Sure," said Bob. He moved closer to the armrest.

"Will you hold me?" asked Cathy.

She climbed into his lap and nuzzled her head against his chest. He patted her back and she moved his hand into her hair. He caressed the blonde hair between his fingers and stroked her.

"I hope I'm not giving you mixed signals. I need to be touched and I trust you. I haven't slept or eaten for the last few days and I can't calm down," said Cathy.

Bob nodded. He felt a little warm. A less intense feeling than the one he experienced at Gloria's. One of these days he'd understand all these feelings himself and he wouldn't have to keep divulging the daily events of his life to his therapist for a play-by-play analysis.

"Please," said Cathy, "I want you to hold me and stroke me but I can't go any further with you."

"It's all right. I'll hold you and nothing will happen. Just remember a hospital is a safe place too. No shame in going to a psych ward," said Bob. "Just to be honest, though, I think you are very pretty."

Cathy replied softly, "I know you do. I'm attracted to you also."

When the waves of shivering stopped, Bob walked her out to the kitchen and showed her the bouquet of marigolds. She picked them up, felt the soil, and sniffed a flower. She sighed deeply.

"Are you sure they're not for someone else?" asked Cathy, half-joking.

"Oh no," Bob assured her. "I was too embarrassed to bring them over your house."

"Thank you. They're beautiful," said Cathy.

They embraced. They exchanged long tight hugs. Bob didn't need to bend at all. Cathy's neck rested in the crook of his shoulder and he rubbed his cheek against hers.

Bob asked Cathy to the Group dance but she declined. She was too sick emotionally to rock and roll with a bunch of people she hardly knew. She preferred contra dancing with the granola crowd and she hinted to him that she might be available for the next get-together at the Fiston Grange Hall. Then she thanked him "for being there" with another tight hug, and left for home.

✦ ✦ ✦

Bob went to the dance. He entered the basement of St. Mary's Church where a hundred plus people gyrated in near darkness and music blared from a live DJ. The Group, a community of like-minded fellow-sufferers, sponsored a dance for the area three or four times a year. Bob received a lot of support for his emotional condition through group-sponsored activities. Eventually, Bob saw his friends and he spotted Gloria. She was slow dancing with one of her other admirers. Apparently, she had convinced her live-in boyfriend of ten years not to attend. Bob wondered how to sweep such a popular woman off her feet. He was having a very confusing day.

Bob ignored Gloria to pique her interest. The DJ played a mixture of fast and slow oldies. Bob mingled easily because the place was so crowded and most of the people knew each other from the area. Everyone was looking for a new face. Then Bob saw one of his friends dance with Gloria. She was slow dancing again. He watched her body as it swayed with the music. Her arms were clasped around his friend's neck. Her head rested against his chest.

The tune faded, Bob walked out to the dance floor, and asked Gloria to join him for the next song. It was a fast beat. They rock n' rolled a few feet apart, smiling at one another. The next tune was a slow dance. Bob asked her to dance again but she declined. She was too tired. Yet as soon as Bob turned around she was back out on the dance floor, slow stepping with someone else. She slow danced with several other men that night before she finally agreed to dance with Bob again. To the fast, pulsing beat of 70s disco, Bob asked for an explanation and she shouted over the music the new limits of their complicated relationship.

Disgusted, Bob walked off the dance floor. He felt sick. He danced with a few other women, just for show, then left. Being in love with a coquettish girl was for boys. He knew he had to grow up. When he arrived home, he found Cathy had left a message on his answering machine. He could call her back tonight, if he got in before 10:30 pm. On the message, she thanked him for his kindness and said she felt calmer. Bob thought about Cathy—the way she made him feel—and then about Gloria. He made a choice, looked at his watch, and picked up the phone.

The Highlander

Bob O'Neil shivered as a chill ran down between his shoulders and a pit opened in his stomach. Keeping one eye on the highway, he glanced at his passenger. The woman's face was wrinkled, with high cheekbones and a wide forehead. Their eyes met. She broke contact by smoothing out her ankle-length orange skirt. A pearl necklace bounced against her ample breasts, a fullness that pressed through flowered print blouse. The woman cleared her throat and moistened her lips.

"Bob, I said they eat the brains raw—while the monkey is still alive. That's what they do in Hong-Kong. They buy a monkey at the market, hang it upside down, then bash in the skull and scoop out the brains—and the monkey screams and screams," said Nikki.

Bob shuddered. Nikki Walsh and Bob were traveling to Dartmouth College to hear lectures on alien abduction and crop circle phenomena. They had met in church. The church attracted people in recovery from life. Fellow members practiced hands-on healing, listened to guided meditation, talked to spirits, and shared an interest in the unexplained. Nikki had been relating highlights of her world travels while Bob drove the two hours from Fiston to Hanover, New Hampshire.

She was fortunate, she explained, her late husband had been transferred out of the submarine service and put into a cushy job; he became a naval attaché assigned to foreign posts. She knew many wives of submariners who had lost their men to the sea—subs weren't very safe back in the forties. She had lived all over the world. She told him the worst place to live was Taiwan. The smell was what she noticed first. Then she saw dogs sold at market. They cooked the dogs. But eating dog didn't bother her as much as the way they prepared the meal. They pounded the live dog with a stone for two hours. If the dog died before the passing of the first hour, they had to buy a new dog, and toss out the worthless carcass. Aside from tenderizing the flesh, the live pounding enriched the meat with valued secretions. Memories of the yelping kept her awake nights.

Bob wiped his moist forehead with the back of his hand.

"There's Concord," he said, changing the subject. He pointed to the miniature skyline of New Hampshire's state capital. To his left, he flinched at seeing another statie pulled up behind the bridge abutment. The cops were out, he thought; after all, it was Memorial Day weekend.

"Another hour to Hanover," said Nikki. "What do you do, Bob?"

Bob paused for a fraction of a second.

"I am an unpublished writer, computer programmer, and environmental workshop facilitator at the University," said Bob.

Although he did do these things, he wasn't paid. His real income came from a couple of disability checks each month. But his therapist told him these activities would help him develop a new identity to replace the shattered one based on his lost engineering career. With his illness in remission, he was once again venturing into the world.

"I've written twenty-six science fiction novels," said Nikki. "Sword and sorcery stuff. I had to use a pseudonym. No one would buy books from women back in the late sixties. I'll show you a copy next week at church," said Nikki.

Bob shook his head. "It's tough to be published. You have to be almost a rock star these days," he said. Then he turned the subject to the upcoming lecture. "Have you ever seen UFOs?" asked Bob.

Nikki nodded.

She was a member of UFOnet, had observed various craft types, and knew extraterrestrial demographics. There were at least four races of aliens: the large-eyed "Grays" with and without genitalia, mysterious "Hairy Dwarfs," seven-foot tall reptilians with greenish skin as rough as sand paper, and the beautiful "Nordics" that could easily pass as Swedes.

Then Nikki related to Bob a sighting. While driving back to her house one dark night, she saw a great glowing orange light beyond the woods in the direction of her home. At first she thought it was on fire. She feared for the house's only occupants: her tabby's kittens and retriever's puppies, a rabbit and a raccoon. But when she turned down her deserted back road, she found the house intact. The glow emanated from a large saucer-like ship that had landed on the field across from her house. The space ship filled the twenty-five acres quite nicely. As she approached the craft, a blonde "man" greeted her. He said his people were concerned about the nuclear weapons stored at the airbase and the nuclear submarines being overhauled at the Fiston Navy Yard. He told her the use of nuclear material should be abolished because radioactive decay burned the "Mother." When she asked whose mother, he had replied "the Earth Mother."

"What else did he say?" asked Bob, squeezing his hands on the steering wheel even tighter.

"Not much," said Nikki, shrugging.

"Were you afraid?" asked Bob. He burped silently to relieve the deepening pit in his stomach.

"I was relieved. No fire. I'm more afraid of meeting one of us in the dark," she said, pointing to the passing cars. "We're not that nice here."

Bob passed a Walsh's grocery truck lumbering along the highway. Nikki jerked her thumb towards the truck.

"Grandpa Walsh started that company in Portland, Maine. My husband's father, you know. He expanded it to all six New England states," said Nikki. "He was very disappointed that Gordon stayed in the Navy. But Gordon retired as a rear-admiral."

Bob recalled his old roommate had worked for Walsh's supermarket in the deli section. He gently tried to bring Nikki back to reality.

"I understand Walsh's is owned by a British company, " he said.

Nikki nodded. "I sold the business to them for ninety million dollars. Of course, I cleared much less with taxes, legal fees, and the like," she said.

"Of course," said Bob, playing along, although that pit in his stomach shook.

"I gave each of my four sons a million dollars. I did have five sons, but I lost one, you know. People thought I was foolish but it's really their money. I receive a million every year. That's the way my son, the marine, set it up. Two stars. His father was furious. A Navy man. You'll never guess how old I am."

Bob turned to size her up. She looked about sixty-five years old. Not real elderly. Very sharp. A tack. But he hesitated with a number. No matter what the age, the guy always gave the wrong answer.

"A gentleman," she laughed. "I'm ninety-five years old."

Bob politely scoffed at the admission. "You don't look it," he said.

"Thank you. Do you watch the *Highlander* series?" asked Nikki.

Bob nodded. The TV show was based on a series of movies about immortals who battled each other with swords for possession of the earth.

According to the show, beheading was the only way to take the life of an immortal.

"The series' producers wrote to me about how to put together the story line," said Nikki.

"Really," said Bob.

"They had read my books. They're still in print. But it's passed fifteen years so I don't receive any royalties," said Nikki.

"Do you believe that immortals actually roam the earth like on *Highlander*?" asked Bob.

"Of course. I'm a Highlander. My mother was Scottish and my father Iroquois. He was a crack shot but posted the family farm because he kept finding half-dead animals crawling around the property," said Nikki.

Before Bob could say another word, she had opened her pocket book and extracted her wallet. First she flashed her license under his nose attempting to prove that she was indeed "Nicole Walsh" who had been born on June 3 in the year 1900. Bob saw a familiar looking picture but wasn't able to clearly see the birth date. He was too polite to insist on a second look and too embarrassed to question her veracity. Then she opened her purse and unfolded some money. Bob took a deep breath. He imagined himself driving a Howard Hughes-type eccentric that might wave a thousand dollar bill beneath his nose as a reward for being an attentive listener.

"Is twenty plenty for gas?" asked Nikki.

Bob nodded. He guessed she was hard up for cash with this being the last week before her birthday. Next, he slowed the car as the exit for Hanover appeared and they followed a winding road into the sleepy college town nestled in the mountains.

"Here we are," said Bob.

They had arrived at the Dartmouth campus. Bob stopped for student pedestrians. He was amazed at how pretty the girls looked—much more attractive than the ones he went to school with.

The pair walked across several quads after asking directions from the students. Nikki hobbled a bit as she walked but said her legs no longer hurt. She said the pain from the operation had disappeared after her son, the general, had told her to go to sleep and pray to God for relief. Then she filled in the details. She had "died" in a car crash, viewed her body from above, and dropped into a coma. Once she awoke from the six month long coma, the doctors performed experimental surgery on her crushed legs. The medical bill was over a million dollars and she didn't carry any insurance. She shrugged and declared what good was money if you didn't spend it. Then she pulled Bob around to face him. She stared up into his eyes.

"I lost four inches. Now I have plastic bones and knees. I used to have beautiful legs," said Nikki. Holding onto the rail before ascending to the auditorium, she pulled up her skirt and revealed the scars that crisscrossed her knees. Next, she asked him if he had ever been married, and Bob shook his head, confused.

The pair ate dinner in the café next to the auditorium. Bob had taped both lectures with a hand-held voice-activated recorder. Previously he had used the mechanism to transcribe the sessions with his astrologer and psychic. He had bought the recorder to support his brief stint as a temp journalist with the *Fiston Daily Herald*. But his first assignment, coverage of a town council meeting, caused a flap. He deserted the meeting, and the job, his body quaking amid the flutter of conflicting views from the councilors. Now he was investigating deeper and more meaningful topics on his own. Eventually, he hoped to bring to light various government cover-ups, resolve worldwide conspiracy theories, and comprehend the paradigm shift in thought required to survive in the next millennium.

"Do you think the CIA is suppressing our knowledge of crop circle phenomena in the US?" asked Bob.

"Of course," said Nikki, "they're into everything. My son, the general, worked for them. Military intelligence actually. He played pro-ball to find out how widespread drug use was. He received a captain's grade pay and all the rest of the money he earned went into their slush fund. Then he retired from the game. Now he's a general and his wife just loves his blue uniform," she said.

Bob poked his chicken dinner with his fork.

"The Illuminati are involved too," said Bob. "Did you hear the professor say a Knight of Malta helped him identify the crop circle glyphs as ancient religious symbols? But now he's dead. Could his brother knights have had him killed as a renegade? The Knights of Malta are very high on the social strata. I understand they possess diplomatic immunity."

Nikki smiled at another recollection.

"Old grandpa Walsh was a thirty-three degree Mason. I remember his wake, all dressed up in a tuxedo with his lamb's skin waistcoat buttoned down his middle," said Nikki.

She nibbled on her chicken, her one concession to a vegetarian diet. She hinted that the special diet and copious amounts of clean fresh spring water were ultimately responsible for her long life. Above all, she told him not to eat pork or drink city water. Pork was full of filth and the city water was contaminated with trace metals that gave old people the disease that made them forget things.

"What did you think of the shrink?" asked Bob, referring to the psychiatrist who had written a definitive book on alien abduction.

"I thought he was boring and inconsistent. You can tell counseling abductees is the most interesting thing that's happened to him because he's got nothing of interest to say about himself – he just rambles on. Then, one minute he's saying alien abduction is a spiritual experience and the next he's comparing it to being tagged like caribou. All I know is I don't want to meet a gray," said Nikki, shivering.

She swept her plate clean with the edge of her fork and plopped the crumbs into her mouth.

Bob paused. He decided to disclose one of his own experiences.

"I met a light being once. I had survived a serious car accident with an eye injury. The translucent light being appeared at the head of my bed in the hospital and gently tapped my injured left eye with a wand," said Bob. He scooped the rest of his salad. "The eye healed without any permanent injury."

"He cured you," confirmed Nikki. "They're healers, you know."

"Only later did I read about that very same type of being in the shrink's book on abduction," said Bob.

Bob looked at his plate, felt his stomach, and decided another chicken dinner would fit. Listening to two distinguished lecturers share about encountering alien beings, resisting pressure from intelligence agencies, as well as discovering that the structure of the crop circle glyphs were a form of harmonic communication energized Bob. The first chicken dinner had only whetted Bob's appetite. He ordered another.

88

Nikki descended the stairs carefully. Bob watched with concern. Slowly, they walked back across the quad to the car. Bob eyed a trim coed then ducked into the automobile. Nikki remarked on how nice his vehicle was. She owned a ten-year-old Camaro. She admitted to caring for the car as you would an old horse. Rather than junking it and buying a new sports car, she had decided to refurbish it with the in-coming million-dollar check.

Bob turned on the radio but scanned past the station playing reggae music. The static caused by mountain interference was deafening. Nikki held up her hand.

"Wait!" she said. "That's Bob Marley. I knew him in Jamaica. The cops shot him right in front of me for no reason at all. The bullet went clean through his shoulder. Lucky I was a nurse. I stripped off a piece of my white evening gown, covered the wound, and ordered the taxi driver to head into the mountains."

"Wow," said Bob, massaging his now tightening yet plump stomach with his right hand.

He turned off the radio. Too much static. Something was interfering with the radio reception.

"I caused that," said Nikki, pointing to the radio. "My husband used to get mad at me every time I walked into a room. The clocks stopped, the TV scrambled, and the appliances went on the blink. 'But honey,' I used to say, 'can I help it if my body contains too much electricity?'"

Bob looked at the sky. He figured between the mountains and the thunderheads, a storm was approaching, and that might explain the bad reception. Or perhaps his radio needed yet another repair job. Too much electricity, Bob tried to laugh but couldn't. He just patted his stomach. Suddenly, lightening sheared the sky. Specks of rain dotted the windshield.

"God will come like this. The year two thousand twelve will bring many changes. The returning Christ. The fire from the clouds above will meet the fire from the upturned earth below. Fire and flood, famine and fear. If you are one of the few to live into the next millennium, you'll have your choice of living on forever in paradise or passing on to spirit," said Nikki.

Bob twitched. He had occasional bouts with millennium fever.

"How do you propose to stay alive?" asked Bob.

"Remember what Daniel Webster told the Devil after he won the debate…'Stay out of New Hampshire!'" said Nikki, laughing shrilly. "I'm staying right here in Fiston."

Bob grimaced. While the bulk of the world perished, he could rest easy in Fiston. New Hampshire was under the protection of God's hand and Daniel Webster's tongue.

"Besides," said Nikki, "God knows who he wants. My husband had a terrible stomachache the morning the O-39 submarine was scheduled to go on sea trials. He called in sick. The boat sailed out—never to return."

The pit in Bob's stomach nearly erupted. He wiped his moist forehead with a quivering hand.

"I remember a summer in Moscow…" said Nikki.

"Nikki, please!" said Bob.

He warded her off with the palm of his hand. Whoever heard of a submarine with an "O" prefix, he thought, everyone knew they were designated "SS," "SSN," or "SSBN." He was on major tranquillizers. He figured she needed minor ones; she needed truth serum.

"I need some quiet, please. No radio, no talking, just peace and quiet," said Bob.

Nikki pouted a little. Then she snuggled back in the electronically controlled seat and dozed. He noticed she wasn't wearing her seatbelt—she had seen a woman trapped in a smashed car frantically trying to unsnap her jammed seatbelt while the car burned up around her. Another memory.

As usual, the drive back was much quicker. Bob's stomach settled. The rain eventually stopped, the sky cleared and the moon shone. Bob stopped the car at the ice cream stand and touched Nikki on the shoulder. She smiled. They had arrived at their rendezvous point. She remarked how the churchgoers might think the missing pair had eloped. Bob laughed in spite of himself, said goodbye, then waited until she was safely in her car before driving home.

At the house, he picked up the *Fiston Sunday Herald* from the front porch and greeted his dog Teddy. After feeding Teddy, he poured himself a drink, sat on the couch, and sipped a ginger ale. He patted Teddy as he unfolded the paper on his knee. He stared at the large black letters, pulled away from the dog, and tightened his stomach so hard that the ginger ale blew out his nose. Still gagging on the soft drink, he patted his now gurgling stomach and read the Memorial Day headlines again—"Fiston Navy Yard Remembers Crew of O-39."

The Babysitter

Bob O'Neil had just come home from the psychic when the phone rang. After being told a potential relationship was around the corner, he answered the call expectantly. Wendy, an ex of one of his friends, greeted him with a cheery "hello." She was calling from a lawyer's office in downtown Fiston. She said she was back in town for brief stay and could really use a friend. Then she proved it.

"This is attorney Kendal and yes, Dr. Wendy Weissman could really use a friend," the lawyer said.

Bob remembered that the psychic suggested the best way to heal oneself was to help others. He had met the scattered psychologist a year ago. She had lost her Maryland license and asked him to go to Baltimore as moral support when she battled her former employer in a sexual discrimination suit. She wanted to go that instant as he recalled. Bob had been willing, but she had chosen another able knight to rescue her instead.

Bob slowly munched his turkey bologna sandwich as she related her latest predicament. He said he'd meet her at the office. Then the lawyer came on to relay directions. He was very precise.

Bob crossed the old bridge, turned right at the first light, and parked illegally in front of the building. Inside sixties rock jammed the air. A blonde secretary in a tight fitting green summer dress ushered him into attorney Kendal's office. Wendy dictated a phone number as the lawyer punched the keys. Then attorney Kendal pointed to the phone and shrugged. She thanked him curtly, took the phone, and waved to Bob. The lawyer rose, extending his arm. Bob shook hands with a middle-aged man in short sleeves and loosened tie. He had thinning red hair and a disarming smile. Wendy was gesturing to the phone, saying to another lawyer something about being kidnapped. Her brown hair rested on her shoulders. Her heavy glasses in tortoise shell frames fitted snugly on her small curved nose. Her dark brown shorts matched her hair but didn't hide the blue varicose veins on her thighs. She had married and divorced six times in rapid succession since high school. At thirty-six she was used to having men around.

"Attorney Kendal referred me to you," she said into the phone. Snippets of conversation floated by as the lawyer measured Bob.

"So Wendy says you're an engineer from Cornell University", he said.

"Yes," said Bob. Bob looked down at his grass-stained sneakers, beige camper shorts, and t-shirt. He rubbed at a smudge on his t-shirt.

"Do you work?" asked the lawyer.

"I'm in transition. I used to be a chemical engineer at the Shipyard..." said Bob.

"Oh," the lawyer nodded knowingly, "you got caught in that lay-off."

Everyone in town knew how the Shipyard had cut back. Bob said nothing more, letting him believe the obvious, although his termination had occurred several years prior to the major cutback. Meanwhile Wendy was talking about how her psychotic mother would not answer the phone and bemoaned the fact her father, the dentist, was stalking her to scare off potential boyfriends. She had requested a restraining order, but they hadn't served her dad.

"Yet," added the lawyer looking at Bob curiously and grinning slightly. Bob wondered why.

Wendy was now screaming into the phone that the case was a conspiracy. Apparently her prospective Baltimore lawyer had just won a $900,000 lawsuit for a woman. Only that woman didn't get her job back. Wendy wanted her job and the money. She couldn't depend on her ex-husband's $5000 per month alimony. It ran out in a couple years. A financial reversal on the ex's end had reduced her payment by $700 per month—just when she could least afford it.

Wendy dropped the phone into its cradle. She smiled brilliantly at Bob and the lawyer.

"When he calls back, will you notify me in writing?" she asked.

"Of course, if he calls," said the lawyer.

"Now you need my address, right?" she asked. "Let me see..."

"I may be parked illegally, can we get started?" asked Bob. Bob moved slightly to the door. He didn't receive many tickets and hated to pay the city the five-dollar fee.

"I'm afraid," said Wendy moaning quietly.

"Don't worry," said the lawyer.

"My address is confidential," said Wendy.

"Of course," said the lawyer.

"I'll leave," said Bob. He stayed. Wendy opened her wallet and extracted a slip of paper. She slowly read her typewritten address. She replaced the paper in a side pocket and closed the wallet.

"I'm afraid to go tomorrow," she said.

"Don't go till next week," suggested the lawyer.

She turned to Bob, saying, "The legal system is so complicated. I need to return to the scene of the crime. Will you go with me next week to Baltimore?"

Bob told her about his upcoming trip to the Baseball Hall of Fame and of his dislike for cities. The lawyer asked where he was taking Wendy to lunch. Bob decided on the Starlet sandwich shop just down the street. As far as planning the rest of the day, he'd drive home to retrieve his phone calls, then walk the beach. He told Wendy she was welcome to join him.

"But the apartment. I still need to see one. I already gave my notice. I've nowhere to go. I'm afraid," she said. She clutched her small leather purse that contained her Rolodex and sunglasses and hefted her black vinyl pack.

"One thing at a time—baby steps," said Bob. He remembered the advice from his support group, which was meeting tonight.

"That's right. Baby steps," she said.

The lawyer looked outside. "Is that your car?"

Bob told him he was afraid to leave the car, they might ticket it.

"Just give me the ticket," said the lawyer as he looked at his watch and ushered him to the door. "I know the right people in town."

Outside, the trees gave some relief from the hot, dry day as they walked to the sandwich shop. They only had to stop once, when Wendy became overwhelmed with fear. After ordering, Bob pulled out his wallet. Wendy said she didn't expect him to pay for lunch but Bob just meant to pay for his iced tea and he did. After she finished eating her tuna sandwich, they visited the rabbi at the temple. Unfortunately, the rabbi was busy with a bar mitzvah student so she couldn't tell him personally how utterly he had failed her. She told the secretary instead.

Then they retrieved both cars and she followed Bob to his house. Bob needed to make a brief pit stop. But she wouldn't go in to use the bathroom, she made Bob drive her to a nice restaurant. Bob thought if she talked more she might settle down, so he took her to the beach. Hardly anyone went there because of the rocks. They walked out around the point to a secluded section.

"Do you know I could have sued my mother for stopping payment on my medical school tuition?" she informed him. "Bob, she owes me $43,000. I'll never get out of debt. Now she won't even speak to me. When she took me out to lunch, it was never Friendly's, we always went to expensive restaurants where she could show off her minks and jewels. Do you know why I had to stop back there and say 'Wendy, W-E-N-D-Y?' It's because my parents never called us anything at home. My parents never called me by my name. They never said it so I have to say it now, over and over again, to remind myself who I am."

She finally told Bob a little about the past few days. She had stopped by Henry's place. He was another friend of her ex's. He had recommended her calling Bob.

"Do you know Henry and I slept together last night? With our clothes on. No sex. Bob, I'm afraid," she said. She stopped walking. She pleaded that he wait for her. He paused and together they continued at a slower pace. The beach was deserted. At the far end two people threw a Frisbee to a large black dog.

"No one," she said ominously, "knows I am with you."

Bob looked around. The pair had moved out of sight and their dog barked in the distance.

"We are alone," said Bob.

"Do you know if I screamed right now no one would hear me."

Bob laughed a little.

"Will you do something for me?" she asked.

"What?" Bob asked.

"I'm afraid to ask because if you refuse me I might do something stupid," she said.

Bob stared at the sea. The wet sand was rippled, exposed from low tide. They both carefully stepped over rocks and driftwood.

"Do you know people die from lack of eye contact, lack of touch, lack of hearing one's own name, from being treated like a thing instead of a person? They proved it in France in the 50's. They won't test that theory now, it's too threatening for people."

Then she quickly changed the subject.

94

"Do you know Henry offered to marry me after he had finished smoking half a joint?"

"Henry likes to exaggerate when he's high," said Bob, frowning at an oddly shaped rock.

Then Bob changed the subject.

"I know you haven't asked, but you can't sleep at my place tonight. Too much is going on," said Bob.

Wendy kicked a pebble. She wore a simple pair of off-white Keds.

"I don't want to stay where I'm not wanted," she said. "Do you know why I waited outside your house? I was afraid if I went in I wouldn't leave."

Bob stopped laughing to be polite. But he didn't take the sincerity of her comment to heart. He was doing his best to treat an abnormal situation normally.

"Do you know about sleeping together?" she asked. "I mean do you like to just sleep? No sex?"

Bob tried to remember the circumstances around the last time he slept with a woman. He stumbled. Lots of rocks were embedded in the white sand in front of him.

"I've been alone a lot so when that happens I usually get pretty excited. I sleep with my dog these days. We get along fine. I'm staying out of relationships until I get healthier," said Bob.

Wendy kept the pace. She skipped a flat rock into the sea and it bounced twice before sinking.

"I believe dogs should play with dogs and people with people," she said.

She told him about a pet she once had, a gold fish. Bob laughed. "Don't laugh," she countered, "that gold fish lived nine years."

Bob whistled.

"But I never named it," she said, puzzled.

"Maybe that was simply a re-enactment of the parental abuse you encountered," said Bob. He stepped over the white belly of an overturned crab.

"An insightful comment," she said and lay down on the beach rocks.

Bob sat down next to her. Little rounded pebbles kneaded their butts. The pale blue sky was littered with tufts of white being blown out to sea.

"I still haven't told you what I wanted you to do for me," she smiled slyly. "I'm afraid Bob."

"You'll be fine," said Bob. He patted her shoulder.

"I wonder what would have happened if I had met you before my ex?" she asked. "Do you realize if you deny me my special request I'll be so overwhelmed that I'll run away from here screaming back to the car and hitch a ride to I don't know where."

Bob's fists dug little pits in the sand as he watched another tuft of white drift slowly east. Then he sat up and smoothed out the rocks beneath his butt.

"You want a hug," said Bob.

A tingling spot grew hot in his chest. The tingling became electric as she wrapped her fingers around his hand. He shivered as her thumbnail brushed against his palm.

"You can't hug me yet. Do you understand that?" she asked.

She placed his hand on her stomach.

"I think that I'm barren. I'm so stressed and depressed that I don't produce eggs and can't enjoy sex like a normal woman. That can really happen, I know."

Bob said nothing so she continued.

"The psychotropic medication I was on didn't help me. Plus the potential side effects are very serious. I discontinued treatment. I'm through with meds and therapy. As you can see I'm as normal as the next person, just more sensitive."

He nodded without looking at her.

"I'm still in treatment," he said to the beach sand between her legs.

Then Bob laid back and watched the clouds. He mentioned how soothing the sound of the breakers was. Like meditation. She seemed interested in meditation but hesitated when he said it brought up a lot of old stuff.

"Bob," she announced, "I'm ready for my hug."

Bob looked around the deserted beach. He grabbed her tightly feeling her breast under his left arm. His chest heaved as he lost a little platonic control.

"Can you squeeze me any tighter?" she asked.

They disengaged but still held hands. She laid back for an instant, then shot back up. She told Bob she needed more stimuli, she stood, pulled Bob to his feet, and led him toward the car. Then she stopped.

"Bob, I'm afraid," she said, "Wendy." She reminded herself, "W-E-N-D-Y spells Wendy."

Holding her hand lightly Bob guided her back to the car. At the house, they both drank cold spring water and ate chocolate éclair bars that Bob bought from the ice cream truck. Then she went to the bathroom and asked to use the phone. Bob told her he had to leave by 7:00 pm, so she would have to hurry up and find a place to stay that night. She made a list of people to call including her father and a guy she had lunch with once. She felt the need to formally break off their one-lunch-long relationship. Bob suggested calling a motel. She was afraid to sleep alone. She called the battered women's shelter but nobody answered. She smiled crookedly.

"I'll need to say I'm being battered by somebody," she said.

Bob held his head in his hands.

"Hello, is this the police? Hi, a former friend is evicting me and now I need the number for the battered women's shelter because I'm in an abusive relationship. Thank you," she said.

She hung up the phone.

"See, I haven't implicated you in anything yet," she said.

Bob groaned.

"You need that meeting. Why don't you just go and let me make a few more calls," she said.

Bob shook his head. She laughed. They both knew she'd be there when he returned. She told him not to worry, she knew she wasn't wanted and hadn't asked to stay anyway. She made another call. Helpmate, the battered women's shelter was filled. The local homeless shelter said they'd call her back. She demanded to stay past 7:00 pm and Bob missed his meeting. He needed one. The tingling in his chest had disappeared. Now his head tingled. While she waited for the call, she held her black Teddy. She asked for an embrace. Bob held her index finger. She said she wanted a child. But first she needed to straighten out her life. Admission to the local nut hospital was out of the question. They wouldn't take her. Then the shelter called. The clerk asked her a series of questions. He said the restraining order against her father ruled her out. But she insisted he hadn't been served. Then she said she didn't want to go to the local nut hospital for a third party eval. They might think she was crazy and give her drugs.

"Don't laugh," she shouted. "Benzodiazapanes uninhibited me."

When the clerk said he'd need to talk with the case manager she slammed down the phone, sick of the bureaucratic bullshit.

"Bob," she said. "I can't go to the ER smelling like this, they'll label me schizo-affective for sure. I'm label-less. I'm my own disease. I have the Wendy Weissman syndrome."

"Let's write a plan," said Bob.

"That's right, a list."

She wrote briefly then looked at Bob. He knew, didn't he, that she had failed her ex, but even so, they weren't right for each other. Bob said nothing.

"Let's review the list," said Bob.

"OK, dissolve the restraining order, call Dad and apologize for saying 'Fuck off,' call the hospital, find a motel to stay the night or at least shower, then call the homeless shelter for admission." She smiled. "I did it," she said.

"Are you ready to leave?" Bob asked. He had bolted the front door unnoticed.

"I'm afraid," she said.

"Baby steps," said Bob.

"Yes, do I have everything?" she asked. She squeezed her black Teddy.

"Can I have a cookie?" she asked. She had drifted into the kitchen near the side door. She grabbed a homemade chocolate chip cookie from the foil plate on the table. Bob handed her two more as she stepped over the threshold of the side door. Bob followed, shutting the door and hearing the spring-loaded lock click behind him. She hesitated next to her baby blue Toyota Camry with sunroof. Bob told her to follow him. Driving a circuitous route, he stopped at a cheap motel on the other side of town. They walked into the Crow's Nest office together.

"I'm not really with him," she said to the clerk, an elderly woman with thinning white hair seated behind the counter. "Bob kindly showed me the way here. Do you charge the same for an hour's stay instead of a night? I may want to just shower."

The clerk gave her a long look and said she'd ask the manager after Wendy filled out a registration form.

"My name is Dr. Wendy Weissman. I live at...I don't know... let me see..." she said and opened her wallet and searched for the small slip of paper containing her address. "This is confidential information," she told the clerk. "I have a restraining order against my father. I'm a trauma victim that lost a job through sexual discrimination and I'm suing my former employer for kidnapping me for nine days."

The clerk blinked and asked if she was safe at present. Wendy said her good friend Bob was the only person who knew where she was. The clerk handed Wendy the key to room 106. Bob refused Wendy's offer to treat him to dinner—he had friends to meet.

"Won't you see my room?" asked Wendy.

"That'll be extra, dear, hour or not," said the clerk.

Wendy and Bob both stared at her then at each other. Bob shook his head.

"I have choices today," said Bob, "I'm afraid of what might happen next if I go in."

She laughed.

"What if I drop my things inside and come back to say goodbye?" she asked.

Bob nodded.

"You know you are waiting outside just like I did the first time at your house," she said, turning around.

Wendy returned. They hugged. Bob's only advice was for her to pray to God for help. She kept squeezing her black Teddy bear as he jumped into his car. Then he pulled out onto the road and drove away.

Bob and Ted's Adventure

Teddy, a black Scottie, squirmed against Bob O'Neil's head on the pillow. The cool breeze tickled Teddy's whiskers. Then Teddy scratched himself. Suddenly his owner awoke briefly, swatted him off the bed, and pulled the covers over his head.

Teddy was hot on this humid July night. He jumped up on the couch with the pretty flower pattern then climbed up the back and rolled into the windowsill. The window was open. But the screen kept him from falling out into the yard. The cool night air chilled his belly.

In the morning, he climbed down from his perch when he heard Bob roll out of bed. Teddy coiled into his round, Scotch plaid bed. A good match for a Scottie with little legs, a big head, and a glossy black coat. Only his glossy black coat was now dull and dirty. His oily skin itched. Then Bob let him outside on his red leash. Teddy used the leash because sometimes he wandered away. Teddy lifted one rear leg slightly and sprinkled the grass. He heard his owner singing in the shower. Trying to stay in tune, Teddy howled softly.

The water kept running but Bob finished showering. Teddy had just guessed the bath was coming when his owner scooped him up from the yard, carried him through the doorway, and gently placed him into the warm soapy water. Teddy sneezed. A heavy doggy smell filled the small bathroom. Teddy permitted his owner to soap him down and rinse him off. His whiskers matted against his snout. His tail became whip-thin. Twice Teddy tried to sneak out with a quick jump. But Bob held his head and shoulders in a tight grip. Then his owner pulled the drain plug, lifted him up, and dropped him into a beige towel. Teddy's hair clung tightly to his body. He looked like a big fat wharf rat.

First a slight shudder rippled through his body. Then he shook out the water as Bob stroked him with towels. When he dried, his hair became fluffy and parted naturally down the middle of his back. Teddy's eyes gleamed. He struggled out of the towels and ran out of the bathroom. He ran through the living room, bumped his rear end against the long low table, and slid into the kitchen. There he turned around so fast on the slick floor he fell side ways. He jumped up unhurt, his little legs churning, as he skidded across the floor hardly moving foreword at all.

Now he felt clean and crisp. He was a little puppy again acting a half-year-old instead of ten and a half. He liked to play. He raced beneath his owner's legs, through the living room and into the bedroom. Then he turned quickly on his heels and ran back chasing his owner into the kitchen where Bob turned suddenly saying, "Gotcha" and Teddy twirled around letting his owner chase him. They chased each other back and forth until Teddy jumped exhausted into his bed and rested his chin on the edge.

Looking up at his owner, he heard him say, "Want to eat? Want to eat Teddy?"

Teddy's head popped to attention. He jumped out of bed and ran to the owner. Teddy was so happy he spun himself in tight circles. Feeding time was always fun. Bob gave him the usual two handfuls of dry dog food, gourmet quality, with just enough water added to cover the flavorful brown nuggets. In no time, Teddy finished his meal.

"Want to go for a walkie?" asked Bob.

Teddy barked. He wagged his tail so hard his muscles ached. Bob placed Teddy in the car with his red leash on. They were going on a special walk. They were traveling to Mt. Aggie. Teddy had never climbed Mt. Aggie before. He watched the rough country pass by. Usually his owner walked him on the beach.

Suddenly the car lost its balance. The car shook as Bob swore and pulled over to the roadside. Bob popped the trunk, extracted the tire iron, and kicked the flat tire. He left the door open. The smells of the forest beckoned to Teddy. He silently jumped out of the car and darted across the road with his red leash trailing on the ground while Bob unscrewed lug nuts on the other side of the car.

First Teddy barked at the horses at the Mt. Aggie riding stable. He spooked one palomino with a white tail. Luckily the little girl in a yellow jersey stayed atop her mount. Next, Teddy rolled in the grass. The horses had trotted in the field and left some dung. Now Teddy smelled. Teddy followed the horse scent and turned left on the path that led up the mountain. He expected lots of adventures. Teddy saw a large yellow butterfly with black spots. He chased the butterfly down the path until it landed on a pink-flowered bush. Teddy stopped and barked at the butterfly but it didn't move and was too far away to eat.

Teddy climbed higher. He rolled on the green moss to cool his hot fur. He panted from the steeper climb, more rock outcroppings to avoid and less shade from the trees. The sun shone brightly in the sky. Then a chipmunk ran across his path. Teddy squealed. He ran regardless of the heat. The chase was on. He followed the reddish brown critter with the white belly until it disappeared into a hole beneath a rock. Teddy missed a meal. He was hungry, thirsty, tired, and lost.

Teddy wandered in the brush. He found a blueberry patch. He nibbled blueberries but some were green so now Teddy's stomach ached. He crawled under the branches of a small tree and felt the leash snag. He was caught. He went to sleep and when he awoke the sun was much lower in the sky. The shadows were longer. A cool breeze blew in his face. He tugged at the leash but it stayed stuck. He missed his owner. He missed his bed.

Teddy whined. At the sound of footsteps, he turned to see a tall blonde woman with green hiking boots and khaki shorts. She let him smell her hand. Then she patted him and untangled his leash. After examining his collar, she started calling out his owner's name. Next she led Teddy through the brush. As they walked down the mountain, the pair found the big riding path that went to the stables. Suddenly Teddy stopped. He listened. He heard a familiar voice calling, "Teddy, Teddy." Bob appeared in the path. Teddy howled and ran. He jumped into Bob's arms. He was home.

"M"

Bob O'Neil dropped the letter from the telephone company on the floor. His eyes glazed. Then he quickly retrieved the document before his dog could eat it. He re-read the letter to check if he had misunderstood the statements. *No,* he thought, *I have to tell them or else I need to give up my account.* He decided to call his local phone company; perhaps the literature describing the new system was in error.

"Hello, this is Sheila, may I have your phone number?" asked a customer service representative.

Bob gave his number including area code to the woman. He liked numbers, the ease of their expression; sometimes he wondered what capital numbers would look like. He had decided to invent capital numbers after finishing the call when the woman suddenly jerked him out of his daydream.

"Is this Robert O'Neil?" she asked.

"My friends call me Bob," he said.

She began calling him Bob and he answered another round of routine billing inquiries. Finally, he was able to ask his nagging question.

"It's about the SUPPER system. I don't think it's fair that we have to answer detailed medical questions. I'm not buying health insurance. I just want to call my friends."

"SUPPER? Oh, you mean SUPER 999. Super Enhanced Response 999. The phone company is very proud to offer this expanded version of 911 to our local communities. I expect Fiston will greatly benefit from its new services."

The woman explained the phone company had a large computer that stored data on its customers in a database, basically a filing system, and everyone's cooperation was needed to make the service work.

"We need to know about you so that we can serve you better," she said.

"I don't mind answering some of these questions," he said, looking down the list of twenty or so. He didn't have a criminal record so he wasn't bothered by the question: Have you ever been arrested? Then his voice rose a notch, "But I don't feel I need to divulge my medical history. Why do you need to know if I have a mental/emotional condition?"

The woman paused for an instant then she sighed and told him to hold. Bob was bumped up to her supervisor. Bob winced at the man's deep clipped voice.

"Sanders, here, how can I help you Mr. O'Neil?"

Bob explained his case. He didn't want to appear uncooperative but he thought some of the questions on the SUPER 999 application form were intrusive regarding medical privacy rights.

"Mr. O'Neil," said Sanders, "you are our first complaint on this issue. Don't you understand we need the data on you and your household to better provide you with emergency service? The information you give us might save your life or the life of a loved one. Lastly, as far as privacy is concerned, anyone with enough diligence could hack through the system to find your insurance premiums, medical bills, and prescription receipts. It's all a matter of public record."

Bob sighed. He didn't like the man's rough voice. Beads of sweat cascaded down the inside of his arms.

"I just don't think it's fair," concluded Bob. He wasn't a legal scholar; he was an ex-engineer on disability for a nervous disorder. He couldn't handle stress.

"Look, there are new laws governing the 911 system. The government is working with hospitals and insurance companies to contain health costs. That's one of many reasons we need to keep a file on our customers. What's so bad about having an "M" appear after your name in the phone book? Someday it may save your life."

"I want an unlisted number!" said Bob.

"Fine, we'll remove the number and when your doctor tells us that you're well—a signed, written and verifiable statement, we'll remove the M beside your name," said Sanders.

"But I don't want to be published at all," said Bob.

"That practice has changed, Mr. O'Neil. Our new policy is to list everyone, the only exceptions being those who can pay a hefty annual fee or qualify for special treatment, to stay off the books—the extra handling charges, you see. If you're alive and own a phone, you'll be in the book." He paused a second. "Judging from the neighborhood you live in, you have no where near those resources."

"My neighborhood?" asked Bob.

"What do you have to hide, anyway?" Sanders cleared his throat. "The SUPER 999 system will demand a lot from everybody. I've had to skip my vacation to maintain the project's schedule. Now you'll have to excuse me. I have work to do."

Bob stared at the phone. An off-white curvaceous orb quite often attached to his ear. He called his therapist. She hadn't run across the problem before, she lived in another community, but she did suggest he contact her friend Judith Spellman, the lawyer he had dealt with before regarding his trust account. Judith took his call on the first attempt. Usually she was very busy and not good at returning phone calls.

"Hi Bob. I've just heard about SUPER 999. Sounds great. Oh, really? I understand your concerns, but lying about your condition will just make matters worse. Your complete history is on the computers. An automatic crosscheck will alarm the system and result in revocation of your right to use the phone. You can then appeal to have that right restored, but if and when that's granted, what have you gained? Actually I'd be more worried about having the phone company sue you for making a false statement. You have a lot to lose and you can't afford to make a mistake. Remember they need to comply with the government's new emergency response laws by having people fill out the questionnaires as completely as possible. I know you're disappointed. Why don't you call the Fiston Legal Advocates? They specialize in this type of law. By the way, have you thought about a will? How about meeting in my office next Thursday? Good luck."

Bob penciled in "will" on his calendar by the phone. The picture above the blocks of days showed a group of black Lab pups nuzzling in the grass. Bob looked out his kitchen window to the sunlit trees in the backyard. A robin darted across the garden. He looked at his watch, walked to the fridge, and withdrew a gallon jug of spring water. He filled a glass, palmed a pill bottle, and dropped the tablet onto his tongue. Then he carried the phone into the living room and sat on the couch.

"Fiston Legal Advocates," said the woman.

Bob explained his story. She filled out an intake request form over the phone. He asked her a number of times if the center was confidential and she assured him of complete privacy. Bob waited on hold for ten minutes until Jeffery, the legal aide, introduced himself. After listening to Bob recount his now familiar story, he agreed that a privacy issue was involved, but although he was not familiar with the details of SUPER 999, he felt that this was a case where the benefits of the majority outweighed the concerns of the minority. He promised to have one of the few remaining lawyers review his opinion. Budget cuts had resulted in loss of staff and hence they were more selective in accepting cases.

Bob hung up the phone. He stared at the instrument of his despair. He doubted the lawyer would ever call back. Lawyers were tough to get a hold of even when you were paying them. This service was free. Bob began to accept the idea that the phone company would have a file on him. Didn't the pharmacy? He fantasized someday everyone's phone conversations would be recorded for posterity, and customers could buy recordings of conversations they especially treasured. Conversations of the departed would be in particular demand. His reverie was broken by the shrill ring of his orbed companion.

"Could I speak to Mr. Bob O'Neil?" asked the man.

"Speaking," answered Bob.

"Bob, I'm Dennis Wilson from Legal Advocates. I reviewed your file, called the local SUPER 999 implementation team, and checked case precedents. Bob, I think we have a case. This action appears to me a blatant disregard for the privacy of the individual. As a test case, we could form a class action suit of affected parties, go to court, and while I don't expect we'd win at the lower court, I believe the case is controversial enough to be pushed to the highest level on appeal where we will ultimately win. All I need from you is a written statement... ah will you excuse me, I have a call from my department head on the other line."

Bob smiled. He always wanted to make a difference. Perhaps after his successful battle with conglomerates, big government, and supercomputers, he would meet a fair maiden enchanted with his heroic deeds. They would sit in the morning sun as he recounted yet another tale of wrong turned right and she would utter a wide-eyed gasp then offer him more herbal tea and farm-fresh honey.

"Hello, Bob, I'm sorry but we can't take your case. Our workload won't allow it. Budget problems. We are a free service. I'm sorry," said the lawyer.

"But you said we could beat them..." cried Bob.

"There are other cases that demand our attention and outweigh your concerns here," said Wilson.

"What else could be more important?" asked Bob. He was shouting into the phone.

"Mr. O'Neil," said Wilson, "we help a lot of people here, they depend on us to serve them."

Bob heard the click, returned the receiver to its cradle, and picked up the questionnaire. He filled out the form as completely and honestly as possible. Then he went to the new phone book to look up his state representative. He had one last card up his sleeve, but as he went through the list of names on the appropriate page, he scratched his head. He checked again. The representative's name was no longer listed.

The Sunny Side of the Street

Bob O'Neil sat at a table in front of Le Cafe, Fiston's fashionable side-walk restaurant. He held his black Scottie Teddy by the leash. Teddy lunged at passing dogs while Bob's eyes lingered over passing women. Bob's head dropped. He studied the surface of the metal table hoping his face would blend into the crowd of "leaf peepers" sipping foam-covered French-brewed coffees and fingering black-encased Japanese-made cameras. He had no desire to confront his ex-roommate on such a warm evening in October, a fine example of Indian summer in New England.

"New sneakers," said a familiar voice.

Bob heard the opposing chair pull out and looked up to see Rudy bend his back with a grunt and slide into the metal seat. His red-and-black plaid lumberjack shirt was open at the sleeves and stretched to bursting around his ample middle. But Bob noticed the eyes most of all, drooping, hungry, and bloody, as if one additional night's sleep might send him into oblivion while a month's worth might not do him any good.

"Hi Rudy," said Bob, "nice shirt."

"Yeah, the Salvation Army major gave me a couple, just need to lose some weight." He touched a straining button, then looked away, "Hey Bob, we're still friends right?" he asked. Hurrying on, he said, "I need some cash."

"I want the two hundred you still owe me for rent," said Bob, feeling the blood pound in his head.

"You'll get that as soon as I get another job," said Rudy. "They ran me out of the apprenticeship program."

"I'm sorry," said Bob. He wiped his forehead. "By the way, the doctor called about your heart exam and stress test."

"Thanks," said Rudy. He rolled up his shirtsleeves and revealed small bruises on the inside of his elbows.

"I acquired another habit since we parted," he said, pointing to the needle tracks.

"You broke out!" said Bob. He whistled. "Heroin?"

Rudy nodded. "Don't blame yourself, Bob, I had to leave your place when I picked the booze up again. Now I'm shooting horse," he said, shrugging.

Bob shook his head as Rudy rolled down his sleeves.

"It's better than sex, Bob, and it's cheaper than ever. My new girlfriend and I were on our way to score when the cops pulled me over. That's how I got the DWI. Cuffed me, printed me, and mug shot me, they did. Then they locked me into a cell. But the nails in the bed shot into my back. I slept on the floor. That was yesterday though. No more DWI's, Protective Custody incarcerations, or Public Intoxication citations for this guy. I'm putting down the booze and the needle. Today is a new day," said Rudy.

Bob patted Teddy. "Today is all we have. I can't give you the money but I will give you a ride to a rehab. After all, they must have confiscated your license," he said.

"I'm driving still, what else can I do? A rehab is a good idea. When I get that bad and need a little R&R, I'll go. But right now I'm back. I'm on the sunny side of the street again. I can lick this. All I need is some pocket money. How about a dollar for a coffee?" he asked.

Bob pulled out a five-dollar bill from his wallet. He looked at Rudy with his fallen face and grizzled-gray hair. Rudy eyed the hand holding the greenback. His fingers tapped the metal tabletop.

"How's Eric?" asked Bob, folding the bill.

Rudy's face softened.

"He's almost eighteen and really has his act together," he said. "He took me out to lunch last week."

Bob extended the bill across the small round green-colored table. He stared at Rudy.

"Rudy, you can use this for food, a bus ride home, a phone call or a coffee. Forget the money you owe me. Just call me when you're ready to ask for help," said Bob.

Rudy snatched the fiver.

"Thanks Bob. I'll make it. You'll see," he said.

Bob watched him struggle to rise, lose his balance, and grip the chair. He turned a shade of white. Then he smiled, joking about the head rush being a freebie.

"I'm going now," said Rudy. He waved to Bob, stepped into traffic, stared down an on-coming car, tripped over an unseen pebble and then crumpled to the asphalt.

Bob and a few leaf peepers ran into the street surrounding him. Kneeling by Rudy, Bob heard a man shout above the din of spectators.

"You," said the man, pointing to an on-looker, "call 911. Clear aside, I'm a doctor."

Bob placed his blue jacket beneath Rudy's head and began unbuttoning his shirt while the doctor felt for a pulse. Rudy's complexion had faded to light blue as the doctor administered CPR.

A few minutes later the ambulance pulled up, sirens blaring. The attendants pulled on latex gloves and relieved the doctor. Bob stood up. He heard them say they were losing him. Bob turned around to check on Teddy, who was tied to the metal table. Then they said, "He's gone." He turned back to take in the scene. The professionals were checking their watches.

Next, Bob saw the flashing blue lights of a police car. A local cop pulled up, pushed through the crowd and bent over to check out the body. The concerned look on the cop's face faded when he recognized Rudy's features.

Playing It Safe in Bermuda

Bob O'Neil didn't have any trouble finding the place. An old black man wearing dark sunglasses directed him with a smile. He sat in a lawn chair beside the road selling junk glassware to passing tourists. Reggie, he said, lived in a red house down the street on the right. The old man added that Reggie had just gone up the road on his new horse. Bob wiped the hot sun out of his eyes, walked over to the house, and sat on the porch stairs to wait. Reggie soon appeared, trotting up the busy road. He was dark, with long brown hair wrapped in a ponytail and had a face creased with a permanent grin. He wore a red shirt open down the front, khaki cut-offs, and army-surplus boots. All he needed, thought Bob, was a patch over one eye. With his pirate look-a-like guide approaching, Bob was ready for a personalized sailing trip along Bermuda's coral reef-encircled shore.

Reggie looked a lot rougher on horseback than the typical island gentlemen of Bermuda that Bob saw scootering around Hamilton. They hunched over their motorbikes dressed in dark wingtip shoes, calf-length socks and knee-high shorts. Their matching ties fluttered over lightweight sport coats. Hubby let the wife drive. Most Bermudans were single car families, if that, although Reggie's parents owned several cars.

"Glad you could make it. Where's your scooter?" he asked.

"Took the bus. Scooters are too dangerous," said Bob. "Besides, you guys drive on the wrong side of the road."

Bob liked to play it safe.

The Bermudan government limited car ownership to residences with the space to park a vehicle. By permit only. Everyone else had to travel by bus or motor scooter. Tourists included. Welcome to Bermuda, boss.

"All set to sail?" asked Reggie. He grinned.

"Aye, Aye, sir!" Bob said. He saluted his captain.

✦ ✦ ✦

From the bar talk the previous night, over Diet Cokes, burgers, and chips, Bob had learned Reggie was ninety days clean and sober. The longest time in five years. Bob had stopped drinking for some time. Reggie had recently acquired a sailboat from a friend tired of the yacht-racing scene. When he heard Bob wanted a boat ride while on his one-week island vacation, he offered his services. A real ride, not one of those mushy tourist affairs. It was free, too. All Bob had to do was buy him a hamburger. Reggie told him where and when to meet, then shook hands and disappeared into the night. Bob just needed to show up at one o'clock and do as he was told on the boat.

Bob knew Reggie was an experienced yachtsman. The more Diet Cokes Bob bought, the more stories Reggie related. He had sailed over 10,000 miles on the North Atlantic, visited his ex-wife on a solo trip to Cape Cod twice, and Joe, the bartender of the Swizzle Stick Inn, highly recommended him. In fact, by the end of the evening, everyone at the bar had said Reggie was an expert.

"But do you know the way through the reefs?" asked Bob. He had a slight case of cold feet. The hotel clerk had told him that morning the island was almost completely surrounded by coral reefs.

"Hell yes, I've been sailing here since I was twelve," said Reggie.

"I haven't sailed for a while," Bob said.

"Oh, you have experience. What's a sheet?" asked Reggie, patting his horse.

"A sail," said Bob.

"A sheet is a rope," corrected Reggie.

"I renounce any claim to sailing knowledge," said Bob wiping the sweat from his forehead.

Reggie scanned the cloudless noon sky. He turned completely around, searching the horizon with his hands, shading his eyes from the sun, and balancing his weight on the horse with his legs. Then he rubbed spit on his palm and held the flat of his hand into the wind.

"Just a little brisk from the southwest. Less than fifteen knots. Good. The boat can't take more than twenty knots the way she's rigged now. We'll blow through Davidson's Bay in a straight shot," said Reggie in nautical talk.

Reggie's natural grace in formulating the weather report reassured Bob. He was comfortable again.

"Let's get our gear and head for the boat," said Reggie.

Reggie carried the heavy outboard; Bob held the gas tank, water bottle, and all-important stereo. The half-mile hike to the bay in the hot humidity sent rivulets of sweat down Bob's face and stained his glasses with salt.

Once at the dinghy, they putted over to the mooring where the yacht floated. He sailed a twenty-six-foot single-mast schooner that seated four. Across the red painted hull with white trim black letters spelled *Magic Eight Ball*. He said he inherited the name from the former owner who might have played pool. Bob joked that the former owner might have run drugs as well.

Reggie took command. First, he directed Bob to get down under the floorboards and drain the bilge using a plastic hand-pump. Bob grunted as he knelt on the wood, sucked up the brine, and dumped the water over the side. The natives were thankful for the rain yesterday. But to Bob the rain wasted a beach day. That's how he met Reggie, complaining about the weather. Reggie told him the rain was the island's only source of fresh water.

Next, he ordered Bob to stow the gear transferred from the dinghy as well as stuff already on board. He stored the gear while Reggie adjusted the rigging. Bob stowed forward below deck two high-pressure aqua-lungs used for diving. He carefully hung two life preservers inside the small cabin. He tossed his pack with his money and camera unsecured beside the cabin door. Then he grappled with the anchor, which Reggie tied to the tiller with a long rope. He deposited Reggie's bottle of bland tap water by the anchor. He shrugged at the bottle. Bob had brought nothing—why drink water when sailing around a tropical island in the middle of the ocean on a hot summer afternoon?

The sailboat did have a radio—an am/fm boom box from which reggae music throbbed and infrequent marine weather reports droned. The sailboat did lack a few things, namely an engine. Bob suggested they tow the dinghy and use its engine in case of trouble. But Reggie laughed off the idea of trouble. He did admit she'd take a real nice tow. Reggie conceded the boat should have an automatic position locator/identifier beacon and when he scraped together the money he'd buy one. Today they'd use visual dead reckoning to locate their position from shore. After all, it was a clear day and the station on the boom box gave updated weather reports from the Naval Air Station. Bob wondered about buying a simple hand compass but said nothing.

Reggie explained the island history while they readied the boat's rigging. The *Sea Venture*, with the original colonists aboard, wrecked in the treacherous reefs off shore in the early 1600s. Left mostly to fend for themselves, they were Britain's oldest self-governing colony. Convoluted limestone rocks etched its pink sand beaches. Reefs practically encircled the volcanic island. Beyond the reefs was an 18,000-foot drop to the ocean floor. Large green and red marker buoys showed safe channels. Reggie said the keel might make it across the coral reef, but he'd play it safe and use the channel. Bob liked the idea of playing it safe.

Finally they unfurled the sails, ran them up the mast, and secured them from below deck. The wind snapped the sails as they let go the mooring, and secured the lines. Reggie took over the tiller. Bob sat next to him with his back in the corner and his long legs resting against the base of the tiller. The craft cut through the gentle waves of the inter-coastal waterway. They left the Sea Rose Hotel beach area and headed toward the causeway and the open water on the other side of the bay. To the west was a destroyed bridge through which they'd sail back to their mooring on the final leg of their journey around the tip of the island. Above the bridge pilings was a historic fort with six sides. To the north, the Naval Air Station with radar sat on the hill. East, past the swing bridge, was a narrow opening in the bay: the channel.

Reggie told him that his father used to own the land from the Sea Rose Hotel to the causeway. He even donated some to the National Park system. That's how Reggie got his house. He relied a lot on mom and dad. His house was not quite finished; he still needed kitchen cabinets. The building inspector demanded his work be sure and true before agreeing the project finished and signing off the permit. Only then could he buy a car. Nobody could own a car unless they lived in an approved residence that had room for one. But how do you build your own home if you don't have a car?

"Hey Bob, pay attention. I'm headed for that causeway. We have to wake up the bridge keeper," said Reggie.

He puffed on a cigarette and tooted his aerosol-activated marine horn.

"We are running with the wind," said Reggie. "That damn bridge keeper ignored us. Damn him."

They made ready to come about tacking smoothly 180 degrees while the bridge opened. The motorboats gave them wide berth as they came about again and ran with the wind through the open swing bridge. Reggie saluted the operator and tooted his horn.

"Can I have some of that water?" asked Bob. The salty spray had dried his mouth out.

"Don't yanks know the word *please*?"

Bob nodded as he gulped the bland water. One of his tour guides had said white limestone coated roofs on houses acted as a catch basin for rainwater. The limestone neutralized acid in the rainwater. Then storage tanks beneath the house collected the water for use. Bob wondered how they flushed their toilets during a drought if water ran low.

"Coming about. We're heading into St. George's. See the replica of the *Sea Venture*."

Bob hardly noticed the replica; the come about was tough, the wind had picked up a notch and the boat handled roughly. They looped around St. George's Harbor under sail only and headed for open water. Bob suggested they return to the mooring, he'd had enough fun, but Reggie wanted the full run around the coastal tip on the open sea.

"See that building there? That's my father's club," he said.

The building stood on a green with a flag, a heavy stone-and-glass structure. He came from money. Houses here started at $400,000 and he owned a duplex. When Reggie finally got his life together, he'd buy a buggy, and become a hackney for rich tourists to tip in Hamilton.

"We're on radar."

He pointed to the control tower up the hill beyond the club.

Reggie gave Bob the tiller with instructions to head for open water outside the mouth of the harbor. The mouth was only about a quarter mile wide. Reggie found a pack of cigarettes, then motioned for the tiller. Bob gratefully let go control. Outside the harbor, Reggie waved to his old fishing boss speeding passed—they didn't see them. The wind and waves got rougher as they followed the channel around the reef.

"I think our draught is low enough to go over the reef, but we better not chance it," said Reggie.

"Let's play it safe," said Bob.

Reggie inhaled his butt deeply.

"I smoked a lot of weed on that boat. That's why they fired me. Then I went like my brothers. Shooting heroin."

Bob snapped to attention.

Reggie's hand inadvertently moved to cover the needle tracks on his left arm. Bob stared at the marks. Reggie went to Delhi, once, although not for spiritual reasons: the Indian government had sentenced one of his brothers to an eighteen-year prison term as a heroin trafficker.

"Are they clean and sober, like you now?" asked Bob.

"No, they both died of AIDS in prison. Prepare to come about and tack," said Reggie.

He swung the tiller around, pulled the jib through, and let the boom swing. Then he pulled the lines in tight, trying to sail a letter-perfect tack. Bob screamed. The boat shuddered and the starboard side dropped deep into the water. A wave sloshed over the side soaking the cockpit; the next wave slid in gracefully. Then the front end pounded through a wave, its spray soaking them both. Swearing, Reggie popped the line to the main sail. The boat righted. Then he gauged the wind and brought them into it again. Bob pleaded with him to stop. They were several miles offshore. He thought about the swim to land but figured the reef might rip him to shreds.

"Get away from the tiller!" shouted Reggie.

"Please go back," begged Bob. He shivered in the brisk fifteen-knot plus wind.

"If we swamp or capsize, remember to stay with the boat. You know that much, don't you?" asked Reggie.

Bob nodded. He looked longingly at the life preservers hanging in the cockpit, but was too afraid to move forward and grab hold of them.

Reggie had a good idea how his boat should sail in light wind on the harbor. He tightened up again into a proper tack—the boat shuddered and bucked and heeled over. Bob jumped up onto the gunwale that lifted up as water spilled in from the other side. He looked at the water surging, his body shaking, and his hands gripping the edge of the cockpit. Then he looked at Reggie, staring into cupped hands trying to light a cigarette.

"Hey Reggie, pay attention," shouted Bob.

Reggie dropped the butt and messed with the radio, scooting it away from the flowing salt water.

"For Chrissakes I'll buy you a radio and cigarettes when we get back to shore," said Bob.

Reggie eased back on the tiller. The waves lapped over the starboard gunwale.

Bob released his grip on the gunwale, placed his hands together for an instant, and asked His Lord Jesus Christ for mercy. He expected the worst: a water-logged list to one side from a gust of wind, a loss of balance, the sudden crack of the boom bouncing off his head, and then oblivion as the sea swallowed him.

"Don't sweat it, we'll sail in a luffing condition. We have too much sail for this wind and I can't modify here," Reggie said.

"Right, screw the sail talk, how many times have you taken this boat out?" asked Bob.

"Four times."

"Just like this?" asked Bob.

"No, never out here," said Reggie.

Bob said nothing. He was soaked, shivering, with salt-blurred glasses. He was sick of that "Hey Mon" Jamaican reggae music. The weather update from the Naval Air Station gave an advisory for small crafts. The warning was delivered in a monotone mid-western accent. Bob saw the heavy clouds ahead. They were coming in with wind at about fifteen to twenty knots. The boat was not safe at all above twenty knots. He shook. Then he remembered to pray. He prayed silently and felt immediate relief. His head cleared.

He grew more confident, riding waves as if on horseback, relaxing his grip on the back of the open cabin. He even stopped looking at the life preservers hanging inside.

"Hey, Reggie are you paying attention?" asked Bob.

Reggie had been at his post for over two hours. He was fading.

Reggie sprung to attention.

"Sure," he said. Then he upped the volume of the boom box and the music beat in tune with the waves breaking over the bow. Next Reggie handed Bob the tiller with instructions to head for a white house on the coast.

"I can't do it! We'll sink," said Bob.

"You can do it. I need to bail. We have too much water," said Reggie.

Bob forgot about everything except where the house was and how the wind and the waves kept it bouncing all across the bow. He was steering with his weak arm. He forgot about starboard and port or any other direction. He felt his way toward the house. Then the feeling disappeared.

"Reggie, bail me out. I've lost the house," said Bob.

"Looks good to me. Try to finish bailing the bilge."

Reggie handled the tiller and Bob bailed. They had three long tacks to go. Reggie fired up his last dry cigarette and smoked it looking down wind. The next wave sprayed over them both.

"Are you paying attention? How are we doing?" asked Bob.

"We're doing fine. Remember, I want to get home as much as you," said Reggie.

They became calmer. Neither one was swearing at each other, themselves, or the boat any more. Reggie had only screamed once for Bob to back off from the tiller. Reggie had developed an annoying habit of letting go the tiller while coming about. Bob kept grabbing it so they wouldn't sink. Bob helped by bringing in the jib when the boat came about. He made the line taut as Reggie ratcheted down on the reel. Then Reggie secured the line to its cleat.

"We're running with the wind again," said Reggie.

"Yes, we're home free," said Bob.

"We're not home yet," said Reggie.

They were headed for the bay from the opposite direction. An old bridge was partly destroyed. Only its twelve-foot diameter pilings remained standing. The clearance was 200 feet wide. The wind played tricks closer to land. The wind disappeared and the boat's forward momentum pushed them toward the pilings on starboard. Reggie yelled "Oh Christ!" and leaned into the tiller to keep the boat from lunging into the concrete. Then the wind returned and the boat made headway until lack of wind nearly bounced them against the concrete again. When they passed the bridge Reggie leaned hard one last time to swerve away from the coral reefs that lay beyond the pillars.

"Now we're home free. You did good. You didn't even get sick. I was just as scared as you were. You see those two unsecured aqualungs? They're equivalent to two sticks of dynamite and if they get knocked around too badly, they'd blow us up. Some things are better off not knowing."

Reggie hesitated, looking above at the mast.

"Racing sails, about a third less area, and this boat would fly real smooth."

Bob just laughed. He had come through the escapade unscathed, except for the friction burn on his elbow that he kept rubbing. Reggie secured the boat to its mooring. They spent an hour pumping brine, mopping boards, and rolling up the sails for storage in its pouch.

"It's getting on to eight o'clock. Would you like a ride back to town by scooter with me or play it safe and wait for the last bus?"

Bob barely hesitated. "Sure, I'll take the ride. What the hell."

The Group Spirit

Bob O'Neil brushed away a hornet from his sunburned face. The frequent walks on the beach, during another summer without work, had speckled his dark hair with blonde highlights. His face was freckled brown and his nose red, although he had given up drinking years ago.

Today Bob felt useful to society. He walked lightly to the Fiston Post Office, gripping a letter to Ann Landers about how the head of the Center of Disease Control had erred in her column last Sunday. The CDC's conclusion about the transmission of AIDS had been flawed. AIDS research was Bob's hobby. He had stopped working after losing his job. The plant could not afford to pay big money to an engineer who had lost control of his nerves. Now Bob found other ways to interact with society. He wrote short stories and editorials, but never expected the stuff to be published.

But this piece was different: lives were at stake. The rebuttal writing the previous night suffused Bob with joy. An electric tingling coursed from his brain to the tips of his fingers. The rush illuminated his mind and enabled him to see subtle connections between seemingly unrelated events. Needing to vent the story to relieve his stupor, he called the editor of the *Fiston Daily Herald*. The reporter covering the "Living in Today" section listened to Bob's excited account of the column, the error, and the new conclusion. The reporter agreed. He confirmed Bob's logic; the conclusions of the AIDS research study presented were flawed and the practices of the study had endangered lives.

Bob, however, had trouble "living in today" since spotting the flaw. In fact, the sheer magnitude of the discovery astounded him. He rarely read the Landers column, yet that day he did. He knew about statistics and AIDS. He had noticed the errors somehow; now he had written the letter. The coincidences had spun in his head all night. He could not let go of the thrill and stay in the moment.

Last night, he listened quietly to his meditation tape, lying on the bed without sleeping. The tape jingled his toes and fingers instead of calming his mind. He may have slept, but he awoke tired. Then he remembered to medicate himself. The pills did something, God only knew what. He had stopped talking to God. He had even stopped asking for help and stopped thanking Him at night. The doctor advised against talking to God. Although at times he had thought he had a direct transmission line to God, he had never believed himself to be His son. "In Doctor We Trust" had become his motto. Appropriately, the doctor was a child psychiatrist for he had never grown up.

While the doctor dispensed pills for his head, the social worker listened to his heart. His Buddhist-minded therapist sat in the lotus position meditating as he poured out his soul to her. He had withdrawn from the community of like-minded and thoroughly medicated fellow sufferers. He stopped attending The Group. They might know him too well. Then they might hate him. Today he felt different from The Group. Smart, nervous, watchful—a medication change did that sometimes. The drier, cooler weather too, altered his cranial hormones. September was coming—memories always surfaced upon the anniversary of his entry to The Group.

As he approached the mailbox, his usual state of fear, anxiety, and depression turned to passion in his expected confrontation with Ann Landers. He thought of the charismatic peasant girl, Joan of Arc, whose muse had her lead the French against the invading English. Bob didn't hear voices at the moment, but he did feel a great obligation to the masses. Bob grinned from ear to ear as he stopped in front of the mailbox. He hesitated slightly then slipped the letter to Landers into the slot. His duty to humanity to be a life-giving savior outweighed any personal responsibility to self.

After mailing the letter, he needed a break. Bob sipped coffee at the outdoor café. He smiled contentedly remembering a recent wrong set right. The previous week he had made amends to Corky, an old gent with a leathery face, whom he had argued with over "table ownership." Fortunately Corky accepted them with a smile because the next day he fell dead of a heart attack while opening the door to his house with an arm full of groceries.

"Excuse me, sir," asked a man wearing a spring jacket, t-shirt, and a day's growth of beard. "Do you know what city this is?"

"Fiston," said Bob.

"Piston?" asked the man.

"No, Fiston. Fiston, New Hampshire," said Bob. He watched the man disappear around the corner.

Bob finished his coffee, tipped the pretty blonde who removed his mug, and then ran into Sajan on the way to the car. Sajan, a Lebanese microbiologist from the University, was too dazed or deep in thought to hear Bob call him. Sajan had curly black hair that needed combing, a mustache in need of trimming, and a five o'clock shadow that darkened his heavy cheeks. His newly acquired belly stuck out over his Dockers slacks. He had stopped drinking and getting high and now started over-eating. He confirmed the Heisenberg Uncertainty Principle as applied to humans: As one aspect of a life is brought under control, another slips away. Of course science ignored the guidance of an all-knowing Higher Power. But where was He?

Sajan was frowning. He still hurt from the break up of his long-term relationship with Rachel, the Israeli millionairess with sixteen personalities, and Bob wondered which personality Sajan was mourning the loss of today. Or was he simply missing the physical stuff?

"Hey Sajan," said Bob. "Do you want to read my letter to Ann Landers rebutting the head of the CDC on their conclusions in AIDS research?"

"Bob," said Sajan. "Do I need to talk to you! How about a coffee at the Starlet Cafe?"

Bob agreed and returned to his table.

Before Sajan read Bob's scientific paper, he dumped all his problems. He had bounced a $40 check at a pet store to buy food for his two cats—reduced to one since the car accident—but Sajan was too troubled to speak of death. Through a series of mishaps, he forgot to pay the resulting $150 court costs. Then, in the confusion of moving, he mislaid the contempt of court letter. Two police officers awoke him one night last week, read him his rights, cuffed him, and took him to jail. He didn't mind jail but he did need his meds. They kept the terrors away. Bob noticed the fear in his eyes; his pupils had dilated into huge dark pools encircled with a thin brown iris. He was addicted to his long-acting painkillers but preferred them to brain numbing neuroleptics. Sajan's new shrink was exploring a psychiatric vacation to detox him from the meds.

"At least the Pizza Den gave me my old job back," said Sajan.

Bob slipped Sajan a twenty along with the letter, then watched as he pocketed the money, and opened the note. First, Sajan tried to dazzle Bob with the latest advances in AIDS research.

"I still think the answer is in prayer and meditation, not the high tech medical sciences," replied Bob.

Bob was quiet about his not knowing to whom to pray.

Sajan scanned the letter. He shook his head a couple times, then smiled.

"You're missing too many details from the study to make these conclusions," said Sajan.

Bob dropped off his high. His face drained, jaw slacked, and hands shook. He gripped the table edge to steady himself.

"Did I make a fool of myself?" he asked.

"No, you qualified with 'given the facts of this study I will prove...' but the FBI still may shoot you for suggesting a government testing conspiracy," said Sajan. He rubbed his hands together, grinning.

Bob sipped his coffee, holding the cup with both hands dwelling on the irretrievable letter on the way to Ann Landers.

"The moral of the story is people shouldn't subject themselves to government test programs," said Sajan. "But you're only partly wrong. The CDC may have compromised the safety of the people in the study. But to conclude improving the performance of condoms alone will impede the transmission of HIV precludes the existence of at least four other infection co-factors."

He drew a graph showing that, as the number of co-factors increased, the rate of HIV transmission increased exponentially.

Bob whined. A short high-pitched squeal that released the fear from his gut. Bob ignored a sidelong glance from the man smoking a butt in the table across from him.

"Don't worry, Bob," said Sajan. "Remember you did the best you could at the time."

"I know, I just can't snap out of it," said Bob.

With his soul vibrating against his chest, systematic deep breathing triggered a self-hypnotic cue provided by his beautiful Buddhist therapist to unknot his guts before he vomited.

"You look better," said Sajan. "It's Monday right? Going to the Group on Wednesday? We need support."

"No, I lost faith," said Bob.

"I could use the company, Bob. It's going to be a rough week, I miss Rachel, and my cat just died. One disaster after another," said Sajan.

Bob looked at his friend's wide-eyed stare and swollen black pupils. If he knew Bob was going to the Group, he might sleep through the night instead of catching two-hour naps here and there.

"OK Sajan, I'll meet you out in front of the hall at 8:30 pm," said Bob.

Tuesday was therapy day. He bought a Coke for the half-hour ride north to jump-start his weary brain. As he sucked down the soda, he meditated for spiritual protection from a God in which he had lost faith. Once the car bumped along the shoulder when he dropped too deep in thought. He hadn't been sleeping since Sajan pointed out the flaw in his Landers letter.

"Hello, Bob," said Trisha. "How are you?"

His tall blonde therapist greeted him in the doorway wearing her hair trimmed above the shoulders. She was bright, cheerful, pretty, and his age, but married to a neurosurgeon with three kids. They spent several sessions deciding the best way for Bob to process his feelings of love for her. He even went out with a girl that looked just like her, but his emotional hang-ups had prevented consummation of the relationship and ultimately led to their break-up.

"I'm OK," said Bob. His voice tingled with excitement.

Bob followed Trisha in her black sleeveless summer dress flowered in purple and gold into a sunlit room. He sat on the couch, laid back a little to collect his thoughts and feelings, while Trisha sat on the floor, brushed out her dress, and squeezed her long legs into the lotus position.

"You look sleepy," said Trisha.

Eyes closed, Bob nodded. He let his mind wander. The spirit of his dead mother stared at him. He asked what she wanted. She worriedly sent him her love.

Bob awoke from the couch while Trisha hummed "Oum" with her palms open and resting on her knees.

"I let you sleep, Bob," said Trisha. "How are you feeling?"

"Fine," said Bob, "Thanks for the session. I'm a lot calmer. I needed the rest."

"Same time next week?" she asked.

"Sure," said Bob.

He pulled out of his wallet the check for the $25 insurance co-payment. She handed him a receipt.

"Thanks for a great session," said Bob.

"Goodbye, Bob," said Trisha.

She waved and smiled brilliantly.

Sajan was definitely late. Bob's anxiety had returned as soon as he left Trisha's office. Bob kicked a pebble as he paced in front of the hall where the Group met. He had "Hi'd" several familiar faces walking past, wondering if he should enter.

"Oh hell," said Bob. "Sajan might have forgotten our talk Monday."

A guy in a suit, probably a newcomer, heard Bob's outburst and did a double take.

"Are you addressing me?" asked the suit.

"No," said Bob. "I'm thinking and my brain has its speakers on."

Bob entered in time to hear the lady chairing finish her qualifying in a short speech about doctors, meds, police, state hospitals, and halfway houses. She was afraid of violating probation and thought God had a vendetta against her.

"Hey, Bob, long time no see," said someone from behind.

Bob turned. He shook hands with Ray, a short chubby CNA in training with a medical history twice as long as Bob's.

"Have you seen Sajan?" asked Bob.

"No," said Ray. "But how are you doing?"

"Shitty," said Bob. "I wrote a letter to Ann Landers that's technically flawed and I'm too confused to write a follow-up apology note to ask forgiveness."

"She doesn't care, Bob," said Ray.

"But you don't understand, I insulted the head of the CDC," said Bob.

"Bob," said Ray, holding Bob's arm. "Let's get a coffee."

"But I'm supposed to meet Sajan here," said Bob.

"Look around," said Ray, "he's not here. He'll make it eventually. But you're in no condition to help him."

They left as the meeting was called back to order. Bob and Ray drank coffee and ate ice cream at the Starlet Cafe. Ray shoveled into a big Sundae and joked about being fat while Bob picked at his vanilla scoop between spasms of shaking.

"I must not be used to the AC," said Bob.

"What else is going on?" asked Ray.

"I haven't slept for three nights," said Bob.

"I get sick when I don't sleep," said Ray.

"I can't calm down," said Bob.

"How do you feel?" asked Ray.

"Guilty. I'm guilty of talking about one of my ex-roommates. He called me today for no reason. I think he wanted an apology.

"I'm guilty of committing a sin of omission with my ex-girlfriend. I saw her today, married with a two-year-old boy, and I never told her she wasn't responsible for my crack up, firing, and lost career. I'm responsible for her broken nose. Her guilt over me allowed that accident to happen."

Ray sipped his coffee.

"Bob, this stuff is tough to deal with," said Ray. "Talking is good therapy."

"But you don't understand," said Bob. "I'm guilty of all kinds of things and I want to pay the price."

"Are you taking your meds?" asked Ray.

"Yes," said Bob.

"Have you asked God for help? On your knees?" asked Ray.

"No," said Bob.

"I always ask for help in the morning, I remember to be grateful during the day, and if I do stress out, I ask that He take it away. At night, I say thanks too," said Ray.

"You do all that?" asked Bob.

"It's that simple," said Ray. "But it's not always easy."

"Just talk to God?" asked Bob.

"He'll listen," said Ray.

Bob's ears popped. He just needed to ask Him for help. Ray had a disability, too, but he still volunteered at the Drop-in center. He said disabled people were more closely connected with God.

"He wants us to be happy, but we need to help others. How best can you serve?" asked Ray. "What do you enjoy doing?"

"I write a little," said Bob.

"Then ask for direction," said Ray. "In the meantime, write."

✦ ✦ ✦

That night kneeling beside his bed on the floor, Bob talked with God. He asked for his nerves to settle and he stopped shaking. He asked for tiredness and he yawned. He realized the planet was a playground where being in tune with God allowed miraculous things to happen.

He awoke after a sound sleep on Thursday morning. He still shook a little but the feeling disappeared when he asked for help while looking for his sneakers under the bed. He cleaned house most of the day.

Then he took a walk in the warm sun and cool breeze. His head cleared; no longer did the urge to confess his faults, real or imagined, grip him. He approached the bridge into town. He stopped halfway across staring down at the fast moving water thirty feet below. But he didn't need to suppress an impulse to jump. He admired the sunset instead: hues of red, orange, and gold tinted the pancake flat clouds in the west. Sparrows pivoted in formation around the mast of a sailboat below, foaming bubbles streaming from its wake. A sea gull cried out. Bob turned to see the bird riding the breeze, its feathers fluttering. The bird stayed suspended, its discolored beak cawed him, then the air whisked him away with the flap of his wings.

Bob asked for direction and a white feather from the passing gull fell at his feet. Bob hefted the feather in his left hand, his writing hand.

Looks like a quill, thought Bob.

He slipped the feather into his shirt pocket and finished crossing the bridge.

Adopted Family Values

Bob O'Neil received a lot of support from the Knights. They were his adopted family from down the street. Sometimes he even managed to help them. Bob babysat the two little boys, complimented the daughter on her looks, and told Shirley Knight how much everyone cared about her—namely Bob.

Bob used to play big brother to Andy, the older boy. They went bowling, saw movies, and ate ice cream. The experience lasted a year, until Andy grew out his little brother role. Andy was nearly ten; now he knew everything. Andy enjoyed his friends' basketball pick-up games more than he did Bob's attention. Bob had a new assignment this year, Shirley's five-year-old, Tuck. He promised to take Tuck on a fishing trip in his canoe. Every time Bob visited Shirley Knight's, Tuck ran to the closet, pulled out his fishing net and waved the net in Bob's face.

Today, Bob and his dog Teddy visited the Knights for emotional support since his roommate had moved out after a squabble. Shirley, a pretty, blonde, blue-eyed divorced mother of three, was very spiritual and understanding. She was the neighborhood mom who naturally assumed the caretaker role. Bob relieved the contents of his irritated soul in the warm air of the living room while Shirley re-filled his coffee cup and nodded sympathetically.

"After the big fight, my roommate found a place to move to the next day," said Bob.

"It must have been time for him to leave," said Shirley.

Bob nodded. Shirley knew how the universe provided.

"Now you have to find out why you let him stay in your house so long and took his abuse," said Shirley.

Bob took a big gulp of coffee.

"More fuel for therapy," said Bob.

"Therapy!" said Shirley.

She yelled at Andy to be ready in thirty minutes for his appointment.

Andy was in the kitchen being tutored by Shirley's live-in boyfriend. Andy was complaining about his homework. School wasn't Andy's favorite subject. Andy brought home fourth-grade homework so complicated that Bob and the live-in, two ivy-league college graduates, couldn't figure out a solution. High-school educated Shirley usually came to everyone's rescue and solved the problems.

Bob stopped griping about his latest ex-roommate. Instead he half-listened to Shirley relate the neighborhood gossip and half-listened to the live-in tutor Andy. He was through being the center of attention.

"Do you want to be stupid the rest of your life?" asked the live-in.

Andy had just given the wrong answer yet again. Clearly, according to the live-in, he hadn't read the assignment.

The live-in was a disabled physician. His mind had cracked before he could make his million. Unfortunately he didn't have a Dale Carnegie attitude with kids. To be fair, he had just recently been released from the hospital, went to therapy twice a week, and kept popping tranquilizers to relieve his ongoing and unidentified anxiety. "Better living through chemistry," he'd mutter to himself.

Bob looked over at the pair. Andy put down his pencil, leaned his face against the kitchen table, and yawned.

"I'm tired," said Andy.

"I don't believe it. I'm fathering a future failure," said the live-in.

"I'm sick," said Andy.

"If you're sick," said Shirley, "go to bed."

Andy closed the notebook and walked away. The live-in looked after him shaking his head. Bob frowned.

"Mommy," screamed Tuck, "look at Teddy."

Everyone looked at Teddy, Bob's dog. Tuck had asked permission to walk Teddy. He held Teddy's red leash and followed the dog around the living room. Apparently, Teddy had mistaken the Knights' living room rug for grass. Ted was squatting in the middle of the living floor doing a bowel movement. Bob gasped. Shirley laughed. The live-in explained to Tuck about bowel movements. Tuck opened his mouth and gagged. Then, as Teddy finished, Tuck lifted his hand to cover his mouth. His stomach convulsed and he vomited.

"Throw up in the bathroom," yelled Shirley.

"Your son is a little over-sensitive," said the live-in.

"Our son," countered Shirley.

Although not in therapy, Tuck certainly had issues.

While Tuck cleaned himself up in the bathroom, the sixteen-year-old daughter made her grand entrance. The front door burst wide open and then slammed shut as an afterthought. The daughter leaned against the door and rotated her hips in, Bob thought, a primitively sexual way. Next she flicked her bleached blonde hair out of her eyes and glared at everyone in the room. Her eyes were glazed and cheeks red.

"Where were you?" asked Shirley.

"Out," said the daughter.

"Have you been drinking?" asked Shirley.

"What is this, the third degree?" asked the daughter.

The live-in stepped out of her way as she hurried to her room. She told him to move aside and called him "loser." The door to the room she shared with Andy and Tuck slammed shut. Tuck usually slept in the other bedroom with the live-in and Shirley; he felt safe there. The daughter hadn't been to school for a month, liked the boys, drank, and shoplifted. She refused therapy. Instead, she was on probation for various offenses with, Bob thought, a good chance that she'd go to jail eventually.

Andy appeared. The daughter had kicked him out of the room.

"Mom," said Andy, "Mrs. Garland's husband died of cancer."

Shirley held Andy. He wrapped his arms around her waist and buried his head against her.

"My poor Andy," said Shirley. "Now I know why you couldn't do your homework. How do you feel?"

Shirley was trying to exchange feelings with her children. She learned about sharing feelings from her own therapy.

Mrs. Garland was the popular second grade teacher. Her husband was the school janitor. He worked every day until the night he died.

"You can go to the service, Andy," said Shirley.

"What service?" asked Andy.

"Everyone has a service when they die. They'll have a wake probably," said Shirley.

Tuck started screaming. He wanted to know about death. He kept asking: Where did he go? Shirley told him the body went into the ground and turned into soil. Tuck looked at the potting soil in which the plants in the living room window grew and screamed again. Shirley told him not to worry, after all, we lived forever. He ran into the bathroom and cried. He didn't want to live forever. Then Shirley told him our bodies turned to dust and our souls went to God. She followed him into the bathroom to comfort him.

Andy shrugged.

"Will you give me a ride to therapy?" asked Andy.

Bob nodded.

"Shirley, I'm leaving with Andy," said Bob.

Shirley was cooing to Tuck in the bathroom and the live-in had retreated to the couple's bedroom to shake on the bed in relative peace.

"But what am I supposed to say to Mrs. Garland?" asked Andy, looking at Bob.

Bob hesitated for a second. Andy had actually asked him a question.

"Andy, my father told me a long time ago what to say to the bereaved family regarding the death of a loved one. I was older than you were when I asked—a senior in high school," said Bob.

"What did he tell you?" asked Andy.

"It's simple. Just say, 'I'm sorry' to Mrs. Garland," said Bob.

"Really? Is that all? Are you sure, Bob?" asked Andy.

Bob nodded.

"Trust me, that's all you have to say," said Bob.

The pair left the warm house and walked into the brisk fall sunshine. Bob grabbed Andy by the shoulders. Bob was thrilled beyond words, yet his mind was filled with unanswered thoughts. The phrase used to express condolences upon life's ending was simple. It was selecting the proper phrases to express oneself in day to day living that was complicated.

Celtic Games

Bob O'Neil bounced his car to a stop on the Tobin Bridge high above the Mystic River in Boston. Traffic was snagged and the height distracted Bob. He hardly ever journeyed down to Boston—much less drove into the city—but this time was different. He had left the relative safety of Fiston to give his charge, Andy, a special birthday present. Andy Knight, his about-to-be-ten-year-old neighbor and avid basketball fan, was going to see his first professional basketball game. Less a fan of the Celtics than curious about seeing the Boston Garden's interior before its scheduled demolition, Bob had become the magician that would toss angels dust into Andy's eyes and convert a dream to reality. A reality with a $150 price tag, thought Bob, and he hoped the angels were watching over him as intently as he intended to watch the boy. Seeing the game was Bob's first attempt at handling a child in the big city.

"Are we there yet?" asked Andy. The car's bouncing stop had awakened him. He rubbed his blue eyes, wiped his pug nose with the back of his hand, and pulled the teal-colored "NC" cap—North Carolina was his favorite team—down to his eyebrows.

"No," said Bob, "We still have to enter the city."

Bob apologized for waking him. Then he looked over the edges of the bridge, over the railing from the single arching lane that stretched out into nothingness. Becoming pencil point thin, it twisted like the rails of a roller coaster, and merged with more traffic that ramped into the city. He understood now why such a bridge spanned the "Mystic" River. Even the most hard-hearted souls might receive a spiritual awakening if they sat long enough in its snarled traffic. His palms stung as he gripped the steering wheel.

He looked down the hundreds of feet below. Sand and gravel machines worked the pit; dock cranes moved containers; ships steamed up the river; and the sun's rays glinted off the roofs of buildings. He looked up: a cloudless blue sky framed a low hung sun, and seagulls whirled around wispy steel girders. He looked across at the far side of the river, near the horizon, miles away, and felt as if he was piloting a 747 into Boston's Logan Airport. Although he was trained as an engineer, he hated to be too dependent on technology. Bob shivered as a shock of fear rippled down his spine like a splash of cold water. He shook silently. Then he stared down at his foot pressing against the brake pedal. He was where his feet were—so the sage said.

"They're going to the game," said Andy. He was staring at the car in front of them.

Bob saw a late-model red Cavalier carrying two young men wearing caps. The car had Maine plates and was obviously heading into Boston.

"What makes you think that?" asked Bob, playing along. He doubted Andy's assertion. But he did believe in coincidences; to him they were evidence that a helpful force existed in the universe and would act in his behalf if called upon.

"The guy on the right is wearing a North Carolina cap like mine," said Andy.

"I guess we'll find out," said Bob.

Traffic started moving, Bob cleared the bridge, banked a right to follow the signs to North Station and drove past the courthouse with the jail beside it. The directions his buddy had given him were right on the money, thought Bob, and it was still daylight. They had two hours to kill before the game. Bob saw the parking garage. "Event parking" was twelve dollars.

"There's the car," shouted Andy. "They're turning into the garage."

"You're right," said Bob with a smile. "They must be going to the game." But, he thought, we'll never know for sure.

Outside the garage, he held Andy's hand as they crossed the street. He pointed to the street sign called "Red Auerbach" and told Andy about the famous Celtics coach. Andy had never heard of him. Then Bob ticked off a half-dozen famous Celtics players from the last twenty years but Andy knew none of them. Andy told Bob about today's players and Bob nodded blankly. He didn't follow sports as much now. He found it difficult to keep up with the new people and trends. He blamed his age. He was, after all, in his thirties. His doctor had assured him that apathy, not memory failure, was a possible side effect of the prescription medication he swallowed daily.

"I want my ticket," said Andy.

Bob gave him his ticket and told him to keep it in his pants pocket at all times.

"If you get lost, show that ticket stub to an usher. He'll take you right back to your seat and to me," said Bob. He replaced his ticket in his jacket pocket.

Before entering the Garden, Bob pointed to the elevated streetcar and asked Andy if he wanted to ride the "T." But Andy shook his head; he'd already done that a few years back. What he really wanted to do was visit the Celtics souvenir shop. Bob bought him a North Carolina t-shirt. The cashier rang the sale.

"Let's buy ice creams," said Bob. He bought himself a black raspberry double scoop and Andy a strawberry and vanilla mix. They sat on a bench in North Station, ate their ice cream, and people-watched while waiting for the Garden to open.

"Excuse me, sir. How is your family this evening?" asked a smiling young black man. "Would you care to contribute to our homeless shelter by purchasing a complimentary copy of this newspaper?"

Bob couldn't help but smile. He looked over his shoulder to locate Andy, then opened his wallet and gave the well-spoken man a dollar for the "free" paper. He read the political cartoons while Andy watched a juggler practice throwing his batons. Every few seconds a baton clattered loudly to the floor.

"Why is he dropping his batons?" asked Andy.

"He must need practice," said Bob, chuckling over a Republican riding a donkey.

"But why are people dropping money into his black hat?" asked Andy.

"They're giving him money so he can eat and pay rent and practice more," said Bob.

"What happens after he gets really good from practicing?" asked Andy.

"People will give him more and more money until maybe he appears on the *Tonight Show*," said Bob.

"Wow, who knows what will happen if I keep practicing basketball?" asked Andy.

Bob told him he might make out better if he practiced his math tables instead. Then Andy needed to use the john. Bob walked him to the one bathroom servicing all North Station, its suited executives, blue-shirted workers, and down-and-out drunks. The smell hit them first—the heavy ammonia-like smell of urine. Their sneakers, sticking to the glossy floor, made sucking sounds. Bob took a look at the single yellow-stained urinal and led Andy back out into the terminal. They could wait.

But they wouldn't wait long. A line had formed in front of the gate. Red-jacketed ushers tore their tickets in half. The pair climbed higher and higher up the stairs. The popcorn man said they had to climb to the balcony, the highest seating in the building, some seventy feet from the floor. An usher told Bob he was down near the balcony's rim, above the "Bud" sign. The sign reminded Bob that they needed to visit the john. After using the much cleaner facilities, Andy scurried down the steep sloped stairway while Bob froze. The parquet floor below looked about the size of a chessboard. The "pawns" bounced a little ball through a hoop. Bob gripped the railing with both hands, crouched down, and stepped down the stairs like an ape looking for a lost banana.

"What took you so long?" asked Andy. He had found his seat, but said he wanted to move into the next row—the one directly over the balcony railing.

Bob ignored the first question and simply replied, "We're sitting where the tickets say."

A college-aged couple sat next to Bob by the aisle. Three city kids were kicking the backs of the chairs behind Bob. He turned and gave them a scowl. Suddenly the announcer broke the silence and everyone rose for "The Star Spangled Banner." Bob didn't rise to his full height: he was trying to keep as much balcony as he could between him and the low-slung railing a few feet below him. If, perhaps, one of those resentful city kids in the row behind bumped him, Bob's six-foot frame might slide across the buffering row and slip over the railing as neatly as a burial at sea. Little Andy then would need a new ride home.

Bob sat down with a thud before the music ended and removed his jacket. The girl next to him squashed him with her ample rear when she relaxed into her seat. He adjusted himself although he did find the snugness pleasant. Then she coughed. She coughed a little phlegm, which she deposited into a white tissue. She continued to cough, wiping her lips with tissue and dropping the little wads next to Bob's feet. He thought he saw some mucus tinged with blood—a red stained tissue. He knew about super-germs. He also knew about the rise of TB and the other so-called conquered diseases. A well-directed cough could drive a new and more virulent strain of TB up someone's nostril from two yards away. Bob kicked the wadded tissues beneath his chair then rubbed his sneakers together to kill the germs.

"I want a drink," said Andy.

"Let's wait until the half," said Bob.

Just then the horn blared, the teams relaxed with the score tied, and Bob took Andy up to the concession stand. Through the crowd, Bob ordered hot dogs, soda, and popcorn and received some meager change from a twenty-dollar bill. Andy took his food, said thanks, and walked ahead into the crowd. Bob held the rest of the food in a tray. He walked slower than normal to keep from spilling the snacks. When he turned to step down the stairs he had to look away. Vertigo overcame him. Then he checked his bearings. Was this the stairway? Where was Andy? He called Andy's name over the din but no one answered. He searched for an usher, remembering that Andy's mother had entrusted him with her child. The ushers weren't in sight but he saw a cop. The cop had red cheeks, a lantern jaw, and big bear-like hands.

"Excuse me but my little boy is lost," said Bob. He gave a general description while the cop shook his head. Bob couldn't remember the name of the team on the cap that Andy wore.

"The place is full of kids wearing caps. Where are you sitting?" asked the cop, his broad red face scowling.

Bob pointed vaguely over toward the middle of the balcony.

"Near the railing," said Bob.

"Let's see your ticket," said the cop. He was smirking.

Bob felt his face flush. He checked his pockets automatically but remembered that he had left his ticket with his jacket back at his seat.

"I don't have it on me," said Bob shrugging.

The crowd cheered as the Celtics pulled ahead. The cop muttered about missing the game then said they needed to find the seats before making an announcement. He walked Bob, hands on his hips, down the first set of stairs as Bob balanced his snacks in their tray and his body against the railing. Someone yelled, "Sit down—" but the cop stared him down. Bob stopped. No Andy. No seats. Bob crouched back up the stairs and tried another stairway. The cop walked slowly behind him. Bob tripped on a man's outstretched shoe and spilled his popcorn on the guy's shoulder. The covers on both drinks popped off.

"Excuse me," said Bob.

"Christ," said the guy. "Watch yourself."

Now Bob eyed the rims of the drinks, the stairs, the seats and felt his way along the railing with the cop breathing on his shoulder. He gritted his teeth. The first thing Bob noticed was the pile of crumpled tissues.

"Andy," cried Bob. Andy looked over at Bob briefly, bit at his half-eaten hot dog, and returned to watching the game.

"Andy," said the cop, with a wink, "you keep an eye on this guy."

"Andy, I hate to think what may have happened to you," said Bob.

At the same time, the girl he had to squeeze past said to her partner, "I hate to think what the end of spring will be like if my hay fever is this bad now."

Bob paused. A coincidental phrase. The universe had responded to his need. He brightened a little. The Celtics were ahead by ten and looked strong. A succession of time outs by the opposing team caused the fans to boo and merely postponed the home team's eventual win.

Bob held Andy's hand tightly for the walk out of the Garden. They passed the concessionaires locking their stands, the outside vendors selling hats and sausage subs, and the crowds milling about the street people's various one-man acts. The crowd thinned as they crossed the street to the parking garage, climbed the stairs, and jumped into Bob's car.

On the dark street outside the garage, Bob's guts turned. He still needed to get out of the city. The show was not over yet. He saw the light ahead turn green and moved across traffic making a left. Then the traffic stalled. The light turned yellow, then red. Bob's car was in the middle of the dark street with two lanes of traffic converging on him from both sides. A yellow cab pulled up to within an inch of his left rear fender. Then Bob sighed. He noticed from the convergence of headlights that the car in front of him was from Maine. It was the red Cavalier with the two young men wearing ball caps that they had first met on the bridge.

"There they are again," said Bob. "Those two guys from Maine really did see the game and now we'll just follow them home, back up north."

But Andy said nothing. Bob looked over. Andy was fast asleep. The light changed back to green. Traffic moved ahead. Bob gently pushed the accelerator, thanked the universe, and made his way out of the city.

The Party

Bob O'Neil smiled at the pretty check out girl at the supermarket. She returned a blank stare. *Have a nice day,* he thought. Bob pocketed his change with a "Thanks" but declined the plastic bag to be environmentally correct. Then he barehanded the two liter bottle of Diet Coke and twenty-five piece kit of plastic tableware—his contribution to Ned's party. He wondered if Ned could really fit twenty-five partiers in his trailer. Suddenly, he caught the eye of a beautiful and familiar-looking woman. Risk's girlfriend! She waved a long slender hand toward him.

Bob walked over to the tall, dark-haired woman dressed in a long sky-blue dress. A book Bob had just finished reading, *The Heavenly Promise,* indicated he should find the hidden meaning in seemingly chance encounters. So after a quick chat, Bob asked her what was going on in her life.

"My Dad's sick," she said, her eyes filling up. "He's in and out of the hospital and the doctors are scratching their heads."

"I'm sorry," said Bob. He touched her arm gently and she smiled.

As he turned to leave the market, he paused to browse over the newspapers and magazines. The front page of the *Fiston Daily Herald* headlined "Standoff at Hotel Ends." Bob looked down at the photo of police escorting his former investment adviser out of his barricaded hotel room. Drunk and despondent over not being able to speak with his vacationing psychiatrist, he had threatened to take the lives of hostages, then his own. Bob whistled. Witnesses praised the quick action of the police SWAT team in cordoning off the downtown block. The released hostages claimed that out of his suitcase full of weapons he had narrowed the choice of destruction to either blowing them up with a hand grenade or shooting them down with an AK-47 assault rifle. Hostage negotiators used his former girlfriend to talk him out. Observation at the State psychiatric hospital would determine the extent of criminal charges.

Definitely not a confidence-building ad for the investment counseling business, thought Bob. He bought the paper to fill yet another page in his scrapbook.

On the way to the trailer, Bob tapped the steering wheel, wondering how many girls he'd meet. He wasn't really interested in a relationship, just companionship. A relationship at this stage of his development, according to the book, could stunt his growth and inhibit his ability to use fractal analysis to manipulate synchronicity and increase his vibrational frequency. He might never evolve to his true spiritual self if some pretty girl batted her lashes at him.

At the trailer, Bob gave Ned the party ware and Diet Coke. Ned was dressed in his work clothes. The blue and gray garb was clean, with "Ned" embroidered in white letters but his hands were stained with dirt and soot. Ned's brown eyes were dull and his face expressionless. He never laughed and seldom smiled. His business cards were piled on the table beside the ashtray filled with the stubs of filterless Camels. Apparently Ned was using the party as a business deduction for taxes.

Bob met the first party guest while Ned finished preparing the ham dinner. The guest was a trailer park resident, an old man at least seventy, with a lame hand shake and a blind dog named Spanny. Bob shook hands with Spanny too and looked deeply into his luminous brown eyes. Spanny's owner was mourning the loss of his dear wife, which he discussed with anyone who would listen—now it was Bob's turn.

Ned's sister Tish arrived next. Bob's heart skipped a beat. Her navy-blue tent-like dress and cream-colored skin hid her weight and age well. Bob had called her after Ned told him she wanted to see him. Bob scaled down plans of a mountain hike up Gunstock to a cup of coffee downtown after talking to Risk, a mutual friend. Bob considered himself well connected with her. Like her, he was a member of MUFON, the world's most respected UFO research organization. At the last MUFON meeting, Bob had learned they both received therapy partly as a result of an extraterrestrial abduction, except that Bob had conscious memories of the abduction and her's were repressed.

Unfortunately, when he did ask her out for coffee, she countered with, "In what context?" and after his offer of friendship, she finally agreed to the "date" if a third party were present. Bob figured she wasn't interested in getting to know him better so he didn't called her. Now Bob felt a little uncomfortable because she probably thought he was weird. He never did tell Ned that he had called her.

Tish smiled slightly at Bob and sat next to Spanny's owner after patting Spanny on the head. Bob heard her muted, "I'm sorry," then agreed to give a reading on how the old man's wife was doing in the spirit world. Tish dabbled in shamanism.

Henry burst in the door carrying a black suit. He was big and fat and loud. He went into the bathroom to change. He'd been boating all day in his "dollar" boat. His pastoral counselor had sold him a 13-foot fiberglass Boston Whaler with a 35-horse Johnson outboard for a dollar to help cure his depression. Henry had obligingly named the boat "God's Grace." He was high from the fresh fall air, bright sunlight, and from smoking a joint. Henry was a born salesman who had crashed and burned after acquiring a fear of people. Although he had never been able to return to sales, marijuana, a social lubricant, calmed his nerves and eased his pain of not having a career-track job. As an ex-co-founder of Narcotics Anonymous in New Hampshire, he had a nagging suspicion that smoking grass inhibited his growth even though he claimed he was one of the lucky three percent of the population for whom grass acted as a stimulant.

While Henry changed, the women came. Jane, a thin brunette gone gray, and Sue, Ned's date from last week, acknowledged the introductions. Henry yelled greetings from the bathroom then flushed the john. Sue winced.

Ned declared dinner was ready. Apparently the other twenty invited guests had other plans. Bob sat across from Henry who had changed into his wrist bandage so he could reveal a long scar to the inquiring young ladies.

"What happened to your wrist?" asked Jane.

"Carpel tunnel as a result of dialing too many 900 numbers," said Henry.

"What?" asked Sue.

Henry unwrapped the bandage and pointed to the scar.

"The salt spray from today's boating makes it sting," he said wincing.

Jane stepped back nearly blushing. Sue asked what 900 numbers were. Both sat down on Bob's side of the table. Ned excused himself; he needed to phone his ex-wife to ask her why she wasn't at the party. Sue winced again. After being divorced five years, Bob wondered what attracted Ned to the ex.

Jane showed Henry a picture of her husband, currently on a business trip.

"I saw him with a blonde two weeks ago at Joseph's," said Henry.

"Wouldn't be the first time," said Jane.

As Ned returned to the table, Bob saw Tish give the old man her phone number. Tarot and Indian Medicine cards were spread on the coffee table in front of them. Then Ned declared he made the brown bread from scratch using Grandma's recipe. He cheated with the baked beans; they were B&M with a little extra something. He owed the homemade coleslaw to his mother's recipe. The two women marveled at a man cooking. Then Ned sliced the ham.

"When did you learn to cook?" asked Jane.

"After my divorce," said Ned.

"Something good came out of it," said Jane. "You must still be friends with your ex too."

"We're very close," said Ned.

Sue jumped. Suddenly Tish announced that she and the old man were leaving the party. She apologized to Ned for not staying to eat the home-cooked ham dinner but they needed to drum and chant over the grave of the late wife while there was still light. They said goodbye to the guests, then Tish led the feeble old man by the arm as he led Spanny the blind dog by the leash out the door.

"Have you been married?" Jane asked Henry.

"Once was enough," said Henry.

"I agree," said Jane. "Although I'm in my second marriage."

Sue turned her back to Ned. He had just wiped a sneeze with the back of one hand while he cut a hunk of ham with the other. Until then she had ignored his open-mouthed mastication and mysterious telephone flirtation with his ex.

"What do you do Bob?" she asked him.

"I'm into computer software," said Bob vaguely. He decided not to lead into this conversation with a monologue account of his lost career, numerous hobbies, and lack of a fulfilling social life as a result of his emotional instability.

"I teach Latin at the University," said Sue.

"Really, that's impressive. I'm reading a book now whose author is investigating the existence of a manuscript written in another dead language. Archaeologists are finding mysterious scrolls in the ruins of an ancient temple that may hold the key to the future of our civilization," said Bob.

He heaped a third helping on his cleaned-off plate.

"Now I'm impressed. I'll have to read the book," said Sue.

She turned distractedly to Henry.

"Could you lower your voice? I can't hear Bob," said Sue.

"There's a reason why I talk so loud," said Henry, looking at Bob.

"He was in Viet Nam," said Bob sadly.

"I had a mortar shell blow me up. Now I can't hear out of my left ear so well. My shoulder cramps on me too. But I lost my twenty-three percent vet disability with Reagan. He "streamlined" the disability system and eliminated anyone with less than twenty-five percent," said Henry.

"I'm sorry," said Sue. "Usually I'm very tolerant of people with disabilities."

"Want a massage?" asked Jane. "I'm learning the trade courtesy of the state of New Hampshire after my job at the tanning factory went belly up."

Jane walked around the table and grabbed Henry's shoulders.

"This will be completely platonic," she announced. "My father was a doctor."

Henry giggled.

Ned excused himself after burping. "What kind of movie would you guys like to see?" No one said anything. He left for the video store.

Sue turned to Bob. In a whispery voice she related the story of her older brother who had worked in a canning factory in Philadelphia. He had quit for the second time, stopped eating and taking his pills, and had been placed in a private psychiatric hospital involuntarily. They were threatening to send him to the State facility unless he cooperated.

"Do you think that's bad?" she asked.

Bob thought for a minute. He and his family had their problems, should he expose a little of himself or remain aloof the way he usually did? The book he was reading said that aloofness was his "personality pattern" that he needed to overcome.

"State hospitals can be the pits. Compare it to the criminal justice system. Not having health insurance and a private practice doctor is like not making bail, sitting in jail, and being represented by a public defender," said Bob.

Sue nodded.

"What he needs to do is accept his illness, at least while he's there, because cooperation is the key to getting out. He's lost his rights," said Bob.

Henry threw a matchbook at Bob. Henry looked embarrassed—if that were possible.

"Are you uncomfortable, Henry?" asked Bob.

He nodded.

"Henry made me uneasy earlier today at Applebee's after the boat ride and I left. I told him I felt uncomfortable," said Bob.

Sue admitted she had never discussed this concept with her therapist of five years.

Bob looked over at Ned. He had now plugged himself into an "R" rated video after leaving a third message on his ex's answering machine. He stared slack jawed as a police chase ended in a four-car smash up. The movie immediately sped to the next action scene.

"We need to connect more with each other—not with that thing Ned's staring at," said Bob.

"I agree," said Sue. "At school the kids have lost the ability to communicate and interact with each other. We're so passive."

"I think people grow faster if they communicate more," said Bob.

"Is that in the book too?" asked Sue.

Bob nodded.

Then he decided to throw his caution to the wind and forget the book for once. He looked down at her clean plate topped with a wrinkled napkin and wiped his hands.

"Would you like to get a coffee downtown?" he asked.

"Sure," she said simply.

They thanked Ned and he waved back without looking over. Jane stopped massaging Henry's shoulders to wave. Henry said to have fun—he was. Then Bob and Sue stepped into the crisp fall evening.

A Date by the Oak Tree

Sitting stiffly on the bench, Bob O'Neil stared at the spare walls of the building. Sunlight streamed through the large framed window from the east. At this Sunday morning service, Cathy sat tense next to him. As usual, the Quaker meeting was quiet, meditative. Every few minutes, a Friend stood, interrupting the silence, and offered individual insights and reflections to the group. The Friends themselves conducted the service, no preacher intervened. Their motto was "Wait upon the Lord." They valued simplicity.

Bob heard sniffling and saw, from the corner of his eye, Cathy crying. Tears dripped down flushed cheeks. Her left hand mopped them off her face leaving wet streaks on China doll skin. Butterflies tickled Bob's stomach as he reached over to squeeze her right hand. She was a tall, blonde, thirty-year-old woman with a slight frame who constantly ran her fingers through her ear-lobe length hair. A naturalist, she loved the color green. She wore rubber-soled boots topped with green-colored nylon and matching green-cotton laces—no dead animal skin, thank you very much. She pulled her clean but faded long-hemmed green jacket tightly around her thin body in spite of the room's warmth.

"Why are you crying?" Bob whispered.

"I hate my father. He's selling the family house to move to Florida. And my mother agrees with him," said Cathy.

After the meeting, Bob walked Cathy over to the adjoining room where the Friends served snacks. He glanced briefly at the plates of cheddar cheese slices, crackers, grapes, apples, and most important of all, a two-dozen mix of doughnuts fresh from the bakery. A collection plate next to the coffee urn offset this minor extravagance of the Friends.

Bob ignored the collection plate. He already had dropped a dollar during the service. He was tall and thin, a head taller than Cathy. The Friends were the third church he had investigated since becoming sick and losing his job. He had been attending the Meeting for several months yet

Cathy was the only person he had met and he knew her by sight from the contra dances he frequented on the second Friday of every month at the Fiston Grange Hall. The Friends smiled and said hello but kept their opinions to themselves.

"How do you feel now?" he asked Cathy.

"How do you think I feel?" she countered.

"Would you like a snack?" Bob asked.

She ate a cracker and cheese sandwich, then poured herself a Country Mint herbal tea. Bob bit into a doughnut and sipped coffee. He didn't care about fat, cholesterol, and caffeine. But Cathy did. She was a health-conscious vegetarian who studied the environment in a Master's program at the University and practiced good nutrition at home.

"I finally have you eating with me. This is our first date," Bob teased.

"I told you I don't date. Too much pressure. Furthermore, guys never pay my way. Too much control," she said.

Bob took a deep breath.

"Would you care to walk through the town forest with me?" he asked.

"Sure, but we have to walk at my pace," she said.

They left the Meeting House and the Friends. The drive to the public woods was short. The November day hung dimly, overcast, and brisk. They found the trail at the far corner of the parking lot. Once in the woods, away from the street noise, the forest yielded its secrets. The leafless trees shielded them from the breeze, screened their view, but magnified the scampering calls of the small animals and birds.

Suddenly Cathy stooped to examine a frost-damaged plant that she insisted was still alive. She cooed over its drooping form. So what? Bob figured the plant would die soon anyway. Next, she hugged a tree. Cathy told Bob it was her favorite tree—the stubby-needled hemlock. Bob cracked a joke about how Socrates used the tree sap to kill himself.

"No, Bob. Socrates used a fern, also called a hemlock, to poison himself," she said.

"Now you'll have to find me the fern," said Bob.

"Wrong season. Besides, you're in therapy. You're discovering healthy ways to deal with your issues," she said.

"What about you? Have you been accepted at the County Mental Health Center?" asked Bob.

"I'm on the waiting list. I let my school insurance lapse like a fool and

I have no money for private coverage. I'm depressed but at least I don't want to kill myself anymore," she said.

Cathy inspected the ground surrounding her favorite tree and checked the health of its numerous saplings. They were fine, so she continued walking. Bob stumbled on a root, swore, and then heard the chattering of a squirrel he spooked.

"Where are your parents moving to in Florida?" Bob asked.

"They'll rent somewhere then buy. But it's so hot and southern down there. I can't stand the thought," she said.

"I had a chance to visit the Crystal River Valley on a land deal. Foster, my paid friend, wanted me to buy a $25,000 lot by enticing me with visions of bikini-clad bathing beauties, but I was really interested in seeing the manatees in the rough. He thought I was nuts. I first saw those exotic mammals in National Geographic years ago. They're a boyhood fixation of mine," Bob said.

"Funny, I had a chance to teach in Crystal River several years ago. I went against my intuition and refused the offer. The temperature must be terrible in the summer," she said.

"Not at all. Actually that part of the panhandle has a unique New England climate with rolling hills, trees, and lots of fresh water," said Bob.

"I knew I should have taken that job," said Cathy.

They walked the trail again. The squirrel chattered. She answered the squirrel's call, identified a pink flower, and picked a white mushroom next to a stump.

"They're edible," she said.

She bit off a large chunk while holding another towards Bob.

He looked at her.

"No thanks. I just had a doughnut," Bob said.

"Don't you know about junk food?" she asked.

"Oh God, not another food fight. Pretty soon you'll slam beef, poultry, pork, and fish," said Bob.

"Remember, I'm a vegetarian and all those animals are mistreated," said Cathy.

Finally they rested, fatigued more from talking than from walking. They sat on the park bench next to the trail and saw the old Pimpernel house across the wide river. A majestic white Colonial mansion with acres of well-kept grounds.

"Imagine, the beautiful river view, the quiet forest, and the pretty girl sitting next to me," Bob said.

She glanced at him.

"Don't try anything," said Cathy.

"My dear, I'm harmless," said Bob.

Next, the trail passed some cement boundary posts, an old graveyard, and stone monument. Cathy inspected a large, twisted tree while Bob read the inscription in the stone memorial. Apparently, a Scottish soldier named Charles Stewart MacDermont fought the English at the Battle of Dundee, became a prisoner, and after Scotland's defeat, went to the Colonies to start a new life. Cathy estimated that the oak tree was at least a hundred years old when farmer MacDermont arrived 250 years ago.

"Who would ever travel to a foreign land to start over, let alone one controlled by the power you had just fought against?" Bob asked.

"My father did," said Cathy.

"You told me he was in the Hitler Youth Corps. He was too young for the war," Bob said.

"My father fought in North Africa, invaded Russia, and stayed a prisoner there for years. He was one of the few to survive starvation conditions. Then he went home to Germany but didn't feel comfortable there. He took the first chance available to leave and go to America. That's how he met my mother, a French Canadian. Neither one knew English and the people here distrusted them. He never talks about the war years," said Cathy.

"Wow. I could never do anything like that. Besides, home is home," he said.

Walking past the old oak; Cathy stopped short on the trail ahead of Bob. Only half aware of himself, he stumbled against her.

"You bumped me," she cried.

She turned around and giggled. Then she wrapped her long arms around him and squeezed tight. The hug was warm and soft.

"Thanks for brightening my day," she said simply.

Startled, Bob disengaged himself from her embrace and turned away. He walked back over to the stone monument to study the inscription and ponder her response. Then he heard Cathy's footfalls recede into the forest along the leaf-strewn trail. In the background the leafless oak shrugged its gnarled branches.

New Age Lines for
an Age Old Problem

Bob O'Neil sipped coffee in the cool air of Fiston's outdoor cafe. He had switched to decaf a year ago on the casual advice of his pill-pushing MD whom he saw monthly. Surprisingly, he did report a decrease in the frequency of his anxiety attacks—in fact, he hadn't once needed to suppress an insane urge to stop his car in traffic, kill the ignition, and run shrieking into the hills.

Across the table, his buddy Risk warmed his hands around a mug of hot chocolate. Risk trimmed his bushy gray-specked beard to a point and he covered his close-cropped black hair with a beret, giving his head the conical appearance of a child's top. Risk was a free-lance carpenter, but he spent his spare time trying to figure out where the CIA-funded "Black Ops" team would strike next. He knew they had assassinated President Kennedy, covered-up secret communications with extraterrestrials, and sold drugs to school kids. A self-declared psychic, he relied on his spirit guides to help him stay on track as the worldwide paradigm shift exploded to life after the coming millennial apocalypse.

"Risk, I have some hot news. But first, I'm sorry to hear your girlfriend left you," said Bob.

"She didn't understand me," shrugged Risk. "I'm not worried, someone else will come along." He took a deep breath and pounded his rippling stomach with a clenched fist. He added, "I may be forty-five, but I'm in excellent physical condition."

"Hi guys," said Cynthia. She pulled up a chair with her high-test black coffee. She never used sugar and cream, which could bloat her otherwise perfectly curved figure; a figure she maintained with a daily workout schedule. She brushed away short auburn hair and smiled at Risk.

"I heard," said Cynthia, pausing. "How are you feeling?"

"Perfect," replied Risk. "We'll always be friends. I'm more concerned about you."

"The new job's fine," said Cynthia with a smile. Risk shook his head.

"Oh, you mean Jeff? I sleep with him once in a while. But there's nothing there," said Cynthia, waving her hand as if to brush away an irritating fly.

Bob's eyes darted from one to the other as the two accomplished love-players traded sympathies in this new era of AIDS-infested trysts that occurred in spite of the demise of the sexual revolution. He, on the other hand, kept his bed warm with a hot-water bottle-sized dog that usually escaped from the covers before dawn.

"I need to apologize to you," said Risk, looking at Cynthia. "You may not realize it but we have spent many past lives together."

Bob smiled. "Risk and I died together in a Russian peasant revolt in one past life."

Risk stared him down. Bob returned to sipping his coffee. "Many times before I lived as a monk. Once the church condemned me for heresy and sentenced me to be burned at the stake. Before my death, you gave me water—not once but many times—at great peril to your life," said Risk.

"But what was I?" asked Cynthia.

"That's not important," said Risk.

"You were probably some fat and shabby peasant lady," said Bob.

"Shut up, Bob," said Risk. He turned to Cynthia. "For your kindness, I thank you. We knew each other several more times as well and may have even been lovers. But what I need to make amends for is my action as a warrior. Once, I plundered a village and in the ensuing melee, I thrust my sword deep into your chest. I killed you and for that I'm sorry," said Risk.

"What honesty," said Bob. He quickly brought his mug to his lips but didn't drink. He peered over its rim.

Cynthia touched her chest with her fingers.

"Wow. How do you know all this?" she asked.

"I meditate," said Risk. "But you can find out about yourself more simply. I suggest you undergo a past-life soul regression. I know a hypnotist."

Bob spoke up.

"Regression therapy can be dangerous. I have enough trouble dealing with this life."

"Trust me," said Risk, pointedly ignoring Bob. "I care about you. Once you have seen the lives we have lived together in the past, you'll realize how our lives are intertwined now. Cosmic forces are bringing us together. It's unavoidable."

Cynthia broke away from his stare. She sipped her coffee and waved to a passer-by. Then she smiled at Risk: a flash of white teeth and a flutter of eyelids.

"Do you really care about me?" she asked.

"I love you. Friend to friend, of course, but the possibility of more is there. It just needs time to develop," said Risk.

Bob twitched. His body heat was rising in spite of the cool breeze.

"I think I'd better go," he said.

Cynthia grabbed his sleeve.

"No, please stay, Bob," said Cynthia. "What do you mean, Risk?"

"I believe in love," he said, with hard, expressionless eyes and a grim face. "I believe in its healing power and ultimate goodness. I've conquered my demons and I'm ready to help others do the same."

Bob ventured his opinion on love. "When I'm in love, I go psychotic," said Bob.

Cynthia shivered while Risk rolled his eyes.

"You'll always be my friend, Risk," said Cynthia, touching his forearm. "Take care, Bob." Then she left. Graceful steps took the slim figure around the corner of the building and out of sight.

"You weren't much help," accused Risk. "I think I scared her away by bringing up the subject of love a little too quickly."

"A bit more subtlety might help, Risk," agreed Bob.

Risk said nothing. Bob looked into the sky. The sun was low.

"I would have left out the apology for the sword play," said Bob.

"Some expert," muttered Risk.

Risk scanned the tables around him, then reached for the *Fiston Daily Herald*. "I wonder what they're hiding from us today," mused Risk. He hummed to himself while he riffled through the paper.

Bob watched Risk a full minute, then he leaned forward and in a low voice said, "Now here's that hot news I promised you: a blacked-out ship of unknown registry or description—I could just see its huge profile and its tugs—went down the river last night and out to sea. I had my friend, the bridge operator, try to find out more from his co-workers on duty but no one talked," said Bob.

Risk stared at him. "What time?"

Bob paused. "Midnight," he said.

"Interesting. Covert naval operations? A nuclear waste dumping?

Secret rendezvous? I'll make the necessary inquiries," said Risk, restored to his old self.

Bob watched him leave, a spring in his step, chest thrust forward, arms swinging—a conquering knight. Bob glanced at the paper. Good. The tidal charts indicated slack tide was around midnight, just as he figured, an ideal time for a ship's departure. Now he wondered, who would admit to seeing the ship? *What ship?* he asked himself, smiling. He laughed. Then he drank his coffee, sweet but cold, and left.

The Watchers

Bob O'Neil was running late. He was supposed to spend Christmas with his last remaining relatives—Uncle Russ, his cousin Vicky, and her daughter Anna. Relatives that still spoke with him anyway—the rest were either dead, too distant, or in denial that he existed. His cousin told him to come to dinner at 2:00 pm. She meant it. Not that he'd have to eat alone, just that she'd worry about accidents, tie-ups, and make everyone—except the dog—wait until he arrived. Bob eyed the phone.

"Hello, Uncle Russ, it's Bob...." he said. Silence. "Bob O'Neil."

"Bobby, she's not here, she went for Anna," said Uncle Russ.

"Tell her I'll be late," said Bob. "I'm leaving now."

"You're coming? I'll tell her you're coming," said Uncle Russ.

"Tell her I'll be late," said Bob.

"OK, Bobby," said Uncle Russ.

"Are you feeling better?" asked Bob.

"Who? Me? Everything's fine," said Uncle Russ.

"Hello?" asked Bob. He heard the click. A typical response from Uncle Russ, thought Bob. At ninety-one, he hadn't changed despite the broken hip and the recent loss of his wife.

The brief conversation brought back childhood memories of Uncle Russ. He swam the Australian crawl, walked a postman's beat, and liked the ladies. Even as a seventy-five-year-old security guard at the local savings bank, he hadn't outgrown brushing against the breasts of the pretty bank tellers. He said they giggled appreciatively. When Bob did stop by the house Uncle Russ said encouraging things like: "When are you returning to work?" or more subtly, "Are you working yet?" Later, while sitting in his red upholstered chair, he dismissed him with a wave of the hand and said, "You're retired." Uncle Russ had worked sixty-five years straight.

Bob chose to spend the holiday with the family even though they were in various states of emotional disrepair. As his therapist said, he had choices today. He could have spent the day home alone, visited the kids next-door or gone to the dinner party at the home of the professor he worked for at his volunteer job. But he chose to break bread with his blood.

While traveling the interstate, he questioned his own sanity. The drive to Boston was always a horror show. He beeped at the yuppie BMW driver that cut in front of him. He braked gently. "Welcome to Massachusetts!" thought Bob.

Bob swerved to avoid an overturned barrel. A guy in a Saab, passing on the right, gave Bob the bird. "Merry Christmas" muttered Bob. He approached Boston and traffic snarled as four lanes converged to two in the wisdom of some civil engineer.

His mind drifted during the wait. Vicky married an older man, a postal worker like her father. He was Italian. Her family was convinced he was part of The Family. Vicky and her husband both took medication for nerves (before it was chic) while they lived together but never entered counseling. Vicky was too self-conscious and her husband was too proud. They had a typical 70s marriage: a couple of good years, a little girl, and a separation. Vicky returned to Mom and Dad's with her court-awarded daughter. The ex visited Anna every weekend in spite of Vicky's barrage of expletives. Being Catholic, the former couple agreed upon an infinitely long legal separation. They were high-strung, like Bob.

Finally, he merged back on the interstate where four lanes of wild traffic twisted through the southern environs of Boston. Bob veered away from a drifting yellow Cadillac with a couple of blown out windows and driven by a man wearing a purple bandana.

He was fearful Anna would hook up with a guy like that some day, a pimp or drug dealer. Anna, the couple's little girl, matured from a quiet, sensitive child with a temper, to a heavily medicated schizophrenic young woman prone to paranoid delusions. She spent last Christmas escaping from her group home, traveling to Philadelphia and walking the streets at midnight. Luckily the authorities found her and placed her in a private hospital for six weeks. Vicky filed the bills in the trash. Her daughter was a ward of the state. Anna was tall, pretty, poker-faced, and a little overweight from the meds. Having perspective on nervous disorders, Bob thought he could help her.

Bob checked his watch as he pulled into the driveway of the well-kept blue aluminum-sided house in Adamsville. He was thirty minutes late. But that was OK. Uncle Russ had excused him. He strode through the breezeway. The knock on the inner door roused the dog. Movement. Anna answered the knock. She smiled and silently opened the door.

"Is that you, Bobby?" asked Vicky. "You're late. I was worried sick."

"I told Uncle Russ. Didn't he relay the message?" asked Bob.

Bob looked over at Uncle Russ. His head was cocked to one side; eyes focused on his lap, jaw slack, and ear plugged. The jack wired him into the tube while its images silently pulsed on the screen.

"Why didn't you give me the message?" screamed Vicky into her father's face. She wrung her hands as he re-focused his eyes and smiled.

"Is supper ready?" he asked.

"Wait... You just wait!" she screamed. He smiled back.

Apparently Vicky had assumed her late mother's role of chief interrogator of the old man. Anna looked over at Bob. She smiled. She was on leave from the hospital, a four-hour pass.

"Are they giving you good therapy?" asked Bob.

"No one talks to me, they think I'm crazy," she said.

"I don't think you're crazy. Do you trust me?" asked Bob.

"What do you know about surveillance equipment?" asked Anna.

"Not much. Except satellites can see everything," said Bob.

Anna's poker face twisted painfully.

"Really? What about infrared scanners?" she asked.

"You don't have the background in electronics to understand how that stuff works. Besides, it's classified," said Bob.

Vicky blew into the room. She wiped her bleached blonde hair out of her eyes. She ignored Anna.

"Supper's ready," said Vicky softly.

Then she walked over to Uncle Russ and bent down.

"TIME TO EAT!" she yelled.

Then Vicky glided into the kitchen.

"Anna, I made the supper, the least you can do is set the dining room table!" said Vicky.

Bob helped Anna set the dining room table. Uncle Russ shuffled to the head of the table and sat down in slow motion. Expressionless, Anna finished folding the napkins and set the silverware. Bob plopped into the seat opposite Uncle Russ. Vicky darted in from the kitchen with a platter of food. She doled out the food to the crew sitting around the table.

Anna pecked at her tiny plate of food like a bird scavenging a picked-over carcass. Uncle Russ mechanically chewed the turkey, potato, and squash with all his original ninety-one-year-old teeth. Bob knew because he could see all the teeth in action. Then Uncle Russ scraped his plate clean. Bob gobbled his meal like a turkey. Roughage. Everything was tasteless roughage. He saw Vicky give most of her food to the dog waiting patiently beneath the table, a plump cocker spaniel.

Suddenly Anna broke the silence.

"Bob, what if someone could watch you all the time?" asked Anna.

"That's impossible," said Bob. "Such a boring activity anyway."

"I don't feel well," said Anna. "I can't sleep. I know they're interfering with my heart even though the EKG was normal."

"You could have a sleep test done. The doctors could check if you're getting the proper brain wave action," said Bob.

"But if they're always watching me, they'll let me sleep normally for the test," said Anna.

Bob reached over and grabbed twenty-two-year-old Anna by the shoulders.

"There are no people after you. Do you believe me?" asked Bob.

Anna smiled a little.

"I trust you. But the feelings..." she said.

Bob told her what he'd read in one of the latest new age books. Earth was in trouble. Benevolent creatures from another dimension were trying to rescue the planet from the control of the reptiles, humorously known as "Lizzies." The Lizzies created conflict and fear on Earth, then consumed the negative emotions generated. They fed off people's fear and frenzy. Systems-busters were ready to throw out the Lizzies and usher in a new order where peace and harmony would dominate in an age of love. Sensitives like Anna could help push out the Lizzies.

"You're not on my wavelength," said Anna. She looked at him skeptically. "I've done terrible things that thousands of people have found out about."

"Anna, we've all done things we're ashamed of. Talk about it with someone you trust. A therapist. A priest. We need to have faith. Ask God to give you help. You do believe," said Bob.

"Yes. But He doesn't listen. I've tried," said Anna.

"I'm going to call next week to make sure you're asking Him for guidance. In the meantime, follow your doctor's advice and take your meds."

Bob kissed Anna on the cheek, hugged her and wished her a Merry Christmas. She hugged him back weakly. Vicky kissed him on the cheek. Bob waved at his Uncle.

"BYE UNCLE RUSS," yelled Bob.

Uncle Russ flapped his hand in Bob's direction. Vicky gave Bob a take-home turkey sandwich and a slice of mince pie. Anna waved. Bob waved, then leaned his forehead against the steering wheel. The meal had filled his stomach yet his heart remained hollow. Thankfully breaking bread with his blood only occurred on holidays. He snapped to attention, muttered "Merry Christmas," gave one last wave, then gripped the steering wheel tightly, preparing himself for the long drive back.

The Laughing Girl

Bob O'Neil slowly awoke to the racket. He turned slightly and felt the cool air rush in under the covers. He squinted at the dimly lit clock sitting on the nightstand—2:30 am. Another wave of banging shook him out of bed. *Sounds like a rifle butt,* he thought, as he walked to the door. Bob took a deep breath and let the door swing wide open.

Two officers from the Fiston Police Department stood on the porch holding foot-long black-colored flashlights. They said they had come to talk and wanted to do it inside his living room rather than standing in the cold January night air. Bob let them in.

The tall one shut the door behind him and held a pen against a spiral notebook. The short one was heavier, with a face as white as the belly of a flounder. Shorty hefted his pants. Bob saw a belt loop of Shorty's pants had broken and the thick black belt was pinching a roll of fat on his hip.

"Are you Bob O'Neil?" asked Shorty.

Bob hesitated.

The tall one had his pen ready.

"Is your girlfriend missing?" he asked.

"I'm Bob," he said. "But I don't know if she's missing or not. How do you know about me?"

Bob stalled for more time. He really didn't even know if he had a girlfriend any more after their recent fight and her erratic behavior.

"We're asking the questions. A simple 'yes' or 'no' will do. Do you know where she is?" asked Shorty.

Bob looked down at his bare feet peeking from under blue cotton pajamas. The toes wiggled.

"I didn't do anything wrong," said Bob.

His hands shook so hard he bunched them into fists.

"What do you know about the missing woman?" asked the tall cop.

Last year had been full of whirlwind romances. Lilly, a natural blonde, had ditched him when he had become too serious about the relationship and too dependent on her emotional support. He had languished,

157

unloved, briefly. Then he found a seat in a roller coaster of a relationship. The ride was bumpy but he liked thrills. The woman taught romance languages at the University. She was tall, beautiful, and flighty. Just hearing his name uttered from the lips of her gifted soprano voice sent chills down his spine. But when her smile dropped to a frown, his heart flip-flopped. Then she lifted her chin for a kiss and his soul leapt out of his chest.

Bob returned to the present.

"We're dating."

"For how long?" asked Shorty, stepping forward. "And where did you meet her?"

Bob remembered her laughter at the beach that past summer—before he knew about her chemical imbalance and her recent decision to stop taking the meds. Their first meeting was on a warm, cloudless August day. They walked the wet sand beach and climbed the slick granite rocks. Down below they saw the sun's rays glisten against the seawater. As they watched the ebbing tide melt into the sand, she disclosed that she bleached her hair blonde because, as she said, blondes had more fun. Later, at coffee, she told him about her three previous suicide attempts.

"Four months. We met at the beach."

"When did you last see her?" asked Shorty.

The latest episode had begun on Saturday night. Bob decided to put her to bed after she confided to him that she had been catnapping in her clothes. "Please stay," she had said. "My life is a mess and I can't sleep alone." Bob hugged her and told her nobody died from lack of sleep. Then he left, ignoring her threats and obscenities. He thought her doctor should know how depressed she was but figured that might violate her confidence with him. After all, she only threatened to kill herself when he suggested she admit herself to the hospital.

"I left her apartment Saturday night. I briefly saw her Sunday morning, three days ago."

"Today is Thursday," corrected Shorty. "Four days."

"Did she give you a clue about what might be bothering her?" asked Shorty.

He saw her that Sunday morning at church. She wore her dark gray London Fog raincoat over a black sweater and black woolen slacks. She flashed him an optimistic smile, then disappeared. The messages he left on her answering machine were never returned.

Bob saw the impatient look on the tall cop's face as he tapped his flashlight in his palm.

"No," said Bob. "She was a complicated girl that laughed a lot so she wouldn't feel sad."

"Bob," said the tall cop. "We'd like you to come down the station to file a formal statement."

Bob's stomach knotted in pain.

"When?" asked Bob.

The phone rang. Bob excused himself to the far corner of the room. He answered the phone and heard the familiar voice.

"Did you miss me?"

The Lucky Night

Bob O'Neil found the old house beneath the on-ramp to the super-highway without a problem. A cold, dark January afternoon. He ran up the steps to the front door, stumbling on a stair. A dog barked from within the house and the psychic card reader opened the door to let him inside. She caught Bob's attention right away; her blue eyes sparkled intensely against hair that was as yellow as her wizened skin and the blossoming flowers covering her black house frock shimmered with glitter. Bob stared down at the woman because her small stature was accentuated by a curved spine which threw her chest forward, almost horizontal to the floor, and made her twist her head up so she could see straight ahead. Bob smiled. He had a lot of questions about his future, particularly with regard to women, and her unusual appearance reassured him that she might have a few answers.

"Who are you?" she shouted over the barking German shepherd. Bob replied, flinching when the shepherd pushed his nose past her hip and bared his fangs at him, uttering a deep growl. "Brutus!" She slapped the dog on the nose saying,"Go to your bed." The dog scampered away.

She turned to Bob. "He minds me well. We trained with an expert so that he would obey only my commands. The voice," she cleared her throat, "it's all in the voice." She looked at him quizzically, "But you must be cold—come in...please."

Bob looked inside before entering.

"Don't worry about Brutus, he'll stay just where he is, in bed, he'll sleep like a baby—unless he hears me scream for some reason," she said with a grin.

She closed the door and Bob stamped his feet on the rug to warm him-self. His friend, Shirley, had given him the psychic's name. She said Cora was accurate, cheap, but suspicious of strangers. Yet when Bob called her, she asked him over right away. She was eager to begin so that she could help him. She said she liked to help people. The fifteen dollars for the session wouldn't make her rich. The low rate appealed to Bob because he was frugal.

Bob followed her through the living room, past wooden icons and porcelain angels. In the dining room he sat across from her on a long table in a cushioned metal chair.

"I live alone in here. The boarders live downstairs. Do you live alone?" she asked.

Pausing to reflect, Bob wondered why she needed to ask such a question. "No. I live with my dog."

"But your wife, where is she?" asked Cora.

Bob shook his head, playing along. "I'm single. Never married."

"But surely a girlfriend... a handsome man like yourself," she said.

Bob told her he didn't have a girlfriend at the moment.

She laughed like a young girl.

"Then you're alone in the world, just like me," she said.

She told Bob that she had been married, but her husband had died forty years ago. She felt she was to blame because when she took ill a few years before his death, she actually died on the operating table after receiving the last rights. Upon dying, she entered a whirling tunnel that delivered her to heaven where she began searching for God to demand that He send her back. What impressed her most about heaven were the large numbers of people standing in lines waiting to be processed by the angels. She said the bureaucracy there was worse than that of the government. She had always been pushy, so she refused to wait; instead, she went around the corner and up an adjacent stairwell.

"They said," she told Bob, "that I couldn't go in, that God was busy. But I said somebody has to take care of my husband, I must go home." So she knocked on the door and opened it. She said God was very warm, a big bright shiny light that was strangely easy to stare at. She told God the story and He relented, saying only that she must begin again to use her psychic powers because they helped people. She apologized for letting her special powers lapse.

"People let God down when they stop using their gifts," said Cora.

She paused and looked up at Bob, tightening the folds of the frock around her neck, although Bob was quite warm.

"Then I whirled back down to earth. My body, which had been all cut to pieces by the doctors and nearly embalmed, started to pulse and quiver. They rushed me to the operating room where they sewed me back up and I never told my husband the whole story. He was a very sensitive man. But

I thought I cheated death and instead my husband died a few years later. He awoke one morning, couldn't move, and choked a little cry, then nothing. I ran to the phone to call the ambulance. When I returned to his bedside, he whispered my name. He said nothing else. The men came with a stretcher, took him to the hospital, and he died later that day. I still feel responsible," she said. "God wanted someone, so he took my husband instead of me."

"I believe God gave you a few more years with your husband," said Bob. "A gift, not a punishment. It was simply your husband's time."

"I'm not alone," she assured him. She shared her life with friends and neighbors and even the boarders downstairs. She basically raised a few neighbor children and they never forgot her.

Bob nodded his head.

"I'm very safe too," she said. "When one boarder drank too much and beat his pregnant wife, I ran down the stairs and threatened to whack him with an iron poker. When he shoved me to move across the room, I called the police, and they arrested him. Three patrol cars stopped at my house with their lights pulsing and their sirens blaring. The police know me and protect me and they love me too, like their own mother."

Bob cleared his throat. "Do you know what time it is?" he asked. He knew he had already missed his meeting.

"Oh, yes. The reading. Here I am telling you my life story. I'd better start," she said.

She produced an ordinary deck of cards.

"Please cut the deck," said Cora.

She removed the top card, stared at it, then placed it face up on the tabletop. The card produced an image in her mind. She said Bob would do well in his business. She asked what business was he in. Bob wondered himself. He finally said the education business. She skipped a few cards, then stared at a red number card.

"Someone will pay you back the money they owe you."

Bob nodded. The people that owed Bob money from years previous he had forgotten and didn't really even wish to see.

Then she gasped.

"I see a red face card, the queen of hearts, your wish will come true. Do you have a special wish, Bob?" she asked.

Bob nodded. He had written God a letter, qualified a number of times and in many ways, that he wanted a girlfriend by the end of the month. The month was almost over and still a woman had not appeared. He ached for a relationship even though he had been unlucky in love all his life. Bob was frustrated, hence the visit to the reader; he wanted to rattle God's cage a little. Some of Bob's friends had cautioned against writing the letter. They said acting like God was the manager of a candy store was risky because He might grant your request in an undesirable manner. But Bob had written the note like it was a legal document, covering all the angles he could think of, and felt Miss Right would come into his life.

"I see a dark-haired woman in your future. But beware of the blonde. The hair may be bleached and she'll give you a lot of trouble. She's greedy. Not with money, no, but she likes to be the center of attention," warned Cora.

Bob asked for the dark-haired woman's name or what she looked like. "I bet it's Brenda, she has dark hair, and she's been noticing me more lately."

Cora didn't pause to explain or affirm, but spoke on rapidly.

"My, the cards are good tonight, so many red ones, never have I seen a man be as lucky as you," she said.

Bob smiled.

"You will help a man with brown hair and be rewarded. You will move into a better neighborhood," said Cora.

She stood.

"I am finished and a little tired. I am very impressed by your good fortune. Even Brutus wants to be near you now," said Cora.

The large dog had curled up at Bob's feet without Bob even noticing.

"Thank you," said Bob. He gave her a twenty-dollar bill.

"I will be right back," she said. "I have change in the other room."

She disappeared down the hall while Bob stood waiting. A few minutes passed. Then five more passed. Bob became a little uneasy.

"I think I'll be going," he yelled down the hall.

"Oh no, I will be there with your money in a minute," she shouted back.

Another minute went by and Bob decided five dollars wasn't worth the wait. He hated to part with the cash but he wanted to leave. She had kept him for three hours and treated him like her long lost son. She could keep the money. He walked toward the front door in the living room. The dog stood in front of it.

"Good Brutus, nice boy, get out of the way," said Bob.

The dog growled at Bob, shoulders hunched up, ears flattened. Bob stopped. He heard footsteps behind him.

"I have your change," said the old lady in that same girlish way as before when she laughed about them both being single.

Bob turned around. He stared.

"Didn't I tell you you were a lucky man tonight," she drawled.

Like a wind blown rose, the stooped-over Cora walked slowly toward him in a pink chiffon see-through nightgown, her gnarled hand sweeping back long blonde locks.

Hang in There

Bob O'Neil stopped the car in front of the small blue aluminum-sided house. The committee of voices in his head whispered, "She's dead and you could have stopped it." He had talked to Anna for two Sundays in a row. He had tried to reassure Anna of her safety. No one was after her. Actually, no one really cared. Now he had come down to Adamsville for a third time, to say goodbye.

Bob unhooked the seat belt, opened the door, and twisted out of his tight, loaded, brand-new Ford. "Something's happened to Anna," her mother had said on the answering machine. Answering machines made life so efficient. He called back after five to save a few pennies. He had wondered if Anna had run away again. Last year at this time, she had been found penniless and psychotic on the streets of Philadelphia. This year, after Thanksgiving, her group home had admitted her to the psych unit of a local hospital. They said she smirked at the nurses and told them she was fine. She said nothing else. She sat in the lounge silently putting together puzzles. She said she never told the staff about the voices in her head that shamed her or the infra-red scanners locked on her body that constantly monitored her every move. They didn't understand.

Bob looked at his car, a self-conscious Christmas present to himself. Anna would never ride with him now, he thought. Christmas brought up memories, she'd said. Unfulfilled expectations of joy. Anniversaries. Bob knew about anniversaries. Anna's mother, legally separated soon after her birth, had said, "Oh" when he mentioned the importance of special dates, emotional triggers that sent the mentally ill back to the hospital.

Bob plodded up the steps in front of the blue house. He remembered calling his cousin back to find out what was wrong with Anna. "Bobby," Anna's mother had said, "Anna's dead." Silence. "She hung herself in the cellar." Bob had said he was sorry. He had asked what he could do for her. He'd talked to Anna for four hours, two Sundays in a row. He'd done his best to calm her. "We all talked to her, it did no good. She was more upset after you finished talking with her anyway," Anna's mother had said with a nervous laugh.

Bob paused at the porch door. He had told Anna he would call again on the third Sunday, New Year's Day, to make sure she was praying to God for help and guidance. Instead he had cooked chili, partied with his friends, and watched the New England Patriots lose a close game to Cleveland. He had blown her off. The 'if onlys' churned in his head.

Bob knocked twice then entered. He walked across the porch breeze-way to the front door. The door was cracked open so he yelled. Uncle Russ yelled back, "Come in Bobby." Bob shut the door behind him.

Uncle Russ turned back to the TV where yet another talk show guest expounded upon his unique life problem. A wire trailed from the silent TV to a plug in Uncle Russ's ear. His jaw hung open but his eyes focused intently on the flickering tube. At ninety-one, Uncle Russ had survived a broken hip, a minor stroke, and the passing of his wife. He still had all his teeth and he used them efficiently on three meals a day. Uncle Russ intend-ed to hang in there.

Vicky, Anna's mother, hurried across the room to greet Bob. She tripped over one of the many cats mewing, scolding it, then apologized immediately. She was wearing her blonde hair up in a bun, a sterling silver cat pin on her blouse, and shiny leather boots beneath a navy blue knee-high skirt. Her wide-open sky-blue eyes had seen more life than her unlined forehead would lead one to believe.

"I'm sorry," said Bob.

"She was never right, Bob," said Vicky, "ever since the eighth grade when she insisted she had worms—not pin worms, large ones—that twist-ed their way up her intestines and wriggled in her stomach."

"How's Uncle Russ taking it?" asked Bob.

"When I told him she hung herself, he said, 'Why didn't I think of that?' He's old. He might sound like he wants to die but all he really cares about is his next meal," she said.

Bob looked around the living room. The mantel above the fireplace held a beautiful picture of Anna smiling. She was free of her inner tor-ment. Her mother went on to say that the picture was a lie. She was a sad unhappy girl who lived a wasted life. She never went to her prom, never had a boyfriend, never knew how to function in the real world. The few mother-daughter baby photos Bob noticed were placed in the far corners of the room. Then he noticed the pet pictures, as if for the first time. They were surrounded by images of the family's past and present pets, mounted and framed. His cousin had six cats and a dog named Goldy. She pointed to one of the pictures.

"That's Goldy as a puppy. Right now she's in the hospital, the best one in Boston, Angel Memorial. The poor dear had trouble with both ear canals. Not just one. They called a few minutes ago. They wanted permission to operate on the second one today. They're so backed up. Just like a regular hospital. They're operating at five, an hour after Anna's afternoon showing," said Vicky.

"Did his first ear canal operation go OK?" asked Bob.

"Her," corrected Vicky, "Goldy is a she. Her right ear is fine. But cocker spaniels are known for having ear problems. I just never knew. She's five years old and falling apart. How old is your dog?" she asked.

"Teddy's eleven in March and not on any prescription medication," said Bob. Unlike myself, he thought.

"Amazing. If I ever lose my job as a secretary, I'll always be able to become a vet assistant. Between Goldy's care, two cats on heart medication, the two cats with kidney infections, and the special diets all six cats require as well as Goldy's special dinners, why I certainly know how to care for pets," said Vicky.

Bob stared at his cousin.

"The vet said when Goldy comes home, she'll have a floppy bandage that will protect her ears," said Vicky.

"Just like the Flying Nun," said Bob.

For lunch, Vicky made Bob a corned beef on rye sandwich. She drank a glass of milk. Afterwards, Bob asked her about the details of the death. Vicky said Anna had been on a three-day pass from the hospital. She didn't know what medicine Anna was taking, but it wasn't working. She had known something was up that day. Anna had acted funny. Happier. Like she had made up her mind. They had just finished lunch, eating corned beef on rye sandwiches.

Bob looked down at his empty plate and stared at the crumbs left over from his sandwich. Vicky paused for his attention. Bob suppressed a wave of nausea and caught Vicky's eye. She continued with her account. After eating lunch, Vicky had decided to give Goldy a bath. Then Vicky noticed the hot water had started to fade while the dog shook and moaned in the sink. Bob interrupted Vicky and asked where Anna was at that time. Vicky thought a moment. Anna had asked her if she was going down the cellar. Vicky told her not right away; she had to finish giving Goldy a bath. So then Anna had smiled and laughed a little short girlish laugh, said she'd see her downstairs in a few minutes, and closed the door to the cellar behind her.

Bob asked Vicky how long it was before she went down to check the hot water furnace. His cousin thought for a minute. The directions for shampooing Goldy had said the medication needed to stay on her fur about five minutes before rinsing. Then Vicky had to rinse and dry Goldy. Vicky guessed ten minutes had passed before going down the steps to the cellar.

"Then what happened?" Bob asked.

"I saw her hanging from a tangle of rope. The dog's rope. She had stood on a pink box, the one she used to put her toys in when she was a little girl, and tied the ends of the rope around a rafter across the unfinished ceiling. She looped the rope many times around her neck as you would a necklace until the line was taut. Then she kicked the pink box out from under her feet and died. The man at the meat market said that she died quickly."

Bob nodded.

"I knew Anna was dead. I walked up to the body and got close enough to see her hands clenched into tight fists at her sides. I even screamed, "Oh my God she's dead!" Then I turned around and struggled up the cellar steps to call the police. I almost forgot their number," she giggled as if she'd nearly missed a trick question on a pop quiz.

Bob asked if they had done an autopsy. She told him they hadn't. The authorities had skipped it. They had intended to do one, but after talking to her, the attending psychiatrist, and the hospital staff, they decided to just take a blood test. Vicky wrung her fingers together, as if trying to wash her hands clean. They left her hanging there all afternoon, she told him. Everyone showed up, the detectives, the local police, the state police, the medical examiner, so many people inspected the body; she concluded with a bemused smile that her daughter had caused as much inconvenience in death as in life. Then Vicky excused herself. It was time to give the cats their daily treat.

✦ ✦ ✦

The door opened and the grim-faced father shuffled in. Bob could feel the tension in the room soar. The tall, broad-shouldered man was bent and his blue eyes were red rimmed. His left hand squeezed an invisible ball rhythmically. He wore a dark suit and heavy winter overcoat.

"I'm sorry," said Bob.

"I know," he choked out. "Are you ready?" He looked at his ex-wife.

"Just a minute. The animals...." she said and ran into the kitchen. The cats mewed after her.

Vicky returned an instant later. Uncle Russ excused himself from the wake. He was too old to be walking around on his four-legged cane. Bob said he'd follow the couple in his own car. The little procession arrived at the funeral home. Strangely enough, as Catholics, they now had buried five relatives at this place—a Protestant funeral home. Bob hung the coats while the pair composed themselves in the lobby. The father moaned when he saw the name above the arrow that pointed them toward the room in which the wake was being held. They walked up a flight of steps and turned the corner. They all stared at the beautiful young woman lying in the casket. Anna's torso was dressed in a rose-white turtleneck sweater.

The father whimpered quietly and said he'd be no good after this ordeal. He kissed his daughter on the cheek for the last time as she lay in the casket while Bob averted his eyes out of respect. Then the father knelt before the casket to say a prayer. The mother walked over too but didn't kneel. She simply touched Anna's forehead with her finger tips as if to determine whether she just had a temperature and would get up to have lunch after a brief nap. But the forehead, Bob imagined, was cold.

Bob knelt by the body and looked at the restful unlined face below him. She was too pretty and too young for death to take her; even if she did have paranoid schizophrenia. He remembered taking her to see *Forrest Gump* last summer to sort of show her that even people with problems can lead accomplished lives. He looked at his flowers. When he had ordered the flowers the day before, his heart crumpled. That was when he had begun to let go. His stomach twisted around like he was in a bad dream and he had to say the name Anna a second time to the flower girl clerk with the spiked blonde hair and heavy gauge steel necklace. He felt like he had lost his little sister. He had tried to protect her as a big brother. He should have called more. Bob crossed himself and rose.

He heard the mother telling the newly arriving visitors that she had been a very sad unhappy girl who had never been right since the eighth grade. She told them her life was a waste, that it was finally over. Bob asked if Vicky had saved any of the poems she had written, he wanted copies for his scrapbook. The mother announced that the writings were missing, that Anna had hidden them God knows where, and that although she only wrote sad poems, five had been published anonymously in Anna's college newspaper.

But the mother hadn't a clue as to where the copies of the published poems were. Anna had also drawn sad pictures, and had continuously given verbal instructions regarding her funeral. She wanted a solemn black and white silhouette picture of herself next to a closed casket. The parent ceded partially to her wishes and put the solemn picture next to a happy one.

Bob was glad the casket was open so he could pay his final respects in person. For the parents, Bob imagined, it was a little different. The father had wanted to kiss her one last time before he saw her again in Heaven while the mother had wanted to touch her one last time to be sure she would never see her again on Earth.

Off to See the Wizard

Bob O'Neil pulled away from the ocean-side house where his friend Gary lived with his grandparents. With Gary riding shotgun, they passed the drug store where Bob fed his daily prescription habit, circled the convenience store where Bob bought two stale coffees, and turned up the on-ramp where they connected to the superhighway. Driving west, they were off to see the spiritual healer that lived in a gingerbread house more than two hours away from Fiston. Bob had lost confidence in the established medical profession. They treated symptoms, not root causes.

Bob crinkled his eyes behind the thick glasses. His eyes were heavy-lidded and he sighed several times. Suddenly, he took his hand off the steering wheel and slapped himself across the face. Gary looked over sharply. He had blue eyes, curly brown hair, and an easy GQ smile that twitched spasmodically from tardive dyskinesia—a side affect of his meds. Gary was in limbo, unable to work while not yet classified by the system as completely disabled so he could qualify for a monthly check from Social Security.

"Hey, what's wrong?" asked Gary.

"I'm tired. A late night. Now I work. I get up at 6:30 am every morning to drive a guy to his job site. I make two hundred a month doing a humanitarian service when I used to make four thousand a month polluting the environment and building armaments," said Bob, a former corporate engineer and ex-defense department employee.

"I like sleeping in," said Gary. He opened his pill bottle into his cupped hand and tossed some pills into his mouth. Then he gulped his coffee. "I'd ask for a raise," said Gary, burping.

"He doesn't have the money. Besides, my medium told me the beach next to the Inn where he works was my power center. Being there at dawn will draw energy to me," said Bob.

"Why are you seeing this other lady, this spiritual healer?" asked Gary.

"Nettie is a highly respected practitioner of New Age medicine. She treated my medium's insomnia, gave advice to my New Age friends on

171

diet, and counseled my church pastor. On my last trip, she removed four mischievous entities that entered my energy field after my psychotic breaks. Now she might incorporate the two remaining helpful entities into my higher self as well as integrate my mind, body, and soul. She might even help you," said Bob.

"Maybe," said Gary. He liked his state-supplied German-born psychiatrist.

They stopped at Dunkin Donuts for more coffee, donuts, and a quick stretch thirty minutes into the three-hour trip. Gary commented diplomatically on Bob's bleary-eyed driving.

"You nearly hit two cars back there. Are you using your blinker?" asked Gary.

"Are you finished?" asked Bob looking at Gary's donut and coffee.

At the gas station, Bob filled the tank. The cold February air mixed with the hot coffee and heavy smell of unleaded gas. Bob steadied himself against the car. Then he asked Gary to drive. Gary was supposed to come along just for company and maybe a therapeutic talk with the healer. He was an afterthought guest when Bob's two scheduled companions cancelled out. Jane had injured her back when an amorous massage client inadvertently fell on top of her and the other, Henry, was scheduled to enter the University hospital for an angioplasty. Besides having clinical depression, he was dying of a broken heart.

Back on the Interstate, Gary drove the staid rental, which he referred to as a "runtal," with the steering wheel between his knees while he lit a butt and sucked coffee. The loaner replaced Bob's brand new Ford that he cracked up on the way to the funeral of his paranoid-schizophrenic once-and-forever-removed cousin, Anna. She hung herself with the family pet's leash—a desperate act designed to steal attention away from the true center of family interest—the dog.

Bob liked the Tempo. It was a peppy gas-efficient economy car, but Gary complained about its poor suspension on curves and its wind-out at 55 mph. Bob thanked Gary with a yawn for taking the wheel. Then he curled up on the seat with his arm tucked under his chin and his jacket pulled up the back of his head. An instant later, it seemed, Gary grabbed his knee. "Bob, we're getting close. Where is this place?" he asked.

"We're nearly there. A couple of exits more," said Bob.

Bob was awake. He had slept nearly two hours. The State Prison, all silver with its surrounding concertina wire, glided past. Gary whistled.

"That's where I'm afraid of going," said Gary.

"But you live in New Hampshire," said Bob sleepily.

"No, prison in general. Especially a forensic psychiatric unit. There's no freedom for those guys."

"When those thoughts come, ask for God's protection," said Bob.

"I just have an intuitive feeling..."

"As your friend, I'm telling you to ask for help, don't drink, and take your meds. You'll have as good a chance as any of us to stay on the outside," said Bob. "Talk to the healer."

Twenty minutes later they pulled into the driveway of the healer's gingerbread house. The house was a dark brown, old colonial, two-story structure with its rotted porch now repaired. Bob stared at the familiar icons he had seen with Henry on his last visit. He gazed at the large ice covered pond whose swift-flowing stream emptied over a nearby spillway, paid homage to the St. Francis of Assisi statue in the front yard that now wore a cap of snow, and listened to the wind chime with metal spheres that hung from the porch. Birds alighted on a glass-lined feeder.

Nettie stepped out. She waved her hand from the porch, beckoning, and showed Bob and Gary into the living room. The air filled with classical music from the three B's as Nettie pointed to a couple of stuffed chairs where they could wait until she finished with her client.

Bob had waited two hours last time he went with Henry. A spiritual emergency had superseded his scheduled appointment. Apparently a little boy was sick and his parents came to ask for help. Henry had insisted on sitting in the car holding a smoke with the want ads draped across his protruding belly. He missed his job interview as a result of the spiritual emergency, refused to talk to the healer, and, while driving Bob's car on the return trip, said he'd buy a gun with his next disability check, pay off his loan to Bob, then blow his brains out. He said no one cared if he lived. Bob told him he cared. But after hearing a suicide plan, Bob tensed with a sidelong glance at the steering wheel each time they passed by a bridge abutment.

"Please wait here until I'm through with my client," said Nettie. She was a bright-eyed, gnome-like woman with black hair tinged with gray. Covering her white blouse and purple slacks was a black house frock that repeated a pattern of white crescent moons in a cluster of gold five-pointed stars.

After she disappeared down the hall, Bob used the facilities. The coffee called after the long trip. Gary stepped outside to smoke a butt. Back in the living room, Bob touched a white Teddy bear that wore a red woolen hat. A host of angels danced on top of the wall-length bookshelf. Indian medicine cards were spread out in the desk next to the color charts. Two shelves of books, from the art of healing to the universal laws of metaphysics covered the wall below the dancing angels.

No book in particular sparked Bob this time. He had replaced the book he had borrowed from the previous visit. A channeled work from extraterrestrials who wanted to help the good guys here shift the planet into its next higher spiritual level. Rather than a rare find, Bob noticed this book was the current rage in his favorite New Age bookstore. He intended to buy the book for the two pages of instruction on how to develop spiritually—which included whirling like a dervish clockwise. Bob wondered if he'd regress if he spun counter-clockwise.

A door shut softly with muffled goodbyes. Bob turned.

"We're ready to begin," said Nettie. She pointed through the old wooden door made for short Englishmen. He walked up the small twisting wooden steps, following a string of Christmas bulbs that lighted the way. Smiling angels lit from within by candles sat on every other step. Bob looked up. Gold stars, painted with a reflective coating, hung from the ceiling. Bob paused at the top of the stairs. *Welcome to Nettie's Haven* greeted a woodcut sign that hung from the entry door. Bending beneath the doorframe, Bob stepped into a small room with a ceiling bent with the slope of the roof, lit brightly with the noon sun, and sat on a couch facing a gurney and small desk.

"I can see the two entities are still hovering around you," she said.

"I want to know today if they help with my writing," said Bob.

"We can ask permission to ask that question," said Nettie. "What is it you want to cover this time? How have you been?"

Bob told her about his bout with psychosis that he thwarted with increased medication after his cousin killed herself, how his new car crashed, and that his newly formed relationship broke into pieces. He had suicidal feelings, anxiety attacks, and trouble sleeping. Then, after the psychosis lifted, the depression lingered. Only now, a month later, did Bob feel like his old self.

"My main problem is emotional maturity," said Bob.

"Are you sure you don't want to honor the child within?" asked Nettie.

"I can't remember my childhood," said Bob. "Hell, I can't remember much of anything anymore. In a way it's comforting to live so simply. I used to have a great imagination."

Nettie listened a little more to his complaints then asked him to lie on the gurney. She turned on his brain's computer with a sweep of her hands across his armpits. Then she asked permission to do reprogramming. She made sure the circuitry was sure and true by having him extend his arms and simply asking the higher self for confirmation. When Bob's forearms bent down, the higher self meant "no;" when his forearms resisted her pressure on his wrists, and stayed motionless, the higher self meant "yes." Nettie asked several questions a number of ways to successfully test the connection.

"Now I'll check for equilibrium among the fourteen meridians," said Nettie.

She found disharmony. As a result, she muttered an incantation and sprinkled invisible powder in a circular motion around his belly where all the meridians intersected. Bob was a little disturbed since last time he had been in balance. But he did feel more comfortable today than he did last time. After spending ten minutes revealing himself to her, he mounted the gurney and shook so violently that she squeezed ten drops of extract, alcohol-based, into each palm. He felt the calming effect immediately; a warm glow suffused his body. Idly he wondered if he'd start drinking again.

"You're voice is stronger, eyes clearer and face calmer. I believe removing those four entities last time really made a difference," said Nettie.

Bob nodded.

"A lot of people have complimented me. I even bounced more quickly out of my psychotic depression in January. I don't feel depressed now, just a little anxious," said Bob.

We can fix that," said Nettie. She asked Bob's higher self if a relaxant was needed; it was, and she squeezed five drops of perfumed brandy into each palm.

"Now rub them together," said Nettie.

Nettie determined emotional maturity was not Bob's problem; he actually had an emotional blockage. She sprinkled water on his chest, prayed, and wrote out an incantation that he needed to recite.

"You must say 'I cleanse my emotions and allow them to flow' six times a day for ten weeks," she said.

Then she checked to see if Bob would actually say the prayer and Bob's higher self predicted he would indeed. She held the prayer on a sheet of paper next to Bob and together they said it aloud six times.

"Would you like to integrate the two entities into your higher self?" asked Nettie.

"Will they improve my writing?" countered Bob.

"Let's see just what they will improve," said Nettie.

She asked Bob's higher self if the two discarnates affected his writing. They did not. Bob's writing was a gift from God Himself and the two hangers-on had nothing to do with it. Then she discovered they helped with decisions. Except they were helpful only thirty percent of the time. They contributed to poor decision making the other seventy percent. They also were clinging to his imagination. It was frozen under their influence.

"Would you like them removed? You could do better calling on God and His angels for help," said Nettie.

"I could have sworn that last time we decided they were helpful entities. My memory must really be playing tricks on me," said Bob.

"I'm sure they're influencing your decision making even now. Just remember you have free will and can ask for God's help," said Nettie smiling.

Bob nodded for her to proceed with their removal from his prone position.

With the wave of her arm, and several raisings of Bob's arms, she pronounced the discarnates removed and his imagination restored.

Bob smiled gratefully.

"If only I wasn't sick," said Bob regarding his disability. "At least now the entities aren't draining my energy."

Nettie offered to see how sick he was. Bob's higher self indicated his brain was functioning normally, except for the lack of protein uptake. Bob wasn't using his protein efficiently. After a few more taps against his wrist, she determined RNA was the answer. He needed to take ten tablets of yeast-derived RNA daily. It cured mental aberrations, improved memory, as well as affecting a number of other bodily functions, which Nettie read from a fact sheet. She hinted he might even find a suitable partner after using the supplement.

"As long as one's brain is receiving the proper nutrients, it can make any chemical the body needs," said Nettie.

176

"Are you saying, if I take RNA, I won't need my meds?" asked Bob.

"Of course not. That's between you and your doctor," said Nettie. "You'll know when the RNA takes effect and you can give up your meds."

Nettie waved her hands and determined Bob would not take the RNA. A touch of the wrist predicted this.

Bob folded his arms against his chest.

"I will too take them. Just to prove it, I'll buy a bottle," said Bob.

Nettie withdrew a bottle from her desk.

"I just happen to have that supplement in stock. This is a nine-day supply. Just $17.50," she said, "I can send more to you by mail."

Bob asked Nettie how to bind the strands of his broken life. She told him to use creative visualization. He had to set a goal and plan objectives, then make a mental collage with his goal at the center.

"Write a list of wants. Not a wish list. A want list. Just be discerning. You will be given them. The universe provides. Remember though, each of those wants you get has consequences," said Nettie.

She smiled.

Bob shook his head.

"I believe in being grateful for what I have, not in using God as a candy store for satisfying what I want," said Bob.

"We are placed here to live our dreams," said Nettie.

"I live one day at a time in the hope of doing His will," said Bob.

"We all have free will," said Nettie shrugging. "We've spent enough time talking. How's $60 sound? Plus $17.50 for the pills," said Nettie.

Bob wasn't through. But he wrote the check for $77.50.

He thought of the way he ran his life before he became sick and found spirituality. He was self-will run riot. None of the goals he set out to achieve ever meant much once they were accomplished. True, he did have some form of emotional imbalance that might heal in time. But even that had been a gift to help him develop spiritually and be closer to God.

Bob stood facing Nettie.

"If I start thinking I'm in control, I'll go crazy. I don't know what's best for me. I don't always like getting what I want. God provides. I have to continue trusting that God will provide what I need. Serendipity is His gift. All I need is to be grateful for what I have and ask for peace of mind," said Bob.

Bob walked down the steps, opened the little wooden door, and entered the sunlit living room. Gary sat on the couch asleep.

"Hey Gary, wake up," said Bob. "We're leaving."

"Did you want to talk to me?" asked Nettie, looking at Gary.

"I don't have any money," said Gary—he was too sick to work and he hadn't been approved for disability yet.

"Oh," said Nettie looking at her watch. "I'm expecting a client any minute."

"Let's go Gary, we're leaving," said Bob.

"Have a good trip back," said Nettie.

Nettie opened the front door for them. She addressed Bob with her bright eyes.

"Don't forget your higher self wants you to make an appointment in ten weeks," said Nettie.

Bob snorted.

"I'll write that on my 'want' list," said Bob, grinning.

He left the gingerbread house with Gary in tow. He winked at the St. Francis statue, nodded to the waterfall, and waved goodbye to the feeding birds. Then he looked at the bottle of pills—he smiled, and thought his higher self was part right after all. He wouldn't take the pills, and began to toss the package into the clear, ice-cold rippling stream. Then he hesitated. He saw the factory one hundred yards downstream from Nettie's house and decided not to add to the stream's pollution loading. Instead, he threw the pill bottle into the Tempo's plastic rubbish bag. Then he sat in the driver's seat. Gary sat beside him.

"Are you going back to her?" asked Gary.

"I don't agree with her methods," said Bob.

"Good. The place gave me the creeps," said Gary.

Bob felt alone again. He felt so responsible for his life situation; he trembled. He put his palms together. What Bob really needed was G. O. D.— Good Orderly Direction and he sent Him a prayer. Beside him, Gary snored. Bob stared at his friend's unlined face—Gary thought less and smiled more than Bob.

"Surely God takes care of us if we ask Him," Bob muttered to himself. Then he gripped the steering wheel, put the car in gear, and settled in the seat for the long ride back to Fiston.

The Wish

Bob O'Neil heard light tapping on the side door while punching keys in the computer room, an extra bedroom in his house that he had converted to a work area. He pondered a moment over a final key stroke, then pulled himself away from the dull, staring eye of his passionless lover, to walk past Teddy sleeping on the couch—some watchdog, he thought, and approached the pane-glass side door where a slim, tall figure waved.

"Cathy!" he said.

He opened wide the door for his ex-girlfriend to shuffle into the kitchen, using fine-boned fingers to wipe tears back into her short blonde hair. She held Bob close and sobbed on his shoulder. Bob patted her back with his right hand while he drew her away with his left. He noticed the blue eyes right away: drawn, hollow, haunted. She had aged, he thought, twenty years in the last three she had been away from Fiston.

"He doesn't love me, I made a place for him in my heart but he doesn't care," she cried.

"I care," he said.

He guided his old love to the couch where Teddy lay sleeping. The dog jumped down for the two humans to sit and talk. Cathy's on-again, off-again relationship with the farmer was finally off for good. The long, cold winter had killed their flowering love: its blossoms wilted, petals crumpled, and roots froze. The farmer didn't even answer her letters or calls. A complete break. With the coming of spring, she was afraid to be alone, and had come back to Fiston to visit friends who could help her forget her isolation. But deep inside, she knew she was unlovable. She would spend the rest of her life within herself, childless and alone.

Listening to her recount her broken love affair twisted Bob's heart. He tried to remember what had ended their relationship. One day she simply stopped answering his calls. He had survived the break-up, but had never quite let her go. Now he was, as she put it, a "friend." He felt more than that though, as she poured out her heart and held his hand. Of all his ex-girlfriends, she was the one he thought about most, she was the one who got away. Although she was always direct with him, unlike the others, he did remember she could be critical, controlling, and uncompromising. But the ache in his chest overshadowed those thoughts. He broke her train of talk by releasing her hand and standing beside her.

"Would you like something? A snack or drink?" asked Bob, to change the subject.

"Do you have any spring water?" she asked, wiping her eyes.

Bob shook his head.

"No, nothing, thank you," she said.

"How about we walk Teddy and look for meteors? I just read on the Internet that they'll be especially bright this week due to the new moon," said Bob.

She nodded, pulled one of Bob's heavy sweatshirts over her head to protect her thin blood from the night air, and grabbed his arm for support down the newly built steps of his house. Bob's free hand held Teddy's leash.

They walked in perfect step to the end of the dead end street, then turned to the north where they might best see the meteor shower. Teddy whined as Bob pointed out the Big Dipper and Little Dipper to Cathy. She turned to reply that she knew the constellations, that she really wanted to talk about the love of her life, her soul mate, who finally had ditched her forever, when Bob let out a yell.

"Did you see it?" he asked, grabbing her.

"See what?" asked Cathy.

"The shooting star," said Bob. He made a wish. Holding her slim figure in the dark, he forgot about how her eyes had appeared, and wished that she would love him as deeply as she now loved the uninterested farmer.

"I didn't see a meteor, are you sure?" she asked. She turned to face him. "I'm cold," she said.

Bob mentioned they might return to his house but she shook her head. She wanted to be warmed up right away. Bob put her hands in his then she slid her arms around his middle. He embraced her, looked down at her small, soft face, and kissed her. She returned his kiss with one of her own, then squeezed him against her tightly.

"I need to be held," she said.

Bob's face flushed hot, as he brushed her hair with his hand. She sighed, then, stepping back, placed a finger under her nose, and sneezed. She looked at Teddy and said he had stirred up her allergies. Next, holding Bob tightly, she told him how she went clothes shopping at her favorite Fiston shops but couldn't find anything that suited her. She needed clothes but they had to be just so. She did find, she said, a nice looking pair of sneakers and although the store stocked a complete range of sizes, they weren't able to fit her particularly shaped feet.

Bob groaned. He led her under a streetlight to tell her she looked just fine the way she stood before him. But she spoke first.

"Why don't you ever comb your hair?" she asked him, peering at it under the light.

He grabbed a tuft with his fingers and, using his hand like a comb, parted it to one side of his forehead.

"Not that side. The other one. Otherwise your face will look crooked," she said, then she sneezed again. "Teddy needs a bath. Now my nose is running."

"He just had a bath."

"Then I must be allergic to *him*," said Cathy.

Bob walked Cathy away from the streetlight, away from the prying eyes of neighbors, toward a secluded section of the road. While Teddy sniffed a bush, Bob put his arm around his new old girl. He held her close and she nuzzled between his shoulder and neck.

"What type of aftershave do you wear?" she asked.

"Why?" replied Bob in a hushed voice as he dizzily closed his eyes and hugged Cathy.

"None of my men wear aftershave. I can feel my eyes beginning to tear. You'll need to bathe with hypo-allergenic soaps as well. Now I'm a little hungry. Do you have any all-natural foods at home?" asked Cathy.

Bob opened his eyes with a start and wondered about the meaning of love. Then Teddy tugged at the leash so he turned toward the darkened sky with the girl in his arms and saw another meteor arc across the sky. Bob closed his eyes and wished anew.

Cathy stiffened and sidestepped out of his arms.

"Thanks for warming me up, I guess we'd better be going," she said.

Bob grabbed her arm; she wriggled out of his grip, and they walked back to the house, each deep in thought.

Cathy smiled at him once inside, her now tear-dried face creased with wrinkles. Bob found himself smiling with her, loving even the wrinkles and not understanding why.

"Thanks for being a friend and listening to my endless complaints about life," she said. Then she yawned and peered at the wall clock. She had to be going, she said, and began twisting out of his sweatshirt.

As Bob caught the sight of flesh arc across her middle, he told her not to bother, that the night air was cold, and she could keep it, but Cathy shook her head. She shrugged out of the sweatshirt, and handed it back to him neatly folded.

"Thanks for the offer Bob, but it just doesn't fit me," she said.

Bob nodded, smiled a thin smile, and knew that although spring was approaching, they both would be alone for a while longer.

Cool Routes in Ireland

Bob O'Neil stepped off the Irish tour bus and looked down the wrong side of the road to check for speeding cars. His therapist thought the vacation would improve his self-esteem; his psychic told him the trip would allow him to reconnect with his past lives (claiming Bob had lived there as a monk in an isolated monastery); and his shaman, who had performed a soul cleansing and identified his animal guides before he left, said the trip would give him the balm to heal his racing mind.

While he loved Ireland—its quaint towns, the easy-going hospitality of its citizenry, and its bucolic ways—he noted the bus driver's warning to be alert: Irish behind the wheel of a vehicle became irritable and impulsive maniacs. He thought that Ireland needed more lawyers and liability laws to slow down traffic. But he didn't need to try to collect. He had money. His dead relatives' money enabled him to visit "the old sod." All his blood relatives of the preceding generations were dead. They had left a small legacy—dusty photograph albums, rusty tools, a tarnished silver spoon. All dead except one: Johnnie Daley. By going to Ireland, his country of origin, and meeting Johnnie, his oldest living relative, he hoped to gain the essential kernel of wisdom about life that his parents had failed to tell him. He wanted an answer. Perhaps the past can explain the future, he thought, and then he walked toward the tour group standing in front of an abbey quietly listening to the tour guide.

So far Bob had witnessed a shearing on a working sheep farm, stood beneath several monoliths where the "little people" buried their dead before the Celts invaded, and strolled through a lovely old church predating the Cromwellian War. The tour guide explained how the people kept the church open throughout the years of British-imposed anti-worship laws. He lingered at the church imagining himself conducting an illegal Mass before a frightened flock of peasants. A single denunciation would have brought his death with a bounty for the priest-killer. Bob decided next time at the psychic's he would request the day-long past-life healing to remove any ill effects of a violent death. Although five times as expensive as a reading, friends commented that the warm, snuggly feeling lasted for days. Then he wondered if his parish priest would approve.

While the tour group boarded the bus—or "boos" as the Irish said—Bob approached Fionna, the fair-skinned and freckled-faced church tour guide. She had a musical voice, thin frame, and a stunning command of history. Bob asked a few historical questions while his eyes danced over her body and his ears resonated to the tone of her replies. By the time the bus driver started tooting the horn, Bob had bought a video costing thirty Irish pounds that explained the abbey history and its associated pilgrim walk into the mountains; had posed for a picture with Fionna's arm around his shoulder; and had donated a twenty-pound note to the abbey restoration fund. In all the rush to return to the bus, Bob forgot to ask Fionna for her telephone number. But that was just his speed, and after all, he figured she probably had a boyfriend anyway.

At the bus Bob met his hooting tour group; they pounded their seats and stamped their feet upon his arrival. They were upset that he had delayed them and worried that he might cause them to miss their dinner reservation at the hotel.

When they pulled into town, Bob drew in a tight breath. He pressed the scrap of paper in his pocket. The telephone number he did have was for his cousin. He had written to Johnnie Daley, the son of Grandmother O'Neil's sister, six months earlier and had received a carefully printed letter inviting him to visit. Now Bob re-read the copy of the letter and noticed Johnnie, his grand-cousin-once-removed from somewhere had misspelled the word "comming" and had scrawled his phone number across the bottom of the printed one-page letter almost as an afterthought. In the hotel room, Bob held the letter with one hand and picked up the phone with the other. Next he sputtered out a request to speak with Johnnie Daley like a man asking for a blind date.

"Do you know who this is?" asked the scratchy voice of an old man.

Bob mentioned his cousin's name.

"So you flew across the pond. How do you like your vacation thus far?" asked Johnnie.

"I didn't expect the brilliant sunshine," replied Bob. "And the people are so friendly, the grass is so green, the air is so clean."

"Yes, yes, spring is very green when we see the sun. But every day, I have to face the usually cold, damp, cloudy weather. A depressed person would jump over the edge of a cliff. Lucky for me I'm not depressed because we have a lot of beautiful cliffs."

He paused and Bob heard gulping sounds.

"Do you know what the difference here is between winter and summer?" asked Johnnie.

"The temperature?" replied Bob.

"No, that stays the same year round, about 55 of your degrees. No, actually the difference is you just have a longer overcast day," said Johnnie. He laughed. A tight, measured, twisting sound that made Bob think of bending metal.

"That's because you're so far out, I mean, up, ah—north," said Bob and he laughed too, with a quiver in his voice.

"What exactly do you want?" asked Johnnie.

Bob blinked at the phone. "Can we visit?" inquired Bob.

"Now?" asked Johnnie.

"Tonight. I'll buy you dinner. I'll take a cab to your house and we'll go out," said Bob.

"I ate already. I could use a drink. As for coming here, a cabbie could never find the place and he'd charge you an arm and a leg doing it," said Johnnie.

Johnnie gulped something, burped, and sighed.

Bob frowned.

"I came a long way to meet you. But..." Bob's voice trailed off into silence.

"You came across the pond," said Johnnie, pausing. "All right, I'll try to meet you, if my neighbor is home and willing to drive to town. It's a long drive. Almost an hour. And I have to work tomorrow. I have animals to feed. I'm an old man. If I do come, I'll meet you at Mike's Black Ale Pub. Ask anyone in town. I'll be there at 7:00 pm if I'm coming at all. But I ask you, if I don't meet you, don't think badly of me. Can you promise me that?" asked Johnnie.

Bob winced a little. He covered his disappointment with an "OK." Then he said his goodbyes and hung up the phone.

The hotel desk clerk, a bright-eyed cheery-faced woman, suggested he either eat at the hotel and take a cab to town, or, since he had the time, he could just as well see the sights by walking into town through the woods and eating at the pub. The path to town was only about a one-hour walk.

After reviewing the hotel dinner fare and prices, Bob decided to walk now and eat later. He needed to move to rid himself of jet lag and bus cramp. He would also distance himself from the tour group, which was filled with old fossils hungry for wool and linens and tiny high-priced meals served at four-star hotels. A walk through the woods and snack at the bar would clear Bob's head from the overnight flight, tone his body, and conserve the pounds in his wallet.

He followed the clerk's directions. He went out the main lobby, followed the path down the hill toward the lake and as he looked up over the lake to the western mountains, the sun dipped from behind the clouds and glowed between the peaks. Bob stepped off the path, awed, and slipped in something gooey. He looked down. Deer dung. He wiped off his sneakers in the grass. On the lookout for wildlife, he followed the path into the woods, remembering the clerk's instructions to bear to the left. The sun sunk deeper beneath the mountains. The shadows lengthened. Bob heard a bird twitter. The woods then broke into a field and Bob caught sight of an island, or "innish" in Gaelic, across the lake where the sun-polished ruins of a monastery and chapel shown briefly. Bob imagined himself in his previous life, a monk, dressed in a simple wool robe, hard at work beneath a spreading yew tree in the afternoon sun. As a learned man, he would transcribe old Latin manuscripts onto stretched sheepskin to save remnants of wisdom from a lost civilization for later generations. In exchange for food, he would teach visitors the classics.

Stepping back into the wood and out of his evening dream, he paused at a crossing where the path split off into four directions. One path, a sloping downward trail to the right, he imagined led to the lake; another path, sloping up the hill to the left, led to where he couldn't guess. He discounted the two extreme paths and narrowed his choice to the two well-worn paths in front of him. "Bear to the left," echoed the clerk's voice. "But which left? Which path shall I follow?" he asked himself. Bob looked around, seeing no one except the still and darkening forest, he shivered and pulled his jacket around himself, realizing that, if needed, the jacket might serve as a useful blanket with which to bed down for the night. He knew enough about survival in the forest to be sure to sleep on the trail and not wander into the dark woods alone.

Crossing his fingers, Bob chose the well-worn path veering to the left.

He walked fast. He noticed less the now shadowy wood and more the dull gray light still emanating from behind the mountains. Quicker and quicker he walked, almost trotting, while carrying a sinking feeling in his stomach that he was traveling the wrong path, walking deeper into the heart of Irish darkness. Finally he came to a clearing where he noticed the path split into another "v" but this time he was relieved to see a sign. Bob peered at the sign in the dim light, then sighed. He didn't understand Gaelic.

"What could 'Ballin' mean?" he asked himself aloud.

"That depends on what you want it to mean and where you want to go," replied a voice.

Bob turned. An old man with a large, red, once-broken nose sat on a log sipping liquid from a steel flask. He nodded in Bob's direction. His eyes gleamed.

"I want to go to town," said Bob, looking past the sign. He saw both paths twist into the wood with about equal wear.

"Then 'Ballin' means town," he said, smiling.

"But what does the other word mean?" asked Bob, pointing to the strange word that identified the path to the right.

"If you know where you want to go and how to get there, why ask fruitless questions about paths that are for others to take?" asked the man.

Bob stared. The man grinned. He was dressed in wool from head to foot, a woolen cap, jacket, trousers, and even wool-lined leather slippers.

"I'm lost," said Bob. He kicked at the dirt.

"But I found you!" said the man.

"I think you might not be telling the truth," said Bob.

"Haven't you ever told a lie?" asked the man.

"It's a matter of degree," said Bob.

"What kind of degree? Thermometer, compass heading, or university—that's the worst of them—there they teach you to lie and then to believe your own lies. A true fool. Are you a fool or are you willing to walk your path?" asked the man.

"I do want to walk further down the path but I need direction," said Bob.

"I find my direction from the sun and the stars, from the whisper of the wind on the leaves of trees, from the rain drop that weaves its way to the flowing stream," said the man.

"I give up," said Bob. "Thank you for your help."

"In this country, it is customary to give a man who freely offers you help a token of your appreciation," said the stranger, smiling.

Bob threw him a large coin, an Irish pound, and chose the left side of the "v." He walked fast, hearing the sharp crunch of his feet on the leaf-strewn path, while the man called on him to stay true to his course. Suddenly Bob scared up a rabbit that ran across the trail. *A good omen*, he thought, *my personal animal guide*. Soon Bob heard traffic, blaring horns, and a clock sound seven bells. He was in town, the path led out the gates of the park, and he asked the first person he saw about the pub. Mike's pub, they said, was around the corner. Bob rushed around the corner, saw the sign for Mike's Black Ale Pub and gently pushed past an old man and middle-aged woman. He twisted his way to the noisy bar that smelled of stale beer and hard liquor, and waved to the barman.

"I'm looking for someone," said Bob.

"He's outside," said the stone-faced barman with a nod.

Bob rushed back outside and called to the departing pair. They turned.

"So you've come to visit us after all, late but here now. Meet my neighbor, Tara, who was kind enough to drive me on short notice," said Johnnie Daley.

Bob shook both their hands. Johnnie had small yet thick and powerful fingers that gripped his larger hand with machine-like firmness. Johnnie was short, just over five feet tall, with red cheeks and sharp piercing eyes. He adjusted his cap and pulled at his tie, then invited Bob and his neighbor, Tara, into the pub for drinks. Johnnie ordered a whiskey and lit a cigar. Tara drank beer. Bob asked for ginger ale.

"Ginger ale? You came 3500 miles to drink that with me?" he asked.

"But Guinness isn't healthy for me to drink," said Bob.

"Guinness is the healthiest drink that Ireland produces," said Johnnie. "Look at me, I'm a hearty old man that has drank and smoked his whole life. Let me buy you a Guinness."

He motioned to the bartender, "Pete, bring my relative here a Guinness."

Bob ignored the dark, tall, stout as foam bubbled over the edge of the mug and spilt on the counter.

"Really, I don't drink. I used to but I don't now," said Bob.

"An Irishman who doesn't drink," grumbled Johnnie.

He tossed off a whiskey and chased it with the stout in front of Bob. Bob told them about the adventure getting to the bar.

"So? If you slept in the woods you'd be warm enough. There are no wild animals in Ireland to bother you," said Johnnie. "And no wild people, either."

Then Bob told them about meeting the odd old man with the wool-lined slippers.

"You met the hermit. No one sees the hermit much these days and seldom has the fortune to talk to him. What did he say?" asked Johnnie.

"Let him be quiet, Johnnie, you know it's unlucky to divulge his sayings. 'Tis his fortune to hear the hermit and misfortune to tell of the hermit," said Tara.

"Wives' tales," muttered Johnnie.

"He just asked a lot of questions," said Bob.

"But knowing the right questions to ask puts us on the path to find needed answers," said Tara.

Bob looked at Tara again. Although a plain-faced round-figured woman, she held his glance with a depth that surprised him. Next he looked at his cousin as he puffed a cigar between sips of Guinness. He was grinning. He held Bob's glance for an instant then he caught Pete's eye for another beer. Bob wondered if blood was thicker than Guinness.

During the next round, the conversation turned to more controversial subjects like the division between church and state, the newly instituted divorce law, and, of course, a free and united island, a republic that had finally cast off the yoke of the stranger. On the advice of his therapist, Bob said little about the political and religious situation. He might elicit strong feelings about subjects that he didn't fully understand. However, he did have a weakness for the alcohol his cousin was consuming.

Bob focused on his cousin again, hearing that he had raised twelve children on a small farm with cows and sheep. But now the children were grown and living overseas, the wife had passed on, and Johnnie was tired. The land was tired. And luckily the European Union sent him a monthly check to help him make ends meet. Johnnie looked at Bob sharply.

"Have you eaten?" He waved the barman over to the counter.

"Sir, I want you to prepare the thickest sandwich from the thinnest and most tender beef you have for my guest here. Do you like gravy?" asked Johnnie.

Bob nodded.

Johnnie laughed, "And another drink for my cousin. Ginger ale." He laughed again and slapped Bob on the back.

The barman returned soon with a large sandwich platter with gravy-covered french-fries. As Bob chewed the tasty mass of roasted flesh, he relinquished his newly acquired vegetarian instincts that had arisen in response to the emergence of "Mad Cow" disease in the British Isles. While he questioned whether Irish beef was safe to eat he knew that a refusal was sure to disappoint his cousin. The world was, he thought, already quite mad and he fit right in.

Dinner over, he bade farewell to his cousin and friend with a promise to write but his cousin shook his head. He told Bob not to expect an answer because he wasn't much with a pen. Outside, the trio heard music, fiddles from afar, that inspired Johnnie to tap out a few bars of an Irish step dance. His cousin was as spry as a man half his age even with three or four whiskeys churning in his stomach. When Tara brought the car around, Johnnie shook Bob's hand, reminded him with a chuckle to stay out of the woods, and suggested he board the bus that stopped up the corner for the ride back to the hotel so he could save money on cab fare. Bob waved goodbye to the pair, then walked down the sidewalk, slick with dampness from a light rain, to the corner where the bus stopped on cue.

"Are you passing by Hotel Rose?" Bob asked the bus driver.

He nodded.

As Bob strode down the aisle, the bus accelerated forward and Bob gripped the seat next to him to keep from falling down.

"Fionna!" Bob said.

Fionna looked up and smiled.

"Bob, the American. Have a seat," she said. "Our paths cross again."

Bob cocked his head at the word "path," remembering his walk through the woods, but thoughts of the hermit melted at the sight of the pretty girl.

Fionna was returning home from a trip to town. He told her about his visit with his cousin, his search for his roots, and admitted he was less than satisfied.

"But roots are buried beneath the tree, 'tis better, I think, to look for the blossoms on the bough of the tree," said Fionna.

She smiled.

Bob drew a breath and decided to pick a blossom.

"I'm returning to my hotel, would you care to join me for a cup of tea?" asked Bob.

"Love to," said Fionna.

Bob smiled in response, stretched with a yawn from the long day of touring and visiting, then sank deep into his seat.

A Different State

Bob O'Neil tapped his foot. He needed to leave on time for the facilitator's training session. They were traveling to the big city to learn how to run a mental illness support group. He hoped the lecture would interest them as well. Boston always put on a nice show. His group needed serious help.

He doubted Kittie would show because he had told her the departure time was 4:00 pm exactly and she had complained. Too bad if she took offence. He had other problems with the local mental illness support group. Bob and several other concerned members had overthrown Ned, the manic control freak who had served as local meeting dictator for four years. He threatened to show the Boston board a petition signed by several of his supporters. Bob smiled. The letter was the last chance the sick people had to take over the meeting from the duly elected officers. "Here she comes," he said and stared at Kittie exiting Fiston's psychiatric hospital. She was at the rendezvous site on time.

"I'm here. You said you wouldn't wait five minutes... I nearly broke my neck in the bathroom changing into my dress clothes. That's not a very compassionate attitude, Bob. My therapist said I need to express my feelings and I felt fear that you would leave me behind."

Bob nodded to Kittie, overweight and frumpish, glanced at her rumpled green sweatshirt and orange sweat pants, and thought she looked like an over-ripe pumpkin. He told her to sit in the backseat because he expected two more people, one an especially large man. She replied that the hospital receptionist had told her they wouldn't be coming. Upon further questioning, Bob discovered Kittie was an outpatient in the partial hospitalization program and decided to see the receptionist himself to check her story about the change in plans of his two friends.

"OK Kittie. I guess it's just you and me. Take the front seat," said Bob.

Kittie ran her fingers across the dashboard.

"A Ford," she said. She told him her father used to own a Chrysler dealership. Bob nodded. She asked him how he could afford to own such a luxurious car with his disability check. He shrugged and said the payments took out a big bite.

Bob wheeled the car out of the hospital parking lot and onto the highway. Traffic was mild on this spring afternoon. The bright sun shone through a skin of powder white clouds, just thick enough to remove the glare.

Bob reminded Kittie that she would have an hour of free time before the lecture to eat dinner while he sat in on the training session. Kittie cried she had no money. She pulled open her pocket book and removed a hairpin, a penny, and an expired credit card.

"Oh," she said, "Here's two dollars. I'm rich. Now I can eat." Then her face twisted. "Where are my keys?"

She upturned her purse in her ample lap to aid in the search for the keys. No keys.

"Here are my pills. Don't let me forget to take my dose at 6:00 pm. It's very important. If I skip the pills, I'll turn into a toad." She laughed.

Bob laughed a little and said, "I'll try to remember to remind you but that's your responsibility."

Kittie looked behind her seat to the rear. "I can't believe you wanted me to sit in the back. That seat has less room than the rear seat of a police car. Have you ever sat in the rear seat of a police car?" asked Kittie.

Bob ignored her, remembering a time in a manic state when he had demanded a cop arrest him and so the cop had complied. Luckily Bob faked a fainting spell to break out of jail before he could be processed officially.

"HAVE YOU?" She shouted. "WELL I HAVE."

Bob told her to lower her voice. She picked up a magazine lying on the floor with a deer photo on the front cover and decided to look at the pictures because she developed motion sickness when she read in a moving car.

"Can I smoke?" asked Kittie. She held a pipe in her hand. Bob answered no. "What about music? Can I listen to a song? Can I sing?" asked Kittie.

Bob pushed a button on his stereo but muffled the volume.

"Wow. You listen to SEA 102, the wave of the future. I like new music too."

"Let's relax. We're almost there," said Bob.

Kittie nodded. She had been there before. "Did you know they banned me from this meeting? At the annual summer picnic, I accused a woman of being paid under the table for editing the Boston newsletter while on disability. I threatened to report her to the IRS and Social Security. I accidentally dumped potato salad on her lap. They banned me but you know what, they put her on the books the next month." She smiled.

Bob stopped the car. The meeting was at a famous and expensive hospital in Boston, atop a high hill, called MacLeod's. Bob walked Kittie to the smoking area and pointed to the cafeteria. "I'll be there," he said, "The general meeting starts in an hour."

The training session inside bored Bob. A few board members greeted him. But they discussed how to organize their particular group and not how to implement principles of group control in general. He had a special control problem: Ned—a guy that smelled of sweat, cigarettes, and stale coffee who wouldn't stop interrupting people. Then Kittie entered the meeting, saying she just wanted to observe, and she left as soon as she had seconded a motion. The next time she entered, she asked Bob for two extra dollars in a loud whisper. Heads turned. Bob opened his wallet, found a five, and she left with it humming.

After the meeting adjourned, Kittie buttonholed an exiting board member with white hair and clear blue eyes. Bob watched as she hugged the old man. He feebly resisted a few moments, and then draped his hands over her arms. His lips made soundless circles like a fish trapped in a net as she spoke. She told him she now lived in another state with archaic mental health policies. In fact, after being hospitalized over twenty-five times in a space of five years in a state facility, she now was only released conditionally. She maintained her freedom as long as she took her medication.

Bob stared. He excused her from the relieved listener and whispered, "Did you take your pills?"

She shook her head. "I'm in a different state. Those rules about medication don't apply to me here." Her face brightened, "Oh look, here's Ned."

Bob saw Ned. He was dark, with graying black hair, and broad shoulders. He carried copies of the letter in hand which he gave to the board members. Kittie hugged all her old friends and some new ones while Ned shook hands. His hand, Bob saw, made a lot of stabbing motions toward the white sheet of paper he was holding and his mouth never stopped moving. Next, the speaker brought the meeting to order. Ned and Kittie found seats. Bob listened to the black-haired, stern-faced woman with MD and PhD degrees. She outlined the newest treatment of seasonal affective disorder. Special sun lamps fooled the brain into thinking winter had not yet come to avoid feeling depressed. Bob sighed. Even summer depressed him.

At intermission Kittie came by and asked him if she could smoke in his car for the return trip. Bob shook his head. Bob asked Kittie if she had taken her pills. She said no. Then Kittie smiled.

"I'm going back with Ned," she said. "I can smoke with him. He's even starting a new meeting in Palmer."

She walked away with Ned. Down the hall and out the door. Bob sighed. The man with white hair and clear blue eyes sitting next to Bob put a hand on his shoulder.

"Letters don't mean shit. But people do have choices. Are you staying for the group sharing and caring half of the meeting?" he asked.

Bob watched through the window as a set of headlights disappeared from the parking lot. Then he turned and followed the white-haired man to the group of people sitting around a folding table.

The Helper

Bob O'Neil answered Henry's call for help without thinking twice. He was Bob's best friend. Henry's car engine had blown the day before and he was without food so Bob and Teddy, his twenty-pound Scotty, went to the rural northern edge of Fiston to be Henry's wheels for the day. When Bob arrived, Henry was sitting on the steps of his trailer smoking a cigarette. He was down to about ten a day but his heart doctor was still dismayed. Upon seeing Bob, he crunched the butt under his sneaker and swayed over to the side door.

"You're late," he said.

Bob shrugged.

"Traffic was heavy and Teddy needed a walk. How's your car?"

"My car's dead and I'm broke."

Henry climbed into the car with his 350-pound bulk sagging the suspension. He smelled of stale coffee and tobacco. Bob drove across the street to the supermarket, parked in the front where the fire trucks were supposed to stay, and let Henry out to do his shopping.

"Do you need any help with the cart?" asked Bob.

"No, for Chrissakes that's what I'm going to lean on."

Henry shut the door and shuffled away. Bob watched him enter the market through the electronic doors and disappear.

After waiting twenty minutes, Bob decided to find Henry and assist him regardless of his wishes. The warm sun was welcomed but the car had become much too hot for him and the panting Teddy. Bob found Henry by the diet soda.

"You need some help?" Bob asked.

Henry's face quivered.

"In a hurry? I can't move any faster. I'm sick. And I can't deal with any more of your crap. Get out and wait for me instead of pestering me if you really want to help."

Bob left the supermarket. He needed to forgive Henry because he was

196

ill and a good friend in need. So he and Teddy went for a walk around the side of the market where the grass was green and a pleasant breeze blew. Teddy sniffed and lifted his leg several times. Then Bob decided to wander back to the car. As he approached the front of the market, he heard screaming.

"You tell me to hurry up then you make me wait here under the sun in front of this building for you to take a dog walk. What the hell is wrong with you? Are you trying to kill me? I've had it. Take me home now."

Bob nodded to Henry. He tried to think of something to say but couldn't. He simply waved his hand and muttered, "it's OK", more to himself and the people around him than to Henry. His friend had confided to Bob that his multiple personality disorder incapacitated him more than his depression or heart condition. Bob wondered what personality was emitting the expletives now. He had names for them all. When Henry arrived home he began having an angina attack so Bob carried in the bundles of groceries. Henry swallowed his nitro and went to bed while Bob sorted through the plastic bags.

"All done, Henry. The perishables are in the refrigerator and the rest is laid out on the counter like you wanted."

"Bob, I'm sick. I think I'm having a heart attack. Call me an ambulance. Call 911."

"Are you sure?"

"Call the friggin' number!"

Bob's hands started to shake when he dialed the number. He knew his voice would be recorded and the address would light up on the computer screen.

"What is the nature of your emergency?" asked the operator.

"My friend might be having a heart attack."

"Is your friend conscious?" Bob affirmed that and told them Henry's name.

"Is Henry being treated for a heart condition?"

"Yes."

"Who is his doctor?" Bob yelled the question to Henry and he yelled back an Arabic-sounding name.

Then the operator asked about Henry's medications. Bob shouted for a listing.

Henry groaned, "Hang up the phone."

"What?" asked Bob.

"Tell him the address and hang up the phone."

Bob said, "Look, he's in too much pain to talk any more. If you need to call us back we are at ...?" Although Bob called Henry almost every night, his mind had slipped into low gear. He had to break off and ask Henry for the phone number and address. Then he echoed Henry's reply and dropped the receiver in its cradle.

Next Bob sat down on the couch and listened for the coming of the ambulance. About fifteen minutes later a wailing police car sped by the trailer down the dead end road. They had missed the house. Bob walked out onto the street and waved. Neighbors started gathering on their front porches to watch the show. By the time the cop car had turned around, the ambulance arrived. Bob escorted the two paramedics and police officer into the house where they found Henry sitting on the couch with an overnight bag. The paramedics took his vital signs and asked for his medical history. Henry related the information in such a concise and offhand manner, that Bob imagined him in a job interview summarizing his resume for a position in the medical field. He had stopped swearing and even joked with the technicians about being fat as they unfolded a heavy-duty metal chair. They insisted that he sit in the chair so they could carry him to the waiting ambulance. He protested weakly, then sat down with a sigh and allowed himself to be strapped in. Before they lifted him off the floor, he gave Bob his key and told him to lock the trailer before leaving. The cop asked Bob if he was a relative. Henry told them Bob was his brother.

When the ambulance was ready to begin the journey to Fiston Regional Hospital, the police officer walked into the busy street and held up his hands. Bob watched as the policeman waved the ambulance through the stopped traffic and admired how much power he wielded.

"I hope your brother makes out OK."

Bob nodded. "He's actually my good friend. But I hope so too."

They shook hands. Then Bob gave Teddy some water and a little walk before deciding he should go to the hospital to check on his friend before ending the day.

On the way to the hospital, Bob drove carefully, trying to calm his nerves. Henry would be OK, he told himself, but if he passed away, that was OK too; he was not the one in charge. Just as Bob felt better, he saw a small object drop out of the sky ahead of him. Looking closer, he saw the still feathers of a dead sparrow fall under his wheels. He crossed himself and prayed for Henry's soul, for it surely must have departed.

At the hospital, Bob had to wait two hours before the staff would tell him about Henry's condition. He was stable. Luckily for Teddy, the afternoon clouds had rolled in so the car was not that hot.

"When can I see Henry?" Bob asked the middle-aged nurse.

She shook her head. "We'll let you know as soon as possible."

Bob decided to leave when the phone rang at the desk.

"Just a minute…sir. Would you like to see Henry?"

Bob nodded. He listened as the nurse explained the situation. Apparently, Henry was becoming a reluctant patient. He had hurled his snack at the TV screen, abused the nurses and refused to take any more medication.

"Have you spoken with his psychiatrist?" asked Bob.

Bob gave her the name, which was easy to remember because he was also a patient. In fact, he was responsible for coaxing Henry back in treatment. The effects of emotion-numbing childhood abuse, flashbacks from combat in Vietnam, trauma from the untimely loss of loved ones, not to mention the loss of self-esteem from a shattered sales career, had all conspired to make Henry a social outcast. He was also an enigma to the psychiatric profession because none of the drugs available worked for any length of time. Fortunately, he trusted Bob and the shrink.

"We'll try to contact her. Henry's room is just around the corner."

She led the way through a series of double swinging doors. The first thing Bob heard was shouting. A nurse waved at them to hurry. Bob frowned at the swearing. Henry's vocabulary had regressed to the sailor he used to be. At the nurse's station, another middle-aged nurse briefed Bob about the situation. Bob wondered which shift the twenty-somethings worked.

"Henry is in crisis. He fell off the bed and is now demanding to be released. We want you to try to calm him down."

Bob entered the room while the professionals stayed back.

"Henry, how's your heart?"

Henry was face down on the floor, struggling to rise with about as much success as a turtle on its back waving its flippers.

"I'm going to sue that friggin' doctor. He's responsible for this."

Slowly, Henry tucked his arms under his chest and brought his legs under his midsection. Bob grabbed an elbow for a little support and the big-framed man righted himself. Then Henry stepped outside the door shouting obscenities at the nurses and yelling for the doctor. The nurse at the desk called for a code blue. The staff gathered around the hallway; about thirty people showed up to witness the event. No one touched Henry. When the doctor entered through the double doors, Henry snapped.

"I want you for breakfast. You are history. I'm eating you alive." Henry glided toward the doctor in his white johnny with his hands up and fingers pointed.

"Let's rock and roll, Doc," said Henry.

The doctor tried to hold his ground but the nurses intervened.

"Get out of the ER doctor. Get out."

"I have patients to attend!"

The nurses pushed the doctor back through the double doors, stepped in front of Henry, and called the police a second time.

Within five minutes, three police officers had secured the scene. One cop sat Henry down and asked him questions back in the room while another talked with Bob out in the hallway.

"I need a statement about this incident for my report. What's your name, address, and social security number?"

Bob asked why he needed his social and the cop said it was strictly routine. Bob looked around blankly at the dispersing staffers and shrugged. He gave the information.

"Where do you work?"

Bob balked at this question, too. At first, he said he worked at the university, but when the cop wanted the phone number, he spilled his secret.

"I don't work, really. I'm on disability."

The cop nodded. "I know that."

Then he went to see how his partner was doing with Henry. When he returned, he had Bob confirm Henry's address on his license and asked Bob another question.

"What's your friend's phone number?"

"It's unlisted."

"Listen, I need this number for my report and Henry is too drugged up to give it. You know the number, so cooperate, and we can get on with business."

Bob quivered. Did loyalty to a friend outweigh his obligation to the law?

"I can't remember."

"Just give me the number."

"Where's a phone?"

A nurse lent Bob a phone and he let his mind and finger fly across the buttons. Then he gave the results to the officer. Doubt plagued him. Perhaps the "nine" should have been an "eight." But if he made a mistake, and they issued a warrant against him for making a false statement, he'd plead innocent—he had a stress-induced memory lapse.

"Did Henry point his finger at the doctor or make any other threatening gestures?"

"No. I didn't see anything like that," Bob lied.

"Good, because that's classified as assault, which can be a felony."

Suddenly the three cops gathered around Henry one last time but he paid them no attention. He simply told them he knew nothing and remembered nothing. They all sauntered over to Bob. He could see Henry was fully dressed and held his overnight bag.

"We are now going to escort you and Henry out of the hospital. He says he needs physical assistance to leave so either you help him or we'll arrest him."

Bob nodded and grabbed Henry's shoulder as he stood up. Henry grunted, then they both walked out through the electronic doors and into the fresh afternoon air, one cop on either side. Henry tapped out a cigarette and broke his silence by asking the cop on his right for a light. The officer shook his head.

"You are banned from this hospital forever," said the cop pointing at Henry. Then he looked at Bob.

"And you...pull your car over here."

Bob ran for his car, greeted Teddy, and drove up next to Henry. As Henry climbed in and the car sagged, the officer bent over the edge of the open window.

"Henry, you better be gone in less than a minute or we'll arrest you. And if you ever drive him back here, we'll arrest the both of you, get that Bob?"

Bob nodded. He pulled away in a daze. At the main road, he blindly turned right instead of left. Henry snickered.

"What a joke those cops were. I want to see my lawyer to report that doctor. I'll sue him. And my neck hurts. I need to go to another hospital."

"No."

"What?"

Bob had finally turned himself around and was heading north again, toward Henry's home.

"I'm driving you back to the trailer."

Henry said nothing. The two sat in silence as Bob's mind replayed the day's events. He needed a break.

"We're still friends, Bob, right?" asked Henry.

"I don't know," replied Bob.

Bob felt like he was awakening from a dream, like a swimmer emerging from the depths after a deep dive. The pressure in his head was easing. When Bob pulled into the driveway, Henry extended his hand. Bob grasped it, always amazed at the strength of the big man's grip.

"Friends, right?"

"I'll try, Henry."

"That's not good enough."

"That's the best I can do."

Henry took back the key, shut the car door, and shuffled up the steps of his trailer. Bob put the car in reverse, and pulled away. As he looked back, Henry's free hand went up in a feeble attempt at a wave. Bob didn't wave back.

Comfortable Poverty

Bob O'Neil first heard the phrase "comfortable poverty" the same day he heard Thomas died. Bob's friend Jessie, the poet, said this was how William James had described a highly spiritual lifestyle. He proposed just living for the moment without trying to accumulate any wealth for a rainy day as the easiest way to keep a clear head. He must have meant: live in a low-end room, eat out but at greasy spoons, drive a junker, and wait on people who have money to spend.

But today it is raining.

And Thomas's eight-unit apartment building leaked. In one room, wet gobs of plaster dropped from the ceiling onto a water-soaked rug. Last week the fire department rescued a first-floor tenant living on a disability pension. The gas line had ruptured to her stove filling several apartments with a fishy smell in the early morning hours. Last month, children played potty in the broken toilets smeared with feces left next to the building's trash dumpster which the whole neighborhood seems to use. The city's department of public health removed the extra toilets after an in-person visit. Not everyone can afford a phone.

Thomas wasn't a good tenant. He didn't pay rent. The landlord took him to court and Thomas told the judge he didn't feel he could pay a dollar for rent when he lived in a cockroach-infested, lead-painted building. The judge was sympathetic. Case continued.

Thomas wasn't a model citizen. Bob assumed he ate out a lot, probably at fast food joints, because his trash was mostly empty beer bottles. Though sometimes during a blackout he threw out full ones too. The neighborhood kids played with these. Yet the beer didn't fill him. He was skinny, about 37 years old, with inquisitive dark eyes. This summer he overdosed on heroin. The rehab hospital offered him an expensive day program. Too much for someone without health insurance. A friend gave him the book *Alcoholics Anonymous* and a local meeting list. He chose his own road, but he didn't drive a Saab. He walked.

Thomas did work. He was painting a big house down the street where he lived. He was proud of his work. He'd scrape and paint, scrape and paint, only taking long breaks on those really God-awful hot, hazy, humid days. He'd climb up a forty-foot adjustable aluminum ladder to work on the third story. When he wasn't working on the building, he'd tape a tall window shutter to the bottom of the ladder to prevent little kids from climbing into trouble.

The *Fiston Daily Herald* reported Thomas died in a thumbnail column next to the school budget debate. The police say the case is still under investigation. Driving down the street where Thomas lived and worked, Bob saw his ladder with the taped wooden shutter lying against the building. No one was working there now, it was raining.

A No Life Story

Bob O'Neil awoke with a headache. He hadn't slept well with the extra medication. Depressed as ever, he dimly wondered why the doctor he had been seeing for five years had waited so long to prescribe the new antidepressant. After collecting sixty months of insurance checks, she had finally decided that his work-disabling psychiatric condition could be treated with pills that had been around for years. She might be slow with new ideas, but at least she didn't pester him about finding a job bussing dishes. As an ex-engineer highly skilled in out-of-date technology, he was grateful for the little he did have.

In the bathroom, he swallowed aspirin. *More drugs*, he thought, then he showered. Bob dressed, putting on yesterday's clothes. That trick saved on laundry time and expense, and hell, he didn't see that many people in a day. Who'd remember? He went into his office, located in the second bedroom, where he worked on his fake job. A dozen diskettes with wording scrawled across their labels littered the desktop. One tiny corner of clear space held his mouse and pad. Embossed on the pad was a photo of his dog. The underside hid a photo of his ex-girlfriend. *Almost time to get another pad*, thought Bob, wondering if his new love interest would go out with him. He needed time to recover from his ex, so he decided to ask out the new prospect in about three months. Until then, he'd just smile and stare at her.

Bob checked his e-mail—no word from his fake boss. Just another message from his psychic friends on HealNet about needing to heal a man dying from a brain tumor in Texas. Bob printed the message and tossed the paper into his prayer box. At night when he was about to fall asleep, he'd perform Reiki and ask his spirit guides to bless him and the box filled with paper pleas for prayers. He hoped the psychics on HealNet were praying for him too. One hand washes the other. He needed a new life because he had no life. I'm just a no life, he thought. The box was nearly empty at present due to a mishap. The cleaning lady assumed the paper pleas for help were trash and emptied them in the office paper-recycling bin at the Fiston dump. Those guys were beyond Bob's help. Bob needed the cleaning lady because between working on his fake job, lying in bed pretending to sleep, and simply doing nothing, he had no time to scrub his house.

Surfing the Web on his computer, Bob found interesting visuals about pending environmental catastrophes like ozone depletion, global warming, and frog deformities. His fake boss was presenting a paper to a group of potential clients and he told Bob he wanted to scare the willies out of them. The shakened chumps would then support his projects. Bob copied charts and graphs whose lines went up and up and up. He saved one-eyed frog pictures and five-legged frog pictures and even a frog Siamese twin. He found pictures of receding glaciers and of rising oceans.

As soon as Bob finished a couple of hours of fake work, he logged off the Web and began the tedious process of saving files. Just then the phone rang. The fake boss thanked him for the graphs he'd already received. He figured a few more photos might make the whole presentation as gripping as a Stephen King novel. Bob assured him more were coming. Then the fake boss told Bob he really appreciated the ozone depletion graph Bob had made over Fiston. "Twenty years from now, all those Fiston sun worshippers receiving skin grafts will wish to hell they had paid fifty dollars to attend my dog and pony show," said the fake boss. Bob was glad his forty hours of fake work had paid off with a verbal pat on the head.

Bob had felt guilty all yesterday after sending an e-mail requesting reimbursement for his fake job-related expenses so he was glad that his fake boss brought up the subject. After telling Bob about the millions of dollars being spent to refurbish a rundown section of Fiston to create the Education Tech Center, he told Bob a sad story. The Center's bean counters had him over a barrel on expenses. He probably could not pay Bob's expenses from last year. However, he hoped that this year's expenses might be paid some time next year—as long as the Tech Center opened on schedule. But he expected delays coordinating such a massive project. The fake boss did tell him to re-submit the expenses on a new form, something about burying the bean counters in make-work. Bob asked about discretionary funds at his disposal, but he was told airtight project controls could trace a missing nickel. Bob wanted about $500; he could have the nickel. On a bright note, the fake boss said he was very appreciative of Bob's couple of hundred hours spent finishing an ambitious environmental project which would raise awareness that man's technology was slowly killing the planet and its people.

Bob hung up the phone with a sad face. He needed to mail this last diskette of environmental horrors for the upcoming presentation but he wanted to slip in a love note to his fake boss concerning his unpaid expenses. He scrawled some really heart-rending words when his pen went dry. He picked up another and scrawled away. When that pen went dry a few words later, he picked up a third lying on the coffee table and finished the letter. He reviewed it. Two different colored inks weaved together in a drunken scrawl. He shook his head. Maybe, he thought, God wanted him to mail the letter after he talked to someone. Looking at the clock, he decided to hit the noon twelve-step meeting in downtown Fiston.

At the nooner, Bob rubbed elbows with fellow no lifes to obtain his daily dose of social contact. One of them each day sat in a chair in the middle of the room and told everyone how great life was, then afterwards everyone else raised their hands and agreed. Sometimes a no life told everyone a sad story. Everyone would slap him on the shoulder and tell him, "It gets better!" Today Bob raised his hand and he heard the same thing, knowing inside that the "it" meant him. Later, an experienced no life told Bob he hadn't been meant to send that letter. He said "restraint of pen and tongue" was a useful phrase to live by. Bob decided to rewrite the note.

On the way out of the nooner, Bob stopped in the copy store to retrieve his duplicated magazine article for his fake boss. The clerk, a fellow no life, told him the article still wasn't ready. Bob scowled and told the no life clerk he was very upset with the delay and took back the magazine. Inwardly he smiled at the outburst: fifteen years of therapy was starting to make a difference. Changing the subject, the clerk asked if Bob had heard from the publisher about a story he had submitted. Bob shook his head and left.

Still grumpy, Bob decided to run up a mountain before going home. Two-dollar sub in hand, he spent twenty minutes running up the face of Mt. Little. They used to say only chicken-littles climbed it but Bob huffed and puffed at the top. Then he ate his lunch while surveying his domain. Yesterday he had paid a psychic sixty dollars to tell him the world was going to end. After preparing the visuals for his fake boss's presentation he could certainly believe it. However, she wanted him to share this news with his friends. The last time Bob had entertained that same apocalyptic

notion he had run screaming through the dark streets of his neighborhood alternatively shouting "The world is ending" and howling like a
wolf. In a moment of clarity he had admitted himself to the locked ward
at Fiston Regional Hospital. The psychic had also told him to explore survival living. He had found a hand-operated pump that could dispense 200
gallons of pure water from pond scum at one gallon per hour; located
germicidal tablets to add to canteens; and discovered bleach could purify
and preserve water stored in gallon jugs. Before going to the trouble of
saving 50 gallons of bleach-preserved water in his crawl space, he knew he
should pour a little into the gallon jug to test the recipe he had read in the
survivalist store. But he was scared that he'd miscalculate and poison
himself. What would the ambulance guys think when he told them he
mistakenly added too much bleach to a gallon jug to preserve water for
long-term storage in case of a sudden natural disaster like the earth slip-
ping on its axis? With his history of breakdowns, they'd send him to the
locked ward for sure, if he survived.

Back home, he turned on the classical music station that his receiver
obtained from an illicit hook-up to the cable box. He didn't like the make-
believe violence on TV. He preferred the up-to-date real-life violence available on the local and network news shows. He sat for a moment in front
of the blank TV screen trying to compose himself for his tutoring session
with a fourth-grader. The phone rang; his ex wanted to talk. She asked him
if he missed her and he told her after several pauses and gasps for air that
it was over. He said the relationship hadn't worked. What more was there
to talk about? She wanted to see him. He remembered the last time he'd
seen her seven weeks ago when, in a tirade, she had screamed and
screamed in his face for canceling a proposed outing. She had sent back his
letter ending the relationship, opened but unread. She had no phone and
he feared for his safety in a one-on-one encounter. Now she told him she
wanted to walk on the beach, have dinner, and be friends. Bob remembered the skulking in-a-box feeling he experienced with her at the end.
Between gasps of air he said, "No thanks," cringing a little in the shoulders,
bracing for the tirade. She ended by telling him she would stop by. "Why?"
he asked. Then she offered to call, and by this time he just said suit yourself, told her he had to tutor a child, and hung up like people do to tele-
marketers.

At the newly opened Fiston community center, reporters clustered around the busybody chairwoman of the committee that oversaw the activities of the executive director who ran the place. She reeled off statistics to the reporters showing how successful the center was and how well the residents liked it. She saw Bob. She waved. Then she told them Bob, a volunteer tutor, was a brilliant computer wizard who programmed all their software. Bob grinned a little thinking about her exaggerated half-truths and outright lies about him and the center, which showed how great everything worked. Praise was over-abundant today. Bob waited for his charge. Five minutes passed. The kid was late. The busybody told Bob in front of the news people where the pink sheet was pinned in the office and asked him to call the parents at home. Bob looked in the office, forgot where the sheet was, then went back to the busybody and asked again for the exact location. He wondered if the news people were taking notes at this lapse of brilliance or better yet, why he was even there at 3:30 pm on a workday? He found the sheet and called but the mother said she didn't know where her kid was. Bob told the busybody exactly what the mom had said and hoped the news people wrote that down too.

Next, Henry came by. He was a no life who had given up. They talked a little about his impending death and the inability to overcome the fear of suicide. Henry had severe heart disease, diabetes, high blood pressure, and untreatable depression. He weighed in at a ringing 350 pounds and couldn't stop eating or start exercising. He smoked two packs a day. Bob told him he hoped his bad day would improve. Henry doubted it. Bob told Henry about his upcoming performance. He was going to read a story to a group of fellow writers at a cafe downtown. Henry listened to the story, Bob revised a few words, and then he read again. Henry didn't like the story but did offer him a place to stay inland in case a natural disaster flooded the coast. He said the main problem wasn't storing water but staying warm. Bob couldn't heat his place if he lost power. The stored water would freeze. So would Bob. Since Henry couldn't attend the reading, Bob called another no life who had to decline due to a prior commitment.

Alone, Bob sat in the chair of the cafe rigidly. His heart fluttered. He'd heard students read about grizzlies scratching their backs, farmers haying fields, and a grown-up Gretel, of Hansel and Gretel, copping a bag of dope from a drug dealer. The audience had giggled a little. Now the teacher introduced Bob as a comedy writer and announced he had just seven minutes to read his piece before she buzzed him off the podium. Bob improvised. Once at the podium, he had a bright idea: he decided to start in the middle of his piece. Bob knew the story happened to be funny but he wondered how well the gag lines from his abbreviated piece might strike an expectant audience. Holding the papers in a shaking hand, he felt the silence. He swallowed back nausea, setup the story scene, and began. The silence continued. Halfway through his piece someone yelled, "Speak up." Looking down into the papers, Bob heard a throat clear, silverware clatter, and a magazine page rustle. No one even chuckled. The story finished flat. Its start was unrecited, its middle muddled, and its ending a mystery. The warning buzzer never sounded. With time to spare, Bob acknowledged his automatic applause and sat down. He was numb.

At the break no one looked at Bob. No one said anything. He saw a couple of real lifes that he knew from class: a good-natured intellectual whose children were half-grown traded baby stories with a smiling new dad. Suddenly, the teacher reached across the table and shook the new dad's hand vigorously for a great read; she wished the intellectual luck on her up-coming read; and she ignored Bob completely. The two real lifes returned to a conversation about their defined careers and nuclear families. Bob tried to participate in the discussion but didn't fit in. They knew he had a fake job and a childless relationship with a four-legged partner. Their thick shells of wellness squeezed him out. His thin shell had cracked a long time ago. He listened to them for a few minutes, pretending to take part in the animated conversation. Then he said his goodbyes.

Bob walked down Fiston's main avenue wanting to punch an old lady or kick a cat. As luck would have it, he found a fellow no life instead; that no life took him by the arm to a large gathering of no lifes in a "beat" restaurant. Among the suggestively painted mannequins and hijacked road signs, Bob told his no life pals that the day had had a few low spots. They listened and agreed. They all had experienced similar days like that. They hooted over a number of sad stories and laughed out loud over a couple of tragedies. Pretty soon Bob laughed too. He ordered another chocolate frappe. Then they gave the waitress a big tip and lots of compliments. Outside Bob looked up. He saw a full moon. "So that's why," he said to the others. They all joked about being "loony" on the way to their cars. The end of the world seemed very far away to Bob.

Growing Pains

Bob O'Neil's eyes gazed across the empty room and fixed themselves on the framed-photograph of Teddy and himself. The sitting with the professional photographer had cost Bob $350. Teddy's hair was rich and dark; neither of them had much gray. He remembered the treats Teddy had consumed as an incentive to pose for snapshots—pictures which now adorned four of Bob's coffee mugs. Memories flooded into Bob's mind about Teddy and the times they enjoyed together.

◆ ◆ ◆

Teddy was a small black Scotty dog. He had little legs, a medium-sized body, and a very large head with very white teeth. He lived with the O'Neil family: Mrs. O'Neil and her son, Bob. Mrs. O'Neil kept a neat house. Nothing was out of place and everything had to be put away. But Teddy was a little guy, full of energy, and wanted to play all the time. He pulled out Mrs. O'Neil's newspapers and shredded them like a mouse; he pulled out his toys and scattered them like a baby; he pulled out Bob's books and chewed them like a beaver. When Mrs. O'Neil came back from the donut shop, she'd scream at Teddy, tape up a roll of newspaper, and hit him for making a mess. Teddy was so scared he tinkled on the rug and she would hit him even harder with her bare hand. Teddy made lots of mistakes in the house and his nickname was "Dirty Dog."

Mrs. O'Neil finally decided to pen Teddy in the kitchen using plastic gates. She laughed and said he was "confined to quarters." Then she went to the refrigerator for a drink, popped open the can, and cringed as the cold foamy golden liquid streamed down her throat. After finishing the drink, she rinsed the can, stacked it away, and lit a cigarette. The smoke she inhaled burnt her throat too, and she coughed, but not even having a little mouth cancer could make her stop smoking. At night, Teddy stopped barking and jumping and went to sleep on the bare kitchen tile. Mrs.

O'Neil slept on the couch. Mr. O'Neil had given Teddy to his wife; but he had died suddenly the year before. No one ever talked about the cause of death.

In the evenings, when Bob arrived home, the house was dark because Mrs. O'Neil went to bed early. Teddy stirred. Bob said, "Easy Teddy, don't wake her up." Then he went to bed. Being back home felt funny. He touched his head. All through school Bob studied very hard, but did little else. His head slowly became bigger than the other kids. At the end of high school, he graduated with honors wearing the largest sized cap available. In college Bob passed all his tests but never found time to play with his friends so his head grew even larger. By the end of college, he had found a very important job where having a big head didn't matter. The managers at the company only valued hard work. Bob earned lots of money. One day a few people he used to know from college visited and warned him that his head looked awfully big. Bob cast aside their concern with a wave of his hand. Soon after the visit, Bob's head was so big he had trouble holding it up and his pace at work slowed. The managers met and decided Bob had to leave their company. That's how Bob lost his big job.

Bob moved back home with his mother and after awhile he found another job, a little job, and he wanted to keep it. He hoped the change might help nurse his head back to normal size. Home-cooked food, his old bed, and the small town all would help heal him. But problems existed. Mrs. O'Neil was sick. He really didn't know Teddy. His brother had married. His friends had moved away with their new families. He didn't exercise much. He didn't have a girlfriend either. Bob worked, read, and watched TV. No one called him.

One Saturday morning Bob slept late. He awoke to smell bacon and eggs cooking. Mrs. O'Neil had set the table and Bob sat down in his pajamas, waiting to be served. Teddy stayed under the table watching as Mrs. O'Neil demanded to know if Bob thought she was some kind of slave that was supposed to serve him for the rest of her life. Bob said no, and moved to the counter to make toast. She exploded in anger, told him to stay away from the bread—he'd make a mess. He opened the fridge door for the butter but she grabbed the butter away from him and raised back her clenched fist to strike a blow. Bob flinched, cowering in the corner against the counter top and stove. Mrs. O'Neil laughed, "How could a big young man like you be afraid of a frail old woman like me?" Then she told Bob she was putting the house up for sale. She was moving into a trailer park for retired people. They didn't allow young men or dogs. She was giving up Teddy. He could take Teddy or she would give him away to some woman she knew from the coffee shop.

Bob didn't mind leaving home again—he was used to living by himself. The idea of caring for a pet scared him, though. Being totally responsible for a helpless life form—he shook his head. When the big head condition became a problem, Bob had headed back home to rest. But Mrs. O'Neil didn't give him much rest time. Now Bob had to move out. He left without Teddy. He wasn't sure he could even take care of himself. When Bob settled in near his little job, he decided to buy his own house. He called his mother to tell her his new address. She said she gave Teddy away to the woman she knew from the coffee shop. He didn't feel sad and he didn't feel glad. He didn't feel anything. Just cold, like his stomach was full of three large ice cream sundaes. The next time Bob called Mrs. O'Neil, he heard Teddy barking. He was back. Bob smiled. She told him he could take Teddy home if he picked him up by tomorrow. So Bob drove down to the trailer and picked up Teddy. Mrs. O'Neil smiled and said "Happy Birthday." She said Teddy was his birthday present. His card was in the mail. Bob brought Teddy home. He never received the card and didn't have a cake to eat. Teddy whimpered as he put up the big plastic gate. Bob opened a can of foul-smelling dog food and held his nose from the smell. Teddy ate the food and drank some water and went to bed on the cold floor just like before. Bob tried to sleep too. He shook because of the cold ice cream sundae feeling in his stomach. His head grew even bigger.

That night Bob dreamed about Teddy and the dogs he'd grown up with and what life was like with dogs. When he awoke, he didn't remember much about the dream, but he did remember to put Teddy outside. Teddy went to the bathroom on the backyard grass; he wasn't a dirty dog after all. Then Bob threw out the foul-smelling dog food that he'd taken from Mrs. O'Neil and visited the vet to ask what was the best dog food that he could buy for Teddy. Teddy liked the vet and wagged his tail the whole time he was there.

After the vet visit, Bob went to the pet store with Teddy. They walked through the store together and tossed into the basket a forty-pound bag of food for mature dogs because Teddy was an older yet very active male. Bob dangled a brand new red collar and six-foot leash in front of Teddy and he sniffed them. In the sleeping area, they found a bed with a cover full of teddy bears. It had a round bottom and high sides to let a little dog nestle and stay warm.

Teddy liked his presents. The two meals a day were a treat; he jumped and bobbed his head as Bob scooped food and the big bag rustled. After eating, they went for a walk around the neighborhood. Teddy went out at least three times a day. Long walks with little legs made Teddy tired. He slipped into his new bed, twisted his body in a little circle, then put his head on the bed rim and closed his eyes. Soon he stopped yipping and jittering and jumping and barking every time Bob twisted his long legs over the gate. Teddy went to the bathroom outside, too. He never asked to go out. Bob just knew. They went out three or four times a day: before work, after work, after dinner, and before bed. So, one day just before Christmas, Bob removed the gate and Teddy tore through the rest of the house. He ran back and forth from the kitchen, past the living room and into the bedroom. Bob chased Teddy out of the bedroom and around the corner of the kitchen. Then Teddy turned on his heel, little legs spinning out from under him, and he chased Bob back through to the bedroom. Teddy howled and panted and Bob shrieked when Teddy tried to nip his heels. The gate was gone, never to reappear.

Christmas was fun. It was just the two of them. Bob bought toys for Teddy, a squeaky cat, a mushy tennis ball, and a twist of rope. Teddy hated cats and chewed the squeaky toy right away. He caught the tennis ball in his mouth after it bounced on the floor, then gave it back to Bob. Teddy was unique because terriers hardly ever retrieve.

Christmas was lonely, too. Bob and Mrs. O'Neil had a fight after she got sick from a stroke. Mrs. O'Neil yelled a lot and Bob decided not to call her for a while. Then he figured out what to say but went out dancing instead of calling her one Friday night. He'd do it tomorrow, he thought. When tomorrow came, the phone rang. His cousin said his mother had died that night. The ice cream sundae feeling in Bob's stomach numbed his entire body. His lungs contracted and his hands shook and his head expanded. He wished he had made peace with her, but then again who knows, she may have blown up at him over the phone and died right then.

While making the funeral arrangements, Bob talked to a priest about his big head problem. The priest directed him to a support group for people with that condition. Bob kept things simple. He just made sure to eat, sleep, go to meetings where other people with big heads talked about their lives. As they talked, somehow their heads became smaller. They too felt as though there were ice cream sundaes stuck in their stomachs but they assured Bob the ice cream melted a little in time. Bob felt better after the meetings. He didn't go to work for a week, but that gave him more time to play with Teddy. They walked in the wet sand on the beach, sniffed the dry leaves strewn on the trail in the woods, and looked for wild animals on top of a near-by mountain.

Now Teddy and Bob were all alone in the world, except for the occasional pet they'd meet on the trail or the people Bob met in the support meetings. One day, with work going poorly, something inside Bob's big head exploded causing Teddy and him to be involved in a big car accident. The car they were riding in was totally destroyed, but they were alive. A guy in a pickup truck drove Bob to the hospital. Luckily neither was badly hurt, but Bob knew that from now on, he'd have to have a doctor treat his big head problem or something even worse might happen to Teddy and him.

As a result of the accident, Bob lost his job. They didn't want a person around an important job site who couldn't control a big head problem. He couldn't find another job because everyone could now guess that his big head had exploded. No one wanted him around. No one except Teddy. Bob realized that he and Teddy were a lot alike—they both had extremely big heads for their bodies.

After the accident, Bob visited the support group. The people at the big head meetings didn't exclude him, but they didn't talk to him either. During the breaks he would walk up to a small group and wait for eye contact or a break in the conversation, but it never came. His hovering made everyone uncomfortable, so Bob stood alone a lot in a room full of big-headed people. But now Bob's big head was different – it had exploded.

He missed being included in the parties, the movies, the outings, and the friendly chatter. Nevertheless, he still kept coming to the meetings— they were his friends – and he brought Teddy, too. Once he invited people to a party of his own. After rushing around to make all the final preparations, he was so tired that he fell asleep on the couch. No one came. If they did come, they may have seen him asleep and were afraid to wake him. So Teddy and he shared the party treats together.

The big snowstorms came in January and February. Bob shoveled his driveway, then they walked the neighborhood streets. The plows had dropped salt and sand and cinders and the road glistened black with melting mush. Ice crinkled underfoot. After a couple of streets, Teddy bounced up and down on his paws and cried. Ice and salt stung his paws. Bob lifted him up and carried him home. Once in the back yard, Teddy peed, then Bob let him off the leash. Teddy hopped across the snow like a rabbit, his two rear legs pushing off together and little chin lifted high. White flakes of snow stained his chest. Chunks of ice hung from his black beard.

After losing one volunteer job after another, Bob might lie for hours on the couch. When Teddy was hungry or needed to go out, he barked. By now, Teddy was so self-contained that he never barked unless it served a good purpose. Bob knew he needed to care for Teddy. He didn't have much else to do, yet things seemed very hard. Life was gray. The glint in Teddy's eye when they played ball, or tag, or squeaky cat, or find the cookie, was about all the light that filled Bob.

Spring came one day. It lasted only the day because spring is the shortest season in New England. Bob and Teddy noticed the smell most of all. They went to the beach. They hadn't been on many walks around the Fiston area all winter. But hibernation was over; both Bob and Teddy crawled out of their cave to see a brighter, warmer sky. Bob even smiled a little down at the beach. Teddy scavenged old dead crabs, a rotten lobster claw, pieces of dried-out sponge. A lady behind Bob told him Teddy might get sick eating such treats. Bob introduced himself to the attractive woman. Her name was Liza and she was new in town. She worked a volunteer job for the mayor; he needed to be re-elected in November. She wore a white wool sweater, a black skirt, leather boots and a purple raincoat. She said she liked purple because the color was spiritual.

Bob decided to volunteer for the mayor, too. Liza expected to receive a real job with the mayor later. Bob thought he might find one too. At the end of the walk, she patted Teddy with the tip of her left index finger and pulled away before he could brush his wet nose against it. She peered at Bob's car and said it was just as handsome as Teddy. Bob lifted Teddy into the front seat, brushed off his paws, and waved to Liza while driving away.

On their first date, Liza complained the car smelled of dog. She put a napkin from her purse between her rear end and the seat because the beach sand and dog oil on the cushion might stain her suit.

Bob went to several parties for the mayor. He met a lot of people with extra horsepower who ran the city. They talked and talked, mostly about

216

themselves and all the good deeds they had done for the community. Bob stayed close to Liza, but other people wanted her attention, too. She began not answering his calls as fast as usual and started talking with a hushed voice to Brian King, the city attorney. Then it happened. She found a couple of hairs on her white silk dress shirt and accused Teddy of shedding them. Bob said Teddy didn't shed, that they were probably her own. When she denied that, he snickered and said they might be from Brian King instead. She broke up with him that night. While he didn't find a job, she became Brian King's personal secretary.

Teddy had missed Bob. They hadn't palled around as much since he met Liza. But now he decided to do more fun things. The weather was warmer, summer had almost arrived. Bob had bought Teddy an extra bed. He put the new bed in the bedroom. Teddy always slept with Bob. But he never stayed the night. The bed might keep him in the room a little longer. When Teddy did sleep with Bob, he liked to nest in the blanket between Bob's legs; other times he slept next to Bob's hip. He was about the size of a hot water bottle and just as warm.

During the summer, Bob tried a new doctor to help him with his big head problem. The doctor had a few new ideas and Bob gave them a try. Bob became a tutor for kids and he always told them a story about Teddy. Bob still walked Teddy every day. They went to the beach, to the woods, and to the mountains. During a hot day, Teddy climbed up onto the couch, peered out the open window with his nose against the screen, and then jumped on to the back of the couch and rolled into the windowsill. He lay against the screen, listening to the passing cars and feeling the breeze blow past his whiskers.

Bob noticed Teddy was a little gray around the ears in July. He had forgotten dogs age faster than people. They went to the beach and met a cute, frisky, Cairn terrier named Misty. She was small and white, lithe and light. Teddy ran back and forth to find Misty. Usually, Bob never let Teddy off his leash, but Misty's owner, an auburn-haired woman with many laugh lines creasing her face, said not to worry. After meeting her blue eyes, Bob noticed the manatee pictured on her T-shirt with the words "endangered species" below it. She wore faded jeans torn at the knee and white sneakers. She assured Bob that Misty could take care of herself. The two racing little dogs ran between lots of big Labs and Shepherds. Teddy finally tired first. Misty sniffed him. Then Bob found out Misty's owner was named

Katie and taught at the University part-time. Bob said he was a part-time tutor.

Bob and Katie arranged to meet at the beach a number of times and Misty and Teddy had loads of fun running free. Bob never quite gave up being the nervous parent with a wild and love struck kid, but he tried to let go as best he could.

Bob still went to the support meetings too. But a funny thing was happening there. All the people who knew Bob from before and snubbed him had started switching to other meetings, leaving the area for new jobs, or settling down with new spouses. The constant flow of new people that Bob tried to help and stay close to grew to accept and help Bob also. He still had a big head, but people had a much harder time knowing that it had actually exploded at one time. Bob would mention in his story that he had an experience with an exploding head problem and if anyone in the meeting wanted to know more about it, they could talk to him. And they did. Bob decided talking about a problem wasn't as intimidating to people as actually living in the problem.

In August, Teddy slowed down a little. Misty ran circles around him and he stumbled on the wet sand chasing her. Katie wiped away some tears. Bob said Teddy would be OK, he just needed a rest. But Katie said the University, at the last minute, had cancelled her contract and told her to find employment elsewhere. She had friends out of state that might give her a job, but she'd have to move. Bob felt a shaky feeling come over him. His hands shook and his voice cracked. He felt that cold, hard ice cream fill his stomach. His head enlarged too. But all he could say was, "Gee that's too bad; I'm sorry you can't stay." She looked at him expecting that he might say more, but he didn't. Goodbyes were always tough for him. What was he supposed to say? Then Teddy barked.

"Why is he barking?" asked Bob. Misty barked, too.

Katie said he might know Misty was moving away. Animals were very intuitive. Bob had an idea. He asked for her address so Teddy and Misty could keep in touch. Katie gave Bob a slip of paper, smiled, and wiped her eyes. Bob waved goodbye. Shaking a little, he put Teddy in the car and drove home to the empty house.

On Labor Day, Teddy had a stroke. Bob found Teddy in the kitchen, lying down, frothing at the mouth. His little legs paddled back and forth. Bob rushed Teddy to the clinic. He thought Teddy had eaten some of his medicine that dropped on the floor but the seizures continued, nearly boiling his brain, and he started traveling in clock-wise circles. Teddy needed to see a specialist. The brain doctor said that Teddy might have a tumor inside his skull. The brain doctor put Teddy through a CAT scan and found that neither hemisphere of his brain was normal. He recommended an operation to remove the possible tumor. Bob agreed. Unfortunately, the doctor couldn't find a tumor. Teddy's recovery was slow but steady. He even stopped circling. After a while, he ate all his food and slept in his own bed. He slowed down a lot more. He could not go up or down stairs or walk more than fifty feet. Bob carried him everywhere.

At the end of the summer, with Teddy feeling better, Bob had a party. He invited all his new friends from his big-headed support group, the dog people from the beach, and some of the people he tutored. And they came. They saw Teddy convalescing. Sometimes he walked in circles, but mostly he walked straight and he loved eating pieces of striped sea bass and sirloin steak strips. Bob wished Katie and Misty had been able to come but she was busy teaching and Misty needed to see the vet about some ailment.

The brain surgery healed on the outside but the seizures continued on the inside. Teddy received higher and higher doses of medicine from the brain doctor. Bob performed Reiki on Teddy, he took him to a reflexologist way up state, and he even inquired with psychics about what to do next. Finally, in the first week of October, Teddy cried so much, and wouldn't eat his food or drink his water or swallow his grape jelly-coated pills, that Bob had to bring him to the clinic. Bob cried. Teddy was groaning in his arms, wrapped in his favorite blanket. They said he had a grave condition and doubted he'd snap out of it, but Bob said he had seen Teddy like this several times before. They kept him two nights and Bob visited him both days. He brought Teddy's favorite bed and lots of food. Then, early Monday morning, on Bob's birthday, he went to the clinic to make a decision on what to do with Teddy. They said he was in a coma. The vet tech went back to check on Teddy again, as Bob waited in the exam room. Then the doctor came in. She said Teddy had passed away a moment ago. She said he knew Bob couldn't bear to put him to sleep, so he had died just as Bob arrived, taking the decision out of his hands. Bob patted Teddy's body when they brought him in. He cut off a lock of his hair for safekeeping, unbuckled his collar, and told the doctor he wanted Teddy's body cremated.

After a careful drive home, Bob sat on the couch and cried again. The ice cream sundae feeling in his stomach melted. The mixture oozed up into his head and dripped down his face as tears. His heart melted. But if it could melt, it could also mend. His head enlarged also. Then he went to the big-headed support meeting and told them that Teddy had died on his birthday. He said of all the time Teddy had lived with him, that this had been the best. He loved Teddy, he missed him, but he knew he'd see him again one day, and he thanked them all for being his friends.

"Happy Birthday, Bob!"

Bob O'Neil sat with a friend at a table gazing through the six-foot high window of the dockside restaurant. He stared at the long, thin, dark blue line between sea and sky that was rapidly vanishing as the evening passed. The sun had set an hour before on this chilly November day. Now the only light remaining came from the red and green glowing bow lamps of passing homeward-bound fishing boats being guided by the constant flash of the Wood Island lighthouse a mile offshore. Bob ignored his former girlfriend, Cathy, a petite blonde, who still turned heads when she entered a room. From the reflection of the glass, he studied her red turtleneck, black slacks, and shiny white Keds sneakers. They stayed in touch in spite of the break-up. Today the occasion for the get-together was his birthday, but the topic of the evening's conversation was her constant thoughts of suicide.

"Earth to Bob. Are you still with me?" Cathy giggled. "If you keep wandering away I may sing "Happy Birthday" to you. I bet the whole restaurant will join in. They may even bring a cake," she said.

Bob stiffened. The thought of her little girl voice quavering off-key in public gave him a new incentive to pay close attention to her morbid confession.

"As I was saying, you've helped me a great deal," said Cathy. Bob noted the crinkles around her eyes were deeper and darker from lack of sleep.

She thanked him for being such a patient listener. As she saw it, and her therapist agreed, the problem was that her old boyfriend, the one she had met before Bob, and who had continued to love her while she dated Bob, and who pined away loving her for years more—even after her latest fling—still loved her.

"What's so terrible about that?" asked Bob.

"He didn't call me Thursday night. He always calls on Thursdays. So I called him Friday and left a message. He still didn't call back. So I called Sunday. I knew he'd be home Sunday. He reads the newspaper, watches the panel shows, and drinks beer," she said.

Cathy sipped hot water from her mug. The waitress said they were out of herbal tea. Bob let his decaf steam.

"He said he wasn't interested. In me, that is. He doesn't love me any more. And he doesn't have a girlfriend. He doesn't, you know. I heard his voice and he's telling the truth," she said, arching her eyebrows.

Cathy continued, "I thought about it for a week, lying in bed sleepless night after night, crying in the bathroom at work, and I finally I realized I did love him. After ten years of being pursued and feeling nothing, I truly love him. Just like the love I had for my first boyfriend. The one I ran away from."

Bob closed his eyes for a moment. He thought a little about Cathy's past experience with boyfriends, their own romantic dance, and his limited experience with women.

"When the first guy began to love you, you ran. Now, when this guy disappears, you start loving him. You're repeating a pattern," said Bob.

Cathy shook her head. "I was just a kid then. Now I'm an adult. I may even stop my twelve-step support group. Nobody cares there and meetings are beginning to bore me," she said.

But Cathy did confide that she liked therapy better, in fact she would prefer to see her therapist every day if she could afford the bill.

"What does your therapist say?" asked Bob.

"He says I should see him every week for the time being, considering what happened, and I agreed," said Cathy.

"What happened?" asked Bob.

Cathy told him by the end of the week the pain in her chest wouldn't go away. She pointed to her heart. Sometimes the pain dropped to just above the groin, where she would now remain forever childless, and other times the pain rose to her throat, where she muzzled her grief. She tried herbal remedies to no avail. She refused to self-medicate with pills or alcohol. She called her therapist, but his secretary said he was busy and told her he was completely booked for the week. All her friends were either away or too distant for the kind of intimate conversation she craved. So she dwelled on a permanent solution.

She grinned.

"I did make one phone call. I thought of you and the crisis center card you keep next to the phone in case of an emergency. I decided to call the Samaritans, but, guess what?—the line was busy at 2:00 am. I laughed out

222

loud, I figured God was giving me the go ahead sign. Then I planned it out," said Cathy.

"Why didn't you call me?" asked Bob.

Cathy shrugged.

Bob hesitated. "How were you going to do it?" he asked.

"Here we are," cackled the harried waitress with the big bust and enormous behind. She wore an apron embossed with a lobster that seemed to crawl as she flitted from table to table. She served Bob a fried bay scallop and native shrimp combination plate. The heavy, grease-laden aroma of the tiny local delicacies sickened Bob. Next the waitress attended Cathy, laying out a side of fried onion rings, a bowl of coleslaw, and a pile of steaming broccoli on top of edible seaweed.

Cathy's eyebrows knotted as she stared at her vegetable dish.

"More hot water?" asked the waitress, trying to read her expression.

"Yes, please," replied Cathy, looking up. "Excuse me but do you know if any sea creatures were killed or injured in the gathering of this seaweed?"

Startled, the waitress finished pouring her hot water, "Really I have no idea. I never gave it a thought. I could find out for you but I really don't know who to ask at the moment," she said.

Cathy smiled politely, "No problem, I just won't eat the seaweed."

Not only was Cathy a strict vegetarian, thought Bob, she didn't believe in eating or using anything that may have harmed an innocent animal.

Bob held out his mug for a refill, and returned his attention to Cathy.

"So how were you going to do it?" he asked, not touching his food.

"Simple," said Cathy. Bob watched her pick up her fork and knife, strip the oily batter from an onion ring, slice the bare onion with a nervous sawing motion, gather the segments on her fork, and shovel them in her mouth.

"After I failed to reach the Samaritans on Thursday night, I planned to rise early Friday morning and, not having to go to work because of the new flex time schedule, drive north to a lake near the home of my lost love. I'd write him a short note about how I felt, settle my affairs, and give away my few possessions to friends. Then I'd walk to the edge of the lake, lay on the sand, remember the good times we had there, roll up my sleeves, and slice both my wrists with the razor blade I keep in my jewelry box," said Cathy.

Bob shook a little. He looked at her. He looked at his combination platter cooling down below him.

"I'm glad you didn't do it," he said, gripping his fork to steady his hand to delve into his scallops and shrimp.

"Bob, you haven't eaten a thing. It's your favorite dish. My treat, remember," she said.

Bob nodded. It was a free dinner. His favorite meal. He nibbled.

"I think I'm going to need a doggie bag. Too much excitement, I guess. The time around my birthday brings up a lot of stress that's hard to deal with," Bob said. He figured that it was the truth in some twisted way.

Bravely, Bob took another bite, but he struggled to swallow one mouthful twice and still the scallop felt stuck in his throat. He sipped his coffee.

Cathy nodded to herself.

"The call stopped me," she said.

"What call?" asked Bob. He put down the mug, grateful for the interruption.

"An elderly lady I hardly knew in my twelve-step group called me Friday morning to ask if I'd go shopping with her that day. She said she was feeling crummy and needed to be with people from the group. I guess I mentioned my new flex-time schedule at the meeting that week. I really don't remember. Everything is such a blur," said Cathy.

"How are we doing?" asked a cheerful voice.

Cathy let the waitress take away her plates, clean but for the mound of seaweed. The waitress looked at Bob with concern. Was he satisfied with the cooking? Bob nodded. He needed a box. The waitress bustled away.

"Will you promise me something?" pleaded Bob. "Will you promise to call someone, to ask for help next time?"

Cathy nodded. "I promised my therapist to stay alive. He gave me his home phone number and his beeper number and told me to call any time," she said.

"Good. I hope you do. Meetings help me; sounds like one in particular helped you. I think we receive help by helping others," said Bob.

"I guess I could go back to the meeting again, to give back a little," said Cathy.

Bob rose from the table, took Cathy's hand, and pointed to the ship channel. Cathy followed his stare. The lighthouse silhouetted a large, ocean-going tanker, lit like a Christmas tree. Three tugboats, one at the stern and two at the bow, pushed the slow moving tanker upstream, guiding her toward port. They watched the procession pass in silence. Then Bob touched her shoulder, saying, "Everything needs a little help finding the way home."

Cathy smiled.

When they left their table, Bob lagged behind. He shrugged as heads turned to watch the blonde exit the restaurant. Then he hurried along to say goodbye with tomorrow's dinner, enclosed in a large, grease-stained paper bag, flapping against his leg.

Mexico

Bob O'Neil stared at the blinking light of his answering machine. Hope filled his heart as he pressed the button. Perhaps, he thought, the chemistry professor from last week's blind date had returned his call. He frowned upon hearing the voice. Then he cringed. The voice was singsong with inflection. A lonely, depressed, and wounded female was issuing a distress call. A married female, he reminded himself. Bob's eyes glazed over as he remembered another day about a year ago when a similar message warmed the winter chill out of his bones.

"Hello," said Bob.

"I'm afraid, Bob. I booked a trip to Mexico because my life is such a wreck here and now I'm afraid to go on vacation. I'll lose my $1500 and sit home all week—if I don't lose my mind first."

"Now Doreen, you'll have a great trip. Just think of all the wonderful sites you'll visit and interesting people you'll meet."

Bob helped Doreen over the rough spots in her life. She had girl-friends but liked to ask his opinion too. They had been communing over the phone almost daily for over a year. She thought of him as just one of the girls and even confided her love trysts with other men. Nevertheless, Bob thought some day he might deflower their platonic relationship. He imagined himself swooping in and rescuing her from some insensitive brute.

"Bob, I'm scared. I'm scared to go alone and I'm scared to stay home. My job is a bore, my boss is a bitch, my boyfriend didn't understand me, and I feel like I'm going to pieces. I can't go on like this."

"Just do the next right thing."

Bob knew there was safety and strength in platitudes.

Doreen began to cry. Bob's heart twisted a little in sympathetic motion. She broke through the sniffles in a little girl type voice: sad, seductive, and unsure but surprisingly clear.

"Will you come to Mexico with me?"

Bob hesitated. He always was slow to decide matters but Doreen mistook his silence for outright rejection. She cried on. Between sniffles, she begged him to go. She knew he had the money and time to travel and she was in desperate need of a travel companion.

Bob had been to yet another psychic the week before and she had said a woman with very dark hair was coming into his life. Bob was starting to tire of handing the reins of his life over to strangers gifted with second sight and thought the twenty dollars paid wasn't worth the one hour sitting. She told him more than he wanted to know. He felt the elderly woman was grateful more for the company than for the money. Yet the prediction popped into his head and made his heart ache. Doreen not only had very dark hair, she had a cupie-doll body laced with unmarked curves.

"Yes," Bob said.

"Really!"

"Yes, I'll go with you. I've always wanted to see Mexico. What part are you traveling to?"

She told Bob about the particulars of her trip and warned him that seats were selling fast. He needed to call the travel agent immediately. She also stipulated that he book separate accommodations. Bob took this as a temporary setback; they were friends now; what might happen down there was anybody's guess. Then she said she had to get dressed for work. She thanked him and gave him the direct number to her office phone.

Bob smiled. He called the agent, let her describe the trip, told her he'd think about it, then hung up. He didn't bother to call his friends. They were busy at work. He waited about ten minutes and called the agent again. He told her he had thought enough. She giggled. He read his credit card number to her over the phone and purchased a $1500 non-refundable reservation.

Doreen called him thirty minutes later.

"Did you give her your credit card number?"

"Yes."

"I can't believe it. You're going with me," she said.

Doreen's enthusiasm infected Bob. The day was a blur of excitement. Bob received several Doreen calls. She had recovered herself and now was taking charge of finding airport parking, locating helpful web pages of local sites through the Internet, and giving advice on clothing.

"You'll need a sport jacket for dinner and lots of clean underwear. One for every day. And wash all your old summer clothes before you pack them..."

Bob laughed.

"My camera was stolen...I may need to buy a camera. Do you..."

"No. I'm borrowing my ex's. By the way, did you read my 'Friendly Tip' e-mail?"

Bob suppressed another laugh. She had sent him a half dozen e-mails, suggested he buy summer casuals, and was finishing his sentences. *That's pretty tight*, he thought.

The next day they left for Playa del Mar on the mainland coast with the island of Cozumel off shore, a pearly sand beach on Mexico's Riviera. She asked several more times if he had read her e-mail but he just put her off. All the books, maps, and trip tickets were together with his passport and e-mail print outs in his black carry-on travel bag. He was the best-dressed guy on the plane. He wore a navy blue sport jacket he picked up at Goodwill for ten dollars, a pair of new lightweight beige trousers bought on sale, and a blue button-down dress shirt. Doreen looked comfortable in a pair of white shorts, a flowered blouse, and red sweater. Once they settled in their seats, she asked yet again if he had read her "Friendly Tip" e-mail.

While Doreen stared out the window watching the ground pass by like an episode from a silent movie, Bob opened his carry-on and read his friendly tip.

"Is this really true?" he asked with a frog in his voice; he could feel a cold coming.

"You do smell. Although today I don't notice it as much as usual."

"But..." he looked down at the note, quoting..."Is it really 'an unwashed smell similar to that of a homeless person'?"

She nodded, looking away.

Bob sneezed. Doreen flinched as some aerosol particles landed on the exposed flesh of her leg. As Bob blew his nose into the tissue provided by the passing flight attendant, Doreen swiped the box on his lap to wipe herself dry.

By the time the trip was half over, Bob had repaired his wounded ego. His heart would quicken upon seeing Doreen's lithe figure in a sheer gown. He enjoyed her swimming stunts in her skimpy bathing suit. They had spent hours together.

Getting up from the bed, Bob muttered to himself, "Something might happen yet." Then he shut the door to his room, sauntered over to dinner, and reminded himself that he was having a great time. The night sky sparkled with stars, the ocean lapped on the white sand beach less than a hundred yards from where he stood, and a sea breeze cooled off the hot, moist tropical air. At the lobby, he met Doreen and they went to dinner. The food was wonderful, served in a buffet style. Doreen looked stunning in a loose fitting evening gown, but she was sad. Phone service was poor and she had been trying to reach her ex, who was on vacation in New Orleans, to convince him to come to Cancun and Playa with her. The trouble was, she couldn't remember if he was joining that woman he met in Aruba last fall or if he was alone. After hearing her predicament, Bob returned to the buffet for seconds. When he returned, she was flirting with a dark-skinned Mexican waiter named Pablo. Pablo's wife was a hotel maid and they had a three-year-old daughter that the mother-in-law babysat. Doreen mourned to him about the lack of such a sweet family in her life then Pablo pointed over to Bob. Doreen shook her head and dismissed Bob's potential with a flourish of her hand.

Bob turned away. Upon seeing the time on the wall clock, he indicated they had better hurry and finish the meal.

"The meeting is in twenty minutes, we need to catch a cab," said Bob.

Doreen nodded to Pablo, inviting him to grasp her outstretched hand. Pablo declined. After he left, Bob told her they each should leave a dollar tip for Pablo's trouble. She frowned, then agreed. Bob had seen how the workers crossed themselves each time they received a dollar tip from an American. One dollar was equivalent to a week's wages. Bob regretted not giving a dollar to the attendant who showed him to his room on the first day. He simply thanked him but the Mexican still managed to smile back as though the oversight was a simple case of amnesia.

Back at the lobby, they caught a cab for town. Bob remembered the first time they went to town. Doreen had wanted to save three dollars and walk the two miles. On a sunny afternoon at the edge of the main street, past the guard shack, she stopped a number of tired, depressed-looking Mexicans on their way home from work. She spread the map out and asked them in which direction they should proceed to town. The group stopped and looked at one another in silence. Then she asked them again in slow, perfect English, her lips over-enunciating each syllable in the kind of style reserved for illiterates and children. The Mexicans stood wiping their brows and looking at each other miserably. Some pointed to the right, others, the left. A couple even pointed across the street to the golf course. She was about to ask again, in a higher pitch when Bob hailed a passing cab. He waved "Gracias" to the small group before they left.

Even Doreen had thanked him that time. Now she was over-tired and needed a meeting. The cabby spoke Spanish to Bob. But Bob said he only knew a few words. In English, the cabby asked if they were married. They both said no. Then he asked if they had any children. Doreen murmured no, then asked Bob in a loud whiny voice if he had any children. Bob said no and the cabby stopped asking questions.

The pair arrived at the meeting with time to spare. They talked with other Americans, drank coffee, and listened to other fellow sufferers share their mistakes of the past, problems of today, and hopes of the future. Bob's hopes turned on introducing himself to two women on his right from Arizona. But by the end of the meeting, one had left and the other was holding her boyfriend's hand. Bob saw that Doreen was having better luck. Three men crowded around her. She was in the middle of telling them the story of her life when they noticed Bob staring at her. She glanced in his direction briefly to introduce him as "my friend Bob." She was in high spirits and told them that after asking numerous friends to accompany her on the big trip, she had thought of Bob, and they went together— although they occupied separate rooms. Bob waved a "Hi" in their direction. Doreen then quizzed the photographer from the *Buffalo Daily News* about life on the beat. As an ex-reporter, she could identify. The Texan was building a multistory condo using cash downtown and he gave her his cell phone number and address. But Doreen was laughing the loudest at the obscene and juvenile jokes of the rugged-looking but penniless cowboy who had the best physique of the bunch. They all agreed to ride scooters on the island of Cozumel the next day or rent a jeep. They would meet at the ferry at 7:00 am.

After Bob and Doreen said goodbye to the trio, she asked Bob if he was mad at her. Bob said nothing. He had made reservations to Chichenitza to see the Mayan ruins the next day, so she knew he couldn't go jeeping with the gang. He ducked into a store full of leather etchings. She followed. He stared at Mayan gods, praying to his, hoping the rage within would subside. She stood behind him and asked which guy he liked the best. He told her the photographer was the nicest and the cowboy was the most dangerous. Giggling, she admitted she liked the dangerous one. Bob made a selection, bargained with the wrinkled woman shopkeeper lamely, then hefted his bag. Doreen chose a larger, more expensive Mayan calendar etching and was determined to pay the same price as Bob. She succeeded. When she counted her change from the shopkeeper, she found a mistake and demanded the missing bills. Upon leaving the shop, she confided in Bob that she hated dishonesty.

They filled more shopping bags and emptied their wallets, then decided to return to the hotel. In the comfort of his room, Bob relaxed. He had a few souvenirs. He was taken with dolphins. Dolphins patrolled the beaches, butting sharks, and making it safe to swim. One tour let you swim with dolphins, but between the steep price tag and the sniffles of his budding cold, he passed. Instead, he held a glittery dolphin bracelet to the light, two silver dolphins melded together swimming in a circle of life. His dark onyx dolphin, cold and powerful, jumped over a rocky outcropping. Dolphins performed a useful service, he thought, they kept the sharks at bay. Just then the phone rang. Doreen wanted him at her room. He walked down the hall and knocked. She had changed into casual clothes, slacks and a blouse. Smiling, she ushered him into the room.

"I have a slight problem with my plumbing," she said simply.

Bob blushed a little but with all the sun he hoped she didn't notice.

"Have a seat," she pointed to the bed. It was the other bed, not hers. Sitting, Bob grew tired. She spoke about her promised jaunt to the island, her inability to awake early and get to the ferry, and Tex's cell phone number being inactive. To top it off, her sink was leaking. Bob could hear the entertainment blaring from the hotel open-air esplanade where college-aged actors staged cultural fare for the hotel guests. Bob smiled grimly; he was beyond such peasant entertainment.

"Bob," said Doreen, "could you wake me tomorrow so I can make the ferry? I'm so afraid I'll just go right back to sleep after the wake-up call."

Bob opened his eyes.

"No. I like my sleep. I have a full day planned. Tell your cowboy friend to call you."

Bob closed his eyes again, slipped his sneakers over the foot of the bed, and began to lie down on the pillow.

Doreen grabbed the pillow just in time, letting Bob's head roll back against the sheets.

"I'm planning to use this pillow tonight."

Bob jumped up and said goodnight. But before he could leave, she implored him to look at her plumbing. Being an experienced homeowner, he squatted beneath the leaky sink and saw water seeping from the cold-water shutoff valve. Just as he grasped the knob to tighten it and stop the leak, the silver orb stripped and dropped to the floor. Water spewed. Bob stood. Doreen pushed him out the door, screaming "Get out! Get out! Bob the plumber, what a joke!" The door slammed shut. Bob listened. He heard shrieking. She had called the desk. "There is a flood in my room! I demand a plumber. My trip is ruined! My clothes will be soaked. Do you understand English? A flood! A flood I tell you. I demand a plumber. Now!" She hung up. Bob knew the stone rooms prevented water damage and the bathroom floor sloped to a drain by the tub. But he walked away, letting her unravel.

A little later that night, while watching the last act of entertainment, before the drunken hotel guests were permitted on stage to perform, he saw Doreen come out wearing a shawl. He walked over, inquired about the condition of her possessions, and asked if everything was OK. He even apologized for the plumbing accident. She accepted his apology and said the leak was fixed. Then she politely asked him to move away. He was, she decided, standing too close to her. Bob turned on his heel and left her alone by the pool, and headed toward the softly breaking waves at the beach. There he ran into a pretty woman in a bathing suit, a few years younger than him, who was at the resort as part of a wedding party. Most everyone was coupled up but she admitted she had no boyfriend. Bob had noticed her at the beginning of the trip; the airlines had lost her luggage for a few days. When she asked him if his wife would object to his spending time with her, he said Doreen wasn't his wife, just his cousin—that was the line they agreed to use, but they didn't always stick to it.

The woman's name was Shawn. They walked the beach. Traded tourist

232

horror stories. Then returned to the hotel. Shawn told Bob that the next day she was leaving with the wedding party to continue their trip. Bob sighed. He got her address but she lived in the Midwest and he knew long distance relationships were a long shot. Then she brushed some brown hair from her eyes and asked if he'd like to come in to her room to visit. Bob thought about the time; it was late, and he had the Mayan ruins to explore the next day, so he said goodnight, and left her leaning against her door frame with the room's light silhouetting her long hair and open-legged stance.

Bob loved Chichenitza despite the three-hour bus drive. Doreen came too. She decided to sleep late and blow off the boys. But they sat in separate seats. Bob was comfortable with that. Once there they explored the city with their group. They saw the Mayan basketball court with its brilliant acoustics and reliefs of athletes playing ball. They stood on an observatory that charted stars. They explored the caverns where the monks and nuns lived. Doreen playfully suggested that was where Bob belonged. They took pictures of the temple and the garden of the hundred columns. The guide explained that the Yucatan was formed by a comet hitting the earth millions of years ago. He said the Mayan calendar was the most accurate one known. The calendar was made into a two-gear mechanical device known as a long count and a short count. He said the long count was coming to a close in 2012. Bob whispered to Doreen that 2012 was the expected arrival of the next killer comet that would blast man back to the Stone Age. Doreen stepped away.

Most of all, Bob enjoyed the celestial clock in the middle of the city. The pyramid had four sides of stairs, one side available for climbing. There were 90 steps about nine inches tall and mounted at almost a 45-degree angle. The platform above had five more steps giving all told, 365 steps that corresponded to the days of the year. Standing at the proper spots during the spring and fall equinoxes, an observer could see a shadow of a snake develop from the sun's rays on the steps, which then slithered into or out of the ground. Bob climbed about six steps before he sensed his vertigo and agoraphobia begin to bubble over in his brain. Doreen scrambled to the top and he snapped a few shots of her butt as she made the climb. The guide warned that going up was easy, but going down such a steep slope required a lot of fortitude. Some people needed to be rescued. Bob saw one athlete run all the way down.

On the way back to the bus, a helpful tourist offered to take Bob and Doreen's picture together. Doreen screamed "No!" and waved him off. As an afterthought she said "Thank you" very politely. Before reaching the exit gate, Doreen came to a dead stop in front of a clothing store. She went in while Bob stood looking at the big clock. Finally he entered.

"Doreen," he said, "we have to go."

"In a minute. Tell me which goes better with my fair complexion. The pale blue gown, or the matching blouse and skirt?"

"All I know is the bus is about to leave and you'd better hurry up."

"Quiet! You're not helping at all. Leave. Leave me alone. Get out!"

Bob left. He jumped into the bus and the guide looked at him grimly.

"Where is your wife?"

"She's not my wife. She's busy in a clothing store."

"It's time to leave. Go find her."

"No."

The guide shrugged. "You all heard me say to meet at the San Martin restaurant if you missed the bus. Let's hope she did, too. She's been late too many times. I have a schedule to keep."

The bus pulled away.

At the restaurant, the group enjoyed a buffet meal and native dances. A woman balanced fruit on her head while tap-dancing to a festive song. The taps echoed off the walls as Bob's group caught sight of Doreen entering the room. Bob noted she had bought the pale blue gown. But her hair was slick with sweat. She sat next to Bob without a word. He noticed wet marks spreading from her armpits and dirt stains on her shorts. Then, eyes widening, his nose sensed the humbling smell of body odor. Bob considered the aroma similar to that found on a peasant who had just spent a day weeding in the fields. As soon as she drank a glass of water, she told Bob her story.

"I remembered the name of the restaurant, but I spent all my money on the gown so I had to hitch a ride here in the back of a farmer's wagon."

Bob smiled. The trip was nearly over.

Bob stared at the red light of his answering machine—it no longer blinked. He remembered how later she apologized for her behavior during the trip, how she stopped talking to him when he told her she was making bad choices about her lovers, and how she introduced him to her fiancé. They had covered a lot of ground together. Years of friendship. But it was a bit one-sided. He had sent a present to the wedding instead of going himself. He thought of another platitude: women stick with women and men stick with men, and if married—so much the truer. He blessed her troubled soul like the priest he should have been and deleted the message.

The Set-up

Bob O'Neil left the poetry recital at the Fiston Book Store and Cafe with three women on his mind. He smiled. Perhaps the third one is the charm, he thought. The psychic had told him he would meet a woman named Dianna suitable for the deep and intimate relationship he craved, and Bob was now on his way to meet his blind date—unfortunately, her name wasn't Dianna. Perhaps she used her middle name, rather than her given name. He sighed. The possibilities were endless since Spiritualism was an inexact science. Actually, he longed for the melodious voice of Bridget, who had just performed her reading to a small but loyal crowd of literary enthusiasts. Yet she simply considered him a "friend." He frowned. Judy, their mutual friend, had come to his rescue. As Bob weaved through the traffic, eyes glazing, he thought about their preparations for the big date.

Judy had made Bob her Pygmalion project after offering to do what no woman had ever done before—set Bob up with a date. She had a friend who she said looked like Sally Field in *The Flying Nun*. She told Bob her friend Connie was a petite and unpretentious 45-year old who taught special education at a nearby grade school. Bob liked "petite," wished she was ten years younger, but thought it might work because he still was in emotional grade school and figured she might have a little patience with him. He needed special attention when it came to relationships.

Bob met Judy earlier in the week at her house in preparation for a clothes-shopping spree. He listened as she sketched out Connie's life and noted some common interests. Then Judy crinkled her nose and suggested he exchange his oversized coke bottle eyeglasses for a more streamlined, lighter pair. Sitting on the couch, her eight year-old son chirped that his mother thought he looked like a geek in the current pair. Judy denied it, but her son then reminded her of the conversation with one of her girl-friends. Bob smiled. "The things kids say," she said. He agreed and went to the optometrist with Judy.

Next, Judy took Bob into a store and picked out three short-sleeved shirts, a pair of khaki shorts, and stylish soft leather shoes. She made Bob promise not to wear white socks with the shoes, it was very uncool. Bob also promised not to wear socks at all when he wore shorts with his stylish shoes. Then Judy asked him where he intended to take Connie. When Bob said "coffee," she made a face and suggested a walk. Bob brightened. He decided to go to Singing Beach where the wind whispered over the unique mix of volcanic ash and beach sand. Judy agreed. But told him he needed one more pair of khakis: long pants were the only acceptable attire for a first date.

Bob called Connie promptly at 9:00 pm on Wednesday. He was nervous, but his fingers didn't shake as he punched the numbers, nor did he feel a constriction in his chest or a seizing in his brain. He was a swimmer, prepared to meet cold water, and just dove in. Connie answered in a gravelly voice. Bob mentioned their mutual friend and she laughed knowingly. She let him steer the conversation and he aimed it at pets and play. They both had dogs and cats and liked to travel. At times the conversation lagged, but their common interest in animals kept the words flowing. If all else failed, there was always pet talk. About halfway through their forty-minute dialogue, she asked for his vocation. Bob was actually without portfolio, a drifter in the super-tight economy of the new century. He worked at his leisure and at his avocations, which were many. Tonight his voice barely broke out of its monotone as he told Connie he worked for the local university. He didn't get pay for this work, but he did obtain from it a sense of satisfaction.

Finally, Bob asked the question. Would she accompany him to Singing Beach? She replied with a delighted laugh. Sure, she said, she'd do anything once. Bob smiled. Then they said their goodnights and retired. Although excited, he slept soundly and during the remainder of the week, he monitored his condition.

Bob broke out of his reflective reverie by blowing his horn. A confused tourist was hesitating at the Fiston rotary, a traffic pattern unique to New England. Bob flushed and cussed, delighted with his newfound emotions, which were activated in real time. Next he felt sorry for the lost motorist and a little embarrassed. The road was wet from the thundershowers the previous hour. Water sprayed across his clean windshield. Yet the sun shone, gleaming off the dashboard. He had cleaned his car. He scrubbed the windows with a homemade vinegar solution, wiped the dirt from the plastic molding, and then sealed the plastic with a smooth shiny finish coat that rejuvenated the material and made it smooth and sparkly. The vacuuming removed a half of a cup of sand from under the driver's side foot mat. The trash filled a green plastic bag the size of a rubbish barrel. Bob even found some surprises. Evidently his new dog had been unable to hold her bowels, something that happened more often than he cared to think about.

He stopped at home, grabbed his new windbreaker, put the leash on Sarah, left again with a wink to Monkey, the cat, for luck. Sarah, he thought, was his ticket to Connie's heart. He brought along a few treats for both dogs. Sarah, a silver and tan Yorky with a blonde head, sat panting on the passenger seat unaware of her supporting role. The day was still sticky and hot.

Once at the beach, he waited. She was late. Perhaps, he thought, she decided not to come. Stood up. Bob sweated in the sun. The beach was hot and smelly. While the storm had driven away the bathers, he felt overdressed in his khaki trousers, navy blue socks and stylish shoes. He did like the blue plaid short-sleeved shirt.

Suddenly, his date appeared from around the bend. He saw a big smile but an even bigger waist. What he thought might be the Flying Nun, turned out to be Alice, the maid, from *The Brady Bunch*. He smiled anyway and waved. Claire and Sarah hit it off right away. Claire, a small white powder ball with curls, actually looked more like an overweight poodle than a traditional Westie.

"I'm Bob," he said. He adjusted his glasses as an afterthought. Today was the first time to wear them and he had been stepping where there were no steps. *I need to visit that thirty-something optometrist,* Bob told himself.

"I'm Connie," she said, outstretching her hand. She wore a simple white blouse, beige shorts, and white sandals.

Bob noted the firm, no-nonsense grip.

238

"I'm sorry about being late. I almost missed the turn for the beach."

Bob nodded, forgiving her. Up close he saw the square jaw, age induced jowls, gray-streaked coarse black hair. He would try to follow his therapist's suggestion and focus on the inner being.

"Shall we walk?" asked Bob, cutting to the chase.

"Let's. Such a lovely beach."

Bob guided Sarah through the big rocks blocking the road's end and began walking through a rock-covered section of beach. Connie caught right up. Bob clattered and slipped more than once on the uneven footing of the polished beach stones. At first, he thought the smooth, hard soles of his new shoes were at fault, then he realized he was also contending with an error in the make-up of his trim and vogue glasses. Somehow they made objects at his feet appear a half-step higher than they really were. Bob frowned as Connie outpaced him.

She turned. "Having trouble?"

Bob shook his head. "Sarah had to pee," he lied.

He looked up across the beach quickly. The rock field stopped a few steps away, but seaweed four-inches deep covered the next stretch of beach. Apparently, a storm washed up this mess, hence the putrid smell. Bob looked down again and groaned to himself.

"Are those new shoes?"

"They're my spares."

Bob's new shoes disappeared in the glistening muck as he stepped through it with Sarah. Suddenly, Sarah, excited by the foreign smells, squatted to empty her bowels. Bob and Connie watched. *Wonderful,* thought Bob.

When the couple reached the sandy half of the beach, Connie kicked off her sandals and crunched her toes into the sand. Bob stumbled along next to her, trying to keep up.

"How long have you had Claire?" he asked, trying to bring the date back to life.

"Three years. She's the only survivor from her litter. One was still-born and the other was put down because of a birth defect—no bones in the rear legs."

Bob's mind drifted to the subject of putting people down for various defects.

"And Sarah?"

"I've had her a year and a half. I picked her up at the Fiston dog shelter. Her owners were elderly and couldn't care for her. When I saw her, she hadn't eaten for three days and was crying constantly."

"Claire's eight. I adopted her from an elderly woman too."

Bob stopped. They were at the end of the beach. He listened to the pulsing roar of the surf.

"There's a great view just over the rise and up to the point through that trail." He pointed into the greenery.

"I don't see a trail, but OK."

Bob entered first. The trail was overgrown with bushes that were dripping from the previous rainstorm. He flinched as water soaked through his pale khakis, turning them flesh colored.

"What a pretty view."

"There's the light house and the islands and a ship on the horizon, probably on its way to the harbor in Fiston."

Bob waited a minute or two then suggested they return to the parking lot along the rise, an asphalt-covered path that paralleled the beach a short distance from the water. He wanted to save his shoes and keep his balance. At the lot he bought Connie an ice cream and gave the two dogs a bowl of water. Then Bob felt the tension mount. His khakis stuck to his rear end and legs.

"How would you like to go to the concert at the Music Hall tomorrow?"

"I promised to attend my nephew's baseball game. And it's a school night. I need my rest."

Bob breathed.

"Maybe we can get together another time this week."

"I'm very busy with school."

He nodded. It was over. They exchanged pleasantries, then Bob bent down to pick up Sarah.

"Wait…" cried Connie.

Bob held Sarah as she gagged. Green bile, strands of grass, variously colored stomach fluids issued out of her gaping mouth. She had been overcome by the heat of the beach and excitement of the date. *Sympathetic vomiting*, thought Bob.

"I think she'll be OK." He waved to the departing Connie.

Bob wiped his sweating face with a napkin.

"Hot enough to swim," he said aloud. Then he thought about "diving in" when he made the call for the date. He had been swimming since Wednesday and hadn't lost his wind. With Sarah tucked under his arm, he walked back to his car whistling.

With a leaning toward 12-step programs, the "Checklist on Recovery from Mood Disorders" offers many helpful suggestions winnowed from hard experience.

Elizabeth Moulton, Psy. D., A.R.N.P.

Afterword

A Checklist
on
Recovery from Mood Disorders—
One Experiencer's View

By
Sarah T.

The following items are thoughtful reminders on how to stay on the beam and recover from a brain illness:

Find a safe place to live with positive nurturing people who love you. They may be from your family, friends, church, or twelve-step group.

Find a medical doctor you feel you can trust. Not every medical doctor is the same. Some have personalities that may conflict with yours, others may not care about you as a person, and some are not competent. They try to stabilize the mind/body with medicine and write prescriptions to treat illness. Talk therapy and other treatments can then be used to change behavior. Medical doctors' expertise is not talk-therapy. I have been satisfied with 2 out of 5. I have tried to talk to my doctors in complete honesty and without reservation. If I don't, they can't help me with my problems and illness.

Adopt a 12-step program to begin to find a pathway to life that is based on a higher power, honesty, and simplicity.

Stay in the moment. Try not to regret yesterday or worry about tomorrow. Things take care of themselves if we just do the next thing in front of us to do.

Take your medicine. This must be emphasized. When people feel better they simply decide they no longer need treatment and quite frequently end up in the hospital. Do what the doctor tells you to do. Stabilize your mind/ body. After about a month the medicine will take effect but it may take your brain's nervous system several years to recover and reach equilibrium with the medicine. Then work with your doctor to optimize the dosage and types to regain more normal living. Remember: After a psychotic break, over 85% of the people need to stay on anti-psychotics for the rest of their lives. It is very dangerous to believe that you are in the slim 15% minority. Continued breakdowns can reduce brain functioning and precipitate an increasing tendency to have additional breakdowns.

Do not drink or use drugs. These substances can induce psychosis, cause depression, precipitate panic attacks, and impair brain functioning as well as interfere with prescribed medication. These substances are also habit forming and may result in dependency.

Acceptance of the illness is the key to recovering from it. We must work out of the denial and anger that we have a problem that makes us different from the norm. Medication, therapy, and special work on our part are required to stay on the beam. We must learn to accept our illness and work with it so that our lives can be more full. From acceptance we can move towards understanding and then action because our minds have been opened. As a result, we are willing to learn to take better care of ourselves. We should remember that most people have some kind of problem that sets them apart from others.

Stay away from caffeine. This is a drug that is abused, out-of-control, and over-used.

Adopt a pet. I found a dog very helpful. When I couldn't connect with people because I was too sick or depressed, my dog always was there. My dog and I formed a special bond that lasted 11 years and helped me bridge the gap I had with people—all people. But don't think a dog is the only answer, try a cat, a mouse, or a fish, or even for starters a plant. Having the responsibility to care for another and allowing oneself to receive the beauty that that other has to offer us is a key part of recovery. Caring for a dog and the companionship he offered probably saved my life.

Help others. Not matter how unfortunate you think you are, someone else has it worse. Not matter how hopeless you feel, you have been given a gift that will bring a little peace to someone else's life. The gift can be as simple as being able to read to another, or sing, play music, drive, fix things, sit with, cook, tutor, or something else that you like to do, that you may do everyday, that you could do for another without any thought of something in return.

Find a therapist that you trust. Therapists are not the same as medical doctors. Doctors take very few courses on how to relate to people while a therapist spends most of his/her time involved with the various ways to relate to people and the dynamics that go on between people. Seeing a therapist once a week is ideal. That time period is short enough to allow for all the week's events to be brought up and possibly work on some issues as well. I've found a therapist who likes to talk but holds back from giving too many suggestions or who tells me what to do. I do feel she recognizes patterns and helps me try to break them. She cares a lot about me and I've found that to be very important.

Don't make any big life changing decisions for a year. If you can, try to postpone as many as possible for as long as possible. It can't be said enough that when our brain's functioning is impaired, we are the last to know it. Make changes in little steps. That may be hard to accept and even harder to put into practice but that it is all what is about: finding a balance in life. Sensitive people need to approach change very gradually. After a while, you yourself will be able to feel the change as it happens inside your gut and then you will know quicker what outside change is now bothering you, what outside change happened too fast for you to process, and when to slow down the speed of change.

Obtain guidance from people you trust. Before making decisions, practice running them by someone else. Try to find one person, preferably someone outside of the family, who you feel has something you want on an emotional and spiritual level. This person may have had problems similar to your own but has some how surmounted them. By confiding in this person, you will find that your strangest thoughts and darkest secrets that seem to make you so different, are really rather commonplace. He or she may hear your problems at a level different from a therapist and offer concrete suggestions based on what he did in a similar situation.

Trust in God. Or try some other spiritual or natural force. It can be as simple as acknowledging a spiritual light in things or as complex as being a practicing member of one of the great religions. After all, everything had to come from somewhere. Believing in something other than oneself takes the pressure off daily living. Do your best in all your endeavors. If you make a mistake, apologize, and if needed make amends. No one is perfect. The imperfections make us human, unique, and lovable. Remembering that we are not perfect helps eliminate another emotional zinger: GUILT. We need to work on our faults with the professionals and people we trust to become better, more useful and helpful people.

Stay out of relationships for at least a year. One of the big stresses is sexual energy. Picking people who will unintentionally hurt us is a big problem. Only hard work around parental/partner issues with professionals and friends will bring the problems into the light on the intellectual level. Knowledge of the problem will bring to light a solution but that still must seep into the feeling level and then we must learn how to act with the new set of feelings. The whole process can take years before a complete personality transformation can occur. Some may require a lot of work and others will learn faster.

Stay around positive, uplifting, decent, caring people who by their actions will bring you up to their level. Selection of the confidant is a key in getting this connection. Sometimes, the people may not seem willing to socialize with you. Don't give up. Try to be available to them. Talk to someone who isn't talking to someone else. Talk to the people talking to your confidant. Talk about feeling disconnected at a twelve-step meeting. Introduce yourself to a new person each day and try to find something that the two of you have in common.

Anniversaries. Be careful of spring (15 March +/-30 days) and fall (1 September +\- 30 days). These two time periods are disrupters to the nervous system due to the accelerated change from light to darkness that occurs during the equinoxes. I have found August 15 that starts the fall a serious stress; the discomfort generally lasts a week. However, for those not taking proper care of themselves and experiencing a lot of emotional stress, these tough times can cause anything from a series of sleepless nights to a serious hospitalization for a major breakdown. Other ones to watch for are the three at year-end: Thanksgiving, Christmas, and New

Year's. Other ones are more personal: a hospital stay for a breakdown, the ending of a relationship, a birthday, or the date of a loved one's death. Or the day of a major life change, whether good or bad—a sobriety date, a wedding, and a career change. When you feel the upwelling of anxiety that is not account for, remember what has gone on in your life during that time for the past number of years. Then you can stop blaming the people, places, things, and situations around you. You can use the phone and talk to your friends and professionals and 24-hour help lines. You can write in a journal, read, play, expect a little less of your self for a few days, talk about it at twelve-step meetings, and ride it out. The better you are taking care of yourself during the rest of the time, the less effect the anniversaries will have on you. A suggestion—put all your personal anniversaries as well as the obvious ones mentioned in your calendar for reference. When the feelings of gloom, doom, and high anxiety come upon you, check your calendar. Don't forget to pray too.

Medicine. Find out how much extra medicine you can take in an emergency to prevent a possible breakdown. More than a few times, my illness overwhelmed my medication and I had to rely on my doctor's instructions and my own instincts to increase the drug dosage to prevent a possible breakdown. This is something that should not be done lightly but emergencies do occur and you must work with your doctor to prevent the illness from overwhelming you. Denial may creep in and prevent you from seeing your own erratic behavior. Living with another person may be helpful. I had a number of roommates, however roommates and coping with them is a book in itself. Another note on medicine... I had to taper off lithium because I realized after several years that particular medicine was clouding my thinking. I am still on another mood stabilizer, but for now I no longer take lithium. I can trace part of my recovery from that medicine change. It must be remembered that all medicines affect us differently and some of my friends get along fine with lithium.

Play. Try to find some fun things to do. Develop a hobby of your own like gardening or cooking or reading. Try a sport like volleyball to play with others: Roller skating, ice skating, contra dancing, walking, golf, tennis, bowling, golf, ping-pong, or basketball. Finding an activity that you can focus on will stop you from focusing on yourself and your problems. Performing the activity with people that are also having fun lifts the spirit as well. Remember physical exertion produces endorphins that give the brain a little high and relieve stress.

Meditation. The benefit of one half-hour of daily meditation is equivalent to a dose of anti-depressant such as Prozac. Try yoga or Tai chi as a spiritual exercise. I found Tai chi a good way to start learning how to move energy through my body. I have practiced it every day for a number of years during my recovery.

Alternate healing forms are moving into the mainstream: Reiki, kinesiology, reflexology, hypnosis, accupuncture and accupressure. I have found Reiki to be very helpful and became a Reiki master so I could perform healing on others and myself.

Try to keep a neat house. Stick to routines. But break them once in a while too.

Sleep. A regular amount of sleep, say 8 hours per day, is needed for maintaining good health. Too little sleep can bring on mania. Also too much activity can bring on mania. Not sleeping for more than a day can indicate mania. Over-sleeping every day and taking frequent naps can indicate depression.

Eating. Learn how to eat a healthy balanced meal. Cook in bulk and freeze to save money. Find a good multi-vitamin. Go out to eat with a friend once a week. Or take yourself out at least once a month. You are worth it.

If you think this checklist is helpful, perhaps you can make a copy and give it to a friend in need.

For more information about this checklist and about learning-type games to prevent substance abuse, check out www.sobergames.com.

About the Author

Bill Pagum's background includes a degree from Cornell University and work experience with the Standard Oil Company. He is a writer, game inventor, and environmentalist. You can visit www.billpagum.com to find out more about the novel and upcoming play based on *A No Life Story* as well as other works. Bill also offers substance abuse prevention and recovery games which many therapists find useful for their groups (see www.sobergames.com). His new efforts involve creating a game on sustainability and showing how to use money to build community. You may contact Bill at billpmail@aol.com. He lives in southern coastal Maine.